To Love a Stranger

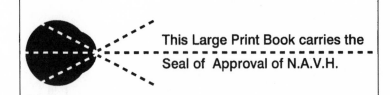

This Large Print Book carries the
Seal of Approval of N.A.V.H.

To Love a Stranger

Connie Mason

Thorndike Press • Waterville, Maine

This is a work of fiction. Names, characters, places, and incidents either are the product of the author's imagination or are used fictitiously. Any resemblance to actual events, locales, organizations, or persons, living or dead, is entirely coincidental and beyond the intent of either the author or the publisher.

Published in 2001 by arrangement with Natasha Kern Literary Agency, Inc.

Thorndike Press Large Print Basic Series.

The tree indicium is a trademark of Thorndike Press.

The text of this Large Print edition is unabridged.
Other aspects of the book may vary from the original edition.

Set in 16 pt. Plantin by Minnie B. Raven.

Printed in the United States on permanent paper.

Library of Congress Cataloging-in-Publication Data

Mason, Connie.
  To love a stranger / Connie Mason.
    p. cm.
  ISBN 0-7862-3393-1 (lg. print : hc : alk. paper)
  1. Large type books.   I. Title.
PS3563.A78786 T56 2001
  813´.54—dc21   2001027519

To Love a Stranger

Chapter 1

Dry Gulch, Montana
1880

Pierce Delaney hammered a nail into the fence he was repairing, nearly shattering the wood with the force of his blow. His face was grim, his vivid green eyes brimming with anger.

"You got something against that particular piece of wood, brother? If I didn't know better, I'd think you were trying to destroy it."

Pierce paused in midstroke, glaring over his shoulder at his brother. His voice was sharp, almost rough, when he answered. "Don't mess with me today, Chad. I'm in no mood for banter." He turned back to the fence post, but Chad wasn't about to let the matter drop. Something was eating at his brother, and he damn well wanted to know what it was.

"You came in awful late last night,

Pierce. You said you were going to stop by the Doolittle spread on your way to town. What happened? Did Cora Lee corner you again?" he asked with a smirk.

"Don't mention that bitch's name to me," Pierce gritted from between clenched teeth. "If it wasn't for her father, I wouldn't bother going over there at all. The man is close to death and his drunken son has run the ranch into the ground. The least I can do, since old man Doolittle and Pa were such good friends, is perform chores around the place. That's the *only* reason I visit the Doolittles."

Chad sent Pierce a cheeky grin. "And here I thought you might be sweet on Cora Lee."

"Shit! You know better than that. Women are a pack of trouble. Can't trust the lot of them. Our own ma proved how faithless women are. Remember what Pa told us? When you need a woman, find a whore, they won't disappoint a man. His advice was sound. There isn't a woman alive I'd trust."

"You don't have to convince me," Chad said grimly. "Hell, I remember what Ma did to Pa. I'll never forget or forgive her for leaving us like she did. The only good thing to come of it was our trekking out

8

west to homestead after the Indian upris-
ings were quelled. What's got you so riled
this morning?"

Pierce flung down his hammer and
leaned his long, muscular frame against
the fence. The bulging muscles of his arms
and torso attested to the fact that he was
no stranger to hard work. Tan and fit,
Pierce Delaney, along with his brothers,
Chad and Ryan, were well known in the
tiny town of Dry Gulch, Montana. Whenever all three brothers rode into town,
trouble usually followed. They were hell-
raisers who relished a good fight. They
drank hard, played hard, and fought hard.
But they could be charming when the oc-
casion warranted.

The Delaney brothers were considered
prime catches despite their wild natures.
Aware of their reputations as troublemakers, parents warned their daughters to
steer clear of the brothers, which made
them dangerously attractive and appealing
to those innocents. The brothers' disdain
for womanhood made them as irresistible.

"Mr. Doolittle was in a bad way last
night," Pierce said. "Cora Lee wouldn't let
me see him. We were alone, don't know
where her no-good brother was right then.
Anyway, she sidled up to me and suggested

9

we go up to her bedroom. She said she'd always had a hankering for me. I turned her down flat, and that set her off."

Chad stifled a smile. "You turned her down? Am I to assume you'd rather pay for it in town?"

"I'd rather pay an honest whore than bed a woman with marriage on her mind."

"So what happened?"

"I was heading for the door when Hal Doolittle walked in from the kitchen. Then things really got out of hand. I don't know what possessed Cora Lee to do such a thing."

Chad sent Pierce an exasperated look. "Dammit, Pierce, don't keep me in suspense. What happened to make you so all-fired mad?"

"All of a sudden Cora Lee bursts into tears and rushes into her brother's arms. Between sobs, she claimed that I seduced her on one of my visits to her father and got her with child."

Chad gave Pierce a startled look. "Did you?"

Pierce looked as if he wanted to smash Chad in the face. "For Christ's sake, Chad! Not you, too? No, I didn't seduce Cora Lee. I have no romantic interest in the woman . . . or any woman."

"What did her brother say to that?"

"He believed her, of course, and demanded that I marry his sister. Do they think I'm stupid? That ranch is going under, and Cora Lee needs a husband with enough money to put them back into business. I happened to fit the bill. But I'm not gullible enough to fall for that. I'm not marrying anyone. Ever!"

Chad shook his head, sending a shower of dark brown hair into his eyes. He brushed it carelessly back into place. "Hal Doolittle has more balls than I gave him credit for. As for Cora Lee, she always was a conniving little bitch. Do you really think she's in the family way?"

"I don't know and I don't care. That's precisely what I told Hal, but he didn't seem to understand. I had to use some . . . uh . . . persuasion to make him back off." He rubbed his bruised knuckles, recalling the fight that had resulted when he tried to leave. He'd left Hal bleeding on the floor and Cora Lee crying.

"I reckon you won't be going back any time soon," Chad predicted. "Too bad, but it can't be helped. Maybe we can send our little brother to help old man Doolittle with the chores. Ryan tends to be more levelheaded than either you or I."

Distractedly Pierce shoved his fingers through his rich, dark hair. "No one in this family is to set foot on Doolittle property. I'm the head of this family and I aim to keep you and Ryan out of trouble."

"Well, maybe there's time to save us, but I'd say you're in a heap of trouble, brother. It appears that Cora Lee is desperate for a husband and has set her sights on you."

"Like hell!" Pierce shouted angrily. "Has Ryan returned from town yet?" he said more calmly. "I'm running out of nails."

"No, but he should be back soon. Relax, Pierce, we all know you didn't get Cora Lee with child. Forget it."

Pierce picked up the hammer, aiming a fierce blow at a nail he'd just set into place. Chad winced as the wood splintered; Pierce's temper was obviously still hot and volatile. Pierce had always been the hot-headed brother, while Ryan, the youngest, wasn't as excitable. Chad liked to think he was the one who looked at things from all angles before reacting. Despite their differences, all three were tough as nails, dead set against marriage, and fiercely protective of one another.

Pierce kept up a steady pounding, venting his anger and frustration on the hapless fence post. If he didn't keep his hands and mind occupied, he'd explode. He could still recall the look on Hal Doolittle's face when he'd refused to agree to marry Cora Lee. He hadn't wanted to hit Hal, but the man drove him to it. Hal was big, but he was soft. He was no match for Pierce, who had decked him with one well-aimed punch.

"There's Ryan now," Chad said, shading his eyes against the glare of the sun. "He's riding hell for leather. Wonder what's wrong."

Pierce looked up, surprised to see Ryan whipping his mount into a fine lather and shouting something they couldn't make out.

"It's not like Ryan to whip his horse like that," Pierce said, tossing the hammer aside and taking off at a run to meet his brother. Chad followed close on his heels.

Ryan reined in sharply, causing his mount to rear up and paw the air. Skillfully bringing the roan gelding under control, Ryan leaped to the ground, his breath coming in harsh pants.

"You've got to get out of town," he gasped as he grasped Pierce's shoulders and pushed him toward the barn. "They're not far behind me."

"Slow down, Ryan," Pierce urged.

"What happened? Why do I have to get out of town? Who's coming?"

"The vigilantes, that's who. Hal Doolittle was in town early this morning, insisting that you seduced his sister, got her with child, and refused to marry her."

"Hell, I never touched the woman," Pierce roared.

"There's more," Ryan said. "Hal brought Cora Lee to town with him. She was roughed up pretty bad. Old Doc Lucas treated her. Hal claims Pierce beat her when she insisted he do the right thing by her."

"That's a lie! I never laid a hand on the woman."

"Tell that to the vigilantes, but don't expect them to believe you. Cora Lee was a pitiful sight. She verified Hal's story. Riley Reed got the men so worked up they formed immediately a vigilante party. Since there's no regular law in this part of Montana, they can pretty much do what they please. They're coming after you. If you don't agree to marry Cora Lee, they're going to string you up. There's no time to lose. You've got to leave until the furor blows over."

"You'd better go," Chad urged. "Unless you plan on getting hitched. There are some in town jealous of our prosperity, including Riley Reed. Others resent us because we won't settle down and marry their daughters."

"I tried marriage once and it didn't work. Hell, I'm not going to run," Pierce said stubbornly. No vigilante party was going to scare him from his land.

"You've got to," Ryan insisted. "You weren't in town. I saw how angry the men were, and how skillfully Hal and Riley incited them. I saw Cora Lee myself. Someone worked her over good. It won't hurt to hide out for a time. Chad and I will handle things here. Between us we might be able to figure out what really happened."

"Ryan is right, Pierce, you've got to leave. You've seen what the vigilantes can do when they're worked up. They're the only law in these parts; no one will stand up to them. Take whatever money we have in the house and go. Send word where we can reach you. Meanwhile we'll do our damnedest to get to the bottom of this."

Ryan cast a nervous glance over his shoulder. "They'll be coming up over the hill any minute now. I'll saddle your horse while you gather a few things to take with you."

15

"And I'll get money from the safe," Chad said. "How long do we have, Ryan?"

"Five minutes, no more. Probably not even that."

"I'm not —" Pierce began.

"Yes you are," Chad said. "You may be the eldest, but you're too hotheaded for your own good. I know you too well. You'd stay here and fight till the bloody end. Riley Reed is the leader of the vigilantes and one mean bastard. He's hated you ever since Polly married you instead of him. They'll burn down the ranch house if we hole up inside and try to fend them off."

He pushed Pierce toward the house just as a cloud of dust appeared over the crest of the hill.

"Dammit, I told you they were hot on my tail," Ryan said as he hurried toward the barn to saddle Pierce's horse. "No time to pack now, just take the money and go. I'll bring your horse around to the back."

Pierce didn't want to flee like a coward, but he had no choice. The ranch was their home and he couldn't let it be destroyed by a bunch of zealots masquerading as the law. He knew Riley Reed. He was a man consumed by his own importance, and men followed him unquestioningly. The vigilantes were quick to lynch and slow to listen to reason. There was talk of a federal marshal being assigned to the territory, but that hadn't happened yet.

Chad went into the house and straight to the wall safe located in the office off the kitchen used to conduct ranch business. He grabbed a handful of cash, found Pierce in the kitchen, and stuffed a wad of bills into the pocket of his leather vest. Then Chad literally shoved Pierce out the back door. The loud tattoo of approaching horses' hooves made haste imperative.

"Hurry," Chad urged. "Ride like hell."

"Dammit, Chad, I'm not guilty. I can't just ride away without defending myself."

"I'm thinking more clearly than you right now. Unless you want to get hitched to Cora Lee, or be hung from the nearest tree, you'd best hightail it for safer parts."

Pierce grabbed his jacket from the hook beside the kitchen door and stepped into the bright sunlight, where Ryan was waiting with a sturdy black mustang gelding from Mexico known for his speed and ability to perform under duress.

"I've saddled Midnight," Ryan said. "Hurry, the vigilantes are riding through the gate. Be sure and keep in touch so we can let you know when it's safe to return home."

Pierce nodded tersely, loath to leave but aware that he had little choice in the matter. He leapt into the saddle and dug his heels into Midnight's sides. The animal hurdled over the fence just as the vigilantes thundered into the yard. Leaning low over Midnight's neck, Pierce headed for open countryside, leading the vigilantes away from the ranch and his brothers.

"Go, Midnight, go," Pierce urged as the stalwart horse stretched his sturdy legs to obey his master.

Pierce glanced back over his shoulder, cursing when he saw that the vigilantes were hard on his heels. They weren't about to give up now that they had him in their sights. Bullets whizzed past him; he bent low over Midnight's withers and dug in his spurs.

Midnight ate up the miles but was unable to shake his determined pursuers. Pierce knew the hectic pace he set was winding Midnight, so he headed for a canyon where he hoped to lose the posse. After an hour of hard riding he deliberately set a slower tempo, hoping the vigilantes would do the same when they realized their horses couldn't take the grinding pace. Unfortunately Pierce's luck ran out. One of the men got off a lucky shot.

A bullet slammed into Pierce's back, entering just below his right shoulder blade. The force of it nearly sent him flying off Midnight's back. He fought to remain conscious as fierce, stabbing pain radiated throughout his body. He felt the wetness of blood, smelled its acrid odor, and felt blackness closing in on him.

Through sheer grit and determination Pierce managed to hang on. He had no idea how long he rode after that, for he may have passed out for a time, but when he looked back the vigilantes were still following.

Through a haze of pain, Pierce noted that he was entering a narrow canyon, whose walls rose high on either side. His brain was fuzzy, making coherent thought extremely difficult, but he managed to keep his seat. Ahead of him the trail curved around a butte and he felt a glimmer of hope. Urging his tired horse to even greater speed, Pierce leaned over Midnight's neck and whispered, "It's up to you now, boy. Run as fast as you can. Lead them away."

Disengaging both feet from the stirrups, Pierce leaned low over Midnight's back, waiting for the right moment. It came when he saw a huge boulder resting at the foot of the butte. Abruptly he dropped off the horse's back, rolling with the momentum of the fall to conceal himself behind the rock. He hit the ground hard, driving the breath from his lungs. The resulting explosion of pain sent him spinning toward unconsciousness. He passed out scant seconds after he landed.

Pierce neither saw nor heard the vigilante party thunder by. The trail of dust raised by Midnight's hooves and the bend in the road had prevented them from noticing that Pierce and his horse had parted company.

Daylight was waning when Pierce opened his eyes. When he tried to move, agony overwhelmed him. He lay back, breathing deeply to control the pain as he tried to recall why he was lying in a pool of blood behind a boulder. It took a moment of intense concentration to remember what had happened. With total recall came the realization that he had to get out of there fast, before the vigilantes doubled back to look for him.

It would soon be dark, Pierce reflected, which would make it difficult to locate him. Of further help was the sound of thunder rumbling in the distance. A pop-up storm would be most welcome, for it would make tracking him difficult.

Dragging himself into a sitting position, Pierce took a moment to gather his strength and get his bearings. There were bound to be ranches in the area. And if he wasn't mistaken, the town of Rolling Prairie was not too far away.

Realizing time was running out, Pierce staggered to his feet. He swayed dangerously, then moved one foot in front of the other by sheer dint of will. Blood soaked his clothing and he wondered how much blood a man could lose before dying from it.

Pierce made slow progress through the canyon, remaining conscious by listing in his head all his reasons why women couldn't be trusted. He began with his own mother, who had abandoned her family for a traveling salesman when they lived in Illinois. Embittered by his wife's desertion, their father had eventually sold their farm and homesteaded to Montana, reminding his sons repeatedly that trusting females could lead to trouble, and more often than not he'd been correct.

Chad had learned his lesson the hard way. He'd courted Loretta Casey, the town beauty, and had even become engaged. But the fickle miss had backed out after Chad had lost his heart to her. Loretta dumped him for an eastern dandy who offered her a chance to live in a big city, which Chad had steadfastly refused to consider. As for Ryan, he found women too demanding for his liking. The one girl Ryan had taken an interest in had insisted that he work in her father's mercantile and stop his wild carousing. Ryan might have been wild, but he loved ranching.

Pierce thought back over his own mistakes, beginning with the day he'd married Polly Summers. He'd been just twenty-one and in love, or so he'd thought. He'd assumed he was getting a shy virgin and discovered he'd married an experienced woman who quickly found other lovers to fill her empty hours. When he'd found her in bed with Riley Reed, her former lover, he'd kicked her out. Trey Delaney, Pierce's father, had wielded his substantial influence to obtain an annulment. His mother and Polly had both left their marks on Pierce. He'd vowed he'd not become a three-time loser.

Stumbling through the dark canyon, Pierce remained conscious by recalling his mother and reliving the anguish her leaving had caused the family. As he'd grown older and wiser, Pierce had never forgotten his lesson. Women could ruin a man's life. He enjoyed sex, and applied himself with zeal each time he went to town, but it was strictly lust-driven. He had his favorites among the women plying their trade above Stumpy's saloon, but none of them meant more to him than a good lay.

Pierce had reached the end of his endurance. It had begun to rain by the time he climbed out of the canyon, and his mind was no longer lucid. Was he hallucinating or did he actually see the dim outline of a ranch house in the distance? He was so parched his throat felt as if it were on fire, and his mouth was drier than a desert. Though lightheaded from loss of blood, he forced himself to continue, knowing that once he stopped he was a goner. If wild animals didn't get him, the vigilantes would.

Pierce stumbled to his knees. Pain exploded through him. He wanted to lie down, to shut his eyes to lose his pain in unconsciousness. He fought the urge to give up as the ranch house took form in the darkness. He blinked. It was no mirage, the structure was real, rising not one hundred yards in front of him.

Light spilled from the downstairs windows, drawing Pierce like a beacon. In a final burst of energy, he staggered forward, halting when he reached the front porch. He wasn't thinking clearly, he realized as he paused to catch his breath. He couldn't just barge in on people he didn't know and wasn't sure he could trust. He needed water and rest before his mind could work clearly enough to assess the situation.

He spied a pump in the yard and approached it with measured steps. No one was around, which seemed strange on a ranch this size. Using the last of his strength, he worked the pump handle and knelt to catch the first rush of water in his mouth. He drank greedily then thrust his head under the flow. When he was sufficiently refreshed, he dragged himself around to the back of the house, seeking a shed or outbuilding in which he could take shelter. He saw something better. The entrance to a root cellar.

Prying open the door, he quickly stumbled down the few steps onto the dirt floor. Once the door was pulled back into place, Pierce was engulfed in total darkness. Using his sense of touch, he located a sack of potatoes and rested his back against it. Having exhausted the reserve of energy he'd drawn upon to reach this place, Pierce finally allowed himself the blessed relief of unconsciousness.

Pierce awoke to more physical pain than he'd ever experienced in his entire twenty-eight years. His mouth tasted of blood and his head felt as if a herd of wild horses were stampeding inside it. The pain in his back was beyond description. He was smart enough to know that if the bullet didn't come out soon, blood poisoning would kill him.

Little pinpoints of light caught Pierce's attention and he glanced upward, noting that the floor-boards were slightly uneven, allowing him glimpses into the room directly overhead. From the amount of daylight visible, Pierce deduced that he had remained unconscious all night and far into the morning. He was thirsty again, and far weaker than he'd been the night before. Then he heard footsteps on the floorboards above and his attention sharpened.

The sound of voices raised in anger filtered down to him. Pierce strained to hear and could just barely make out the words. The voices were those of a man and woman.

"I'm sick of these delays, Zoey. If you don't set a date for our wedding soon, my bank will foreclose on your property."

"You know as well as I, Mr. Willoughby, that there is no mortgage on the Circle F. My father owned the ranch and land free and clear. If your bank holds the mortgage, it's a forgery."

"Are you suggesting I'm dishonest?" Willoughby blustered.

There was a pause and Pierce wondered if the man named Willoughby had frightened the woman into silence. But evidently she had more mettle than he gave her credit for.

"That's exactly what I'm suggesting, Samson Willoughby. You're a liar and a cheat. I wouldn't marry you under any circumstances. Besides, I already have a fiancé whom I love very much. We're to be married soon. He won't let you get away with this game you're playing with me."

"A fiancé," Willoughby sneered. "I don't believe there is a fiancé. Where does he live? Why hasn't he come forward before now? You're a terrible liar, Zoey."

"Look who's calling the kettle black," Zoey retorted.

"You can't hoodwink me, my dear. I've wanted you for as long as I can remember. At first your father stood in our way, but his death changed everything. You love this ranch, don't you? Well, I'm fond of it too. Our lands adjoin, only yours has rich grasslands and water rights that mine lack. Together we'll own a large portion of Montana. If your so-called fiancé doesn't show up soon, you'd better be prepared to marry me or lose your land." He tipped his hat. "Good day, my dear."

Zoey Fuller slammed the door behind Samson Willoughby with enough force to rattle the hinges. Two weeks! She'd been putting him off ever since her father's death six months ago. Zoey knew Willoughby was lying about the mortgage. Yet her search for the title to the ranch had been futile. It had to be here somewhere, but where?

The mortgage papers Willoughby had flashed before her looked like the real thing, but Zoey knew her father wouldn't mortgage the ranch without telling her. Money had been tight, but they'd always come through the hard times without sacrificing the ranch.

Blond and blue-eyed, twenty-two-year-old Zoey Fuller was a rare beauty who didn't comprehend the devastating effect she had on men. She'd had beaus, but none she wanted to spend the rest of her life with. Her father had given her free rein after her mother died when she was twelve, and during those years she'd acquired a mind of her own and a temper to match. She was equally as comfortable in flannel shirt and denim pants as she was in a dress. Since Robert Fuller's death, she'd run the ranch with the help of Cully, a crusty old cowhand who'd worked for her father for as long as she could remember. If he had another name, he'd never divulged it to anyone as far as she knew.

Now Cully was the only hand left on the place. The others had either quit or been driven off by Willoughby's men. Raiders had been systematically stripping her ranch of livestock, and she was on the brink of bankruptcy. After her father's death, Zoey learned that ranch hands were reluctant to work for a woman.

With Willoughby and other ranchers in the area offering higher wages, Zoey was between a rock and a hard place. Willoughby was breathing down her neck, and time was running out. When no fiancé showed up she'd be forced off her land. Marrying Willoughby wasn't even an option she'd consider. She wouldn't have that liar and cheat if he were served up on a silver platter.

Zoey left the house in a wretched mood. There was so much to do and so little time. It was nearly impossible to run a ranch with only Cully to help with the chores. Perhaps she'd go into town later today and try again to recruit hands. Her last two trips had been a waste of time. Willoughby had spread the word that employment at the Circle F would be temporary, that the ranch was in deep trouble financially.

Zoey went to the barn and started pitching hay down from the loft. She noted that Cully had been there earlier to let the horses out into the pasture. She worked tirelessly until her arms began to ache and her stomach rumbled from hunger. She'd only nibbled at breakfast this morning, and lunch sounded good right now. She suspected Cully would be hungry too.

On her way to the house, Zoey remembered that she'd used the last of the potatoes in the bin. She'd have to go to the root cellar for more. Rounding the corner of the house, she noted that the cellar door was slightly ajar but thought little of it. The door was heavy, but Zoey was accustomed to performing difficult tasks and pried it open with ease. Zoey carefully made her way down the steps into the murky darkness.

The sack of potatoes, she recalled, was sitting in the far corner. She felt her way across the dirt floor, nearly falling when she stumbled across an obstacle in her path, an obstacle that hadn't been there yesterday. She dropped to her knees, and her searching hands encountered something warm, something soft . . . something human. She recoiled in alarm. God, why hadn't she brought a lantern down with her?

She stifled a scream when the object moved beneath her hands. Proceeding with caution, she encountered what felt like a bundle of rags. But the bundle of rags had muscles, hard muscles, and a wide chest, and . . . and . . . a face covered with stiff bristles. A man! She sat back on her haunches and stared hard at him. Shocked, she wondered why he was so still and what he was doing in her cellar.

Suddenly he grasped her wrist and she cried out. A moment later a light appeared at the opening of the root cellar.

"Are you down there, Miz Zoey?"

Cully stood at the top of the stairs, holding a lantern.

"Oh, Cully, thank God. Come down here quickly."

"I heard you scream. You find a big rat

30

down there?" He started down the stairs. "I set some traps the other day when I saw they were eating the potatoes and carrots."

"Not a rat," Zoey said, wresting her wrist from the stranger's grasp. "There's a man down here."

The intruder let out a groan and Cully rushed to his side, holding the lantern high. Both he and Zoey got their first good look at the man in the cellar.

"Well, I'll be danged. What's wrong with him?"

"I don't know, Cully. He sure is pale. Maybe he's ill."

Then she saw the pool of congealing blood beneath him and blanched. "Set the lamp down and turn him over slowly," she told Cully.

Cully did as he was bid, cursing beneath his breath when he saw blood soaking the dirt floor. "He's lost a heap of blood, Miz Zoey."

Zoey carefully raised Pierce's jacket, vest, and shirt, finding the bullet wound beneath his shoulder blade. "He's been shot. The bullet is still in him. If it's not removed soon, he'll die of infection." She pulled off Pierce's bandanna and held it to the wound.

"There ain't no decent doctor in Rolling

Prairie since old Doc Tucker took to drink," Cully said. "And it'll take too long to fetch a doctor from another town. The stranger would be dead before the doctor arrived."

Zoey felt a jolt of pity for the man. She'd never considered herself a particularly tenderhearted woman. She couldn't afford to be, but something about this wounded stranger moved her. "Can you remove the bullet, Cully?"

Cully scratched the thatch of grizzled gray hair growing in tufts on his head, and shrugged. "I can try, Miz Zoey, but I can't promise he won't die anyway. We'll have to move him into the house. You sure you want to do this? The man could be dangerous. He could be wanted by the law. You might be letting yourself in for a heap of trouble."

Zoey glanced down at Pierce, more than a little startled to discover that he was quite handsome in a rugged sort of way. And he could be exactly the kind of man Cully described. But somehow she didn't think so.

"I'm sure, Cully. You take his shoulders and I'll take his feet. Together we should be able to get him into the house."

Chapter 2

Pain. Stabbing, excruciating pain. Burning pain. Pierce tried to escape it but was inexorably drawn deeper into torment. Why was he lying on his stomach, pinned down like a sacrificial lamb and suffering beyond human endurance?

"He's coming around, Cully."

"I'm not quite through, Miz Zoey. Don't let him move."

"I'm trying, Cully, but he's awfully strong."

Suddenly Pierce let out a shout and went limp.

"I got it, Miz Zoey!" Cully's voice was exultant as he dropped the bullet he had pried from Pierce's flesh into a basin. "Now hand me that bottle of whiskey so I can disinfect the wound."

"Do you think that's wise?"

"It's all we got."

"Will he live?" Zoey asked with concern.

"Can't tell. He looks healthy enough. No

prison pallor. Don't know who or what he was running from, but he don't look like no outlaw to me. Course, that's my personal opinion."

"I trust your judgment, Cully. I can finish up here. You go get something to eat."

"You sure?"

"Very sure."

After Cully left, Zoey made a bandage from a soft cotton sheet she'd torn into strips and affixed it to the wound. Then she wound another long strip around Pierce's chest to hold it in place. When she finished, she stood back to inspect her handiwork.

Cully had undressed the stranger down to his underwear while she'd boiled water and found the sharp knife Cully asked for. When she returned to the room, the stranger lay on his stomach, a sheet covering him from the waist down.

His back, arms, and chest were darkened from the sun, as if he was accustomed to working outside without benefit of a shirt. He was tall, broad, and splendidly put together. He was lean yet muscular in all the places that counted. There was no layer of fat around his waist. If she could see his legs, she expected they'd match the rest of him.

He wore his straight, dark hair slightly longer than most men, just brushing his shoulders, but it seemed to enhance his rugged good looks. A stray lock of hair had fallen into his eyes, and Zoey reached out unconsciously to push it back into place. It felt soft and thick and clean, and her fingers lingered longer than necessary.

Suddenly realizing what she was doing, Zoey snapped her hand away as if burned. It wasn't like her to fantasize about a man, and a strange man at that. She had no idea who he was, for he had no identification on him, just a wad of money stuffed into his vest pocket. His clothing was of good quality and his boots were practically new. If he was an outlaw, he certainly was a prosperous one.

Cully returned a short time later. "I'll sit with him now, Miz Zoey. Go get yourself some grub. There ain't nothing more we can do for him now but to see that he's kept comfortable."

"I wonder who he is," Zoey reflected aloud.

Cully shrugged his thin shoulders. "Hard telling. We'll just have to wait until he's well enough to speak up."

"I'll return later," Zoey said as she headed toward the door. She stopped a moment and added, "See if you can get some water down him before fever sets in."

"Don't fret, Miz Zoey, I'll take care of him."

Reassured that Cully would watch over the wounded stranger, Zoey left the room. There were still countless chores that needed doing. She had eggs to gather, and while she was at it, she might as well kill a chicken. A rich broth would do the stranger good. When he awoke, if he awoke, he'd probably be ravenous.

Pierce groaned and opened his eyes. Mind-numbing pain permeated every part of his body. Slowly he became aware of his surroundings. He was lying on something soft. A bed? He raised his head slightly and saw a man dozing in a chair beside him. He was spare of frame and wiry, his weather-beaten face the texture of wrinkled shoe leather, attesting to his advanced age and years spent toiling in the sun, wind, and rain. A shock of grizzled gray hair sprouted in every direction atop his head.

Suddenly the old man's eyes opened and met Pierce's gaze.

"So you're awake, are you? Would you like some water?"

Pierce swallowed painfully and gave a slight nod, which set his head to spinning. "Please," he croaked.

The old man supported Pierce's head while he drank. "Take it easy, stranger."

"Thank you," Pierce said weakly. "Where am I?"

"This here is the Circle F ranch." The man asked bluntly, "Who shot you?"

"Oh, he's awake!"

Pierce turned his head toward the voice, set his eyes upon an angel, and thought he was hallucinating. The woman who had just walked into the room was too beautiful to be real. Immediately he grew wary. Women who looked like that were even less trustworthy than the plain-looking ones. He'd learned that one had to be extremely cautious around beautiful women, for they were often too full of themselves.

This woman was extraordinarily lovely. Hair the color of ripe wheat hanging down her back in a single braid, and eyes as blue as the Montana sky on a cloudless day. Her curvaceous body looked as if it had been poured into the tight pants she wore. Her breasts were unfettered beneath her shirt, and Pierce imagined he could see the impression of her nipples pushing against the worn material.

She hurried to the bed. "How do you feel?"

"Like hell. There isn't a place on my body that doesn't hurt. Did you remove the bullet?" The clean, subtly female scent of her teased Pierce's nostrils, shortening his breath until it was an effort to breathe.

"You owe Cully for that."

"You're still not out of the woods," Cully said. "And watch your language around Miz Zoey."

"Sorry," Pierce mumbled. His gaze slid slowly over Zoey's curves. He'd never seen a woman wearing trousers before. What manner of woman was she besides a beautiful one? he wondered.

"Who are you?" Zoey asked curiously. "Who shot you and how did you end up in my root cellar? Most men would have asked for help at the door. Who or what are you hiding from?"

Pierce opened his mouth to answer but never got the words out. The small amount of talking he'd accomplished had exhausted his reservoir of strength. With a sigh, he slid back into unconsciousness.

"Is he all right?" Zoey asked with concern.

"He's still breathing," Cully said, "but I ain't sure for how long."

Zoey placed her hand on Pierce's forehead. "He's burning up. What can we do?"

"I'll fetch water from the stream. I heard somewhere that bathing a feverish person in cold water will bring down their temperature."

He left directly, leaving Zoey alone with Pierce. "Don't die," she whispered, "please don't die." She didn't know why, but the thought of losing this stranger was unthinkable. She had no idea where he came from or who he was, but something about him moved her.

Lost in the depths of pain and shadows, Pierce heard a sweet voice calling him back from the darkness engulfing him. He decided then and there not to die. If this woman who didn't even know him wanted him to live, he owed it to her and to his brothers to comply.

Pierce slowly returned to the world of the living. He had moved in and out of consciousness several times during the critical hours of his recovery, aware that someone was sloshing cool water over his body. Cool water and cool hands. And a voice that defied the devil to save him. His first cognizant thought was that he owed the woman named Zoey his life. His second was that thinking like that could get him into a heap of trouble.

"We almost lost you," Zoey said when she found Pierce staring at her. "Welcome back."

His voice sounded rough and scratchy. "How long have I been out?"

"Three days. We thought the fever would take you for sure. Are you hungry?"

"Not really. Just thirsty."

"You have to eat something. I made some chicken broth. Do you think you can stand being turned over on your back?"

He gritted his teeth. "I reckon, if you help me."

Zoey moved with alacrity, helping him to turn so that his shoulders rested on the pillows she had placed behind him. Pierce found the pain bearable and was glad to change positions after lying on his stomach for so long. Then an urgent need made itself known and Pierce winced with discomfort.

"What's wrong? Did I hurt you?"

"No, I need . . . that is . . . perhaps you could send up that man who's been helping you."

When she realized what Pierce wanted, Zoey's face turned bright pink. "I'll send Cully right up and return later with your

40

soup. Then we need to talk. I don't even know your name."

A half hour later Zoey returned to Pierce's room bearing a tray holding a steaming bowl of soup. She set it carefully down on the nightstand and sat on the edge of the bed to feed him.

"I don't need your help," Pierce said grumpily, unaccustomed to being waited on by a woman.

Zoey let him try, knowing he was still too weak to wield the spoon with any amount of dexterity. After several futile attempts, Pierce handed her the spoon and said, "You win." He hated displaying weakness of any kind in front of women.

Zoey thought him too stubborn for his own good as she took up the spoon, dipped it in the broth, and brought it to his mouth. Pierce swallowed grudgingly. When the bowl was nearly empty, he turned his head away. "Enough."

"Very well," Zoey said, setting the bowl aside. "Now then, who are you?"

Pierce scowled. He didn't like this helpless feeling of being cornered. The way he saw it, he had two choices. He could tell the truth or he could lie. Lying seemed a despicable thing to do in view of Zoey's care of him.

"My name is Pierce Delaney. Who are you?"

"Zoey Fuller. Where are you from, Mr. Delaney?"

"Around. Here and there. Cully said this is the Circle F ranch."

Suddenly Pierce recalled the conversation he'd heard while hiding in the root cellar. "Who is Samson Willoughby and why is he threatening you?"

Zoey recoiled in shock. "Who told you about Samson Willoughby?"

"I heard you and Willoughby arguing while I was hiding in the root cellar. What was that all about?"

Zoey bristled. "It's really none of your concern, Mr. Delaney. Now, where were we? Oh, yes, who shot you?"

"No one you know," Pierce shot back. His eyes were starting to glaze over and Zoey realized enough had been said for now. But they were far from through talking. Pierce Delaney had a way of evading the truth.

The following day Pierce felt stronger than the day before. He was able to feed himself and began to feel real hunger. He was thinking about getting up and trying to move about when he heard riders approaching the house. He knew without being told that the vigilantes had found him. And at a time he was still too weak to leave his bed. There was no help for it now. Dragging himself from bed, he painfully made his way to where his clothes lay, looking for his guns. Unfortunately his guns had been removed and were nowhere in sight.

Pierce's stamina nearly deserted him as he crossed to the window and dropped down to peer over the sill. He'd been right. The vigilante party from Dry Gulch rode into the yard. They reined in sharply when they saw Zoey emerging from the barn. He felt somewhat relieved to see Cully falling in beside her, armed with a shotgun. Pierce feared Zoey would be harmed and he didn't want that to happen. Not on his account.

With a pang of regret, Pierce realized his luck had run out. Once Zoey learned the vigilantes were looking for him and why, she'd gladly hand him over to Riley Reed. He buried his head in his arms and waited.

"Sorry to bother you, ma'am. I'm Riley Reed from up around Dry Gulch. We're vigilantes. We're looking for a fugitive from the law. Have you seen a tall, dark-haired man skulking around here in the last few days? He couldn't have gotten far without a horse."

Zoey and Cully exchanged knowing glances. Cully shrugged his shoulders, his gesture telling Zoey that it was up to her to decide whether to turn Pierce over to these rough men who represented the law in these parts.

Zoey didn't like the looks of the vigilantes. They were a motley crew at best. Their leader looked mean, and fully capable of cold-blooded murder.

"What did this fugitive do?"

"It ain't for tender ears, ma'am," Reed hedged.

"Nevertheless, I want to know if I need to arm myself should this man come around."

"Don't say I didn't warn ya. Pierce Delaney seduced a woman from a prominent family and refused to marry her when he got her with child."

"Is that all?" Zoey asked, relieved to learn that Pierce wasn't a murderer or thief.

"Not exactly, ma'am. When Cora Lee Doolittle insisted that he marry her, he beat her something fierce. It's a wonder she didn't lose the baby. She's a pitiful sight, ma'am."

Zoey gasped and exchanged a look with Cully. "Are you sure?"

"Would he run if he wasn't guilty? Have you seen him?"

Zoey hesitated so long, Reed grew impatient.

"Well? Either you've seen him or you ain't. Pierce Delaney is a vicious, violent man. He and his brothers are hell-raisers who've terrorized the townspeople for years. He's guilty, all right."

Zoey tried to imagine Pierce Delaney beating up a woman, and couldn't. It wasn't difficult to picture him seducing one, though, and taking great pleasure in doing so. Unfortunately she wasn't a good enough judge of men to decide if Pierce Delaney was capable of committing so despicable a crime against a woman. She looked at Cully and received no help from that quarter.

Finally, realizing the vigilantes wouldn't be put off, Zoey gave the answer her conscience demanded. "I'm sorry, no man bearing that description has shown up at the Circle F. In fact, we haven't seen a stranger in these parts for a good long time."

Riley Reed gave Zoey a sharp look, then raised a hand to the brim of his hat and said, "That's all we wanted to know, ma'am. If you see the man we're looking for, I suggest you notify the local law pronto. Can't take no chances with women beaters. You alone here, ma'am?"

The lustful look Reed bestowed upon Zoey made her skin crawl. "My . . . my husband is out chasing mavericks," she lied.

He touched his hand to the brim of his hat. "Good day to you then, ma'am. I reckon we'll head on back to Dry Gulch. Maybe the Delaney brothers will know where Pierce is hiding."

Zoey watched with trepidation as the vigilantes rode through the gate. She prayed she hadn't acted rashly by withholding vital information from the law, even if it was vigilante law.

"I hope you know what you're doing, Miz Zoey," Cully said. "I never did cotton to men beating up on defenseless women."

Zoey spun around to face the old man. "Do you think he did it?"

"It ain't my place to judge. I don't aim to see you get hurt, so I'll be keeping an eye on him."

"Pierce is in no condition to hurt anyone right now. He doesn't look the kind who

46

would do those things that man accused him of."

"Time will tell, Miz Zoey," Cully said cryptically. "I reckon I'll get on with the chores now that those men are gone."

Pierce didn't have the strength to put himself back to bed. He sat beneath the window, waiting for the vigilantes to burst into the room. Dimly he wondered if they would hang him from the nearest tree or wait until they were away from the ranch. He hoped they would wait, for he'd hate to have Zoey witness such a gruesome sight.

He heard the door open and braced himself.

Zoey entered the room, surprised to see Pierce crouched beneath the window in his underwear. "What are you doing out of bed? Do you want your wound to reopen, Mr. Delaney?"

Pierce raised his head and stared at Zoey in confusion. "Where are the vigilantes?"

"Gone."

Pierce couldn't believe his ears. "Why didn't you turn me in?" When women did something unexpected, they usually had a reason.

"Let me help you," Zoey said, wondering herself why she didn't have an answer.

Placing his arm over her shoulders, she supported his weight as he hobbled the few steps to the bed. He sat down on the edge of the mattress, trying to summon the strength to swing his legs up. Zoey bent, lifted his legs onto the bed, and covered him with a sheet.

"Why did you do it, Zoey?"

Zoey knew Pierce wanted an answer, but she still couldn't explain her reluctance to turn him over to the vigilantes. "I'm the one who should be asking questions, Mr. Delaney. For instance, are you or are you not the object of that manhunt?"

Pierce's mouth flattened into a grim line. Lying now would serve no purpose. "I am."

"Did you or did you not severely beat a woman?"

"I did not."

"Do you deny seducing the woman?"

"I deny everything. I never touched Cora Lee. She's lying if she said I did."

"Why did you run?"

"You saw those vigilantes. Do you think they'd stop to ask questions before stringing me up? No woman will ever force me into marriage."

Zoey met the turbulence of Pierce's gaze unflinchingly. Her pulse accelerated, heat curled insidiously through her. What was happening to her? She felt powerless to deny the disturbing chord his words struck in her. He looked and sounded implacable. From his dark hair to the rigid set of his firm jaw to the burning intensity of his green eyes, ruthless and unyielding. She wondered who the woman was that had made him so bitter.

A long silence followed, broken only by the soft groan issuing from Pierce's lips. One burning question reverberated within the silence of Zoey's mind. *Is Pierce Delaney lying?*

"I'm grateful for your help, you have to know that," Pierce said, feeling the effects of his first foray out of bed. "But if you don't mind, I'm about done in and would rather continue this conversation later."

"We will continue it, Mr. Delaney, whether you want to or not. The town of Rolling Prairie has vigilantes, too, and they're every bit as ruthless as those from Dry Gulch. I can easily send Cully for them."

"Do whatever you damn please," Pierce said, too weary to care. "But you'd better do it fast, before I'm well enough to light out of here."

"I may just do that, Mr. Delaney," Zoey

49

said with asperity as she flounced out of the room.

Damn contrary female, Pierce thought grumpily. He wouldn't give a plug nickel for the whole lot of them. He hated the feeling of being beholden to a woman. He couldn't decide if it was good luck or misfortune that had led him to the Circle F and Miss Zoey Fuller. His last thought before he fell into an exhausted sleep was that he'd be damn fortunate if he didn't awaken to find the vigilantes hauling him out of bed to hang him from the nearest tree.

"What did Delaney say about those charges against him?" Cully asked when he encountered Zoey later that day. "Is he guilty?"

"He denied everything, of course, except that he's the man they're after. Frankly, I don't know what to think. It's difficult to believe the man upstairs in that bed is the vicious man Mr. Reed described."

"Looks can be deceiving, Miz Zoey."

"Why didn't you say something if you thought he was guilty of those things?"

Cully aimed a long stream of tobacco juice between his feet. "Never did cotton to vigilantes. They pretend they're the law, and they ain't."

Zoey shuddered. "I couldn't agree more." She couldn't forget the insulting way in which Riley Reed had stared at her. "Unfortunately we have to put up with them until we get regular law in the territory."

"What are you going to do about Delaney?" Cully asked.

"For the moment, nothing. He's much too weak to be a threat to us. I'll make a decision when the time comes. Let's get to work, there's chores waiting."

"Have you forgotten about Willoughby, Miz Zoey? He's gonna want his answer soon. I know how much this ranch means to you."

"I've got to find that deed, Cully. I know Pa wouldn't mortgage the ranch without my knowledge. Where could it be? I've looked everywhere."

Two days later, Samson Willoughby appeared at Zoey's door.

"You look mighty fetching today, Zoey. As good as you look in britches, when we're married you'll wear dresses and act like a lady. Your Pa let you run wild. He was too indulgent."

"State your business, Mr. Willoughby, I have a ranch to run."

51

"Not for long, my dear," he said with a smirk. "Aren't you going to invite me inside?"

"I'm very busy, Mr. Willoughby."

"Indeed, so am I." He pushed past her into the house. "I've always admired this house. Your father had good taste."

Zoey fumed in impotent rage. "What is it you want, Mr. Willoughby?"

"First, you must call me Samson. We'll be husband and wife soon."

"Not as long as I have a breath left in my body."

"And a lovely body it is," Willoughby said, his gaze lingering on her full breasts. "I can't wait to have you in my bed. We'll deal well with one another."

Pierce heard the rumble of voices coming from downstairs, and scowled when he identified the voice of the man speaking with Zoey. He had heard it before. Curious to know what was going on, he managed to drag himself from bed. He paused in the doorway to rest, listening to the conversation wafting up from below.

"Why do you insist on plaguing me, Mr. Willoughby?" he heard Zoey say.

"You forget, my dear, that my bank holds the mortgage on your land. If you don't marry me, I'll be forced to foreclose. The land will be mine whether you decide to marry me or not, but as my wife, you can continue to live here, where you were born and raised. I know how much this land means to you. And you have to know how much I want you."

"When my fiancé arrives, he'll find a way to prove you're a liar and a cheat."

"Dream on, my dear. I vow you'll marry no one but me. Now, since we'll be married soon, I'd like a sample of what I'm getting."

Before Zoey realized what he intended, she found herself clasped against Willoughby's chest. He was stronger than he looked, and her futile attempts to escape served only to arouse him.

"Let me go!"

"Not yet," Willoughby said, clamping his mouth over hers in a bruising kiss.

From his vantage point, Pierce heard the struggle going on between Zoey and Willoughby, and frustration welled up inside him. In his weakened condition he was helpless as a kitten. If only he had his gun. He was wondering if he'd pass out if he tried to negotiate the stairs when Zoey did something that made his intervention unnecessary. Drawing back her knee, she brought it forward into Willoughby's groin with enough force to bring him to his knees. He screamed and clutched himself in agony.

"You'll pay for that," he gasped between sobs. "Once we're married I'll make you sorry you attacked me. I intended to treat you gently, but I can see you need taming."

Pierce let out a chuckle. He'd hate to ruffle Miss Zoey Fuller's feathers. He waited, making no effort to return to bed until he was certain Willoughby wouldn't retaliate. He needn't have worried. Cully burst through the door moments later. He looked mad enough to pull the trigger on the shotgun he carried. Pierce hoped he would.

"Is this polecat bothering you, Miz Zoey?"

"Mr. Willoughby was just leaving, Cully. Bring his horse around, will you?"

Willoughby had finally gained his feet, though he still clutched his groin protectively. "That man has to go when we marry," he ground out, eyeing Cully balefully. "I'm leaving, and when I return it will be with the law to back me up. I know how attached you are to this land, so I'll also bring a preacher along in case you change your mind about marrying me."

"Don't bother," Zoey said with bravado. "I'm marrying my fiancé as soon as he arrives, which should be any day now."

Willoughby laughed harshly. "Choose something nice to wear for our wedding. Get rid of those britches."

Leaning against the door for support, Pierce watched Willoughby leave, curious about Zoey's "fiancé." Pierce didn't like Samson Willoughby's looks. Somewhere in his mid-thirties, Willoughby wasn't unattractive, but his long ferret face had a sly look about it Pierce didn't trust. His eyes were so light a blue as to appear colorless. He was of medium height and build, but Pierce suspected Willoughby was stronger than he looked.

But none of this was any of his business, Pierce told himself. He had his own problems. He'd been accused of something he didn't do, and couldn't return home to his own ranch until his brothers cleared up the mess.

Pierce couldn't blame Zoey for trying to protect her ranch; he'd react in the same way. His home and family meant everything to him. The only difference was that the Delaney brothers were quite prosperous and had no need to mortgage their land.

Pierce was reluctant to return to bed now that he'd gotten this far. His fever wasn't completely gone, but each day he grew a little stronger, though he still had a long way to go. Another week or two and he'd be strong enough to leave the bed permanently. Somehow he had to contact his brothers and find out if Cora Lee had retracted her story yet, and if he was still being hunted by the vigilantes.

"What are you doing out of bed?" Zoey asked as she set the tray of food she was carrying down on the nightstand and assisted Pierce back to bed.

Pierce hated to admit it, but he was still too weak to roam about, no matter how much he detested lying in bed. A scant week ago he'd been knocking at death's door.

"What makes you think Willoughby is lying about the mortgage?" Pierce asked as Zoey set the tray on his lap. "Perhaps your father *did* mortgage the ranch."

"You heard?"

"I couldn't help hearing." He stared at her, thinking she looked beautiful with her face flushed and her vivid blue eyes flashing angrily. "If Willoughby is lying, the deed to your land would be in your possession. Do you have it?"

Zoey shook her head. "I've torn the house apart looking for the deed, but can't find it. But I know Pa wouldn't mortgage the farm without telling me."

"You have no idea what may have happened?"

"None, except . . . shortly after Pa's death, the house was broken into. Nothing seemed to be missing, so I didn't give it another thought. It was such a sad time. The hands were quitting and our livestock was disappearing. Shortly afterward, Samson Willoughby started pestering me about paying the mortgage, insisting that payment was long overdue."

"What about your fiancé? Why isn't he helping you?"

Zoey gave him a startled look. "That's none of your business."

"You're right. In a few days I'll be on my way." But he still couldn't help his curiosity.

"Where will you go? You don't appear to be a man who enjoys being on the run. That Riley Reed fellow mentioned something about your brothers. What about parents?"

"They're gone," he said tersely. "There are just Chad and Ryan at home besides myself. I'm the eldest. Our ranch lies west of the city of Dry Gulch. That's all you need to know, Miss Fuller."

"That's more than I want to know, Mr. Delaney." *Impossible man,* Zoey thought crossly. He wasn't a bit grateful. She should have let him die.

That night Zoey picked at her supper, wracking her brain for a solution to her nearly insurmountable problems. For weeks she'd been taunting Willoughby with a fiancé who didn't exist. What was she going to do when the man failed to arrive? Marrying Samson Willoughby was unfathomable and utterly repulsive. Just the thought of him kissing her, touching her, doing all those things married couples did, made her want to vomit. Yet what choice did she have?

She was willing to do anything — *anything!* — to keep from losing the land her father had worked years to own, toiled tirelessly to make prosper. But marrying Willoughby was where she put her foot down.

Zoey's stomach rebelled as she put down her fork and pushed her plate away. She had to do something, but what? Why couldn't there *really* be a fiancé ready and willing to help her fight Willoughby? Why . . .

Zoey went still as her mind suddenly grasped at the single, lifesaving thread dangling before her. Why hadn't she thought of it before?

Chapter 3

Zoey spent the next twenty-four hours mulling over what she would say to Pierce. It wasn't going to be easy. She perceived in Pierce a hostility toward women. Somewhere, at some time in his past, a woman had hurt him. No matter, she would do whatever was necessary to save her ranch. Her idea was sound. Had Pierce been in possession of his strength, she might have the courage to never approach him with her proposal, but he was more or less captive to whatever she suggested. Pierce was too weak to leave his bed, let alone leave the ranch.

Pierce owed her for saving his life, Zoey tried to convince herself. He would have died if she hadn't found him and rescued him from death's jaws. She could have easily turned him over to the vigilantes when they came for him, but she hadn't. That should count for something. Now all she had to do was convince Pierce that her plan was sound.

Deciding to beard the lion in his den, Zoey slowly climbed the stairs to lay out her plan before Pierce. His mood was anything but pleasant when she entered the room.

"It's about time you showed up," Pierce growled impatiently. "I finished eating hours ago. Where's Cully? Thought maybe we could play some cards. Lying in bed all day staring at the ceiling is killing me."

"And good evening to you," Zoey greeted cheerily. She decided to ignore Pierce's bad humor. Men rarely made good patients.

"I'm getting out of this bed tomorrow," Pierce warned.

"I don't think so. Turn around, let me look at your wound. I haven't changed the bandage yet today."

Pierce glared at her, then eased over on his stomach so she could get to his wound. "How does it look?"

She peeled the bandage away. "It's healing. How do you feel?"

"Tolerable. I'm not ready to ride yet, but it won't be long."

"You're a long way from healed, Mr. Delaney."

He winced as she placed a new bandage upon the wound. Her cool hands felt soothing on his flesh. "Don't you think it's time you called me Pierce? You've probably seen more of me than my own mother."

Zoey flushed. That was certainly true. She had washed every inch of him with cold water, trying to bring down his fever. "Very well, Pierce. You may call me Zoey."

"I already do. Are you embarrassed at seeing so much of me?"

"Not in the least," she lied. She'd never seen a man's naked body before. And this man's body appeared to be an extraordinary specimen. "Your temperament hasn't improved any, Pierce. All finished. You can turn around now."

Carefully he slid around to his back. "Thank you. Are you going to send Cully up here or not?"

"Not," Zoey said succinctly. "There's something I wish to talk to you about."

"I don't like the sound of that. If you're going to ask me to reimburse you for your care, I agree. There's money in my vest. There should be enough there to satisfy you." He should have known money would come into the conversation sooner or later. There wasn't a woman alive who wasn't out to beggar a man.

"I don't want your money."

61

Pierce's eyes narrowed. "What *do* you want, then?"

Zoey flushed but refused to be intimidated by Pierce's bad temper. What she wanted from him was more important to her than money. She drew herself up to her full five foot three and returned his glare.

"Very well, Mr. Delaney, I do want something from you." Her heart hammered loudly inside her chest; she wondered if Pierce could hear it. She swallowed convulsively and continued. "You know that Samson Willoughby is pressuring me to marry him."

Pierce nodded, waiting. He knew he wasn't going to like what Miss Zoey Fuller had to say.

"I despise the man and have steadfastly refused to marry him. You also know I can turn you over to the vigilantes any time I wish. You could run, but in your condition you won't get far."

Jagged shards of green fire stabbed into her. His voice was harsh and derisive. "Are you trying to blackmail me? Tell me what you want."

Zoey exhaled sharply. "I want you to marry me. Now, today, tomorrow at the very latest. In name only, of course. Once Willoughby realizes I'm no longer free to marry, he'll leave me alone. Maybe he'll even forget about the mortgage. At the very least, it will give me time to prove he's a liar and a cheat. After a suitable time you can leave and seek an annulment."

Pierce stared at her as if she had two heads. She could tell he was furious by the stiff way in which he held his body. "Are you loco, lady? What about your fiancé? Wouldn't he object?"

"There is no fiancé. I made him up to buy some time."

"What makes you think I'd agree to marry you?"

"I hold all the cards, Pierce. It wouldn't take much to get that lynching party back here. They didn't appear to be the kind of men willing to listen to lengthy explanations. You've already said you wouldn't marry Cora Lee. What choice do you have?"

Damn conniving female had him over a barrel, Pierce thought, too furious to speak. If Zoey called in the local vigilantes, he'd be sent back to Dry Gulch. He wouldn't stand a chance. If he continued to resist marriage to Cora Lee, he'd be hung before the circuit judge came through town. And he'd be damned before he'd play papa to Cora Lee's bastard, if indeed she was in the family way. He spit out a curse. Women were all schemers, and Zoey was more clever than most. She wasn't above using blackmail to rope him into her harebrained plot.

On the other hand, Pierce knew he was in no condition to flee. If he refused, Zoey threatened to call in the law. Was she capable of doing such a thing? He thought she was. Desperate women were capable of anything. His only hope was to bide his time and pray that his brothers found the man who beat Cora Lee, or convince Cora Lee to tell the truth. The truth would vindicate him.

"Give me your answer," Zoey pressed. God, she hated what she was doing, but she was under tremendous pressure. Her dream was to marry a man she loved, a man who wanted her. And obviously Pierce Delaney was dead set against marrying any woman.

Pierce's eyes turned hard and his lips pulled into a taut smile. "So you want to marry me."

Zoey didn't like the sound of that. "Only for a short time. Until I can find the missing deed and prove Willoughby a liar."

"You want this to be a marriage in name only?" Pierce qualified. His gaze rested on her breasts.

Heat suffused her. What was he getting at? "Of course, I'd have it no other way."

Without warning, Pierce grabbed her arm and pulled her down onto the bed. She fell atop him, but he ignored the pain. "Tell me, Miss Zoey Fuller, what will you do if I demand my husbandly right?"

Zoey looked into the glittering depths of his green eyes and suddenly found it difficult to breathe. "You wouldn't!"

He nodded grimly.

"Why? You don't even know me."

Deliberately trying to frighten her into changing her mind, Pierce said, "I know all I need to know. You're a woman, a damned attractive one, too."

Zoey felt the heat of his gaze searing her. "Let me up!"

Looking deeply into the clear blue depths of her eyes, Pierce very deliberately placed a hand on her breast, squeezing gently, rubbing the unfettered nipple between his thumb and forefinger. With satisfaction, he watched her eyes widen in shock.

"No!"

"That's only a taste of what we'll do if you force me into this marriage."

"But . . ."

Pierce couldn't resist the temptation of

those moist lips, slightly parted and ripely lush. Grabbing a handful of hair in his fist, he pulled her head back and tasted her. Her breath was sweetly scented, and against his will Pierce was drawn deeper into the magic of the kiss. He heard her whimper as his tongue thrust past her teeth into her mouth, but he couldn't have stopped now if he wanted to. And he certainly didn't want to. Surprisingly, he was enjoying the lesson he was teaching Zoey.

Zoey resisted fiercely when Pierce's tongue swept past her teeth into her mouth. Her body stiffened in his arms and she pulled away abruptly. Pierce groaned in frustration. He was enjoying this too much! When she backed away from him, his look of blunt sexual calculation brought heat rushing to her cheeks.

"Are you willing to surrender to me as a wife should?" Pierce asked harshly. "Because if we marry, I'll damn sure demand my rights."

Scrambling off the bed, Zoey backed away, glaring at him in confusion. Her face was flushed, her chest rising and falling with each angry breath she took. A distinct sense of unreality engulfed her, as if this were all a bad dream. But she wasn't stupid, she knew Pierce was trying to frighten her. Yet she couldn't deny his kiss had sent her stomach into a wild whirl. The fact that she had responded to his kiss, even for a moment, stunned her. It wouldn't happen again.

Hands on hips, she challenged him boldly. "If you do anything like that again, I'll bring the vigilantes here faster than you can say your name. I know what you're doing and it won't work. You have no choice, Mr. Delaney. We'll marry under my terms or you'll find yourself facing a noose."

"Like hell! If you want me, it's my terms we'll agree upon." He gave her a smile ripe with sexual innuendo. "I won't be this weak forever."

"Forget it, Mr. Delaney. I'm the one calling the shots."

"No way, lady!" He struggled into an upright position, swung his feet over the side of the bed, and managed to stand. "I'm getting the hell out of here."

He made it through the door and just beyond it before collapsing a few steps short of the stairs. Zoey had to force herself not to go to him. She had to stick to her guns if she wanted to win this battle of wills. Otherwise she'd have to choose between losing her ranch and marrying Samson Willoughby. Marrying Pierce made sense. Willoughby couldn't demand that she marry him if she was already married, and Pierce could remain here until his brothers solved his problems back home.

"Are you ready to listen to reason, Pierce?" Zoey asked sweetly. "You're still weak as a kitten." She helped him to his feet and back to bed. "I know how badly you want to get out of that bed, but you still have a way to go before you're well enough to ride. After we marry you can leave anytime you wish. All I need is your name. In time, you can apply for an annulment."

He gave her a bleak, tight-lipped smile. "You seem to hold the upper hand, lady, for now. Women are all alike. Pretty or plain, smart or dumb, you always find a way to get what you want. And it's the man who usually pays the price."

"You sure do have a low opinion of women."

Pierce gave her a slow, sensual smile. "Oh, I like women well enough . . . for certain things, at certain times. In fact," he said, reaching for her, "I could use one right now."

Zoey scooted out of his reach. "The only

thing you can use right now is sleep. Good night, Pierce. I'll send Cully to town for the preacher first thing in the morning. Is that agreeable?"

"It's your call, Zoey."

Though soft, his voice was edged with steel. Zoey prayed she wasn't making a mistake. Entering into a marriage in name only was the lesser of two evils.

"So be it. Rest well, Pierce." She turned to leave.

"Zoey."

She paused at the door.

"Do you think you can find a dress to wear at our wedding? And I'd appreciate it if you'd find me a decent pair of pants and shirt that aren't bloodstained."

She nodded curtly and continued out the door.

"Zoey," he called after her. "Bring my guns."

Though she was out of sight, he heard her answer clearly.

"No."

Damn conniving female, Pierce raged. Zoey Fuller had done nothing to allay his distrust of women. She'd saved his life only to turn around and demand his freedom in payment. She should have let him die, he thought, then immediately changed his mind. Death was too final, and this marriage needn't be. Besides, he'd already come to despise Samson Willoughby. And he had nowhere else to go right now. Dry Gulch certainly offered no option.

Pierce knew he was at a disadvantage and hated it. He was too weak to ride away from the Circle F, and unable to prove his innocence if he did. Only Cora Lee could free him with the truth, and he prayed his brothers would convince her to do so.

Damn, he wished he had his guns.

Zoey appeared in Pierce's room bright and early the next morning. She carried a basin of water and shaving gear that had belonged to her father.

Pierce's brow slanted upward. "I assume that's for me." He rubbed a hand over the beginnings of a fine beard. "I was getting kind of fond of this."

Zoey placed a towel on his chest and worked up a lather in a cup. Then she tested the razor with the edge of her thumb.

"Whoa, you're not going to use that on me, are you?"

"That's what it's for. I can't shave you with a dull razor. This one has a fine edge. Pa kept it clean and sharp."

"Get me a mirror, I'll do it myself."

"I don't think so." She slapped the lather on his face and nearly laughed aloud when it got into his mouth and he began to sputter. "Lie still," she warned. "I'm very good at this, but only if you don't make me nervous."

Pierce went still, his eyes never leaving Zoey's face as she shaved him. Zoey was right, he thought grudgingly, she was very good at this. She finished and stepped back to inspect her handiwork.

"You'll do."

"All this for a wedding neither of us wants?" he asked with a hint of mockery.

She gave him a mischievous grin. "A girl doesn't get married every day."

"Neither does a man. My first marriage was attended by the entire town of Dry Gulch."

Zoey went still. "You've been married before?" A terrible thought suddenly occurred to her. "You're not married now, are you?"

"No. After the first time, I swore I'd never marry again."

"Pierce, I'm truly sorry to force you like this. But it's either that or . . . well, you know the alternative. I wish it didn't have to be like this."

71

"No more than I do," he said with a hint of sarcasm. "Like most women, all that matters are your own selfish needs. You don't give a tinker's damn that I'm tied to this bed, unable to travel more than ten feet on my own. *Blackmail* isn't a pretty word, Zoey."

Zoey's chin rose stubbornly. She was doing the right thing, she knew she was. At least for her. "Hate me all you like, Pierce, I don't blame you. But I do need you. I swear I'll never bother you again once this mess is cleared up. Besides, where would you go if you left? Obviously you can't return to Dry Gulch. You've nothing to lose by remaining here for a time."

"Nothing except my freedom," Pierce said harshly. "You've got it all worked out, haven't you? Beware, lady." His voice was low and strident. "You might get more than you bargained for."

Zoey blanched, struggling to keep her voice even. "I'll bring up a basin of water and the clean clothes you requested. I assume you're strong enough to wash and dress yourself. Don't dawdle, Cully should return with the preacher soon."

When Zoey, Cully, and the preacher walked into the room two hours later,

72

Pierce was dressed in Robert Fuller's cast-off clothing and sitting up in bed. He smiled ruefully, thinking that at least Zoey had obeyed him in one thing. She wore a lovely blue dress fashioned of silk and lace that matched the bright blue of her eyes.

"This is somewhat irregular," Reverend Tolly said when he was introduced to the bridegroom. "I understand you've suffered an injury." He pursed his lips. "Young people, always in such a hurry. Can't seem to wait. Very well, take your places."

Pierce stared at the tall, gaunt reverend, convinced at last that this wasn't a bad dream. He never thought he'd find himself in this position again. He'd sworn he wouldn't. Time and luck had run out. Zoey took his arm and helped him to his feet. Cully stood as witness.

When it came time to say "I do," Pierce balked. Until Cully poked a gun in his ribs and whispered into his ear, "Make up your mind fast, Delaney. Miz Zoey needs you, and I aim to see that she gets what she wants. You ain't gonna like the consequences."

It was done. Pierce and Zoey were husband and wife. Zoey saw Reverend Tolly to the door, and Pierce collapsed on the bed. He had a wife but could expect no wedding night. He gave a shout of laughter, more bitter than mirthful.

"What in the hell is so funny, Delaney?"

Pierce had all but forgotten Cully, who had remained behind. "This entire scenario is a farce. I never thought I'd live to see the day I'd be railroaded into marriage."

"Them are harsh words, Delaney. Miz Zoey was desperate. She didn't like doing what she did. You don't understand what this ranch means to her. Or how much she hates Samson Willoughby. Play along and you can be on your way again before you know it. If you try to hurt her, you'll answer to me. I promised Robert Fuller I'd take care of his daughter if anything should happen to him."

Pierce felt a hint of admiration for the crusty old man, but that didn't make his situation any easier to swallow. Did Cully actually think he was a match for Pierce once he regained his full strength? As soon as he could ride, he was out of here, marriage or not.

Zoey paid Reverend Tolly from the money she'd found in Pierce's vest and watched the clergyman ride away on his mule, his long legs hanging nearly to the

74

ground. It was a comical sight, but Zoey didn't feel like laughing. Forcing Pierce to marry her didn't sit well with her. Using his money to pay the reverend made her feel like a thief. Unfortunately she had no ready cash. She hoped Pierce would understand. She'd pay him back when her ranch was in working order and the cattle that remained were rounded up and sold. With any luck, Pierce could go on his merry way soon. Even if she couldn't prove there was no mortgage on the Circle F, Willoughby could no longer force her into marriage.

Would she have actually turned Pierce over to the law if he hadn't complied? Zoey wasn't sure and preferred not to speculate.

"Your bridegroom ain't feeling particularly friendly," Cully complained as he came down the stairs to join Zoey.

"I didn't expect he would."

"I sure hope you know what you're doing, Miz Zoey. We still ain't sure Delaney's no woman beater. You better keep your distance. He's getting stronger every day. I can't be around to protect you every minute."

Zoey's eyes grew misty with gratitude. "I can take care of myself, Cully. I know you feel you have to keep an eye on me, but it

75

isn't necessary. I did what I had to do. I'm not too happy with my decision, but I don't regret making it. As for Pierce, I don't believe he'd hurt me. Things will work out." A small sigh slipped past her lips. "I *have* to believe that. Now I'm going to try to placate my bridegroom."

Pierce had known she would return. He'd counted on it. If he had a wife, he might as well enjoy the benefits. Not that he could do much about it right now . . . but eventually, before he left . . .

Zoey walked into the room and closed the door quietly behind her. Pierce's smile sent her pulse racing. He was propped up in bed atop the covers, still fully dressed. She thought he looked handsome and virile . . . too damn virile.

He patted the bed beside him. "Have you come to join me, wife?" His hot gaze ran the length of her; he felt his blood thickening and his groin harden. She had no idea how tempting she was to a man who hadn't had a woman in a very long time. Or did she? Had she come to taunt him with her lush lips and ripe body? It was no more than he expected from her.

"You know I haven't. I came to see if you're all right. Is there anything you need before I finish my chores?"

He gave her his most charming smile. "Would you help me remove my shirt? My left arm isn't working right."

"Of course," she said crisply.

Pierce waited until she bent over him to help him remove his arm from his sleeve before wrapping his right arm around her waist and bringing her hard against him.

Zoey squawked in surprise when his left hand, not nearly as weak as he'd intimated, tugged at the buttons on the front of her dress. "What are you doing?"

"I want to see my wife. It's perfectly legal."

"I thought we agreed that this is to be a marriage in name only."

He had the top three buttons of her bodice undone and moved on to the bottom three, noting with pleasure that the skin visible in the vee of her neckline was creamy white and smooth. "I never agreed to a damn thing, including this marriage. It was forced on me." The bottom three buttons fell open and he shoved the material down her arms. She wore no corset, she had no need of one. Her lacy chemise did little to conceal the rosy pink nipples crowning her full breasts.

"You're too weak for this!" Zoey protested.

"I may be too weak for some things, but I'm certainly strong enough for this." To prove his point, he ripped the fragile chemise down the front, baring her breasts. "Very nice. I'm impressed, Zoey. But not surprised. The way you walk around the ranch, your unfettered breasts bouncing beneath your shirt, gave me a hint of the beauties you were hiding."

"How dare you! Why are you doing this?"

He shot her a twisted smile. Right now he was so angry at being railroaded into an unwanted marriage that being outrageous made him feel better. "You wanted a husband and you got one."

Zoey was so angry she was trembling. But was it really anger that made her body shake? Pierce's hot gaze upon her bare flesh gave her a shivery feeling all the way down to her toes. She'd never felt like this before. All warm and trembly and confused. Her thoughts skittered to a halt when Pierce lowered his head and nuzzled her breasts. His breath was so torrid she feared he might be feverish again. Then he took her right nipple into his mouth, and Zoey felt as if her world had tipped upside down.

Pierce sucked vigorously, moving from nipple to nipple, coaxing them into swollen pink buds with the rough pad of his tongue. Never had Zoey thought it possible to feel this kind of arousal. Never had she imagined that Pierce would be the man to make her feel these things for the first time.

With cunning and obvious expertise, Pierce's hand moved down Zoey's hip, catching the hem of her skirt and slowly raising it as he continued to torment her breasts with his mouth and tongue. By the time she realized what he intended, it was too late. His hand was between her legs, testing the wetness that had seeped through her drawers.

Pierce knew he must stop, for he was in no condition to do either of them any good. But he'd wanted to prove to Zoey precisely what he thought of the "conditions" she'd placed upon this marriage. He'd comply as long as it suited him, if he didn't die from lust first. Soon he'd contact his brothers, then he'd leave with no regrets.

After he'd taken Zoey's virginity.

Suddenly Pierce shoved Zoey away. She sat up, staring up him in confusion.

"I could have had you if I'd wanted you,

lady," Pierce gloated. "You were hot and wet for me. Count yourself lucky that I'm still too weak. If I'm forced to stick around, I'm damn well going to get something out of this short marriage of ours."

Zoey leaped off the bed, angrier than she had ever been in her life. She had made a mistake, a terrible mistake. What was she going to do? Had she traded one devil for another?

"You'll get nothing from me!"

His smile didn't reach his eyes. "Want to bet? I'm quite familiar with a woman's body and the various ways to arouse it. You, lady, were aroused." He fixed his gaze on her breasts. "Look at your nipples. Have you ever seen them so hard or swollen? I could feel your wetness. You were —"

"Stop!" Zoey pulled the gaping edges of her bodice together and backed out of the room. "Don't talk to me like that."

His words were as arousing to her as his mouth and hands had been.

"Heed my words, *wife*," Pierce said in a low, seductive whisper. "I will have you." He wanted her to feel as uncomfortable as he did in this sham of a marriage.

Zoey turned and fled. Abruptly she stopped in the doorway and glanced over her shoulder. "By the way," she said sweetly, "I used the money in your vest pocket to pay the reverend. I know you'd want it that way."

Then she was gone, leaving Pierce with his dark thoughts.

Chapter 4

Eager to regain his full strength, Pierce spent a large portion of each day pacing the small bedroom. By the end of his first week of married life he had regained strength in his legs and was working on his arms. He was also consuming prodigious amounts of food. His first appearance at the breakfast table surprised both Zoey and Cully.

"Should you be downstairs?" Zoey asked with concern. "Less than three weeks ago you lay near death."

"I'm fine now," Pierce answered as he poured himself a cup of coffee. "Thought I'd go outside today and look the place over."

His words gave Zoey pause. "Why? You're not going to try to tell me how to run my ranch, are you?"

"If I'm not mistaken," Pierce said bluntly, "that piece of paper we both signed gave me control over both you and your land."

"No one controls me," Zoey said from between clenched teeth. "You know as well as I that ours isn't a real marriage."

Pierce seated himself at the breakfast table and helped himself to a biscuit. He popped it into his mouth and chewed with relish. "These are good. Are there more?"

Zoey glared at him. "I suppose you'd like some eggs to go with them."

"If it wouldn't be too much trouble," Pierce said complacently. He gave her an enigmatic grin. "It's a wife's duty to serve her husband."

Chuckling to himself, Cully scraped back his chair and rose abruptly. "I reckon I'll mosey on out to the corral, Miz Zoey. Go ahead and feed your husband. I'll saddle your horse and meet you later."

Zoey slammed a frying pan down on the stove. With ill humor she fried eggs and bacon, biting her tongue to keep from flinging angry words back at him.

"Where are you going this morning?" Pierce asked curiously.

"Cully and I are going to round up livestock that have wandered into the mountains. Most of our stock has been stolen or run off, but there are still some around."

Pierce frowned. "Do you think that's wise? Could be dangerous."

"Who's going to do it if I don't? Samson Willoughby has made it all but impossible to hire decent ranch hands. If I can round up enough steers to sell to the army, we can get through the winter."

"What's the use if Willoughby forecloses?"

Zoey sent him a scathing glance. "What would you have me do, sit here and do nothing?"

Pierce's gaze slowly traveled the length of Zoey's trim form. The britches she wore hugged her rounded hips and bottom indecently. The arousing sight made him squirm uncomfortably in his chair. The top buttons on her shirt were open, allowing a tantalizing view of creamy skin and hint of tempting breasts. Pierce was certain his fingers would meet if he tried to span her tiny waist with his hands.

"I'll go with you," Pierce said, digging into his breakfast. "You'll have to loan me a horse."

Zoey looked astounded. "You're not well enough to ride. The section we're going to is rough and mountainous with steep, treacherous trails. I'll be glad to loan you a horse when you're strong enough to sit one."

It rankled Pierce that Zoey was correct in her assessment of his condition. He was growing stronger every day but was not yet ready to tackle a mountain trail. Getting himself wounded had been damn inconvenient. Look at the mess he was in because of it. Here he was, married against his will to a tempting vixen and allowed none of the benefits.

"What are you thinking?" Zoey asked when she noticed the odd look on Pierce's face.

"I'm thinking you're too damn pushy for a woman so desperate for a husband that she railroaded a stranger into marriage."

Zoey's chin rose fractionally. "I *was* desperate, as you well know." She could see anger burning beneath the dark flesh of his jaw. "Cully is waiting for me." She picked up the lunch she had prepared earlier. "We'll return by sundown, hopefully with some of our missing livestock."

"What am I supposed to do in the meantime?" Pierce asked, feeling useless for the first time in his life.

With an impatient motion, Zoey jammed on her hat. "Rest," she threw over her shoulder as she walked out the door. "Ask again after you've regained your full strength."

His gaze lingering on the twin mounds of her round bottom, Pierce watched her stride through the back door. His body reacted predictably and he cursed beneath his breath when he realized he wanted Zoey Fuller Delaney. Wanted her spread beneath him, naked. He wanted to be inside her. Before he left the Circle F he'd damn well have her on his own terms.

Later that day Pierce wandered outside, intending to have a look around. It had been so dark the night he'd arrived that he'd seen little of the ranch itself.

Pierce's chest expanded as he breathed in fresh mountain air for the first time in three weeks, drinking in the sights and sounds of the Circle F. The first thing he noticed was that the weathered paddock fence begged for a coat of paint. Twenty feet beyond, a hip-roofed barn with peeling paint added to the sense of neglect. To the left, a sturdy log bunkhouse stood forlorn and deserted. He sniffed appreciatively of the mingled scent of horses, hay, dust, and manure. The familiar odors made him homesick for his own ranch, and he couldn't help wondering how his brothers were faring without him.

Pierce gazed for a moment toward the mountains where Zoey and Cully had gone earlier in the morning, then followed a path around to the rear of the house. Several yards from the back door a pipe dribbled water into a trough, dragged up from the well by a pump.

The ranch house was solidly constructed, Pierce thought, admiring the sawed wood and log two-story structure. Obviously Zoey's father had taken great pride in his land, for he had built sturdy structures upon it. Taking into account the sparkling stream, meandering river, and lush grasslands, Pierce decided the Circle F possessed everything necessary to make it a prosperous spread. Unfortunately Zoey's father had died before the ranch could realize its full potential, and Zoey was hard put to keep it in operation with Willoughby dead set on gaining possession of it.

Pierce glanced briefly at the corral and several paddocks, deciding to leave further inspection for another day. He returned to the front of the house. The sound of pounding hooves brought his gaze around to the road approaching the ranch. Shading his eyes against the glare of the setting sun, he saw a lone rider appear over a slight rise. Curious, Pierce leaned against the porch railing to wait.

By the time the rider passed through the

gate, Pierce knew the Circle F was being honored by a visit from Samson Willoughby. He cursed beneath his breath, wondering what the bastard wanted now. Had he heard about Zoey's marriage?

Willoughby reined in sharply at the front steps and dismounted, glaring at Pierce with outright hostility. "Who are you?" he asked harshly.

"Who are you?" Pierce shot back, knowing full well what and who the banker was.

Willoughby drew himself up huffily. "I'm Samson Willoughby. Where is Zoey?"

"You mean Mrs. Delaney?"

Willoughby blanched. "Wha . . . what did you say?"

"I assume you were referring to my wife."

"Your . . . your wife!" Willoughby sputtered. "What kind of game are you playing? Zoey has no husband."

Pierce smiled without mirth. "She does now. We were married a week ago. I assume you knew she had a fiancé."

"I knew, but . . . See here . . ." He searched for a name.

"Delaney, Pierce Delaney."

"See here, Mr. Delaney, I'm sure you know who I am."

"You're the bas— er, banker who's trying to steal my wife's land."

Willoughby shifted uncomfortably. "My bank holds the mortgage on this land."

"So you say. As Zoey's legal husband, I'll attend to any problems pertaining to my wife's land. If you've come to intimidate her, you'll have to deal with me first. And I'm not as easily frightened as Zoey."

Willoughby's colorless eyes settled on Pierce, conveying his hatred and disbelief. "You're lying. I don't believe you and Zoey are married."

"I don't lie," Pierce said softly. Had Willoughby known Pierce better, he would have realized that the softness was a prelude to violence. "Neither does Zoey."

"Zoey said many things, most of which I chose to ignore."

"You should have listened to her. Zoey and I are indeed married. Reverend Tolly came to the house over a week ago and married us. Ask him if you don't believe me."

"I believe I *will* speak with the reverend. Unfortunately he's out of town right now. Tell Zoey I was here, and that I'll be back."

"I'll tell my *wife* that you were here, but if I were you, I'd think twice about returning any time soon."

"Are you threatening me, Delaney?"

"Call it what you like, Willoughby. If Zoey says you're lying about the mortgage, I believe her."

"Look here, Delaney," Willoughby sputtered. "I'm a respected businessman. Maybe you can talk to respectable citizens like that where you come from, but not here. By the way," he asked curiously, "where *are* you from?"

"Wyoming," Pierce lied. "How much will it take to pay off the mortgage?"

Willoughby gave Pierce a disparaging look, unimpressed by the ill-fitting, patched clothing he wore. "More than you can afford."

Pierce snorted with disgust. He had no intention of paying off a mortgage that could be fraudulent. "I suggest you ride out while you still can, Willoughby."

Willoughby's expression turned sly. "Did you know your wife and I have been . . . close? You didn't think a hot little piece like Zoey would wait around for you to claim her, did you?"

Pierce fought to keep his clenched fists at his sides. "Whatever you're implying doesn't wash with me, Willoughby. If you utter one more word against my wife's character, I'll see you in hell. Understand?" His quiet words belied his raging temper.

Pierce didn't need to raise his voice. His deceptive calm and threatening tone gave hint to his fury. So much so that Willoughby took a cautious step backward. "The only thing I understand is power and money," Willoughby spouted. "Obviously you lack both of those commodities. I'll leave, but if I find out you're lying about your marriage to Zoey, you'd better be prepared to pay the consequences. I laid claim to Zoey long before her pa died, but the old man was stubborn. He didn't think I was good enough for his daughter, but I showed him." His smile turned nasty. "It's dangerous to thwart Samson Willoughby."

"Dangerous?" Pierce's eyes narrowed. "How so?"

Willoughby smiled grimly. "Thwart me and find out," he hissed as he mounted up and prepared to ride off. The arrival of Zoey and Cully delayed Willoughby's departure. They were driving about thirty head of cows and steers ahead of them. It appeared as if their day had been successful.

Leaving the livestock to Cully, Zoey dismounted and walked briskly to join Pierce.

Suddenly Pierce wished he had listened to her and spent the day resting.

He'd reached the end of his endurance, having overestimated his strength on his first full day out of bed. His wound ached something fierce and his legs felt rubbery, but he wasn't about to display weakness to a conniving bastard like Willoughby.

"What's going on here?" Zoey asked, looking from Pierce to Willoughby.

"Banker Willoughby came calling, darling," Pierce said, casually placing his arm around Zoey and pulling her against him. When he placed a chaste kiss on her cheek, Zoey went along with him.

She returned his kiss, and turned to Willoughby.

"Mr. Willoughby doesn't believe we're husband and wife," Pierce explained.

Zoey smiled sweetly at Willoughby. "I told you I was engaged, but you chose not to believe me."

"Your father never said a word about an engagement in the weeks before he died. I approached him several times about a match between us. Never once did he mention a fiancé."

"It was none of your business," Zoey declared. "Why are you here?"

"I thought we could discuss . . . arrangements, but I see I'm too late for what I had in mind. I had intended to bring the preacher back with me to perform our marriage ceremony, but the good reverend is out of town."

"You're too late. I'm already married."

"So you say. I refuse to believe it until I speak personally with Reverend Tolly. He's expected back in a few days. I'll bide my time till then, but if you're lying to me . . ." His implied threat hung in the air like pungent autumn smoke.

"Would you care to see our license?" Pierce asked. "It won't take a minute to get it."

"I don't want to see your damn license," Willoughby spat, obviously rattled by this surprising turn of events. "You'll be hearing from me." Fuming in impotent rage, he mounted, dug his spurs into his horse's flanks, and rode off.

"Good riddance," Pierce said unevenly. He was beginning to give in to his exhaustion.

"Are you all right?" Zoey could feel his arm around her trembling.

"More than all right. It felt good to tell that bastard where to go. But I fear we haven't heard the last from him. Without proof showing otherwise, the mortgage he holds must be taken seriously. Come on, let's go inside. I find myself in need of a chair."

"You've overdone it!" Zoey charged. "I warned you about pushing yourself. You need more time to recuperate." Placing her arm around his waist, she helped him inside to the nearest chair. "I'll call Cully. He can help you up to bed."

"No, I'll be fine in a minute." Pierce didn't want help. He'd never regain his full strength if Zoey insisted on coddling him. "I'm not going back to bed. Unless," he added, giving her a scorching look, "you'd like to join me, *wife*."

Zoey stepped away from him as if burned. "Is that all you can think of?"

"You owe me a wedding night. You've managed to avoid me but my day will come."

"There will be no wedding night," Zoey said evenly.

"We'll see, won't we?"

"I've got to clean up and start supper." She started to leave.

"Zoey."

She paused but did not turn around to face him.

"What?"

"I'm well acquainted with women's wiles

94

and machinations. And I always get my way."

As she strode off, Pierce closed his eyes and rested his head against the backrest of the chair as his strength slowly returned. Another day or two and he'd be ready to mount a horse. It rankled to sit around the house like an invalid all day. This inactivity was killing him. Maybe he'd ride into town tomorrow and mail a letter to his brothers. They must be worried sick about him.

Zoey was too rattled to come up with a proper retort as she left the room. Pierce was too damn handsome and too damn sure of himself for his own good, and for hers. If she hadn't seen him at his weakest, she'd never suspect he'd sustained a life-threatening injury. He looked too strong, too virile. Had he been operating at his full potential, she'd have been in serious trouble. It surprised Zoey that Pierce wanted her sexually. How could he want a woman he didn't trust? For her own peace of mind she preferred to think he was only tormenting her for forcing a marriage between them. She could take everything he dished out as long as he stayed at the Circle F long enough to foil Willoughby's plans for her.

* * *

Cully joined them for supper that night. Zoey had changed into a gingham dress, which suited her perfectly.

"You look quite fetching tonight," Pierce complimented.

Almost anything looked fetching on Zoey, Pierce reflected, or nothing at all. For lack of something better to do, Pierce had spent long hours dreaming about slowly undressing Zoey, arousing her to passion's peak, and then thrusting himself inside her. If he concentrated hard enough, he could feel himself fill her. Her entrance would be small and tight and he'd have to take his time, arousing her first with slow, drugging kisses and tender caresses. His groin grew heavy and he stifled a groan. Damn, if he didn't have her soon, he'd burst.

When Pierce continued to stare at Zoey, Cully asked, "Is something wrong, Delaney?"

Pierce tore his gaze away. "Nothing's wrong. Why do you ask?"

"Miz Zoey said Willoughby left in a huff today. Reckon he'll be back?"

It took a moment for Pierce to address Cully's question, distracted as he was. "He'll be back, all right. Tell me, Cully,

96

what are our chances of hiring extra hands for the Circle F?"

"Three weeks ago I'd say not a chance in hell." He gave Zoey a sheepish look. "Sorry, Miz Zoey, but that's the God's truth." He returned his gaze to Pierce. "When you and Zoey got hitched, the odds changed. Having a man in charge will make a heap of difference."

"I can run this ranch as well as any man," Zoey retorted. "Pa made sure of that."

"I reckon you can, Miz Zoey, but that ain't the way of things and you know it. Men don't want to take orders from a woman. And they're afraid of Willoughby."

"Hmmm," Pierce said thoughtfully. "I thought I'd ride into town tomorrow and have a look around. I want to mail a letter to my brothers and let them know I'm all right."

"Is that wise?" Zoey questioned. He certainly looked fit enough to ride. In fact, he looked fit enough to . . . God! What was she thinking?

"What do you mean by that?" Pierce asked with deceptive calm. "Are you afraid I'll keep on riding once I leave the ranch? Nothing or no one can keep me cooped up here now that I'm well enough to sit a horse. Are you worried about my health, wife?"

Zoey bit her lip in consternation. What would happen if Pierce simply rode away? "I don't know you well enough to know what you'll do. You owe me for saving your life, but I don't suppose that means anything to you."

He gave her a look of controlled fury. "Should it, after the way you railroaded me into marriage?"

"I'd hoped . . . Never mind, Cully will ride into town with you. Or better yet, he can go alone and mail your letter."

"Don't worry, *wife*, I'm not going anywhere yet." He gave her a scorching look that set her heart to pounding. "You and I have unfinished business to attend to before I leave. Cully will remain here with you. I don't like leaving you alone on the ranch."

Zoey found it difficult to breathe. What was the matter with her? The inherent promise of Pierce's words made her feel hot and cold at the same time. "Unfinished business" was a polite way of saying he still expected a wedding night, and before he left, he intended to have it. How long could she hold him off? Long enough to serve her purpose, she hoped. She was convinced that once Pierce relieved her of her virginity, he'd leave the ranch and never look back.

"Very well, go to town. But be forewarned that if you fail to return by suppertime, I'll send the vigilantes after you. You won't get far."

"Trusting soul, aren't you?" Pierce said sarcastically.

"I can't afford to be trusting."

"I said I'd return and I will. Cully can . . ." Pierce turned to Cully, surprised that the cagey ranch hand had slipped out while he and Zoey were arguing.

Pierce rose abruptly. "I reckon I'll hit the sack. If it's all right with you, I'll ride one of the spare horses into town. By the way, can you afford to pay top wages to potential ranch hands?"

Zoey thought of her empty coffers and frowned. She couldn't afford to pay *any* wages, let alone top wages. "The only ready cash I have is that which I removed from your vest."

"Nothing else?"

"Not until I sell my beeves to the army. That's assuming we can flush more of our scattered stock from the mountains to sell. Can't do it without ranch hands, and can't get ranch hands without money to pay them."

"You'll have your ranch hands," Pierce promised with grim determination.

No matter how he might feel about this forced marriage, he couldn't up and leave Zoey without solving at least some of her problems. He was alive because of her. He had money in the bank, the Delaney ranch was on solid ground, and he had two brothers to rely upon. Zoey had no one except . . . her husband.

Damn, what a tangle.

Accused of seducing and beating Cora Lee, railroaded into marriage by Zoey, and pursued by vigilantes who really didn't care what he had done as long as they could hang a Delaney. And as if that weren't enough, Cora Lee named him the father of the bastard she carried.

Pierce mounted the stairs slowly, tired but satisfied with his recovery thus far. As he prepared for sleep, he wondered what Zoey would do if he burst into her bedroom to claim his bride. The thought brought a smile to his lips. She'd probably scream like an outraged virgin. He wondered how long it would take before she welcomed him, nay, invited him into her bed.

Zoey's thoughts were poles apart from

Pierce's. She really didn't know if Pierce would return from town tomorrow. There was a good chance he would simply ride away and keep riding. His failure to return would mean that she'd lose her land, but at least Willoughby could no longer force her into marriage.

Zoey finished the dishes and dragged herself up the stairs to bed, weary to the bone. Rounding up stray livestock from the hills was hard work. Nearly impossible for two people to accomplish. Eight to ten men would be the least she could make do with to run the ranch efficiently. A dozen would be better.

Who was she kidding? Zoey chided herself. If Pierce managed to hire two or three men, she'd count herself lucky. It was certainly more than she had now.

Zoey's steps faltered when she neared Pierce's room. Was he sleeping? she wondered. His first day out of bed had been quite eventful. Forcing her mind to release the strangely arousing image of Pierce reclining in bed, Zoey continued on to her room. She undressed, washed, and donned a prim white nightgown that enveloped her like a shroud. Then she sat at her dressing table, unwinding her braid and brushing out her hair. Her thoughts wandered as she stared dreamily into the mirror.

Suddenly her thoughts scattered when the door to her room opened and Pierce stepped inside. She leaped to her feet, her eyes wide with uncertainty.

"What do you want? Don't you believe in knocking?"

"I did knock, but you didn't hear me. I saw a light coming from beneath your door and knew you weren't sleeping yet."

She stared at him. He was wearing trousers and nothing else. His feet were bare and so was his chest. "You shouldn't be here."

Pierce sent her a mocking grin. "I'm your husband. Who has more right than I?"

"You're my husband in name only," Zoey countered. "What do you want?"

His gaze traveled the length of her. "You look like a nun, wrapped in that white shroud."

"What does it matter to you what I wear to bed? State your business and leave. I'm tired."

He raised a dark brow. "I'll buy something in town more appropriate for a bride."

"Don't bother. What's your purpose in this visit? I know it wasn't merely to taunt me about my choice of nightwear."

"You're right, my love. You don't mind if I call you that, do you?" he asked. When he received no answer, he continued. "I changed my mind about riding to town alone. I think you should accompany me."

"For what reason?"

"Being seen together will help to convince Willoughby and the townspeople that you have a husband now to see to the running of the ranch."

She eyed him suspiciously. "Why do you care? You can't wait to leave."

"True, but you did save my life despite the high payment you demanded in return. I do concede, however, that I owe you something for your trouble. I've developed an intense dislike for Samson Willoughby. Therefore I've decided to stay long enough to put an end to his meddling."

"How magnanimous of you," Zoey said cynically.

"Don't get me wrong, my love. We both know our marriage is a farce. When the time comes, I'll be able to leave with no regrets and no looking back."

"That's more than I have a right to expect," Zoey allowed. "I used you, and I'm not proud of it." She turned away from him. "Good night, Pierce."

Pierce reached for her. "Not so fast. Don't I rate a good-night kiss for the anguish you've put me through? How much does this ranch mean to you?"

"My land means everything to me! It's all I have in this world," Zoey declared hotly. "I'd do anything to keep Willoughby from claiming it."

"Anything?" Pierce asked softly.

The breath left her lungs. "Almost anything."

Pierce's eyes glowed like emeralds as he grasped her shoulders and pulled her against him. "You know what I want."

Zoey felt his heat through the soft linen of her nightgown. Her heart pounded as she dragged in a painful breath. Why did Pierce have to be so blasted attractive? she wondered with the one rational bit of her brain that still functioned.

Her hands came up between them to rest on his chest. Her original intention was to push herself free, but when her palms flattened on his smooth, heated flesh, she could no longer think. With his blunt words and positively scorching gaze, a sizzling heat welled up from somewhere deep inside her.

Pierce ground himself against her, letting her feel the weight of him, the shape, length, and hardness of him. Showing her how much his body wanted her.

Zoey felt the daunting strength of Pierce's hard body, and her mouth fell open in wordless protest. She didn't want this. Succumbing to his desires frightened her in so many ways. It wasn't just the intimacy she feared, it went far deeper than that. Letting Pierce love her would have devastating consequences. She knew intuitively that once Pierce rode out of her life, she'd no longer be the same woman. She couldn't allow herself to feel anything for this man.

"Let me go, Pierce."

His answer was to place nipping little kisses along the side of her neck, and to tease her earlobe with his mouth and his tongue, taunting her with what he wanted to do to her.

"Are you a virgin?" he asked, startling her.

"What makes you think I'm not?"

The breath slammed from him. "I'll be careful with you," he promised. "I've never had a virgin. I wasn't even the first with my wife."

Then his mouth settled over hers, hard yet gentle, but oh so determined. Zoey fought the urge to give in to his unspoken demands, but something inside her resisted. This wasn't a real marriage, it was never meant to be. Then her thoughts scattered as his kiss deepened and his hands found her breasts. Her mouth opened against the pressure of his probing tongue and he thrust inside, savoring her sweet essence.

Realizing she was flirting with fire, Zoey broke off the kiss and pulled away. "No, I won't let you do that to me!"

Struggling to quell his nearly painful arousal, Pierce took several deep breaths before speaking. His words were clipped and edged with steel. "I've never forced a woman in my life. Before I leave, you'll beg me to bed you. Good night, my love. I wish you the joy of your cold bed."

Chapter 5

Zoey was waiting for Pierce in the kitchen when he came down to breakfast the next morning. Her greeting was less than enthusiastic. Pierce pretended not to notice, assuming she was still piqued over last night.

"Cully is saddling the horses," she said. "We can leave for town as soon as you've eaten. I've made a list of supplies I need. Mr. Schultz, the grocer, is very good about giving credit. Have you written your letter?"

"I wrote it last night after I left your room." He gave her an evocative glance. "For some reason, I couldn't sleep." Half the night had passed before his arousal allowed him to seek his bed.

Zoey's heart skipped a beat. Pierce wasn't the only one who couldn't sleep last night. The way his hands had burned her flesh aroused her still. She had tossed and turned far into the night, recalling everything she found attractive and exciting about Pierce . . . every tiny detail. When sleep finally claimed her she dreamed she was lying in Pierce's arms, experiencing all those things he had promised, even though she had to guess about most of them.

Zoey placed a plate of ham and eggs before Pierce, grateful that he couldn't read her thoughts. "I'll wait outside. Come out when you're ready."

"Have you eaten?"

"I ate with Cully."

He eyed her critically. "You're not going to town dressed like that, are you?" He didn't mind seeing her in those tight britches, but he didn't want anyone else staring at her curvy bottom. "You're a wife now. Dress like one."

"I beg your pardon?" Her voice shook with anger. "I'll dress any way I please. You have no right to dictate to me."

Pierce's eyebrows shot upward. "Am I or am I not your husband?"

"You are," she admitted grudgingly.

"Then I suggest you do as I say. I won't have men looking at you with lust in their eyes. You belong to me. No man has a right to see what's mine alone to view."

Zoey nearly laughed aloud. If she didn't know better, she'd think Pierce was jealous. How absurd. "Have you ever tried riding in skirts?"

"Don't you have a riding outfit?"

"Britches are more comfortable."

"Would you rather change with or without my help?"

Hands on hips, Zoey glared at him. "Very well, have it your way." Then she whirled and marched up the stairs, her bottom swaying provocatively. She didn't hear Pierce's frustrated groan.

By the time Pierce finished his breakfast, Zoey had returned to the kitchen wearing a split skirt and crisp white blouse. "Does this suit you, *husband?*"

Pierce stifled a grin. "That will do quite nicely, *wife.*" He rose and took her arm. "Shall we go?"

The trip into town was short and uneventful. Within thirty minutes they were riding down the dusty street of Rolling Prairie, dodging dogs, children, and mud puddles.

"I'll meet you later for lunch. Where's a good place to eat?" Pierce asked as they separated at the corner.

"The Montana Hotel has the best meals."

"Meet me there at noon. There are several things I need to do besides mail my letter."

"Try to stay out of trouble," Zoey advised.

"I'm not promising anything," he returned with a grin. "Be sure to tell Mr. Schultz about your new husband. Word will spread fast if it's fed to the right person. Maybe I'll stop in to see Willoughby."

Pierce posted the letter to his brothers first. He had written to ask Chad to send a letter of credit on their bank account in care of general delivery, Rolling Prairie, Montana, as quickly as possible. He also gave a brief explanation of what had happened to him and where he was staying. He made no mention of his marriage.

Pierce left the post office and wandered down the street, introducing himself to each shopkeeper he encountered along the way. When he came to the town's only saloon, he entered through the swinging door, ambled up to the bar, and ordered a beer. Though the day was still young, several men sat around a table, shooting the breeze.

The bartender slid a beer toward Pierce and asked, "You new in town, mister?"

"You could say that. I married the owner of the Circle F."

The man's mouth dropped open. "You

married Miss Zoey? Rumor had it she was set to marry Samson Willoughby."

"Can't believe everything you hear," Pierce said. "Reverend Tolly married us over a week ago. I'm looking to hire competent ranch hands for the Circle F. Know anyone who would fit the bill?"

"I'll ask around." He stuck out his hand. "I'm Morris Kent. People around these parts call me Dude because I'm from back east. Where are you from?"

Pierce shook Dude's hand. "Pierce Delaney. I hail from Wyoming."

A man sidled up to the bar beside Pierce. "Did I hear you say you married Miss Zoey? Are you running the Circle F now?"

"You heard right. I'm Pierce Delaney, Zoey Fuller's husband."

"I'm Bud Prichard. I was ramrod on the Circle F before Robert Fuller up and got himself killed."

"You're one of the men who left my wife high and dry when she needed you." His voice held a note of accusation.

Prichard shifted uncomfortably. "I can't afford to work for nothing, Mr. Delaney. All the hands up and left when banker Willoughby spread the word that the Circle F was in deep financial trouble and about to

111

go belly-up. I stayed longer than the others, but in the end I was forced to seek work elsewhere."

Pierce studied Prichard's face and liked what he saw. Prichard returned his gaze with unwavering honesty. Prichard wasn't young, but neither was he old. Tough and wiry, the ramrod looked as steady as a rock and fully capable of handling his job.

"Where are you working now?"

"Unfortunately the new job didn't work out. I'm looking for work."

"I'm hiring," Pierce said. "Can you round up a half dozen or so men to work the Circle F? I'm offering top wages. The work won't be easy. What livestock remains is scattered throughout the hills and must be flushed out. Three hundred head are needed to fulfill the army contract. If you can do that, you can have your old job of ramrod back."

"Is Cully still at the Circle F?" Prichard wanted to know.

"He's still there."

"He's a good man. A mite old but still a good man to have around. I'll see what I can do, Mr. Delaney. When do you want us?"

"As soon as possible. Bring them out to the ranch and I'll decide if they fit the bill."

"Sure thing, Mr. Delaney." They shook on it and Pierce left to join Zoey at the hotel. His steps slowed when he passed the bank. A devious smile spread across his face as he opened the door and stepped inside.

Several people were waiting to conduct business. Pierce waited his turn at a teller's cage.

"May I help you, sir?" the clerk asked when Pierce reached the window.

"I'm thinking of depositing a large sum of money soon and wanted to know how safe my money will be."

"This is the safest bank in Montana," the clerk bragged. "All our accounts are strictly confidential and we've never had a successful robbery. Is there anything else you require, Mr. . . ."

"Delaney. Pierce Delaney. I married Zoey Fuller from the Circle F."

The clerk's eyes widened. This was indeed news. "Will you be handling Circle F business?"

"I will indeed. I'm infusing some of my own money into the operation. My wife has had a run of bad luck."

"So I've heard," the clerk said, lowering his gaze.

"Things are changing fast. I've taken

steps to hire competent help."

"Excuse me a moment, Mr. Delaney, I'm going to the back room to get some forms for you to fill out. You'll want your name on the Circle F account."

The clerk disappeared, returning a few moments later with Samson Willoughby. The banker's face was mottled with rage.

"Come into my office, Delaney. I'd like a private word with you."

"Of course, as long as it won't take too long. My wife is waiting for me at the hotel."

Pierce strolled into Willoughby's office as if he didn't have a care in the world. The door slammed shut with a loud bang, giving testimony to Willoughby's anger.

"I understand you're hiring hands to work the Circle F." Willoughby looked at Pierce with loathing. "Ranch hands expect to get paid at the end of each month. What's all this crap about making a large deposit in my bank? You look like an opportunist to me, Delaney. You married Zoey with the intention of living off the profits from the ranch. Forget it. There are no profits. The ranch will soon be mine, and you can't do a thing about it."

Pierce hung on to the tattered remnants of his temper with admirable restraint. "I want you to stop harassing my wife."

"Zoey was to be my wife. Both the Circle F and Zoey should belong to me. I've wanted them both for as long as I can remember. Robert Fuller didn't approve of me as Zoey's husband. There isn't a man in town more suitable than I, but he wanted his little princess to love the man she married." He gave Pierce a shrewd look. "Does Zoey love you, Delaney? Or did she marry you simply to thwart me?"

Pierce chose not to answer. "You'll just have to live with that question, Willoughby. But as long as I'm here, I'd like a look at that mortgage you're holding on the Circle F."

"Very well, if you insist." He opened a file cabinet and took a document from it and removed a folder. He briefly flashed it before Pierce. Pierce caught a glimpse of a signature but had no way of knowing if it belonged to Robert Fuller.

"Believe me when I say this document is authentic," Willoughby declared as he returned the folder to the file cabinet. "And you'll know it's legal when I serve you with foreclosure papers."

"What if I pay the mortgage off before you foreclose?"

Willoughby gave a snort of laughter.

115

"You don't look like a man who can scrape up two cents, let alone seven thousand dollars."

Pierce whistled. Seven thousand dollars was a lot of money, but the ranch was worth three or four times that amount. The acreage was prime, with water and lush grasslands that stretched out endlessly. Zoey's father had chosen the land with foresight and wisdom.

"Zoey says the land isn't mortgaged, and I believe her."

"Zoey is a woman, she doesn't know everything. Her father preferred not to tell her. A few years back severe weather decimated his entire herd. Then there was a fire that destroyed all the buildings but the main house. The following year his wheat crop failed. He mortgaged the land to pay for new livestock and build the outbuildings now standing."

All Willoughby's arguments were sound, Pierce thought. Could Zoey have been mistaken about the mortgage? Pierce didn't like Willoughby, and didn't particularly believe him, but everything he said made sense. On the other hand, if Willoughby spoke the truth, why hadn't Robert Fuller told Zoey about the mortgage? Or at the very least, discussed the problems he was having making ends meet? Zoey swore the mortgage was forged. Somehow Pierce had to obtain the mortgage papers and let Zoey verify the signature.

Of course, Pierce could pay off the mortgage, but it would mean stripping the family holdings of money that belonged to all three brothers. Pierce couldn't do that.

"Have I managed to convince you that my claim is legal?" Willoughby asked. "It's senseless to hire men you can't pay. Besides, they'll be out of jobs when I foreclose."

"We'll just have to wait and see, won't we, Willoughby? Good day to you. I've kept my wife waiting too long as it is."

"Your wife!" Willoughby spat. "How long will you stick around when she no longer has the ranch?" He was too close to the truth to suit Pierce. One day soon he'd have to leave.

"I can see you're already thinking about leaving. You don't look like husband material to me. Your marriage won't stop me from getting what I want. Men like you don't stick around. I'll be here to pick up the pieces long after you're gone. One way or another, Zoey will be mine. Wife or lover, it doesn't matter to me. She'll need a protector after you're gone."

Pierce tensed. He didn't like the sound of that. The thought of Zoey with Willoughby set his teeth on edge. "I can't stop you from dreaming, Willoughby, but I can and will stop you from hurting Zoey." His expression was hard and ruthless, giving Willoughby pause. "Now I really must be going. I have one more stop to make."

Willoughby watched Pierce storm from his office, thinking that there was more to Pierce Delaney than met the eye.

"You're late," Zoey said as Pierce joined her in the dining room of the Montana Hotel. "What happened?"

"I hired a ramrod. You know him. His name is Bud Prichard. He promised to round up some cowhands and bring them out to the ranch."

"Bud Prichard worked for us at one time. Pa trusted him. But how are we going to pay him and the men he brings with him?" Zoey wanted to know. "And what about Willoughby? We don't know how long we have before he forecloses."

"We'll worry about that when the time comes. Have you actually inspected the mortgage document? Have you looked closely at your father's signature?"

"I saw it briefly. Willoughby showed it to me soon after Pa's funeral. I was too stunned to do more than glance at it. I was grieving for my father at the time and couldn't think clearly. Later, when I asked to see it again, he refused."

"I had a look at the document today. There was a signature, but I can't confirm if it was your father's."

"What can we do?"

"Let's order first. I'm starved. I've got a plan, but it's not foolproof. I need to think about it some more."

"Pierce, I . . . don't know how to thank you."

He bared his teeth in a feral smile. "I can think of a way. Share my bed tonight."

Pierce didn't want Zoey's gratitude. He wanted her body. He wanted to be inside it. He wanted her naked beneath him, hot and willing, wet and eager for him.

Zoey flushed and looked away. Pierce's provocative words both thrilled and frightened her. "You know I can't do that," she said evasively.

"You're a coward, Zoey Delaney. I'm not going to wait much longer."

Just then the waitress came to take their order and Zoey was relieved to turn her attention to something besides Pierce. He was as compelling and complex as the land she loved so dearly.

Pierce sought out Cully when he and Zoey returned home later that afternoon. He found the old man in the barn, repairing tack.

"What kind of shape is the bunkhouse in, Cully?"

Surprised by the question, Cully studied Pierce's face. "Tolerable. Why?"

"I'm expecting some hands to arrive in the next day or two. See what can be done to make it liveable."

"Well, I'll be hog-tied. You done it, Delaney. Never thought I'd live to see the day when good hands would return to the Circle F. How'd you do it?"

"I met Bud Prichard in town. He agreed to round up some hands and bring them out for me to look at. I hired Prichard on the spot and promised him the job of ramrod."

Cully looked thoughtful. "Prichard's a good man. He didn't want to leave when he did, but a man can't work for nothing. He stayed around longer than the others and left when he was offered another job."

"I liked him. I hope he doesn't have trouble finding top ranch hands."

"I don't mean to be nosy, but how are you planning to pay for top hands? I know for a fact that Miz Zoey is plumb broke."

"I have some money," Pierce said. "I wrote my brothers, asking them to send me a letter of credit. Once the beeves are sold to the army, Zoey will be in good shape financially."

"Providing enough beeves can be found. What about Willoughby and the mortgage?"

"I'm working on that."

"I've got to hand it to you, Delaney, you're doing right by Miz Zoey. I figured you'd be bitter at the way she railroaded you into marriage."

"I admit I'm not happy about being used. Women have always meant trouble, and Zoey has done nothing to change my mind. Once I repay Zoey for saving my life, I'm out of here. I'm not a marrying man."

"I reckon Miz Zoey knows how you feel. She won't hold you back when the time comes for you to leave. Just a word of advice. Don't hurt her. She's an innocent. I expect you to leave her in the same condition you found her."

Pierce searched Cully's weathered face, surprised at the fierce loyalty and protectiveness the old man had for his employer.

"I'll take your advice under consideration."

Cully stared at Pierce's departing back, wondering how this whole mess would end. He worried about Zoey. She was becoming too fond of Pierce Delaney, a man neither of them knew. Cully had warned Zoey that her scheme might backfire, and it looked like he wasn't just flapping his lips. It didn't take a prophet to know that Zoey and Pierce were explosive together. She was bound to be hurt when Pierce up and left her.

Three days later Bud Prichard arrived at the Circle F, accompanied by seven men, some young, some old, all of them experienced hands.

"I'm here just like I promised, Mr. Delaney," Bud said as Pierce came out of the house to greet him.

"So I see. Introduce the men to me."

Pierce studied each man carefully. He considered himself a tolerable judge of character and didn't want to hire any troublemakers.

Bud started with the Consuelos brothers, Dom and Hector, a pair of young Mexicans with honest, eager faces. Next came Pete, Shorty, Lefty, Herm, and Mac.

Herm was a cook who seemed inordinately proud of his ability to master a cookstove. All but Pete met with Pierce's approval, and Pierce couldn't put his finger on a reason for his dislike of that particular man. After the introductions Pierce decided his reservations weren't important enough to reject Pete, so he hired the lot on the spot. Each was to receive thirty dollars a month and board, with Sundays off. All accepted with alacrity. Cully took over then, taking everyone but Bud to the bunkhouse.

At that point Zoey came out to join Pierce and Bud. Already acquainted, Bud and Zoey exchanged greetings.

"There are chores to be done around the paddocks and barn, as you can plainly see," Pierce explained, "but I think the ranch will be better served if the men are put to work rounding up livestock. I recently suffered an injury, but in a few more days I should be fit enough to ride along with the men. Oh, one more thing. One man is to be left behind to protect my wife when I'm not around to do it myself!"

Bud sent Zoey a curious look but did not question Pierce's orders. It wasn't his place. "Sure thing, Mr. Delaney. The men will need the rest of the day to settle in, but we'll start out bright and early to-morrow to find your cattle. I know this land like the back of my hand."

"It's good to see men riding Circle F land again," Zoey said once they were alone. "Cully told me you wrote your brothers for money. I'll pay you back, Pierce, I swear it. Every single dime."

Pierce gave her an inscrutable look but said nothing. There was only one thing he wanted from her in return. And if he didn't get it soon, he was going to turn to ash.

Pierce drove the buckboard into town two days later to purchase supplies for the cookhouse and to pick up mail. To his de-light he found a letter from Chad waiting for him. Chad had enclosed a letter of credit on a Billings bank in which they kept an account. It was a smart move, Pierce thought, for a banker in a distant city wouldn't know about his trouble in Dry Gulch.

The rest of Chad's letter was less than comforting. Evidently Cora Lee was stick-ing to her story. She still insisted Pierce had seduced her, gotten her with child, and beaten her when she insisted that he marry her. Chad wrote that Cora Lee's brother was trying to extort money from them to pay for his sister's doctoring. So far Chad and Ryan had resisted the scam. They were being watched by members of the vigilantes but were still trying to find the person responsible for Cora Lee's injuries.

Chad also expressed concern for Pierce's health and prayed for his speedy recovery. He also wanted to know more about Miss Zoey Fuller, and how long Pierce expected to remain at the Circle F ranch.

Although Pierce hated to keep the truth from his brothers about his marriage, he still felt some things were better left unsaid.

Pierce's next stop was the bank, where he used the letter of credit to open an account. The deposit he made was sufficient to pay expenses for at least six months, despite the fact that he'd be long gone by then. He had fond hopes of returning home soon. Willoughby was nowhere in sight, and Pierce didn't ask for him. He finished his business and left.

Pierce was surprised to note that he was greeted in a friendly manner by the townspeople he encountered. Just as he expected, word had spread about his marriage to Zoey. Since Zoey was well known and popular about Rolling Prairie, congratulations were sincere and profuse. It made Pierce feel like a heel. He knew he'd be despised after he up and left Zoey, but that was the way it had to be. He wasn't a marrying man and didn't intend to remain one very long. Women had no permanent place in his life. It was as if Cora Lee and Zoey had conspired together to steal his freedom.

From the moment of their first meeting, Pierce knew Zoey was different from Cora Lee, but he couldn't forgive her for railroading him into marriage. If he hadn't been too weak to ride away, he'd still be a free man. Women were insidious creatures. Once a man gave them an inch, they took a mile.

Pierce was in a particularly foul mood when he arrived back at the ranch. The longer he thought about the way women had fouled up his life, the angrier he became. By the time he drove into the yard, he regretted ever having crawled into Zoey Fuller's root cellar. Furthermore, he regretted offering to help old man Doolittle with the chores. And last but not least, he wished Cora Lee and her family to hell.

Zoey rode up to meet Pierce. She had been out with the hands and looked dusty and tired. Pierce took one look at her tight little buttocks bouncing in the saddle and her unfettered breasts beneath her plaid shirt, and hit the roof.

"Dammit, Zoey, why can't you behave like a lady?"

Zoey's mouth fell open. "What are you talking about?"

"Look at you. You might as well be naked the way those britches hug your bottom and hips. And I can see your nipples pushing through the material of your shirt. You're distracting the hands. It's a wonder they can get any work done, the way you flaunt yourself around them."

"Who put the burr under your saddle? I always dress like this when I'm riding the range."

"You have men now to do that kind of work, and I'm fit enough to ride with them. Your place is in the house."

Zoey's temper exploded. "You have no right to tell me what to do. Who do you think ran this place before you came? Who will run it when you're gone?"

"Until I leave, you'll do as I say. I'm your husband, in case you've forgotten." His smoldering gaze bored into her. "Perhaps you need to be reminded that you have a husband."

From the way Zoey visibly tensed, it was clear his meaning was not lost on her.

"Why do you enjoy tormenting me? I don't like being married any more than you do. Unfortunately you were my only hope of foiling Willoughby's plans for me."

Pierce leaped off the buckboard, reached Zoey in three long strides, and pulled her off her horse. She let out a squawk of surprise and tumbled into his arms. Pierce caught her handily, bent her over his arm, and planted his mouth firmly over hers. He kissed her thoroughly, his mouth hard and demanding, his tongue sweeping past her lips and teeth to suck the very breath from her.

Pierce felt his groin tighten, felt his blood run hot and heavy, and knew if he didn't have Zoey soon, he'd explode. She was driving him mad, strutting before him in tight britches, displaying her ample charms to the best advantage, baiting him, goading him. He'd learned long ago that women were teases, and Zoey was an expert. She pretended she didn't want him sexually, but her body told him otherwise.

Suddenly aware that Zoey was pounding on his chest, Pierce broke off the kiss.

"What was that for?" Zoey asked, still shaking from Pierce's unprovoked attack.

"That's just a prelude to what you're asking for."

"I'm not asking for a darn thing."

"You could have fooled me. You have only to ask and I'll gladly accommodate you. No need to be coy about it. Virgins can want it as badly as their more experienced sisters."

"Don't be crude. Let me go."

Pierce's arms dropped away. Zoey felt so natural in his embrace, he'd forgotten she was there. She was a distraction that was quickly becoming an obsession. He'd been in full possession of his strength for days now and still hadn't relieved Zoey of her virginity or satisfied his lust. He must be slipping.

"It won't be long now, love," he predicted. "I'll be waiting. All you have to do is ask and I'll teach you all about passion."

"When hell freezes over. Excuse me, I'm tired and dirty from the trail. Supper will be late tonight."

Pierce watched her walk away, admiring the way her tight little bottom swayed when she walked. His hands itched to caress those sweet mounds, to strip her naked and teach her body to enjoy all the things he'd do to her.

Soon, he promised himself. Very soon. He remembered the purchase he'd made on his last trip to town and smiled.

Chapter 6

Supper that night was a quiet affair, until Pierce said with amazing calm, "I'm going to break into Willoughby's office tomorrow night."

Zoey's fork clattered into her plate. "You're what!"

"I said I'm going to —"

Zoey made an impatient gesture with her hand. "I know what you said. What do you hope to gain by placing your life in danger?"

"There won't be any danger if it's done right."

Cully said nothing, merely continued eating.

Zoey sent Pierce a scathing glance. "How many banks have you broken into?"

"It's not the same. I'm going to break into Willoughby's office, not rob a bank. He keeps the mortgages in a filing cabinet in his office. You need to take a good look at your father's signature. If it's a forgery as you claim, you should be able to compare it with your father's writing. Do you have a sample of his writing in the house?"

"There are papers in Pa's desk bearing his signature. Unfortunately none of them is the deed to the ranch. That's been missing since shortly after his death. I've turned the house upside down and can't find it."

"What do you think happened to it?"

"I've given it a lot of thought. I'm convinced it was stolen when the house was broken into shortly after Pa's death, but at the time I thought nothing of it because nothing appeared to be missing."

Pierce stared at Zoey, his expression pensive. "If Willoughby holds the mortgage on the land, it would be natural for him to hold the deed as security. If he has it, I'd bet my bottom dollar your father never gave it to him."

"You think Willoughby broke into the house?" Zoey asked.

"He wouldn't do it himself. He'd hire someone else to do the dirty work. A man like Willoughby would find it easy to cheat a woman. While your father was alive, Willoughby had no hope of obtaining either you or your land. Your father's death worked in Willoughby's favor." Pierce grew thoughtful. "How did your father die?"

"He was killed by a band of renegade Sioux. No one even knew Indians were in the area. He was riding in the foothills collecting strays. It was a strange thing. They killed Pa and never struck again. They just disappeared. Pa was in his prime. His health was good, he had everything to live for."

"How do you know it was Indians?"

"We found Sioux arrows in and around Pa's body."

Pierce's brow furrowed in thought. He had grave reservations about the Indian theory but kept them to himself.

Cully jumped in to offer an opinion. "Weren't no Injuns, if you ask me. The whole incident was just too isolated. No one saw hide nor hair of Injuns, just that arrow sticking in Robert's back. Couldn't prove otherwise, though."

"Please," Zoey said, swallowing her tears, "I can't bear to think of it. Indians or no, Pa is dead."

"You're right," Pierce concurred. "Until we have concrete proof, it's best not to dwell on something that only serves to make Zoey sad."

"When are you going into town?" Zoey asked, concerned about Pierce's dangerous mission.

"After the hands have retired for the night. The fewer people who know about this the better. When I was in Willoughby's office the other day I noticed that the rear door opened into the alley. I'm quite good at picking locks. My brothers and I used to rob the candy store when we were wild kids. The next day Pa would whip us good, then pay for the candy we took."

"If you're dead set on this, I reckon there's nothing I can do to talk you out of it," Cully said, rising from the table. "Reckon I'll hit the sack."

No one saw the man edge away from the window, nor knew that he heard nearly every word spoken by the trio inside.

"You don't have to do this," Zoey said.

"The sooner this mess is settled, the sooner I can be on my way. You saved my life and I aim to pay my debt. When I leave it's going to be with a clear conscience."

Zoey should have known Pierce was thinking of himself, not about her problems. He wanted to be free of her, but for some unexplained reason he felt the need to repay her for saving his life before he left.

Zoey rose abruptly. "I'd try to talk you out of this, but I can see your mind is made up. I'll pray for your success."

Pierce sat at the table long after Zoey had cleaned up the kitchen and retired for the night. He pictured her lying in her bed, wearing that white linen shroud that served as a nightgown, and wondered why he hadn't given her the gift he'd bought for her in town last week. He smiled in acknowledgment of his selfish reason for buying her the gift. He wanted to be with her when she wore it. He wanted her to put it on the first time they made love. *Soon,* he thought, *very soon.* Lust was about to kill him.

Zoey was so nervous the next day she could barely function. She could think of nothing but the danger Pierce courted by seeking illegal entrance to Willoughby's office. Somehow she got through the day, but the supper she prepared that evening left much to be desired.

Pierce was unusually quiet at the supper table, mentally preparing himself for what lay ahead. He ate automatically, tasting little of what he chewed and swallowed, mulling over his plans. He planned to enter town after midnight and stay out of sight by using the back street behind the buildings to reach the bank. He'd already found the tools he needed to pick the lock and had them in his room.

"I've been thinking," Cully said, clearing his throat. "I oughta go with you tonight. I could be your lookout."

"I appreciate your offer, Cully, but it's too dangerous. You're needed on the ranch. If I end up in jail, I don't want to take you with me."

Curiously, Zoey had little to say. She'd made a decision the night before, one she knew Pierce wouldn't like. But this was her land, her problem. She'd involved Pierce in her problems by force. An unwilling participant. If he was going to place his life in jeopardy, she was going to be with him.

Pierce retired to his room early. He lay on his bed fully dressed. He dozed off and on until eleven-thirty, then rose, dressed in black shirt and denims he'd purchased in town, and quietly left the room. The house was silent as Pierce stole down the stairs. A quick glance at the bunkhouse before entering the barn assured him that all the lights were out and the men sleeping. He saddled a horse, walked it through the gate, then mounted up and rode off.

Zoey wasn't far behind him, dressed in almost identical dark clothing. She was mounted and heading for town a scant ten minutes behind Pierce. She had scarcely cleared the gate when the bunkhouse door opened and a man stepped out. A few minutes later he rode through the gate and was swallowed up by darkness.

Pierce reached town right on schedule and paused to get his bearings. The only light came from the saloon, which appeared to be doing a lively business. He watched a drunk man stagger out of the saloon and meander down the street. He reined his mount into the alley behind the bank.

On his previous visits to town, Pierce had noted that the bank was the sixth building from the corner. He found it with little trouble, dismounted, and tethered his horse to one of the iron bars covering the small office window. Removing his tools from his pocket, Pierce knelt and began fiddling with the lock.

Darkness aided Zoey as she trailed Pierce. When he reached town and turned in to the alley, she realized he was headed for the back street that ran behind the bank. Zoey entered the alley and lost herself in the shadows, where she had a good view of the street. Should danger threaten, she wanted to be in a position to warn Pierce. If all went well, he'd never know she had been there.

Pierce cursed the lock's resistance. After

ten minutes he'd begun to question his skill. Then he heard the lock give way. The breath left his lungs in a loud whoosh as he eased the door open and stepped inside. He lit a match and crept across the room to the file cabinet.

Hidden in the shadows, Zoey watched as a lone rider, his wide-brimmed hat pulled low over his forehead concealing his features, passed by the alley and continued down the street. She watched in trepidation until he turned a corner and dropped from sight. After ten minutes Zoey grew worried. Pierce should have completed his mission by now.

Suddenly two riders rounded a corner and headed in her direction. Zoey held her breath, hoping their destination was the saloon. When they stopped in front of the bank, her apprehension grew. Peeking around the corner, Zoey knew real panic when she recognized Willoughby and the unidentified man who had entered town not ten minutes earlier.

Spurring her horse forward, Zoey raced around to the rear of the bank to warn Pierce of the danger. If he was found breaking into the bank, all hell would break loose. She saw his horse and knew he was still inside Willoughby's office. She leapt from her mount and burst through the door. He blew out the match and jumped to his feet.

Her voice hissed through the darkness. "Pierce, Willoughby is at the front door. You've got to leave — now!"

"What in God's name are you doing here?"

"There's no time for that. Just get out of here before you're discovered."

Pierce spit out a curse. He hadn't had time to pull the Fuller file from the cabinet, and it was too late now. He couldn't let Zoey be found anywhere near the premises. Grasping her hand, he pulled her out the door and threw her atop her horse. "Get the hell out of here." He slapped the horse's rump. Zoey grabbed the reins as the animal surged forward.

"Aren't you coming?" she called over her shoulder.

"In a minute."

Closing the door carefully behind him, Pierce knelt and, plying the tool he used to break in, jiggled the lock until it fell back into place. And not a minute too soon. He was racing down the alley when a light went on in Willoughby's office.

"There's no one here," Willoughby

grouched. "You woke me from a sound sleep for nothing."

"I tell you I followed them, boss. I saw them leave the Circle F."

"You must have been dreaming." Willoughby went to the door and tried the handle. The door was still locked. "Go on back before you're missed. Next time you wake me up, it had better be for a good reason."

Pierce and Zoey rode hell for leather back to the ranch. Once in the barn, Pierce ordered her into the house while he unsaddled and rubbed down their horses. Zoey went gladly, aware that Pierce was furious with her. She went upstairs immediately, hoping to reach her room before his temper exploded. She breathed a sigh of relief once she was safely inside with the door closed. She lit a lamp and started to undress. She didn't think Pierce would follow her into her room.

She was wrong.

Minutes later the door slammed open. Zoey spun around, holding the shirt she'd just removed in front of her like a shield. Pierce stood in the doorway, his face a mask of rage . . . and something else she couldn't decipher. She'd never seen that

139

look before on his face.

"You little fool! What did you hope to gain by following me tonight?"

Zoey couldn't believe what she was hearing. "I saved your life . . . again."

"That's besides the point. Can't you understand? I didn't want to drag you into this. I didn't want to endanger your life."

"You didn't have to drag me into this, this is my fight. It's my land at risk. I forced you to involve yourself in my problems, but I didn't ask you to die for me. I followed you because I wanted to help. And I did. If I hadn't been there, you would have been discovered."

Pierce's eyes narrowed. "What in the hell do you suppose brought Willoughby to the bank that time of night?"

"Someone had to know about your plans," Zoey guessed. "Someone from the ranch must have followed us. When I saw a rider enter town and disappear around a corner, I thought it was just a coincidence. Whoever it was, though, must have warned Willoughby."

"Are you sure?"

"I'm reasonably sure the man who rode into town minutes behind me was the same one who arrived with Willoughby. Do you think it could be one of our hands?"

"I'll look into it in the morning."

Pierce's expression eased. He couldn't describe how frightened he'd been when Zoey burst into Willoughby's office. He couldn't stop shaking all the way home. Now, seeing her safe, he wanted to take her into his arms, to crush her against him, to kiss her until she begged him to stop. God, he must be growing soft in the head. Is that what marriage did to a man?

Pierce walked into the room, halting scant inches from Zoey. His green eyes glittered like jewels as he took the shirt from her hands and tossed it aside. Her breasts rose and fell rapidly with the intake of her breath beneath the lacy barrier of the camisole she wore. With shaking hands, Pierce reached out and released the ties, slowly easing the garment open and pushing it aside to reveal her breasts. He muttered something beneath his breath and gently touched her nipple with a fingertip.

Zoey inhaled sharply. His touch set off a firestorm inside her. She wanted to throw herself into his arms, feel the hard, arousing length of him impressed upon her skin. She wanted him to do all those things to her that husbands did to wives.

Pierce was experienced enough to know

that Zoey wanted him, and he exulted in the knowledge. His hands curved around her breasts, molding them against his palms, caressing the nipples with the rough pads of his thumbs. Every muscle throbbed with need, screaming at him to lay her down, spread her legs, and thrust inside her. He wanted to take her fast and hard, deep and fierce, then ride her to his own release.

"Do you want me?" he whispered against her lips.

"It makes no difference what I want. I won't give myself to a man who will leave me and never look back."

An odd pain rippled through Pierce, a tightness that contracted and made his throat ache. He wouldn't lie. "I can promise you nothing, love. I never wanted to be married. You saved my life, but regardless, I will leave once my debt is repaid in full. Neither of us expected more from this marriage. I'm only asking that you let me give you pleasure while I'm here."

"What it you leave me with child?" The thought of carrying Pierce's child was disturbing but not unpleasant. Under any other circumstances she'd have loved to have Pierce's baby.

His hard features softened, his eyes

moving over her with something that might have been yearning. "I'll try to prevent that from happening. Let me love you, Zoey."

His lips came down hard upon hers, stealing away her protests and cries as he kissed her with searing fervor, thrusting his tongue into her mouth and exploring it with unleashed passion. He kissed her again and again, leaving her gasping and breathless. Then he dropped to his knees and took the swollen bud of one breast into his wet, warm mouth, drawing on her with exquisite tenderness. The stubble on his chin scraped the tender flesh of her ribs as he paid homage to the other breast.

Zoey's knees grew weak and she would have collapsed but for Pierce's strong hands holding her upright. Then she felt his hand between her legs, and acute embarrassment made her whimper. She knew she was damp there and hoped Pierce couldn't feel it through her denims.

"Tell me you want me, love."

Zoey wanted him, oh, yes, she wanted him. But letting him love her would make his leaving all the more painful. She couldn't bear the thought of all those nights to come when she'd remember his loving and face the emptiness in her soul.

"Don't do this to me. Ours isn't a real marriage. I don't want to know passion with you. You don't love me and I . . . I don't love you."

Slowly Pierce's hands dropped away. His face was contorted with anguish, his pain very real. He'd never taken a woman by force and he didn't intend to start now. He never doubted for a minute that Zoey would come to him on his terms before he left.

"You're killing me. Are you sure?"

No, not sure at all, but it's the way it has to be. "Yes, very sure."

Zoey could almost feel the pain in Pierce's tormented body. Her pain was nearly as great. She turned away from him, pulling her camisole up to cover her breasts. She felt deep shame for giving Pierce so much of herself before stopping him. But his mouth on her had been so sweetly arousing. It had felt so right that she'd been momentarily distracted and unable to stop him. She'd always known Pierce wanted her sexually, for he'd never hid that from her. Tonight his seduction of her had been nearly accomplished. He was so sure of himself, so determined that she'd succumb to temptation. Fortunately she was made of sterner stuff than he gave her credit for.

Men like Pierce wanted sex without attachments. Pierce thought women were treacherous and untrustworthy. And she'd done nothing to change his mind. Railroading him into marriage served only to reinforce his low opinion of women.

Bringing her mental ruminations to a halt, Zoey turned to confront Pierce, surprised that he had already left.

Pierce paced the length of his room and back, too aroused to sleep. Suddenly nothing in his life made sense. Why did this woman, of all the women he'd known, move him in a way he hadn't been moved in more years than he cared to count? Why did he want Zoey more than he could ever recall wanting another woman? He wanted her sexually, he couldn't deny that, but it went deeper than that. God, what was happening to him?

Whatever it was, he didn't like it. He wasn't going to leave until Zoey gave him what he wanted so he could purge her from his system. Soon his brothers would have the truth from Cora Lee and he'd be free to return to Dry Gulch, to the comfortable life he had led before meeting Zoey Fuller.

Abruptly Pierce's gaze fell on the gift he

had purchased in town for Zoey the same day he'd bought new clothing for himself. He'd intended to let her wear it long enough for him to admire her in it, then strip it off her and gently initiate her to passion. Suddenly he grew angry, angry at himself, at Zoey, at all females in general. He ought to give her the damn gift and let her do with it as she pleased.

Grabbing the package from the top of his bureau, he flung the door open and stormed down the hall to Zoey's room. He burst inside without knocking. Zoey was seated at her dressing table, brushing her long blond hair. The breath caught in Pierce's chest. He found the simple sight of Zoey brushing her hair somehow more erotic than if she had greeted him naked. Gaining his wits, he tossed the neatly wrapped package on the bed.

"I hoped we might enjoy this together, but I was mistaken. Consider it a wedding gift," he flung out sarcastically.

He whirled on his heel and disappeared as quickly as he had appeared.

Zoey paused in midstroke, the brush poised in her blond tresses. She eyed the package he'd tossed carelessly upon the bed with misgiving. She rose slowly, approaching the small package wrapped in brown paper and tied with a string as if she expected it to explode. She touched it gingerly, trying to decide if she should open it or return it sight unseen. Curiosity overcame her reservations.

Zoey opened the package with shaking hands, gasping in dismay and no little surprise when she drew out the loveliest nightgown she'd ever seen. She hadn't even known such garments existed. It appeared to be made of cobwebs, all silvery and shimmery. She held it up to the light, and her breath caught when light filtered through its transparent folds. The demure high neck was deceptive, for nothing beneath it would be withheld from view. Three tiny buttons held it together at the bodice. The lower half was split from the waist down.

Zoey stared at the diaphanous nightgown and burst into tears. Had she married a man she loved, this was exactly the kind of garment she'd have chosen for her wedding night. How could Pierce have known?

Seduction took many forms, she supposed, and obviously Pierce Delaney was an expert.

In the days that followed, neither Pierce nor Zoey mentioned the nightgown or what had transpired the night he had given it to her. Pierce arose early, rode out with the men, returned late, and ate in the cookhouse with the hands. Zoey was already in bed by the time Pierce returned to the house.

Zoey missed him but told herself the coldness between them was for the best. She was putty in Pierce's hands. Whenever he touched her she went up in smoke. She'd had no idea she possessed a passionate nature until Pierce touched her. Perhaps it was because no man had ever attracted her like Pierce.

A week after the aborted attempt to break into Willoughby's office, the banker arrived at the ranch, accompanied by a deputy. Zoey met him at the front door.

"What do you want?"

"Where is your husband?"

"In the barn."

"Get him," he told the deputy.

Zoey eyed the deputy warily. "What is this all about?"

"You'll see soon enough."

Willoughby continued to smile complacently while the deputy strode to the barn for Pierce. A few minutes later Pierce appeared, taking a stance beside Zoey. The look he gave Willoughby was daunting.

"State your business, Willoughby."

"Of course, that's why I'm here. I brought a deputy to make things nice and legal."

He removed a sheet of paper from his pocket and shoved it under Pierce's nose.

"These are foreclosure orders, in case you can't read. All legal and signed by the judge. You have two weeks to vacate the premises. Take only your personal belongings and keepsakes. The furnishings go with the house."

"You . . . you can't do that," Zoey sputtered. Though she'd known it was coming, it was still a shock.

Pierce's arm crept around her and she leaned into him, welcoming his support.

"It's legal and binding, Zoey," Willoughby declared. "Had you married me, none of this would be necessary. You and I could be sharing this land and house. But you deliberately chose to thwart me."

He turned glittering eyes on Pierce. "Something strange went on in my office one night last week. What do you know about it?"

Pierce's lips flattened. "I don't know what you're talking about."

"I can't prove a damn thing, Delaney, but I'm warning you, don't mess with me."

Then he smiled at Zoey. It wasn't a pleasant smile. "What are you going to do when your husband leaves you, my dear? He will, you know. His kind never sticks around long. Just remember, I'll be here long after he's gone. I'll still welcome you into my home and bed when you have no one to turn to."

"Don't hold your breath," Zoey retorted. "I'll find a job if I need to."

"Not in this town." He tipped his hat. "Good day to you. I'll return in two weeks to claim my land."

"Oh, God," Zoey sobbed after Willoughby and the deputy rode off. "How I hate that smug bastard!"

"Don't give up yet," Pierce consoled. He brushed a strand of golden hair from her forehead and kissed her temple. He wasn't going to let Willoughby force Zoey off her land without trying one last time to prove that the mortgage had been forged. Only this time he would reveal his plans to no one. Not even Cully. Especially not Zoey.

"He's taken everything from me," Zoey whispered, feeling as if the weight of the world rested on her shoulders. She was going to lose her home, and Pierce would move on soon afterward. The one good thing to come of this was that it was impossible for Willoughby to force her into marriage. And she would starve before turning to him for comfort after Pierce left.

"There's always something that can be done," Pierce mused thoughtfully. "Don't say anything about this to the hands, it might affect their work. We've made great progress these past weeks. The paddocks are nearly filled with Circle F livestock. When it comes time to fulfill your contract to the army, you'll have those three hundred head that were promised to them."

Zoey laughed bitterly. "This is too much! How can you act as if nothing will change? Why should the hands round up the cattle for Willoughby's benefit? That's what it amounts to. Besides, this isn't your problem."

"You made it my problem," Pierce reminded her.

Zoey was too upset to listen to what he was saying. "Perhaps you should leave now. In two weeks you'll no longer have a roof over your head."

"Neither will you. What will you do? Where will you go?"

If it comes down to it, I could always send her to my brothers, Pierce decided.

"I'm not sure. I'll get a room in town and find a job. I've never lived in town." Her chin rose stubbornly. "I'll get by. I'd prefer that you get the annulment. Getting it in Rolling Prairie would give Willoughby more ammunition to use against me."

"Since I never intend to remarry, there's no hurry."

Pierce turned her toward him, wiping away her tears with his fingertips. She gave him a watery smile. Pierce felt something inside him burst. She was so brave it nearly broke his heart. It was the first time in many years he acknowledged possessing a heart, and it startled him.

"Don't despair, love. We still have two weeks. All isn't lost yet."

"You don't have to cheer me up, Pierce. I've reconciled myself to losing the land my father gave his life for. It was all he had to leave me. He died protecting it. I'll survive."

Pierce's determination to help Zoey grew by leaps and bounds. His own problems could wait. He couldn't return to Dry Gulch yet anyway. Not if he wanted to live. Riley Reed would love to put a rope around his neck.

Pierce had a plan. Someone at the Circle F was a spy; unfortunately he had yet to find that man. Bud had questioned everyone in the bunkhouse about the night Pierce had broken into Willoughby's office, but no one had noticed anyone missing. This time Pierce was taking no chances. He'd do what he had to do without interference from a damn spy.

Chapter 7

Zoey tried to present a brave face at supper that night and failed miserably. Though neither Cully nor Pierce mentioned Willoughby's visit or the foreclosure, it was on their minds, making for a subdued meal. Finally Zoey could stand it no longer. Leaving her untouched meal on her plate, she scraped back her chair and ran from the kitchen.

Pierce started to go after her, but Cully grasped his arm and said, "Let her go. There ain't nothing you can do now. Ain't nothing nobody can do. Don't worry none about Zoey after you leave, I'll see to her. Always have, always will." His sharp-eyed gaze speared into Pierce. "You *are* leaving, ain't you? If you are, you oughta do it soon, before Miz Zoey gets too fond of you."

Pierce gazed at Cully through hooded eyes. Why did he feel like such a heel? "I reckon I'll be moving on soon, but not quite yet. I have some unfinished business."

"That business ain't Miz Zoey, is it? It better not be what I'm thinking it is."

"What if it is?" Pierce challenged. "Zoey and I are husband and wife. She's old enough to make up her own mind." Though bedding Zoey wasn't what Pierce meant when he referred to unfinished business, Cully's words came too close to the truth.

"Don't get all hot under the collar, Delaney. I know Miz Zoey is a grown woman, but she's been protected by her pa most of her life."

Pierce snorted in derision. "You could have fooled me. She was the one who used threats to force me to marry her. I would have been on my way a long time ago if she hadn't involved me in her problems."

"She saved your life," Cully reminded him.

"I'm aware of that. Why do you think I'm still here? Words spoken over us by a preacher wouldn't keep me around if I didn't feel I owed Zoey for saving my life. You're a good man, Cully. Zoey could have no better protector. Well . . ." He stretched and yawned. "Reckon I'll turn in."

Though the night was young, Pierce had plans to make. Tonight he was going to make another stab at breaking into Willoughby's office and stealing the mortgage.

Her eyes burning with unshed tears, Zoey peered into the darkness through her bedroom window. Her land, the land upon which she'd been born, the land that her father had toiled to hold for her, was lost. Rich grassland, fertile valleys, bubbling springs, rushing rivers against a backdrop of majestic snowcapped mountains. God, she loved this land and the house upon it.

Zoey's musing turned to Pierce — he was never far from her thoughts — wondering if he was relieved that this whole mess had come to a head so soon. He could leave now, without guilt or recriminations. He had remained her husband long enough to thwart Willoughby's plans for her, and that was all she could ask of him. She had to let him go just as she'd promised. He had problems of his own to resolve.

Zoey knew Pierce well enough to realize he would never beat a woman. Getting Cora Lee with child was another matter. If the way he'd tried to seduce her was any indication, Pierce was fully capable of planning and carrying out a seduction. She hoped all would end well for him even if her own situation was beyond help.

Suddenly her gaze fell on the nightgown Pierce had given her. She had folded it and left it on her bureau where she could admire it. She touched it reverently, wondering how she would look in it. Her skin tingled and her fingers itched to try it on, even if no one but her ever saw her in it. She needed comforting, and for reasons she didn't understand, the nightgown offered that. The thought that Pierce had picked it out and bought it for her brought renewed tears to her eyes.

She'd lost the land, the house, and now she was going to lose Pierce. She was a wife without knowing the real meaning of the word. She was a woman without having experienced the joy of becoming one. Would she ever know a man's love?

Determination tautened her jaw; her blue eyes darkened with resolve. She might never know a man's love, but she could know his passion. All she had to do was walk out one door and into another . . . to Pierce. She didn't know if she loved Pierce, and he obviously didn't love her, but she needed someone tonight, someone who understood what she was going through. She gazed at the nightgown with longing and came to a decision she hoped she wouldn't live to regret.

Zoey stripped off her clothes, washed thoroughly, and slipped into the gossamer gown. Slowly she turned and gazed at herself in the mirror, her eyes widening at the way the material hugged her figure, as if specifically created with her in mind. Her hair didn't look right, so she pulled out her braids and ran her fingers through the silken strands, releasing it into soft waves that hung down her back. Dimly she wondered if Pierce would like the way she looked in the nightgown. She'd never know if she remained in her room staring at her image.

Dragging in a shuddering breath, Zoey opened the door and stepped into the hall. Light flowed from beneath Pierce's door, drawing her like a moth to flame. She reached his door and paused, her hand on the doorknob. She was shaking from the inside out, frightened yet strangely elated. Anticipation had set up a clamor inside her only Pierce could quell.

Gathering her courage, she turned the knob, opened the door, and stepped inside. A single lamp was turned down low, casting the room into a dark and mysterious haven. She didn't see him immediately and feared he'd left without her knowledge. Then she saw a movement and turned her head just as he stepped out from the shadows. He was dressed all in black.

He stared at her and prayed he wasn't dreaming. He hadn't heard the door open, merely sensed her presence. She was dressed in shimmering cobwebs, her beauty rivaling the moon and the stars. Bathed in lamplight, her body withheld no secrets from him. The world paled. His heart and mind were filled with the woman he'd lusted after with every fiber of his being. He faltered over the word *lust,* but could think of no other explanation for the way he felt about Zoey.

Zoey trembled. She felt alive as never before, seared by the green fire of Pierce's eyes. She returned his stare, shivering as she felt the sensual heat of his gaze roam over her. Her nerves were drawn taut. She was on the verge of fleeing when she heard Pierce's whisper.

Pierce tried to speak, but managed only to whisper her name. All of him turned to stone. He'd fantasized about seeing Zoey in the nightgown, but his imagination did not do her justice. She was exquisite. Her body was perfection. From her high, firm breasts crowned with delicate pink nipples to the dark blond patch shielding her womanhood, Zoey was the kind of woman men dreamed about. Her legs were long and shapely, her ankles delicately turned. Her hips flared out gently from a minuscule waist. He wanted her with a passion unequaled to anything he'd ever felt in the past.

He reached out to her, and the gesture unleashed the words building inside him. "Zoey, you're lovelier than I ever could have imagined you'd be."

"It's the nightgown," Zoey replied nervously. "I shouldn't have come." She took a hesitant step toward the door.

"No, don't go!" He reached her in two strides. "It's time for us to be together." Unfortunately Zoey had picked a most inopportune time to come to him. In a few short hours he'd be on his way into town to break into the bank.

Zoey licked moisture onto her lips, which had suddenly gone dry. Abruptly her reasons for being here seemed inappropriate. "The nightgown is lovely," she said, stalling for time. "Thank you."

"What's inside it is lovely." He pulled her against him, smiling down at her.

Zoey shivered; the raw, exciting power emanating from him lit fires within her. She wanted this, she told herself. She wanted him. She wanted to have something to warm her lonely nights when Pierce was gone.

"You surprise me, love," Pierce said. He gave her a slow, sensual smile. "Tell me I'm not dreaming. I've wanted you for a very long time. What made you decide to come to me tonight?"

Zoey shrugged; her reasons no longer made sense. "Perhaps it wasn't a good idea."

"It was a *very* good idea," he whispered against her lips. His tongue traced the line of her mouth, and she trembled. He nibbled at her bottom lip, and she whimpered. Then he covered her mouth and his tongue dipped inside, and she grasped his shirtfront for support.

His hands roamed over her body, the silken nightgown creating an arousing friction along her flesh. He deepened the kiss, his palms touching lightly upon her breasts. When his mouth left hers at last, it was to travel to her earlobe, where he whispered how delicious she tasted, and how he'd like to taste her in other places. Then his mouth was on her breast, laving the nipple through the gauzy material of her gown. Suddenly she was free of the gown as it floated to her feet.

Sweeping her high in his arms, Pierce carried Zoey to his bed, then stepped back to admire her.

"Why are you dressed like that?" Zoey asked, suddenly aware that Pierce was dressed differently than he had been at supper.

"You talk too much," Pierce hedged as he dropped to the bed beside her and kissed her again, driving all thought from her mind but this man's arousing kisses.

"Do you want me, Zoey?" His hands skimmed her body, his touch promising unimaginable delights.

Zoey swallowed reflexively. She couldn't lie. "Yes, I want you. Are you gloating now?"

"Not gloating, love, elated." He rose abruptly and tore off his clothes. Then he stood very still, allowing her gaze to traverse the length of his body slowly.

Despite the languorous haze she was in, her mind registered his arousal, the beauty of his naked body, and she ached in that place where she wanted him to be.

"You've seen me before, love," he reminded her softly when he saw her mouth fall open in wordless wonder.

"Not like this."

The longer she stared at that male part of him, the larger and harder it grew. It rose now like a solid column of marble against his stomach, amid a forest of dark, curling hair. The air about him seemed charged with vitality. There was no denying the extraordinary power of his chest, arms, and thighs, for they rippled with muscles. His stomach was whipcord-lean, and his legs long and sturdy. Yet there was a grace about him despite the latent promise of incredible strength.

Zoey had always admired Pierce's features, and she did so again. Strongly chiseled, rugged, implacably handsome, his face was graced with vivid green eyes that seemed to plumb the depths of her soul.

Those eyes were now crinkled with amusement. "Do you like what you see?"

A spreading warmth tinged Zoey's cheeks. "As you said, I've seen it before." She looked away, focusing on anything but Pierce's daunting erection.

"Don't be frightened, love, I'll try not to hurt you."

The bedsprings creaked as he stretched out beside her and took her into his arms. Zoey's breath caught in her throat; she was surprised at the softness of Pierce's body beneath his muscles. She'd never felt anything more satisfying than her flesh meshed with his.

His hands caressed her as he stared into her eyes, telling her without words that he wanted to please her. His head lowered and he took her nipple into his mouth, laving the taut bud with his tongue, sweeping it into his mouth, grazing it with his teeth. Zoey grasped his head, not to push him away but to bring him closer. She surged against him, moaning softly as he plied his mouth, lips, and tongue to her other nipple, lavishing it with the same attention.

He licked a trail of fire between her breasts, traveling down the length of her belly, planting his weight firmly between her legs as he kissed the insides of her thighs.

"Dim the lamp," Zoey said anxiously. "It isn't right for you to . . . to look at . . . me."

His eyes were glazed with passion as he raised his head and gazed into her eyes. "I want to look at you. You're beautiful all over." Then his strong hands slid beneath her thighs, parting them as he began to slowly caress the moist petals of her womanhood. He moved his hand gently, massaging and pressing and plying his fingers in the most amazing ways.

Zoey shuddered. His touch was light, exploring, thoroughly intoxicating, so seductive she could deny him nothing. She arched upward, and he obliged the sweet demand of her body by taunting her with the swift thrust and withdrawal of a finger inside her tight sheath.

Zoey cried out, consumed by raw, arousing feelings she'd only imagined in her dreams. Deep within her secret being she knew that this kind of overwhelming desire could only be experienced with one man. No other man but Pierce could make her feel like this.

Pierce removed his finger, smiling when Zoey uttered a cry of protest. Then he placed his mouth where his fingers had been and kissed her there. Zoey nearly flew off the bed. After several agonizing minutes Pierce abandoned his succulent meal and moved upward along her body. Soon he'd kiss her more fully there, but not now. He was too hot for that kind of play. Unless he wanted to disappoint Zoey, he had to keep a cool head about him. He wanted her first time to be memorable.

"You're hot and wet and nearly ready," he murmured as he rose above her.

Lost in pleasure, Zoey moaned a senseless reply. She wanted to touch him, to feel his warm flesh against her hands and mouth. Raising her head, she pressed kisses against his chest, his neck, his shoulders, anywhere she could reach, while her hands roamed over his body from his shoulders to his buttocks. Now it was Pierce's turn to moan.

"You're driving me crazy, love," he gritted from between clenched teeth.

"I want you, Pierce, all of you." Cupping his face with her hands, she brought his lips to hers, touching them with a sweeping, savage kiss. Doing as Pierce had earlier, she flicked her tongue seductively against his lips, then delved past the barrier of his teeth, to stroke his tongue.

A guttural groan escaped him, shattering the silence of the night. "Enough!" He raised himself slightly and guided himself to the portals of her sex, where he was welcomed by the sweet moisture of her arousal.

Zoey tensed, fear gripping her. He felt hard, and much too large. He wouldn't fit! He'd tear her in two. She should have thought about the consequences instead of acting impulsively.

Pierce sensed her fear and tried to soothe her with gentle words as he eased inside her. "It will only hurt for a moment," he whispered into her ear. "Relax, it will be much easier if you don't tense up."

She bit her lip in consternation. "You're too . . . I mean, are you sure we'll fit?"

Pierce chuckled. "Women have been doing this since the beginning of time. Trust me."

"I —"

He took her mouth in a searing kiss, kissing her again and again, distracting her from her fears, moving down her neck to her breasts, suckling and licking her nipples. He continued his tender torment until she was arching against him, expressing her need without words. When she surged upward again, he thrust into her, breaking through her barrier in one swift stroke.

Zoey screamed and tried to push him away. The pain was nearly unbearable. All the pleasure up to this moment was forgotten as Pierce's punishing weapon tore into her.

"I'm sorry," Pierce crooned. "The hurt won't last long, I promise." He held her down with the force of his body as she struggled against him. When she had quieted, he began to move slowly.

Pain consumed Zoey. She tried to escape, but Pierce held her down with the sheer strength of his body. But after a few minutes a strange thing happened. The pain began to recede, replaced by something far more pleasurable. She felt him inside her, *really felt him*. He was huge, but she was stretching to accommodate him. Then he flexed his hips, pressing deeper, creating a friction that wasn't unpleasant. He moved again, nearly leaving her body, then thrusting into her once more, gently but forcefully.

His whispers encouraged her to move with him, to take him deeper. Strangely, Pierce had evoked something savage inside Zoey. And as the pain turned to pleasure, she offered herself up to him, arching sharply to meet his thrusts, taking him as deeply as she dared. His passion swept her upward and beyond as he gripped her buttocks in strong, callused hands and lifted her.

"Am I hurting you?"

She caught her breath. "No."

"Then take all of me, Zoey," he said as he ground himself against her. "Take everything I've got."

She flung her head back as she rode the storm of his passion, cresting the waves of pleasure, one after another, swelling and expanding with each thrust. Higher and higher they flew, each plunge of his hips coming stronger and faster than the one before. Until there was a constant ebbing and flowing, hot, bright, emerging into a need so violent it nearly overwhelmed her.

Pierce was lost to the heat and unexpected violence of Zoey's response. Never in his wildest dreams did he imagine she could be like quicksilver in his arms. She was everything he could hope for and more than he deserved.

A growling cry strained the tendons of Pierce's throat, mingling with Zoey's gasping breaths. Striving for the stars, Zoey stiffened as a light burst inside her, sending excruciating pleasure spiraling through her. She heard Pierce cry out, then knew nothing more as she went from sunlight into darkness.

Pierce dropped his head into the crook of Zoey's neck, his heartbeat pounding against her breasts. Damp tendrils of hair clung to her forehead, and he brushed them aside with a trembling hand. Then he lifted his head and rolled weakly to his back, one arm flung over his eyes. He felt Zoey stirring and rose up on one elbow to stare at her. Her eyes opened slowly and she smiled at him.

"I didn't mean to be so rough. Are you all right?"

Tears burned her throat. She hadn't known it would be like this. She'd expected the pain and hoped there would be pleasure, but she'd imagined nothing like the brilliance Pierce had shown her. How was she ever to live without him now that she'd experienced the splendor he was capable of giving her? She tried to move but found she was too weak to do more than lie limply beside him.

At length she said, "I'm fine. I had no idea it could be like this."

"Why, Zoey? Why come to me now, when we could have been enjoying one another all these weeks?"

His eyes glowed with predatory brilliance in the yellow light from the lamp. His body glistened with the sweat of his exertions, and his fierce expression told her there was still more to come this night, much more.

"You'll be leaving soon." Zoey shrugged, as if that explained everything. "I . . . I wanted to know what it felt like to be a wife before you left." *Your wife,* she thought but did not say.

"You'll be a wife again one day," Pierce predicted, wondering why his words sounded hollow. "Some man will come along and sweep you off your feet. In time one of us will get an annulment and you'll be free to experience this with another man."

Impossible, Zoey thought. "What about you, Pierce? Will you find another wife?"

"Never!" Pierce vowed with such fervor, Zoey was inclined to believe him. "You know how I feel about marriage. My mother wanted out of her marriage so desperately she left three small boys behind. I'll give no woman a chance to abandon any children of mine. Do you have any idea how devastated we were? I was the oldest and capable of dealing with the loss, but Chad and Ryan never got over the loss of our mother. The knowledge that she loved them so little still affects them today."

"I'm sorry, Pierce."

"So am I."

"But you did marry. You said yourself you were married once. You must have loved a woman at some time or other."

Pierce gave a snort of laughter. "I tried to replace my mother with another woman, but it didn't work. I chose the wrong woman. After our annulment I gave up all thought of having a woman in my life on a permanent basis."

"What happened?"

"You don't want to know. I just chalked

up the experience to bad judgment. It won't happen again . . . ever. Marriage isn't for me."

"When are you leaving?"

"Soon," he temporized. He gave her a heart-stopping smile. "Did anyone ever tell you you talk too much?"

She opened her mouth to reply, and he slanted his lips over hers, stealing her words. He kissed her long and hard, angling his body over hers, letting her feel how much he wanted her again. Suddenly he rose, went to the washstand, found a soft cloth, dipped it in water, and returned to her. Then he gently wiped away all traces of blood and seed.

"You're not too sore, are you?" he asked hopefully. "I want you again."

The thickness of his sex rose against her hip. The strength and power of him were awesome. The thought that he was swelled with need for her again moved her in ways she didn't understand. It pleased her that he wanted her again, and she wouldn't have denied him had she been hurting.

"I want you, too," she admitted shyly. What she really wanted was to touch him. To feel his vibrant flesh beneath her fingertips. Holding her breath, she reached out and closed her hand over him. He jerked in response and spit out an oath.

"We'll save this kind of play for another time," he said hoarsely, removing her hand. "I don't think I can stand your hands on me right now."

He parted her thighs and eased himself between them. Then he rose up on his knees, opening her wider, placing her legs over his own thighs. She waited impatiently as his hungry gaze devoured her. She rocked her hips in invitation, but he still didn't come into her. He gave her a wicked smile as he lowered his mouth to her.

Zoey screamed as his tongue found a place so sensitive she lost the ability to think. Holding her hips in his large hands, he parted her and stroked her with the roughness of his tongue.

Her release came suddenly, violently. Her body spasmed and she cried out his name. She was lost in the dark brilliance of her climax when Pierce flexed his hips and thrust into her.

Sinking high and deep, he lifted her hips to bring him deeper. He felt her spasms squeezing him all the way to the root of his sex. He kissed her mouth, knowing she tasted herself on his lips and pleased that he'd been able to pleasure her in that manner. Then he thrust once, again, and felt his own release overtaking him.

He shouted his climax into the darkness, his throat working spasmodically. Then he covered her mouth with his to drink in her cries when she surprised him by coming again to pleasure.

"I knew there was passion inside you, but I had no idea how much," he said as he eased his weight off her.

"Are you disappointed?"

"Good God, no! A passionate wife is a man's dream come true." Then he realized what he'd just said and added, "As long as that passion is reserved for her husband. To my regret, I've learned that women are often too eager to share their passion indiscriminately."

Zoey said nothing. She realized it had taken a lifetime to bring Pierce to this philosophy, and nothing she could say would change his mind. He didn't want a wife, and she didn't want a husband who thought so little of women. She wondered if his opinion of her would be different if she hadn't forced him to marry her.

Pierce winced, smote by a twinge of guilt. He couldn't help feeling the way he did about women. Nevertheless, he'd already decided to help Zoey, and that

174

wasn't going to change. His success tonight meant all Zoey's problems would be solved, and he could leave, feeling he had repaid her.

"Go to sleep, love," he said, pulling her against him. "Your body needs to rest now and heal."

Zoey closed her eyes, content in a way she'd never been before, even though she knew Pierce wouldn't be hers for long. Pierce's low opinion of women made it impossible to reach him on any level other than that which they had just experienced. She wasn't sorry she had given of herself, though. It was high time she lost her virginity, and she was glad she'd lost it to Pierce.

Hours later Pierce rose stealthily from the bed, leaving Zoey sleeping soundly. He dressed with haste in the clothes he had discarded earlier. He stood beside the bed, looking down on Zoey with a mixture of confusion and tenderness. No woman had ever made him feel the kind of emotion Zoey did. The least he could do for her before he left was save her ranch. He hoped to hell Zoey wasn't mistaken about the mortgage papers being forged.

Picking up his boots and gun belt, Pierce

tiptoed out the door and down the stairs, grateful that no telltale squeak gave him away. Once outside, he pulled on his boots, buckled on his guns, and strode to the barn.

"Your horse is already saddled."

Pierce swore, his hand going for his gun. Then he relaxed when he recognized the voice. "Dammit, Cully, what are you doing here?"

"I'm going with you."

"No, you're not. How did you know what I was going to do tonight?"

"You ain't all that hard to read. After Willoughby left, I knew you'd try to break into his office again. We're wasting time standing around jawing. Our horses are saddled, let's go."

"What if we're followed like the last time? Someone on the ranch is a spy."

"Bud is keeping an eye on the hands. Trust me, nobody will leave the ranch tonight. You ain't getting shed of me, Delaney, so you'd best set your mind to having me tagging along. Mount up."

Pierce could think of nothing to say that would change Cully's mind. Nodding curtly, he mounted up and walked the horse to the front gate. Cully followed close on his heels. Once they were far

176

enough away to avoid attracting the attention of the sleeping hands, they gave their horses their heads.

Dawn was a faint blush on the horizon when Pierce and Cully returned to the ranch. Bud met them at the barn.

"No one left the ranch tonight, Mr. Delaney," Bud said. "I've been in the barn since you left, and not a horse is missing. I don't know what this is all about and I don't want to know. Cully said it was important; that's good enough for me."

"Thanks, Bud, I appreciate your loyalty," Pierce said, dredging up a smile. The night had turned brisk and he shivered from both the cold and his exhaustion. Not to mention the tension he'd been under during this little jaunt tonight. So much had depended upon his success. "I'm going to hit the sack, I'm beat."

Cully gave him an inscrutable look, started to say something, then changed his mind. Finally he walked from the barn, muttering to himself.

Pierce strode briskly toward the house, eager to rejoin Zoey in his bed. She had come to him last night out of need, and together they had found Paradise. He never would have suspected Zoey of harboring the kind of passion she'd exhibited. It was beyond anything he'd ever dreamed.

The house was quiet as he crept up the stairs and entered his room. The lamp had extinguished itself, and gray light from a pearly predawn filtered through the window. Shedding his clothes, Pierce drew back the blanket and eased into bed beside Zoey. Her flesh was warm and fragrant as he cuddled her against his own chilled flesh, sighing in contentment.

Zoey muttered in her sleep and stirred restlessly. Her innocent movement created a clamoring in Pierce's blood. His hellish lust for Zoey wasn't going to allow him to rest. He caressed her breasts, surprised to find her nipples puckered into tight little buds. He moved his hand lower, between her thighs, and began caressing her there.

Zoey sighed and opened her eyes. "Why are you so cold? Your flesh is like ice."

"I got up a few minutes ago and closed the window," he lied. "It was getting cold in here."

"I'm not cold," Zoey murmured against his chest. "Shall I warm you?" Her voice was as warmly enticing as her body.

Pierce hardened instantly. "I don't know if that's wise. I was rather rough on you last night."

"Today is a whole new day," she murmured as she pulled his head down to meet her lips.

Suddenly Pierce was hot, so hot his flesh was sizzling. He was having difficulty thinking with Zoey's hands roaming over his body. There was serious business to discuss, but it would have to wait until a more persistent need was satisfied. His mouth slanted over hers as he moved atop her, spreading her thighs with his knees. He entered her easily, and just as easily brought them both to shuddering climax.

Chapter 8

Zoey stretched, awakening slowly from a most arousing dream. Then she moved and realized it hadn't been a dream at all. Her body ached in places she never knew existed. Despite those aches and pains, a languorous contentment stole over her body. She smiled, remembering the night and the pleasure it had brought to her. For as long as she lived, she'd never forget Pierce, or this night.

Pierce . . .

She stretched out her hand, searching for him. The place beside her still held his scent, but his warmth was gone. Her face reddened at the memory of his delicious kisses, of how her body had responded to his touch. He had given her ample memories to last a lifetime.

Her next thought made her recoil in fear and horror. Had Pierce left without saying good-bye? It would be just like him to disappear quietly without a word to anyone.

She shouldn't despair, she told herself, she'd known it was coming. From the beginning of their association she'd demanded things of him he'd been unwilling to give. Forgiveness wasn't his way. She'd used him in her battle against Willoughby, and reluctant bridegroom or not, Pierce had fulfilled his part of the bargain. Now she had to fulfill hers and let him go.

Determined to face the day and the rest of her life without Pierce, Zoey rose from bed, momentarily disoriented when she found herself in Pierce's room. Her lovely nightgown lay on the floor, discarded in a moment of unbridled passion. She slipped it on and cautiously opened the door. It wouldn't do for anyone to see her leaving Pierce's room clad in cobwebs, not that anyone but Cully would have reason to enter the house, and he was doing chores this time of day.

Zoey halted abruptly when she saw Pierce standing on the landing. Pierce's steps faltered when he saw Zoey open the bedroom door and step into the hallway. Zoey stared at him and flushed, not knowing what to say after the wanton way she had responded to him last night and early this morning. Pierce found his voice first.

"It's about time you got up, lazybones." He gave her a slow smile that made her flesh tingle with awareness. "I was just coming to awaken you."

"I . . . I thought you'd left." He must have gone down to the stream to bathe, Zoey decided, for droplets of water still clung to his dark hair.

He searched her face, and she grew warm as his gaze traveled the length of her body. "Not yet. There's something I want to show you first." She felt flushed and disheveled, and she knew from his expression he recalled the incredible night they had spent together. "I thought you might enjoy a soak in a hot bath. You're probably pretty sore right now."

Bright pink stained her cheeks, and her gaze slid down to her bare toes. "A gentleman wouldn't remind a lady of her wanton behavior," she murmured, embarrassed.

Pierce gave her a heart-stopping grin. "When have I said I was a gentleman? I filled that tub you keep in the little storeroom off the kitchen with hot water. We can talk while you soak. What I have to tell you is important. You were sleeping so soundly I didn't want to awaken you, otherwise I would have told you earlier."

Zoey's attention sharpened. What was so important about telling her he was going to leave? She'd already guessed that on her own.

"Come downstairs before the water cools."

"Let me get my robe first," Zoey said, turning toward her room.

Zoey dawdled in her room as long as she dared before joining Pierce in the small room off the kitchen that she used as a bathing room.

"About time," Pierce complained. She noticed that he didn't take his eyes off her. "I had to add another bucket of hot water. Go on, climb in the tub. It will ease your discomfort."

Why did he have to be so solicitous? she wondered grumpily. "I can manage my bath by myself," she said when it appeared he wasn't going to leave.

"Zoey, I've seen everything you've got," he reminded her. His green gaze moved slowly over her, smoldering with rekindled passion.

Zoey didn't want to be reminded, but she desperately wanted the bath. And if Pierce wanted to remain, she couldn't do anything about it.

Stripping off her robe, she climbed into

the tub, sinking into the water with a sigh. "Feels wonderful," she said, resting her head against the side and closing her eyes.

"I meant it when I said I didn't mean to be so rough last night," Pierce apologized.

"No need to apologize. You didn't hurt me. Not after the first . . ." She flushed and looked away. "When are you leaving?" she asked bluntly.

He stared at her, mesmerized by the tantalizing glimpse of creamy breasts crowned with pink nipples bobbing above the water. The sweet enticement of her golden woman's triangle almost made him forget that he had something very important to impart to Zoey. Deliberately he turned away as she soaped a cloth and began scrubbing various parts of her body. He waited until he heard her splash from the tub before turning back to her.

Zoey had already pulled on her robe, though it concealed little of her ripe curves from him. Her wet body had dampened the material and it clung to her like a second skin.

"I've made coffee," Pierce said. "We can sit at the table and talk."

Zoey followed Pierce into the kitchen, her expression filled with curiosity. She poured them each a mug of coffee and sat down at the table. Pierce sat across from her, staring into the thick, black brew as he gathered his thoughts.

"What is this all about, Pierce? I know you're going to leave. Why beat around the bush?"

"You knew I couldn't leave until I repaid my debt to you. You saved my life. You could have turned me over to the vigilantes when you found me, but you didn't. I could have been exactly the kind of man Riley Reed described when he came to the ranch looking for me. A woman beater and seducer of innocent virgins. I'm not ungrateful and I always pay my debts."

"What are you getting at, Pierce? I literally forced you to marry me. God knows you didn't want to."

"Would you really have turned me over to the vigilantes if I hadn't agreed? You had me at your mercy. I was too weak to run and had nowhere to go even if I'd been strong enough to flee."

Zoey gave him an inscrutable smile. "You'll never know, will you?"

"It doesn't matter. Last night I paid my debt in full."

"You *what?*" Zoey's brow furrowed in consternation. "What have you done?"

Pierce reached into his vest pocket and

brought forth a sheet of paper, placing it on the table before Zoey. Zoey stared at it for several long minutes, then she gazed up at Pierce through a mist of tears.

She didn't want to cry but couldn't help herself. She had no idea Pierce would do anything like this after he'd failed the first time. When had Pierce stolen the mortgage from Willoughby's office? she wondered.

"Where did this come from? You were with me last night. You couldn't have —"

"I fear I exhausted you last night. I left after you fell asleep. I told no one of my plans. This time I met with success."

Zoey was stunned. "Why didn't you tell me what you intended?"

"And have you tagging along? No, ma'am."

"You went alone?" Zoey gasped.

"Not exactly. Cully was with me."

"You took Cully and not me?"

"It wasn't my idea. Cully must have read my mind, for he was waiting for me in the barn. We both know there's a spy on the ranch. Cully decided to confide in Bud and asked him to keep watch after we left. He was to prevent any of the hands from leaving the ranch last night. We didn't want Willoughby alerted this time. Everything went without a hitch. I also found this."

He extracted another document from his pocket and handed it to Zoey.

"The deed! You found this in Willoughby's office?"

Pierce nodded. "Let's check the signature on the mortgage document against your father's."

Zoey leaped from the chair, excitement coloring her words. "I'll check the signatures now. Oh, Pierce, you don't know what this means to me. If we can prove that the signatures aren't the same, and that Willoughby forged Pa's signature, he can't take my ranch away from me."

She flew from the room, leaving Pierce in her wake. He followed, delighted that his debt had been settled at last. If the document was indeed fraudulent, Willoughby's plan to seize Zoey's land wouldn't hold water. He watched as Zoey tore into her father's desk, searching for documents bearing his signature.

"Here!" she cried, triumphant. "And here's another. Compare them yourself. The signature on the mortgage is a bad copy. Anyone with half a brain can see Pa's signature has been forged." She held the evidence up for Pierce's inspection.

Pierce studied the documents carefully. Zoey was right, the mortgage had been forged, and not too cleverly.

"What are we going to do about it?" Zoey asked. "Wait until the judge comes through town again?"

Pierce pondered the alternatives. "There's a newspaper in town, isn't there?"

"Yes, the *Rolling Prairie Weekly*. Why?"

"Do you trust me to handle this for you?" he asked.

Zoey stared at him. "I thought you were leaving."

"I am, but not just yet. Thought I'd stick around for a spell. There are enough steers in the pens to satisfy your commitment to the army. Bud and the hands plan to drive them to the army post in a few days. Thought I'd stay until they return with the money from the sale. Meanwhile, there are enough brood cows left to start a new herd, and funds in the bank to keep the ranch running until the money arrives."

"You don't have to wait around for my sake. I know how anxious you are to leave. Have you heard from your brothers about your situation at home?"

"No. I'm going to post another letter when I go into town to confront Willoughby later today."

"I'm going with you," Zoey insisted. "You're not going to cheat me out of seeing Willoughby's face when you accuse him of forgery."

"I see no harm in that. We have sufficient evidence to force Willoughby to stop the foreclosure." He flashed her a seductive smile. "We can leave after breakfast if you're not feeling too much discomfort."

"I'm fine," Zoey assured him. She returned to the kitchen. Pierce followed. "I'll fix breakfast. I'm anxious to see Willoughby squirm."

Pierce reached for her as she passed by, pulling her into his arms. He placed his hands on either side of her face and lifted it to his. Then he kissed her, the taste of her mouth reminding him of the passion they had shared the night before. She tasted of sweetness and sunlight and magic. His arms tightened around her as he deepened the kiss, slanting his mouth over hers, licking the seam of her lips, then thrusting his tongue past her teeth and into her mouth.

Zoey groaned against his mouth, caught up in the sweet splendor of his reawakened passion. When Pierce opened her robe and sought her breasts, she arched against him, bringing them into his hands.

"Last night was wonderful," Pierce whispered raggedly. God, he shouldn't be doing this. Once he satisfied his lust with a woman, he seldom wanted her again. With Zoey he had broken every one of his rules. He wanted her now, almost as badly as he'd wanted her last night. "I want to love you again, to taste you all over. Come back to bed with me now."

He took her silence for acquiescence as he scooped her into his arms. Her robe fell away from her body and slipped to the floor. Pierce stepped over it and headed for the stairs.

"Is Miz Zoey all right? She's usually up and about before now."

"Oh, God!" Zoey hid her face against Pierce's chest as Cully walked through the back door. Pierce turned his back to hide Zoey's nakedness and glanced over his shoulder at Cully.

Cully saw Zoey in Pierce's arms, spied her robe on the floor, and gave Pierce a look that would have melted ice.

"Looks like I'm intruding," Cully said dryly. "I can see for myself that Miz Zoey is all right." He turned and strode out the door.

Zoey clung to Pierce, her face flaming. "Put me down, Pierce. What must Cully think of me?"

"I'm not putting you down." Pierce's

voice was hard, implacable. "It's not Cully's place to think anything. We're married, remember? You were the one who insisted upon this marriage. Last night we found joy in one another."

"What we did was to satisfy our lust," Zoey argued.

Pierce continued up the stairs. "Long live lust. Do you want me, Zoey?"

Silence.

"Are you going to lie to me?"

Silence.

"You're a coward, love."

"No one ever calls me a coward. Yes, damn you, I want you. Are you happy now?"

"Supremely." He kicked open the bedroom door and placed her on the rumpled bed. Then he unbuckled his belt, pulled off his boots, and divested himself of the rest of his clothing. By the time he was naked, he was hard as a rock. He felt like a green boy with his first woman. He hated surrendering to that kind of helplessness.

Zoey watched him through slumberous eyes. Pierce affected her in ways she couldn't understand. Her flesh burned, her breasts tingled, and she felt embarrassing moisture gathering between her legs. When he lowered himself to the bed, she reached for him.

"Yes, touch me, love. Feel how hard I am for you. You do that to me, you know. One touch, one look, and I'm burning to have you."

She curled her hand around him. He inhaled sharply. She tried to remove her hand but Pierce wouldn't let her. Placing his hand over hers, he moved it up and down the length of his erection, showing her without words what he liked. Suddenly he removed her hand and rolled on top of her. Then he aroused her with slow, sensual strokes of his tongue and hands, sucking and licking her breasts, caressing between her legs, and kissing her there until she begged him to take her.

Finally taking pity on her, he lifted her atop him, placed her legs on either side of his hips, and slowly impaled her. Zoey gasped as he slid full and deep inside her.

"Ride me, love," he urged hoarsely. Spanning her hips with his hands, he maneuvered her up and down, until she was moving of her own accord, seeking her own pleasure.

Head thrown back, lips parted, Zoey felt the pressure building inside her. Higher, tighter, until she felt her insides turning to liquid.

Pierce could wait no longer; his own

climax was coming on fast, and he feared he would leave Zoey behind. His hand crept between them, locating the swollen nub of her desire with his thumb. Smiling up at her, he rotated it gently. Zoey screamed, her body jerking convulsively.

"Come, love, come to me now," Pierce urged as he lost his last coherent thought.

A burst of fire ignited inside Zoey. Flames consumed her. Contractions rippled through her as she submitted to a pleasure so profound she blacked out. Pierce gave a strangled cry and spent himself deep inside her, his hips pumping furiously.

His heart was pounding and his breath was coming fast and hard. He lay still a long time, until Zoey began to stir. Then he lifted her off of him and stared at the ceiling, wondering what in the hell was happening to him. Had he gone soft in the head? He should be rejoicing now that he was free of his debt to Zoey, free to leave and resume his former life. Instead he found himself hoping that Zoey wouldn't be too sore to make love again tonight. If he wasn't careful, he'd find himself hog-tied for good, which was unthinkable. Marriage wasn't for him. These intense feelings he had for Zoey were lust-driven, too hot to last.

"It's getting late," Zoey said languidly. "I'll fix breakfast while you get dressed. We'll take the buckboard. You probably need to buy supplies while we're in town."

"You can cook?"

"I can do a lot of things you're not aware of," he said, giving her bare bottom a swat as he leapt out of bed.

"I'll bet," Zoey said as she watched him dress. *And you won't be around long enough for me to find out what they are.*

An hour later Pierce went to the barn to hitch the horses to the wagon, leaving Zoey to clean up the kitchen. Cully was waiting for him.

"I don't approve of what's going on, Delaney, but I ain't gonna blow my stack over it. Miz Zoey looked happy, but how long will she remain that way? Until you leave?"

"I didn't set out to hurt Zoey deliberately. What happened between us just happened. I won't lie to you, I've wanted to bed Zoey since . . . well, since before I was well enough to actually do it. Zoey is an adult, she knows what she's doing."

"She's an innocent compared to you," Cully grouched.

Pierce ignored the gibe. "We're going to

194

town to call on Willoughby. You can come along if you want."

"Reckon I'll stay here and keep an eye on the hands. Pete rode out a few minutes ago."

Pierce's attention sharpened. "Pete? Did he say where he was going?"

"Said he had business in town."

Zoey entered the barn, putting an end to the conversation. She was somewhat abashed when she saw Pierce talking to Cully. What must Cully think of her? He was as close to her as a father, and she wanted his approval.

Pierce didn't give Cully a chance to say anything to Zoey as he lifted her into the unsprung seat of the buckboard and climbed up beside her. "We'll be back by sundown, Cully," he called as he drove the buckboard from the barn.

"Let me do the talking," Pierce said as they entered the bank. They had arrived in town a few minutes ago and parked the buckboard close to the general store. "Do you have the mortgage and letters bearing your father's signature?"

Zoey nodded, grateful for Pierce's clear head. She was so angry with Willoughby, she didn't think she could speak coherently.

Willoughby was in his office. When told of their desire to see him, he himself opened the door and ushered them inside his office.

"Have you come to drop off the key to the ranch house?" Willoughby asked pompously.

"No," Pierce said succinctly. "My wife and I are here to demand that you stop the foreclosure."

"You demand? Why would you do that? Everything is legal and aboveboard."

"Because you forged the mortgage document!" Zoey spit out, unable to hold her tongue.

Pierce sent her a silent warning, and she clamped her lips together. "We'd like to inspect the mortgage."

"It's a little too late for that," Willoughby argued. "The papers are served, the foreclosure is a done deal."

"It's never too late for justice," Pierce said. The cold contempt in his voice should have warned Willoughby.

"You've already seen the mortgage."

"Show it to Zoey."

"She's seen it."

"Not really," Zoey snapped. "I was so distraught when you showed it to me that I barely looked at it."

"What is this all about, Delaney?"

Pierce extracted a packet of papers from his pocket, selected two letters, and shoved them under Willoughby's nose. "Look carefully, Willoughby. The signature on these two letters is authentic." Then he held the mortgage up for Willoughby's perusal. "This signature is a blatant forgery. You thought it would be easy to cheat a grieving woman, didn't you?"

Willoughby gave a startled gasp. He'd assumed the mortgage was safely filed with his private papers. How had they gotten into the wrong hands? "Where did you get that?"

"It doesn't matter. I hold the upper hand right now. I can take the evidence to the newspaper office and expose you to public condemnation. Think how it will look. A respectable citizen and businessman caught bilking a poor grieving woman. Customers will take their money out of your bank and you'll be ruined. Is that what you want? Think it over, Willoughby. I understand you have political aspirations. You may as well forget them unless you cooperate."

Willoughby's mouth worked noiselessly. Turning abruptly, he rushed to his file cabinet, frantically searching for the Fuller file. "You stole it!" he accused, trying to snatch the missing mortgage from Pierce's hand.

Pierce gave him a mirthless grin as he held it just out of Willoughby's reach. "You can't prove that." He took Zoey's arm, as if to usher her out of the office. "Come, love, we have an appointment with the editor of the *Rolling Prairie Weekly.* This kind of news might call for a special edition."

"Wait!" Willoughby began to sweat profusely. "There is no need to expose this to the public."

Pierce smiled. "Isn't there? Suppose we come to an agreement. The forged mortgage will remain safely with Zoey as insurance against this kind of thing happening again. In exchange you will alter your bank records to show that no mortgage exists on the Circle F. In addition, you will destroy the foreclosure document immediately and promise never to pester Zoey again with your unwanted attention."

"Is that all?" Willoughby asked sarcastically.

"That about covers it. Do you agree?"

"Tear up the mortgage," Willoughby implored. "Keeping it will serve no purpose."

"I don't agree. By the way, who did you

pay to steal it for you?"

"What makes you think it was my doing?"

"We're not stupid, Willoughby. Time is running out. Do we go to the newspaper or —"

"I agree, damn you!"

"Oh, yes, one more thing. I want a signed statement from you verifying that no mortgage on the Circle F ranch exists now or ever existed. Be sure and date it."

Willoughby cursed for all of five minutes before taking up pen and paper and writing the statement Pierce had demanded. Pierce read it and tucked it into his pocket. Then he asked Zoey for the foreclosure document, which he tore into tiny pieces, letting them fall to the floor.

"You got what you want, now get the hell out of here. I've kept my part of the bargain, and I expect you to keep yours. If word of this ever comes to light, I'll make you very sorry you messed with Samson Willoughby."

"You don't scare me. Words are cheap, Willoughby," Pierce retorted. "If you ever come sniffing around my wife again, you're the one who's going to regret it."

Having said all that needed to be said on the subject, Pierce opened the door and ushered Zoey from the office. Moments later they stood outside the bank, inhaling deeply of the clean fresh air, clearing the foul scent of Willoughby's deceit from their lungs.

"I can't believe it's over," Zoey said with profound relief. She owed Pierce more than she could ever repay. The least she could do in return was to release Pierce from this marriage as quickly as possible. She had too much pride to hold on to a man who wanted to be free.

"We're even now," Pierce said. "I've repaid my debt and am free now to end this forced marriage."

Zoey nodded solemnly. "We're even. You've accomplished more than I had a right to expect. You've kept my property safe from Willoughby and made it impossible for him to force a marriage between us."

Pierce flushed and looked away. "I'm going to the post office," he said, abruptly changing the subject. The realization that he no longer had a reason to remain with Zoey gave him a sinking feeling in the pit of his stomach.

"I'll pick up the supplies we need and have them loaded in the buckboard." She felt the walls building around him again, as if he was protecting himself from something he found offensive.

His cynicism stood between them and always would, she sadly lamented. Lessons he'd learned through experience, and gritty reminders of his past disappointments, had made him the kind of man he was.

Across the street, Pete leaned against the peeling exterior of the saloon and watched Pierce and Zoey walk away from the bank. He'd come to town earlier to receive instructions from Willoughby, and stopped at the saloon first to quench his thirst. He paid little heed to the man who stopped beside him, until he noticed that the man appeared as interested in the Delaneys as he was.

"Say, ain't that Pierce Delaney?" the stranger asked.

Pete gave the man a cursory glance. "Yeah, what's it to ya?"

"What kind of law do you have in Rolling Prairie?"

"Vigilante law. Why?"

"Ever hear of Dry Gulch?"

Pete nodded, wondering where this was leading. "The vigilantes in Dry Gulch are looking for Pierce Delaney. He attacked a woman and left her in a bad way. He led our vigilantes on a wild chase, but they lost him. I reckon they'd be mighty pleased to know where he is now."

Pete's attention sharpened. "You mean Delaney isn't from Wyoming?"

"Wyoming! He and his brothers run one of the largest spreads in Montana territory. Thought they could do almost anything and get away with it. But Pierce went too far this time."

A sly smile spread across Pete's sharp features. Willoughby would be damn grateful for information like this. "Are you returning to Dry Gulch soon?"

"I'm just riding through on my way south to buy some property from a couple who want to go back east. Can't say how long it'll take. If I had more time, I'd return to Dry Gulch and put the vigilantes on Delaney's trail. Can't afford the delay, though. Don't want the Gaffords to sell to anyone else."

"Much obliged, mister," Pete said, pushing himself away from the wall. Willoughby would be grateful for this important piece of information. He rubbed his hands gleefully, anticipating the generous reward he'd soon be spending.

Willoughby was in a foul mood when Pete entered his office. By the time Pete left, Willoughby was smiling.

Chapter 9

Delaney Ranch
Dry Gulch, Montana

Chad Delaney read Pierce's letter for the tenth time since he'd received it. Why hadn't Pierce written again? Chad wondered. According to the letter, Pierce had been shot. Was it a serious wound? If it was a critical wound, Pierce wouldn't have been able to write, would he? And the letter was in Pierce's own hand.

Just then Ryan charged into the house, slamming the door behind him.

Chad looked up from the letter. "Back from town already? Any news?"

"Nothing good," Ryan allowed. "No word from Pierce. You reckon he's all right?"

"The people at the Circle F would have written if something was wrong with Pierce. I reckon he's biding his time. He should have our second letter by now.

Maybe he'll answer soon. Anything else newsworthy?"

"Riley Reed is keeping the people of Dry Gulch all riled up about Pierce. Seeing Cora Lee prancing around with a big belly doesn't help any. Cora Lee's drunken brother is hanging out in the saloon these days, bitterly complaining about how the vigilantes let Pierce get away. His whining is making Reed mad, and Reed is itching to get his hands on Pierce. Dammit, Chad, it's not fair! Pierce is a better man than you or I will ever be."

"What in God's name can we do to help him that we haven't already done?" Chad wondered, at his wits' end.

"We have to keep working on Cora Lee. Maybe one of us can butter her up a bit, get her to talk."

"Which one of us?" Chad wanted to know, cocking an eyebrow at his younger brother.

"You're older than I. You have to do it, Chad. For Pierce's sake."

Chad sighed. "Very well. I'll do what I can."

Circle F Ranch
Rolling Prairie, Montana

Scanning his brother's letter, Pierce was disheartened. Nothing new had transpired in Dry Gulch. The vigilantes were still looking for him, and Cora Lee hadn't recanted her story. As much as Pierce wanted it, he couldn't go home yet. Nor could he stay here, pretending to be a husband when being married went against everything he believed in.

"I assume the news isn't good," Zoey said as she walked into the parlor and found Pierce reading his letter.

"I'd hoped . . . Ah, well, my brothers are still working in my behalf. Unfortunately they've made little headway. Cora Lee is sticking to her story."

"What are you going to do?" Zoey asked quietly. Deliberately Pierce turned away from the longing visible in the depths of her blue eyes. She was so transparent. He knew precisely what she was thinking. "Don't say it, Zoey, don't even wish it. I'm not staying. I never wanted to be married, remember?"

"You can't go home yet," she reminded him.

"Perhaps not, but there are other places

205

I can go. I have sufficient funds to go any-where I wish until this thing with Cora Lee blows over."

Zoey swallowed convulsively. Despite her good intentions to let Pierce go, she didn't want to lose him. Just the thought of all those empty days and nights without him made her ill. What good was her land without someone special to share it with?

"You're safe here. No one knows who you are."

"We can't be absolutely certain of that."

"How would anyone know?"

"I'm not sure, but no matter what, things haven't changed. I want out."

A small sigh slipped past Zoey's lips. "Do what your heart tells you, Pierce."

"You should know by now I have no heart. I said I'd remain until the men re-turn from the cattle drive, and I will. Then I'll be on my way."

Zoey's pride was seriously breached as she pleaded with him, saying things she knew she'd regret later. "I saved your life. Doesn't that mean something?"

"I saved your ranch. Doesn't *that* mean something?" he shot back.

"I could have let you die, or given you up to the vigilantes."

"But you didn't."

Her chin rose stubbornly. "I still could."

He stared at her, his gaze cool and assessing. "But you won't."

She turned away, unable to withstand the cold fury in his eyes. "No, you're probably right."

"I'm not helpless this time. If I thought you'd do that to me, I'd leave now."

"I don't know why we're arguing," Zoey said. "Especially after all you've done for me. Ours was never meant to be a permanent arrangement, I know that. I'm not happy with myself for using you. I hope you can forgive me one day."

"I'm not happy with that either. It's what I expected from a woman, though."

"You showed me what it felt like to become a woman. I'll always remember that."

Her words took the bite from his anger. "Any man could have done that for you."

"But you did it so well."

Pierce stared at her for a breathless minute, then threw his head back and laughed. "Very well. You used me. I can accept that. That makes us even. I wanted your body and took it. Our short association has been mutually beneficial."

"You took nothing!" Zoey declared hotly. "I gave myself to you. I wanted you to be the first."

The amused look left his eyes. "Are you saying I won't be the last?"

Zoey gave a careless shake of her head. "I'll never remarry. As for taking a lover . . . who knows?"

Having said all she was going to on the subject, Zoey excused herself.

"Wait!" Pierce grasped her arm and pulled her against him. "How long will you wait after I'm gone before taking a lover? Do you already have one picked out? I've noticed how you enjoy flaunting yourself in front of the hands, and the way they ogle you."

"You don't know a damn thing, Pierce. Besides, why should it matter to you?" Zoey knew she was baiting him, but couldn't help it. She didn't want him to know how devastated she'd be without him.

"I reckon it doesn't." He stared at the lush outline of her lips, then slowly lowered his head. His mouth settled over hers, and he pulled her closer, grasping her buttocks and molding her against the hard ridge of his arousal as his mouth plundered hers.

"We shouldn't be doing this," Zoey panted when he released her mouth long enough for her to catch her breath. "You know where it usually leads."

"Indeed I do." Then he kissed her again, not at all concerned.

"It's still daylight," Zoey argued, more shaken than she cared to admit. "There's supper to prepare and —"

"You should hire a woman to help with the cooking and housework. I know you'd rather be doing outside work."

"I've already thought of that. I've spoken with Dom and Hector. They have a sister willing to live in and help with the cooking and chores. They're going to stop by their home on their return from the cattle drive and bring her back with them."

"Good." He tried to kiss her again, but she held him away.

"Later, Pierce. I really do have chores to do. There are chickens to feed, eggs to gather . . ."

"I give up," Pierce said, holding up his hand to stop her nattering. A strange, faintly eager look flashed in his eyes. "I'm pleased that you want to continue our intimate relationship until I leave. We'll take up where we left off tonight."

Turning abruptly, he strode away. Zoey stared at his departing back, unable to utter a word. Since their first night together, an unspoken arrangement between herself and Pierce had been in effect. Each night he waited for her in his room. If she didn't show up, he went to hers. And after each night spent in his arms, Zoey felt the invisible bond between her and Pierce strengthening. She wished Pierce felt the same way; but she was merely an amusing pastime to him. He used her body to release his frustrations and appease his lust. And she let him.

Sighing distractedly, Zoey followed Pierce from the room. She'd certainly gotten herself into a fine mess, she thought. She'd expected being married to Pierce would be a straightforward, no-nonsense arrangement. She hadn't counted on Pierce's attractiveness, his virility, or his determination to get her into his bed. She certainly hadn't expected her eagerness to oblige him.

Pierce had never made a secret of his unwillingness to remain in the marriage she'd forced upon him. Yet, despite knowing the kind of man Pierce was, with his aversion to love and marriage, she had given herself to him freely and would continue to do so until he left. Pierce had more compassion than he gave himself credit for. Despite his protest to the contrary, he did indeed have a heart. She'd experienced his caring in many little ways even he wasn't aware of.

Zoey tried to come up with a reason for her unexpected need for Pierce, and didn't like what her mind and heart were telling her.

The hands began the monthlong cattle drive to the fort. At the last minute Cully joined them. Pete had up and disappeared, leaving the Circle F shorthanded. Pierce would have gone along himself but felt he was better qualified than Cully to protect Zoey should she need protecting. So he had remained behind.

A few days later, after many long hours helping Zoey with the chores, Pierce retired early and waited for her to come to him. On most nights exhaustion got the best of them and they did little more than collapse into bed and go right to sleep. But tonight Pierce was going to make love to Zoey. She had tempted him all day. He closed his eyes and visualized the sensual way in which she moved, the way the thrust of her lush breasts filled out the material of her shirt, the provocative way her denims hugged her taut little bottom. His hunger for her had grown as the day progressed. By now he should have had his fill of Zoey, but instead of growing tired of her, he wanted her more today than he had yesterday, or the day before, or the day before that. He could make no sense of this hot craving he had for Zoey, and decided he shouldn't try to explain it, just enjoy it.

Zoey knew Pierce waited for her, and it wasn't exhaustion that kept her from traveling those few feet down the hallway to his room. It was the knowledge that all Pierce had to do was give her a certain look or beckon and she'd fly into his arms. When had she become so damn accommodating? she wondered. And why?

The answers to her questions were lost to surprise when the door burst open and Pierce stepped into the room. He found her standing beside the bed in a golden puddle of lamplight, and his body turned to stone.

The air around him seemed to vibrate. His eyes had darkened to the deepest emerald, filled with promises and passion. His chest was bare and he carried his shirt, boots, and gun belt with him. He looked dark and dangerous and compelling.

"I waited for you." Huskiness lingered in his tone. "Maintaining separate rooms seems rather ridiculous." He dropped his boots and his gun belt to the floor.

Zoey's mouth went dry. "It seemed . . . best."

"Why, when we both want the same thing?"

"You think you know me so well."

His mouth quirked with amusement. "I know your body." He approached her slowly. "I know what you like. I love the way your nipples pucker and beg for my kisses. I know the exact place behind your knees where you're ticklish. And that tiny little mole on your left buttock I love to kiss. When I put myself inside you, you're hot and wet and tight and —"

Her hands flew up to cover her ears. "Stop it!"

He stepped closer, until she could feel his hot breath brush her cheek. "Why are you still dressed?" His fingers rested on the front of her shirt. Before she could stop him, he'd released the first three buttons. "I've missed you."

Two more buttons fell away and he peeled her shirt down her shoulders and arms, tossing it aside. Then he released the straps of her chemise, covering her bare breasts with his hands. Pleasure washed through her in opulent waves that heated her blood and left a delicious heaviness in its wake.

Pierce fell to his knees, unfastened her denims, and skinned them down her hips and legs. Then he buried his face in the soft down between her legs, savoring the tangy-sweet essence of her arousal. Zoey's legs started to crumple beneath her, but Pierce grasped her buttocks and held her in place as his tongue located a place so sensitive, she jerked violently and cried out. "Pierce, oh God, stop, I can't stand it!"

Rising abruptly, he lifted her into his arms and gently eased her onto the bed. "I'll give you what you want, love." He removed his trousers and lay down beside her. His hands slid down her silken belly, then upward to her breasts. He smiled at her, kissing her with his eyes and then his lips. Her mouth first, then the pulsing hollow at the base of her throat, her breasts, her thighs, between her legs.

Zoey molded herself against him, rubbing her bare breasts against the soft fur of his chest, filling her hands with the firm mounds of his buttocks and the hard thickness of his arms and shoulders. She offered herself up to him, seeking the lush decadence of his mouth and hands on her body.

"Now, Pierce, oh, please, now."

He slid his hand between her legs and found the folds of her sex swollen and heavy. Dewy moisture spilled softly onto his fingertips, feeding the fire inside him.

"You're ready for me, love," he whispered as he fit himself into the cradle of her thighs.

More than ready, Zoey reflected as her thoughts fragmented.

He poised at the sweet entrance into her body, gave a triumphant shout, and thrust into her. Zoey cried out in ardent welcome, arching upward to take him deeper. Then he began to move, thrusting and withdrawing, his breath rasping harshly against her mouth. Zoey felt the hysteria of delight rising like the hottest fire inside her. The turbulence of his passion swirled around her, invaded her entire being as he drove her higher and higher. Then he freed them both in a bursting of incredible sensation.

Pierce shifted to his side, watching Zoey as she spiraled down from the pinnacle to which he had taken her. Tears ran down her cheeks and he gently wiped them away with the pads of his thumbs.

"I hope those tears aren't for me."

She opened her eyes, embarrassed to find him watching her. She sighed. "They're for me. You've ruined me for anyone else, Pierce Delaney. Don't forget me, Pierce. Try to remember me after you leave."

He gave her a wistful smile. "Oh, I'll remember you, Zoey Delaney."

"Then why can't you . . . ?" She bit her lip. "Forget I asked."

"You know why," Pierce said, anticipating her question.

Zoey gazed into the stark depths of his green eyes and saw disillusionment and betrayal. That one glimpse into his naked soul was more than she could bear. The thought that her relationship with Pierce had aided and abetted his distrust of women added to her distress. He had more than repaid her for saving his life, and the least she could do was let him go. But it wasn't going to be easy.

"All women aren't alike," she said in her own defense.

"I have yet to meet one different from the rest," he said cynically.

Aggravated, Zoey turned away, too hurt to reply. What could she say in the face of such skepticism? Why couldn't Pierce see that she wasn't like the women who'd disappointed him?

"Go to sleep," Pierce said. "Tomorrow is going to be a full day."

It was a long time before Pierce drifted

off. Something nagged at his conscience. Something to which he didn't want to put a name.

Pierce jerked upright, rudely awakened by a frantic pounding on the door. The room was awash in a murky gray dawn that appeared almost menacing. He leaped from bed, scrambling for his discarded clothing.

"What is it?" Zoey asked, roused by the racket at the front door.

"I don't know." He pulled on his shirt, pants, and boots, and snatched up his gun belt on his way out the door. "Wait here." He checked the chambers of his gun as he hurried down the stairs.

Fully awake now, Zoey wasn't about to let Pierce deal with their early morning visitor alone. Maybe it had something to do with the hands or the cattle drive. This was her ranch, and the problems hers to deal with. She tugged on a robe, stepped into her slippers, and ran down the stairs.

Pierce flung open the front door, recognized the men standing on the doorstep and felt the color drain from his face.

"Howdy, Delaney. Did ya think we wouldn't track you down?"

"Riley Reed." Pierce's voice was toneless; he was already resigned to his fate. "I should have known you wouldn't give up. How did you find me?"

"Someone ratted on you," Reed said with a sneer. "Hal Doolittle's gonna be mighty pleased. He's been on our butts to find you since you gave us the slip. Keep your hand away from your gun, Delaney. As you can see" — he extended his hand to include the men riding with him — "I'm not alone. You'd best come along quietly."

"What is this all about?" Zoey asked, moving from around Pierce to confront the vigilantes.

"You've been harboring a violent man, ma'am," Riley said, assessing Zoey's night attire with a knowing eye. "We're taking Delaney back to Dry Gulch. He's going to do the right thing by Cora Lee Doolittle or pay the consequences."

Zoey stepped forward to shield Pierce. "No, Pierce is innocent. He's my —"

"Zoey!" Pierce's warning effectively cut off Zoey's sentence as he picked her up bodily and placed her behind him. She looked askance at him, and he shook his head. His expression warned her not to reveal that they were husband and wife just yet.

Pierce scowled. He should have known

that one day Reed would track him down. He wasn't the kind to give up easily. Pierce realized he should have left long ago, before he could be traced or linked to Zoey in any way. He didn't want to involve her in his problems. She had enough troubles of her own without taking on his.

Reed held out his hand for Pierce's gun. "Hand it over, Delaney. You ain't gonna escape this time."

Pierce eyed Reed and the dozen or so men riding with him and knew there was no escape. He removed his gun from his belt and tossed it to Reed.

"Bring a rope," Reed called to one of the men standing behind him.

"No! You can't hang him!" Zoey cried out, dismayed by the turn of events.

Reed grinned nastily. "Could if I wanted to. Vigilante law rules the territory. But I ain't gonna hang him . . . yet."

"But he —"

"It's all right, Zoey," Pierce interrupted. "I'm not going to hang."

"But you heard him."

"Don't worry," Pierce repeated.

Someone produced a rope, and Reed ordered Pierce to turn around. When Pierce complied, Reed tied his hands behind him. Another man walked toward them from the barn, leading a saddled horse.

"Mount up," Reed ordered.

Without his hands, Pierce was virtually helpless. Laughter followed his clumsy attempts to mount. Finally Reed grew bored with Pierce's efforts and motioned two men forward to help him.

"Wait, can I have a moment alone with him?" Zoey asked when Reed grasped the leading reins of Pierce's horse.

Reed's gaze slid over Zoey insultingly. "You gonna miss him in your bed, lady? I heard he was good in that department. Just ask Cora Lee." He laughed at his crude remark.

"Please," Zoey pleaded. "Just a few minutes."

Having finally caught Pierce, Reed was in an expansive mood. "All right, lady, talk. But keep it brief." He moved off to converse with his men.

"I'll come with you," Zoey offered. They couldn't take Pierce away like this. She wouldn't let them.

"No!" he said fiercely. "This is as good a way as any to say good-bye. My death will solve the problem of obtaining an annulment or divorce." He searched her face. "How do you suppose Reed knew where to find me?"

"Pierce, you don't think that I . . . My God, don't talk like that."

Pierce gave a mirthless laugh. "The thought did enter my mind. Were you so angry at my leaving you that you'd betray me to get even? Will it make you happy to see me strung up?"

She couldn't believe Pierce was saying such terrible things to her. "No! Of course not. They can't hang you for so minor an offense."

"These are vigilantes, Zoey. They make their own laws. Reed has a special reason to hate me. I married the woman he wanted. He should be grateful it wasn't him Polly betrayed with just about everyone and then ran off with an actor who promised to get her on the stage."

"I'll follow you to Dry Gulch."

"Why? So you can gloat? Give it up. We enjoyed one another while it lasted. You used me just as I used you. You had the protection of marriage and I had the use of your body. That's all I ever wanted from you," he said, choking on the words. Saying them made him feel like a bastard despite being forced into this marriage.

Dismayed, Zoey stared at him. They had been through so much together. How could he brush her off like this? How could he think she'd betray him? She and Pierce had been as close as a man and woman could get, and she'd thought . . . Whatever she'd thought no longer mattered. Pierce had never lied to her. They both had known he'd leave when the time came. He planned to forget her completely and never look back on their time together.

That thought brought another. Maybe . . . just maybe, Pierce really did seduce Cora Lee and get her with child. Had he beaten her, too?

"Time's up," Reed growled as he and his men mounted up.

"Forget me, Zoey," Pierce said as Reed grasped the reins of his horse and jerked him forward.

Tears blurred her vision as she watched Pierce ride out of her life. She watched as long as she could, then walked slowly back to the house. How could he believe she'd betray him? Despite his hurtful words, her inclination was to follow him to Dry Gulch.

Pierce's face was grim as he rode away from the Circle F. He could still see the hurt look on Zoey's face when he'd accused her of betraying him. He wasn't proud of what he had done, but it was for the best.

They were barely out of sight of the ranch when Pierce saw two riders approaching them. He tensed when he recognized Samson Willoughby and Pete, wondering what else could go wrong. Reed raised his hand and the vigilantes reined in. Willoughby rode directly up to Pierce; he looked cocky and sure of himself.

"Is this your doing, Willoughby?" Pierce said, glowering.

"You could say that." He gave Pierce a nasty grin. "Just paying you back. If not for your interference, both the Circle F and Zoey would be mine by now. I'll still have them, and you can't do a damn thing about it. Thanks to Zoey, I learned you were wanted in Dry Gulch."

A pain shot straight to Pierce's gut. "You lie!"

"You think so? Zoey sent Pete to town with a message for me. When I found out who you really were, Pete rode to Dry Gulch to contact the vigilantes there. He was in my employ from the beginning. He was my eyes and ears on the Circle F."

"I don't believe Zoey told you anything, Willoughby. Zoey hated you. She had no reason to turn on me."

"Perhaps she changed her mind. Women are fickle creatures. One never knows what they're thinking or what they'll do next."

"You're dreaming if you think Zoey wants you."

"Perhaps not." Willoughby moved closer, so that only Pierce could hear. "She'll need a man now to take care of her in bed. Since you're already married and can't marry Cora Lee, my guess is they'll string you up. Reed seems to dislike you. But don't fret, I'll be taking your place in Zoey's bed. You'll go to your grave wondering whether I'm lying about Zoey betraying you. By the way," he said with a salacious grin, "I'm grateful to you for breaking her in for me. Deflowering virgins is rather unpleasant."

"Damn you!" Pierce blasted, lunging at him and nearly unseating himself in the process.

"Here now," Reed said, pushing Pierce back into the saddle. "Don't talk like that to an important man like Mr. Willoughby."

"Never mind, Reed, I'm through conversing with your prisoner. Take him away. I have some pressing business with Miss Fuller."

"Leave Zoey alone, Willoughby," Pierce called as Willoughby rode off laughing. "She can still ruin you."

"She can try, but I doubt she'll succeed,

not without you to back her up," he threw over his shoulder.

Zoey changed into denims and flannel shirt and left the house to do the chores. She tried to erase Pierce's cruel words from her mind, but they kept returning. How could he believe she'd inform on him?

The sound of pounding hooves turned Zoey's gaze toward the road as she shaded her eyes against the sun for a glimpse of her visitor. Had Pierce returned? Her hopes fell when she saw Willoughby ride through the gate. He spied her outside the barn and reined his horse in her direction.

"What do you want?" Zoey asked, glowering at him.

He grinned. "I can't stay long. Just wanted you to know that I'm available when you get to hankering for a man. Your so-called husband won't be back, you know. I harbor grave doubts about Pierce Delaney reaching Dry Gulch alive."

"This is all your fault!" Zoey charged. "Get off my land."

"How long will you be able to survive when your hands learn you're on your own again? They'll quit, just like they did before. Taxes are due soon. When you can't raise the cash to pay your taxes, come see me." His eyes gleamed with barely contained lust as he stared at her breasts. "I'm sure we can come to some kind of 'arrangement' that will be mutually satisfying." Then he tipped his hat. "Good day, my dear."

"Go to hell, Willoughby! I'll have sufficient funds from the sale of my beeves to pay the taxes and keep my ranch solvent. It will be a cold day in hell when I come to you for help."

"I expect that day to come sooner than you think, my dear."

Chapter 10

Dry Gulch, Montana

Chad Delaney, catching a glimpse of one of the hands riding hell for leather toward the house, dropped the hammer he'd been using and ran to the front gate to meet him.

Bill Wise brought his horse to a prancing halt and leaped from the saddle. Chad paled when he noted the look on Bill's face.

"What is it, Bill? Did something happen in town?"

"Someone told the vigilantes where to find Pierce. They left late last night for the Circle F ranch near Rolling Prairie. There's talk of a lynching. If Riley Reed has his way, Pierce won't reach town alive."

Chad swung into action. "Round up the boys, Bill. I'll find Ryan. We ride out in fifteen minutes."

"What are we going to do, boss?"

"Make sure there won't be a hanging."

Fifteen minutes later, twelve armed men rode from the Delaney ranch, their faces grim with purpose.

Circle F Ranch

Zoey couldn't concentrate, couldn't think beyond Pierce's last words to her. Forget him? How could she? He could deny his feelings for her all he wanted, but deep inside she knew he lied. He wasn't rejecting her personally. It was marriage he rejected. No matter, she couldn't let him ride out of her life knowing he might never reach Dry Gulch alive.

There were instances when vigilante law served a real purpose in a town with no regular law. More often it was cruel and unjust, making a mockery of the law it served. Riley Reed struck her as a vindictive man, and according to Pierce, Reed had ample reason to hate him. Pierce seemed resigned to the fact that he might not reach Dry Gulch alive, but Zoey was determined not to let that happen. Resolve stiffened her spine as she prepared for a hasty departure.

Zoey left the Circle F a scant hour behind Pierce and the vigilantes. She made a brief stop at the Culpepper ranch, where she arranged for the Culpeppers' oldest son to tend to the chores on the Circle F during her absence.

Intense rage vibrated through Pierce, and that wasn't a bad thing, he decided. He needed anger if he was to survive. He'd not willingly go to his death. He had serious doubts about his chances of arriving in Dry Gulch alive, and suspected that the only thing Riley Reed was waiting on was a good sturdy tree from which to lynch him. He'd have liked to say good-bye to his brothers before he met his maker, but that didn't seem likely.

His rage intensified. It was so unfair. He knew Cora Lee Doolittle didn't have the brains to hatch this plot against him, so it had to be Hal's doing. Yet according to Chad's letter, Cora Lee was indeed in the family way, and someone had to be guilty of getting her that way. He couldn't recall hearing that Cora Lee was being courted by anyone. It was a lamentable mess, but certainly not one of his making. Pierce had been implicated simply because Hal wanted to get his hands on some of the Delaney wealth.

Pierce's thoughts scattered when he realized that Reed had called a halt at a stream so the horses could drink. The men dismounted and quenched their own thirst, leaving Pierce still mounted.

"Hey, I'm thirsty, too," Pierce said.

Reed turned and gave him a mirthless grin. "Too bad. You won't need water where you're going."

Ignoring him, Pierce raised his leg over the saddle and slid to the ground. His hands still tied behind him, he walked to the stream, knelt, and drank deeply. Rising clumsily, he returned to his horse.

"Someone either untie me or help me remount."

One man detached himself from the group to help him. Pierce recognized him as a man he'd once considered a friend. His name was Jim Haskins. Haskins refused to look Pierce in the eye while he gave him a lift up into the saddle.

"Have you turned against me, too, Jim?" Pierce asked quietly.

Jim looked abashed as he said, "I was kinda sweet on Cora Lee. It hurts to see her walking around with a swollen belly and no husband."

"I didn't do it."

"Cora Lee said you did. Why would she lie?"

Pierce could think of no suitable reply. Visible proof was hard to refute.

"The whole town is aware of how you felt about marriage, but did you have to beat Cora Lee?"

"I swear I didn't do it," Pierce vowed.

"Stop jawing," Reed warned as he shoved Jim away from Pierce's horse. "Delaney can't squirm out of this one. He's guilty as sin."

"Hey, Reed, can't we rest a spell?" one of the men asked, stifling a yawn. "We rode all night. I'm saddle-sore and about to fall off my horse."

Reed seemed to consider the request. "Yeah, all right, I'm beat myself. I reckon Delaney ain't any too anxious to meet his maker." He spat a wad of tobacco juice onto the dusty ground. "Remember that hickory tree we passed on the trail last night? Its branches looked strong enough to support a man the size of Delaney. After an hour's rest we'll be fresh for the lynching."

Jim Haskins paled as he spun around to stare at Reed. "You never said nothing about a lynching. You said we'd bring Delaney back to town and give him a chance to marry Cora Lee all proper like."

"I changed my mind," Reed said. His

chin jutted out and his eyes narrowed dangerously. "Are you challenging me?"

"There must be others who agree with me," Jim dared to suggest.

Reed glared a challenge at his men. "What do you say, boys? Are you for hanging Delaney?" The majority concurred wholeheartedly with Reed. The rest shuffled their feet and stared at the ground, unwilling to voice their opinion even though they obviously disagreed.

"Then it's settled," Reed said with a grin. "Rest, boys, you earned it. Our next stop will be the hanging tree."

Pierce slumped in the saddle. Not one of the vigilantes had the gumption to stand up to Reed. Thank God his brothers were capable of taking care of themselves without him. Their father had taught them valuable lessons about survival, and they had all learned well.

Pierce's mind turned naturally to Zoey, and the thought of never seeing her again, never knowing how she was faring, brought a sinking pain in the pit of his stomach. He was glad she wasn't here to witness his hanging. Would she mourn him? he wondered. She probably wouldn't even know he was dead. He'd always intended to end their marriage, but certainly not like this. It suddenly occurred to him that as his wife, Zoey would be in line to inherit his estate. He really didn't believe she had betrayed him, but even if she had, he still wanted her to have the means to remain free of Samson Willoughby's machinations.

"Reed, I want to talk to you," Pierce called out.

Reed swaggered over to Pierce, his expression positively gloating. "What is it, Delaney? Hanging you is gonna be a real pleasure. Polly should have been mine. Had she married me, she wouldn't have run off like she did. I always wondered what you did to her to make her leave."

"Forget Polly, that's water under the bridge."

"Not to me."

"I want to write a will," Pierce said. "Give it to my brother Chad after . . . after . . ." He couldn't say the word.

Reed pushed his hat up and stared at Pierce curiously. "A will? What for?"

"Why do you care? It's proper to grant a man a last request."

"Very well," Reed allowed grudgingly. "You got paper and pencil?"

"In my vest pocket. You'll have to untie me."

"Hey, Haskins, come and untie Delaney while I hold my gun on him. He wants to write a will."

Jim hurried over to release Pierce's bonds. Once free, Pierce rubbed his wrists to return the circulation to them. Then he reached into his pocket for the stub of pencil and pad of paper he always carried with him. He wrote for several minutes, then tore off the paper and handed it to Jim. "Give this to Chad when you reach town."

Jim nodded and slipped it into his pocket.

"Tie him back up," Reed ordered. Jim did as he was told, sending Pierce an apologetic glance as he did so.

An hour later the vigilantes mounted up and rode out. Each mile brought Pierce closer to the hanging tree and the end of his life.

Zoey rode as if the Devil were on her tail. The terrible consequences of not reaching Pierce in time were too painful to acknowledge. Pierce couldn't die. She hadn't saved Pierce's life only to lose him like this. He was too vital, too alive, to die an ignoble death. Even if he didn't want her, she couldn't live with herself if she didn't try to save his life again.

Zoey didn't know what she would do once she caught up with the vigilantes, but she'd do whatever was necessary to prevent a lynching.

"Here we are," Reed called out when he spotted the hanging tree up ahead. He reined to a halt beneath the sturdy hickory; his men drew up behind him. "Who's got the rope?"

"Right here!" someone said, passing a new rope to Reed.

"This isn't right," Jim Haskins said, placing his horse between Pierce and Reed. "What kind of law hangs a man without a fair trial?"

Reed's upper lip curled into a sneer. "Vigilante law. Out of the way, Haskins, unless you want to join Delaney. There's plenty of room on that limb for two."

"I'm sorry, Pierce," Jim said, backing away. "I tried."

"It's all right, Jim. Reed has nursed a grudge against me for a long time. There's nothing anyone can do. Tell my brothers I'm sorry it ended this way. And don't forget the will."

Jim nodded, too choked up to speak. He turned away from the group and took off down the road. He wasn't going to be a party to this travesty of justice. After speaking with Pierce, he was convinced that Pierce was innocent. There was going to be hell to pay for this deed. The surviving Delaney boys were going to be out for revenge.

Jim Haskins ran into the riders from the Delaney ranch a short way down the trail. Haskins skidded to a halt, weak from relief when he recognized Chad and Ryan. "Hurry, they're fixing to lynch Pierce."

Chad's blood froze in his veins. "Where are they?"

"Not far. Just down the trail a few miles."

No reply was forthcoming as the riders left Haskins in their dust.

Zoey rode into a scene straight out of her worst nightmare. It would haunt her for the rest of her life. Pierce stared straight ahead as Riley Reed placed a rope around his neck. Rage and fear drove Zoey when she saw Reed toss the rope over a tree limb and order one of his men into the tree to attach it. Yanking her shotgun from the saddle boot, she fired into the air as she rode fearlessly into the group of men milling around the tree.

"Stop! You can't hang him. It's against the law."

Her random shots sent the vigilantes ducking for cover. Before they gained their wits, she pulled the rope away from Pierce's neck and flung it away. Then she made a desperate grab for the leading reins of Pierce's horse. Her plan, which in retrospect seemed feeble and ill conceived, was to get them both away without coming to harm. Her courage nearly deserted her when she realized how stacked the odds were against success. But valiant to the core, she gave it her best try.

Unfortunately her best wasn't good enough. Reed and a good half dozen of his men surrounded her before she made good her escape.

"Little fool," Pierce muttered bleakly. "Why can't you just let go? You've really done it now."

Pierce knew a moment of raw fear when he saw Zoey ride like a madwoman, firing in the air and shouting. No other woman but Zoey would attempt such a damnfool thing. All she could hope to accomplish was to place herself in danger while he was in no position to help.

"Look who's here, boys," Reed said, eyeing Zoey boldly. "It's Delaney's little whore. She misses him already. Ain't that a shame. What say we give her what she's panting after, boys?"

Zoey eyed him coolly. "What kind of law are you? You're supposed to keep the peace, not break it."

"We make our own law, don't we, boys?" He grasped her leg and pulled her from the saddle. She landed on her bottom at Reed's feet. Reed gave a hoot of laughter and dragged her upright.

"Leave her alone!" Pierce shouted in a voice hoarse with fear. He pulled at his bonds, but they refused to give. "Hang me if you must, but let Zoey go on her way."

Zoey rounded on him. "I'm not going anywhere, Pierce! I'm not going to let them get away with this."

"What are you gonna do, lady?" Reed smirked. "What can you offer us in exchange for Delaney's life?"

Zoey was too distraught to grasp Reed's meaning. "Offer you? How much do you want? I'm sure Pierce's brothers will add to any sum I can come up with. Name your price."

Pierce groaned in dismay. "Zoey, they want —"

"Shut up, Delaney. Let the little lady have her say. This is getting mighty interesting." He turned back to Zoey. "What if the price I demand is your body? Will you spread your legs for us?"

The color drained from Zoey's face as comprehension dawned. "What? You can't. I won't . . ."

Reed shrugged. "Suit yourself, lady." He turned back to his companions. "String him up."

"No, wait! I need time to think about this."

"For God's sake, Zoey, there's nothing to think about!" Pierce cried fiercely. "Get on your horse and ride out of here."

"And let you hang? I . . . can't."

Reed grinned knowingly. "Thought you might feel that way. He grasped her arm and pulled her along with him toward a copse of dense bushes. "You're gonna get more than you bargained for, lady."

Anguish such as he'd never felt before tore into Pierce. "Don't do it, Zoey. He'll kill me anyway, and probably you along with me."

Things were moving so fast, Zoey couldn't catch her breath, could barely think. She dug her heels in, but Reed's superior strength kept her moving. When he reached the fringe of bushes, he threw her to the ground and fell on top of her.

"Wait! Promise you won't kill Pierce if I let you . . ." Oh, God, she couldn't do this.

"What makes you think I'd bargain with you? Willing or not, I'd still have you. There ain't nothing you can do to stop me from stringing up Delaney or taking you here on the ground. I was just playing along with you, letting you think you could influence me."

He grasped the waistband of her britches and tried to pull them down her thighs. Zoey screamed and he cuffed her, telling her to stop her caterwauling. She fought him, finding a vulnerable spot with the toe of her boot. He cursed and released her. She leapt up and started to run. He grabbed her leg, dragging her back down.

Pierce heard Zoey scream and launched himself off his horse. He had nearly reached the fringe of bushes before he was tackled and brought down. The terrifying image of Riley Reed rutting on Zoey's slender body made him want to kill. If someone handed him a gun, he'd shoot every last one of these bastards without blinking an eye.

Then a miracle occurred. Pierce saw more than a dozen men riding like demons toward them. The vigilantes were too stunned to do more than watch as the riders converged on them, their guns drawn and at the ready.

Pierce wanted to cheer when he recognized his brothers and the hands from the Delaney spread. But greeting his brothers was the last thing on his mind as he ran on wobbly legs toward the fringe of bushes. Moments before he reached the spot where Reed and Zoey had disappeared, Reed came staggering out, holding his crotch and limping.

He saw Pierce's brothers and cursed. "What the hell is this all about?"

"Looks like we interrupted a lynching," Ryan said tersely.

"We're the law in these parts," Reed charged.

"The judge will have something to say about that," Chad growled.

"For God's sake, untie me!" Pierce ordered harshly. "I don't know what Reed did to Zoey. She could be hurt or . . ."

Chad freed Pierce with a slash of his knife. But before Pierce took two steps, Zoey crawled out from the bushes. Pierce raced to her, scooping her up into his arms and cradling her against him.

"Did he hurt you? I'll kill the bastard."

Zoey shook her head, unable to utter a word. She was still shaken over her close

241

call. She'd been naive to think she could stop these ruthless men on her own, but Pierce's life was worth the risk to her.

"I didn't touch her, Delaney," Reed said. "Even if I had, you couldn't do a damn thing about it. You're still not off the hook. Just because your brothers stopped a lynching doesn't mean you'll live through this. Old Judge Walters will have something to say about that."

A friend of Hal Doolittle's stepped forward, thrusting his face into Pierce's. "You bedded my friend's sister, got her with child, and then tried to beat her to death. You're gonna pay, Delaney."

Reed knew a lynching was out of the question now. He'd have to bring Pierce back to town and keep him under lock and key until the judge came through. Anything could happen in town, Reed thought slyly. The townspeople were riled up enough to storm the jail and lynch Delaney on their own. And he'd be helpless to stop it. On the other hand, Hal Doolittle might insist that Delaney marry his sister and cheat the hangman. A damn pity.

Chad stared at Pierce, puzzled by what he'd just seen. It wasn't like Pierce to express so much concern for a woman. He acted as if he truly cared about her. "What happened?" he asked, bursting with curiosity. "Who's the woman?"

"Put me down, Pierce, I can stand on my own."

Reluctantly Pierce placed Zoey on her feet. She held on to him for a moment while composing herself to meet Pierce's brothers. Ryan came up to join them.

"Chad, Ryan," Pierce said solemnly, "this is my wife, Zoey. Zoey, these are my two younger brothers, Chad and Ryan."

Zoey held out her hand. "Pierce has spoken often of you both. Thank God you arrived when you did. Another few moments and . . ." She shuddered delicately. "I think you get the picture."

"Your wife!" Chad and Ryan exclaimed together. Finally remembering his manners, Chad shook Zoey's hand, then released it to Ryan. "When . . . how . . . why . . ." Chad was clearly stunned.

"It's a long story," Pierce said.

"Married? You're married?" This from Reed, who appeared as dumbfounded as Chad and Ryan. "Cora Lee and Hal ain't gonna like this. Cora Lee has her heart set on marrying into the Delaney family. Hal is already planning on asking for a loan once you and Cora Lee get hitched." He shook his head. "The townspeople ain't gonna be happy about this. You should have let us hang him now and get it over with."

"No one is going to hang my brother," Chad announced with authority. "The judge will determine what must be done, if anything. After evidence is presented, there isn't a judge alive who will find him guilty." He didn't for a minute believe that, but he wisely kept his reservations to himself. "Let's go. We'll be right behind you. Nothing is going to happen to my brother while we're here to prevent it."

Ryan nudged Pierce and gestured toward Zoey. "What about her?"

"Zoey is returning to the Circle F," Pierce said in a tone that brooked no argument.

"I'm not!" Her chin jutted out belligerently. "I've come this far, I'm going all the way."

"There's nothing more you can do here," Pierce persisted. "What about your ranch? You're needed there."

"I hired the Culpepper boy to look after things until Cully and the boys return."

"I'd prefer that you returned home where you belong. You risked your life to follow me. Do you realize what almost happened to you? Reed and his men would have raped you and thought nothing of it. There's no real law to stop them from doing what they want."

Chad listened to the exchange between Pierce and his wife and didn't know what to make of it. The very idea that Pierce had a wife was mind-boggling, he couldn't wait to hear how a man dead set against marriage had gotten himself hitched.

"Don't worry about Zoey, Pierce. If she wants to come to Dry Gulch, Ryan and I will see that no harm comes to her."

"Thanks," Pierce said dryly. How could he dissuade Zoey from following him to Dry Gulch when his brothers were so damn accommodating?

"It's settled then," Zoey said smugly. "You're not going to get rid of me yet, Pierce Delaney, not until this mess is over and done with and your name is cleared. I can help your brothers find the man responsible for Cora Lee's predicament."

Pierce glared at her, suddenly recalling Willoughby's words. "Why are you so set on seeing me free when you're the one who told Willoughby about me?"

Zoey's expression registered shock. "You can't really believe that!"

Pierce knew Zoey couldn't be responsible for his capture, not after the way she had risked her life to save his, but he wanted her to return home where she'd be safe. He had no intention of dragging her down with him.

Reed approached Pierce with a rope, clearly intending to tie his hands before heading out. "No need for that, Reed, I'm not going anywhere," Pierce said. "I'm as anxious as you are to find the man responsible for Cora Lee's problems."

"We already got that man," Reed sneered. But he left Pierce's hands free. With the Delaney brothers and their ranch hands forming a protective circle around Pierce, he had no choice but to relent.

Zoey pondered long and hard on Pierce's cruel words as she rode beside him. She had no idea why he thought she'd betrayed him. Did he really think her capable of such duplicity after making love with him? It was true they had bantered about it one day, but she had been jesting. His accusation had hurt her dreadfully, but she tried to ignore the pain. Pierce was under great stress. He'd been so close to being lynched that just thinking about it made her tremble.

"Are you all right, Zoey?" Chad asked, riding up beside her.

"I'm fine, Chad. It's your obstinate brother I'm worried about."

Chad chuckled. "Pierce *is* a mite hard-headed." He pinned Zoey with a hard look. "I'm damn curious about why and how your marriage came about. Pierce isn't . . . That is . . ."

"I prefer to let Pierce do the explaining." Zoey knew it would sound less condemning coming from her, but she wanted the Delaney brothers to hear his version no matter how harshly he dealt with her in the telling.

They camped that night in a clearing. Jerky and hardtack were produced, and Zoey gnawed on hers, not really tasting it. Pierce wasn't allowed to visit with his brothers or Zoey, and Reed set a guard on him to make sure he didn't try to escape during the night. Surrounded by Delaney men, Zoey rolled up in her blanket and tried to sleep.

She closed her eyes, but the image of Pierce making love to her, sharing the most intimate of acts, floated behind her eyelids. He had loved her with such consummate tenderness, she found it difficult to believe his caring hadn't been genuine. Yet it hadn't. Even as he kissed and caressed, his mind rejected her. Even as he spent his seed inside her, he abhorred their marriage. And knowing all that, she had recklessly fallen in love with him.

They left their campsite at dawn the following morning. Zoey felt as bad as she looked. She hadn't slept well last night and wondered if Pierce was as miserable as she. She glanced over at him, but he refused to meet her gaze. She knew he was angry at her for refusing to return to the Circle F, but she didn't care. At least he was alive. If she hadn't arrived when she did, Pierce would have been lynched for sure. His brothers hadn't come until much later. By then it would have been too late to save him.

Pierce wanted to look at Zoey but didn't dare. He had no idea how all this would end, and didn't want Zoey to witness his hanging. Pierce knew if Riley Reed had his way, he wouldn't live to face the judge. Furthermore, old Judge Walters was known throughout the area as the hanging judge. What chance did he have? Pierce wondered. Had he not already been married, he could have gotten himself out of this mess by marrying Cora Lee. Hal Doolittle would have liked that.

Marrying Cora Lee was no longer an

option, not that he would have married her under any circumstances. Pierce could see Hal Doolittle's fine hand in all this. Hal was in desperate need of money, and Pierce was handy. Dimly he wondered who had gotten Cora Lee with child. If he knew that, everything else would fall into place.

The combined group of vigilantes and Delaney men rode into Dry Gulch at high noon. People came out of stores and houses to watch. By the time the group reached the small shed that served as a jailhouse, a large crowd had gathered. Among them was Hal Doolittle. He swaggered up to Pierce, blowing his drunken breath in Pierce's face, shouting, "You made my sister your whore, Delaney! It's time you accepted responsibility and married Cora Lee."

"You've got the wrong man, Doolittle," Pierce argued.

Hal's eyes narrowed. "If you don't own up and do the right thing by my sister, we're gonna have a lynching."

"Shut up, Hal," Riley Reed warned. "I got some bad news for ya."

Hal gave Reed a surly look. "What are you talking about?"

"Pierce Delaney is already married." He pointed to Zoey. "That little lady is his wife."

Hal's face reddened with fury. When Cora Lee turned up pregnant, he'd been furious. Then he'd hatched a plan he felt certain would work. Cora Lee would have a husband and he'd have unlimited use of Delaney funds. He didn't like having his plans thwarted.

The Delaneys would pay for this, and pay big.

Chapter 11

Zoey yearned for a private word with Pierce before Riley Reed locked him in the airless little shed that served as a jailhouse. But things moved fast after Hal Doolittle learned that Pierce was already married. Cora Lee's scheming brother was livid with rage, directed at both Pierce and Zoey. Then the crowd got ugly and Chad and Ryan tossed her into her saddle and led her away from the chaos Doolittle was creating. She was still in shock when she reached the Delaney ranch.

Zoey had no idea feelings would turn violent against Pierce. What had the Delaney boys done in their wild youth to alienate themselves from so many people? she wondered. Returning to Dry Gulch as a married man hadn't helped Pierce's cause any. Hal Doolittle had worked the townspeople into a wild frenzy. Had Pierce returned to Dry Gulch, meekly admitted impregnating Cora Lee, and married her, in time he would have been forgiven. But Pierce had committed the unforgivable, and the general consensus was to lynch him.

Zoey was grateful to Chad and Ryan for organizing the Delaney hands to provide around-the-clock protection for Pierce. It seemed the only way to prevent an illegal hanging before the judge came through town on his regular circuit. With so much to worry about, Zoey's sleep that night was sporadic and fitful.

Zoey wandered into the kitchen the next morning and helped herself to a cup of coffee, carrying it to the table where she could continue her silent musings while she drank.

Chad walked into the kitchen, saw Zoey, and asked, "What do you think of the ranch?"

Zoey had been too exhausted the day of her arrival to do more than eat the excellent dinner the Delaney cook had prepared and go to bed. This morning she'd had time to really look at Pierce's home. In some ways it was grander than the Circle F and in other ways it couldn't compare.

"It's impressive," Zoey admitted, gazing out the window at the snow-topped mountain peaks rising in the distance. "Your house is bigger than mine but missing a woman's touch."

"We have a housekeeper who comes in daily, but the only woman who's lived here since our mother left was Pierce's first wife, and she didn't last three months. This has been an entirely male household for as long as I can remember."

Fearing she had resurrected painful memories, Zoey said, "I'm sorry, I didn't mean to imply . . ."

"Don't apologize," Chad said harshly. "My brothers and I don't need pity. I'd rather hear how you and Pierce came to be married. I know my brother, Zoey, and he isn't the marrying kind."

"I meant it when I said I'd prefer to have Pierce tell you."

"Since he's not able to do so at this time, I'd like to hear it from you."

"What's going on?" Ryan entered the room through the back door, saw Chad and Zoey sitting at the table, and wandered over to them.

"Sit down," Chad invited. "Zoey was just about to tell me how she convinced Pierce to marry her."

"That ought to be some tale worth hearing," Ryan said, pulling out a chair with his booted foot and dropping down into it.

Zoey studied the brothers from beneath hooded lids. Both were handsome, well-built men. A little hard around the edges, but beneath their crusty veneer she detected a layer of caring. She predicted that one day these special men would find women worthy of their love. Right now she couldn't blame them for being concerned about their brother's hasty marriage.

Ryan pierced Zoey with a calculated look. "Go ahead, Zoey, tell us how you coerced Pierce into marrying you."

Zoey stared into Ryan's green eyes, so like Pierce's it was uncanny. The bold slash of his eyebrows above those distinctive eyes was lowered now into a scowl. The hard planes of his face were stark against the taut white lines of his mouth. His hair was a shiny brown, not quite as black as Pierce's but dark enough to enhance his tanned features and give him a certain dangerous appeal.

"What makes you think I coerced Pierce?"

"Because we know Pierce," Ryan explained. "And he's not a marrying man."

Zoey turned her attention to Chad, the middle brother. His hair was lighter than Pierce's, his eyes more hazel than green, but no less striking with those tiny golden flecks floating in the center of his irises. There was something hard and bitterly unforgiving hidden in those fathomless depths. Something told Zoey that of the three, Chad would be the least likely to accept compromise. And the most likely to sacrifice himself for his brothers.

"You're right," Zoey said slowly, wishing she could make the truth not sound so harsh and condemning. But neither Chad nor Ryan seemed willing to settle for anything less than the truth. "I won't lie and say Pierce married me because he fell madly in love."

"Pierce fall madly in love? That's a laugh," Ryan hooted.

Chad said nothing, waiting for Zoey to continue. He remembered the tenderness with which Pierce had treated Zoey, coupled with his anxiety about her well-being. He couldn't ever recall seeing Pierce look at a woman the way he'd looked at Zoey.

Zoey's gaze dropped down to her hands, which were clasped tight on the table. "Pierce had no choice in the matter. I forced him to marry me."

Chad's voice was rigid with controlled fury. "You *forced* Pierce? Somehow that's hard to believe. Why don't you start at the beginning?"

The tension in the room thickened. "I found Pierce in my root cellar. He'd been shot and was near death. Cully removed the bullet, and I nursed him back to health."

"Who's Cully?" Ryan asked.

"He used to be ramrod on the ranch until he got too old. Now he's jack-of-all-trades and my friend."

"Who shot him?" Ryan asked.

"The vigilantes."

"Go on," Chad urged. "What happened after you saved Pierce's life?"

"Riley Reed and the vigilantes showed up on my doorstep. They wanted to know if I'd seen Pierce. They told me Pierce had severely beaten a pregnant woman in Dry Gulch and left her for dead. I didn't believe Pierce capable of such a terrible thing, so I sent them on their way."

"And Pierce married you out of gratitude," Ryan guffawed. "I don't buy it."

"I needed Pierce. I was about to lose my ranch to an unscrupulous banker who wanted both me and my ranch. He said my father had mortgaged the land before his death, but I knew it was a lie. I thought if I married Pierce, Samson Willoughby would lose interest in me."

Chad shook his head in disbelief. "I

can't believe Pierce would agree to such an irrational scheme. He's not the marrying kind under any circumstances."

Zoey swallowed convulsively. "He didn't agree. Pierce was wounded and too weak to leave his bed. I threatened him. I told him I'd send for the vigilantes if he didn't marry me." Chad's sudden intake of breath prompted her to add, "It was never meant to be a permanent arrangement. I made it clear that he'd be free to leave once he served his purpose."

"You used him!" Ryan charged.

Zoey gave him a look of wounded outrage. "Perhaps. But you don't know the whole story. We used one another. I saved Pierce's life. He owed me." She faced Ryan squarely. "His debt was paid in full when he risked his life to steal evidence that proved Willoughby's claim on my ranch was fraudulent. He remained in the marriage beyond the terms of our agreement simply because he had no place else to go."

Both Chad and Ryan remained quiet so long, Zoey feared they didn't believe her. Would they throw her out of their house? More than likely, she decided.

"Just one thing bothers me," Chad said curiously. "Why were you with Pierce and the vigilantes? You should have remained at the Circle F, like Pierce wanted."

"I feared the vigilantes would hang Pierce without a fair trial. I care about Pierce too much to let that happen. I wanted to help, so I followed. I didn't know how, but I intended to stop the vigilantes if they had a lynching on their minds."

"I thought as much," Chad said knowingly. "That was a brave thing to do, and a very foolish one. If we hadn't arrived when we did, Reed would have raped you."

Zoey's head rose pugnaciously. "If I hadn't arrived when I did, Pierce would be dead now."

"My God," Ryan said in sudden comprehension, "you love Pierce."

"That's beside the point," Zoey charged. Until this moment she'd been unwilling to admit it, even to herself. There no longer seemed to be a reason to deny it.

"You're wasting your time if you think Pierce will love you in return," Chad claimed.

Zoey flinched at the harshness of Chad's words, which she knew to be true.

"Don't you think I know that? I'm here to help him, not entrap him. Once he's set free, I'll return to the Circle F and he can go back to doing what he did before I forced this marriage on him. An annulment or divorce should be simple to obtain, given the circumstances of our marriage."

Chad speared Zoey with the bright intensity of his gaze. "Is there a possibility that you're carrying my brother's child? I know Pierce. If you're married, you've shared a bed. Are you trying to bind Pierce to you with a child?"

Startled by his candor, Zoey gave Chad a look that should have turned him to ice. "I would never do such a thing."

Chad appeared undaunted. "But it *is* possible." His relentless probing was a tribute to his tenacity. To Chad, everything had an explanation, even those things that seemed to defy reason.

Zoey faced Chad without flinching. "Yes, it is possible. But that changes nothing. I'd never trap Pierce into a marriage he abhors. My ranch can support both myself and my child, should there be one. But at the moment the question of my pregnancy is moot because it's too early to know."

Ryan shook his head, trying to sort through everything Zoey had just told them. Something in the telling was missing, but he couldn't figure what.

Chad's coldly analytical mind had already sifted through the facts and arrived at one conclusion. He didn't particularly like it, but it solved some of the questions that seemed to have no answer.

"You *do* love Pierce, don't you, Zoey? You may as well admit it."

Zoey's lips thinned. "Perhaps, though your brother isn't exactly lovable."

Ryan gave a shout of laughter. "You've got that right, Zoey."

"It's the truth, isn't it, Zoey?" Chad persisted.

"Yes, dammit, it's the truth! But don't worry, I won't breathe a word of it to Pierce if you don't."

"I thought so. I wondered why you'd risk your life for Pierce. Few women would do that. I don't believe in love myself, but it seems to work for some people."

"Pierce isn't one of those people," Ryan contended. "This talk of love and babies is making me nervous. More importantly, what are we going to do to save Pierce's life? The situation in Dry Gulch is growing ugly."

"I want to help," Zoey volunteered. "What can I do?"

"I got the impression that Pierce doesn't want you here," Ryan contended.

260

Zoey's chin lifted stubbornly. "I'm not leaving. Not yet."

Chad sighed. "I didn't think you would. Very well, we can use all the help we can get. I've tried to pry the truth from Cora Lee, but she insists that Pierce seduced her and got her with child. She maintains that Pierce beat her when she pleaded with him to marry her and give their child a name. Pierce claims he never touched her, and I believe him. Ryan and I are convinced this is Hal Doolittle's plot to get his hands on some of the Delaney wealth."

"Your family is wealthy?" Zoey asked curiously. "I had no idea. Most ranchers in the area are barely eking out a living."

"Pa was smarter than most," Ryan bragged. "He invested a small inheritance in a silver mine that paid off. We're not millionaires, but we're better off than most."

"Then money could very well be the motive behind Cora Lee's charges against Pierce," Zoey mused.

"The fact remains that Cora Lee is carrying a child," Chad said. "Once we find the man responsible, the mystery will be solved."

"What if I talk to Cora Lee?" Zoey wanted to know. "Maybe she'll open up to another woman."

"You're Pierce's wife," Ryan said meaningfully. "Cora Lee will hate you on sight. You married the man she wants."

Zoey grew thoughtful. "This is all very strange. Why would Cora Lee want to marry a man who allegedly beat her?"

Chad gave her a confused look. "I never thought of it that way. For one thing, Hal was pushing her to marry Pierce. For another, marrying the father of her unborn child, woman beater or not, is better than giving birth to an illegitimate child. Hal would never allow that to happen. He's too proud."

Ryan added another daunting thought. "Pierce is already married. Hal isn't happy about that. You can bet he's going to continue stirring up trouble."

Zoey leapt to her feet so fast her chair hit the floor. "We can't let that happen! I'm going to talk to Cora Lee."

"I'll go with you," Chad offered.

"No, just tell me how to get there. It's best if I do this alone. Will her brother be home?"

"Not likely. He spends his time at the saloon these days."

"Is there anyone else I should worry about?"

"Cora Lee's father is bedridden. His

heart is worn-out. There's no one else at home."

"Very well, just give me directions to their ranch."

Chad complied, realizing that Zoey had a mind of her own and used it. He chuckled to himself. Chad could well imagine the sparks that flew when those two came together.

Ryan appeared mesmerized by the provocative sway of Zoey's hips beneath her skintight denims as she walked away. He waited until Zoey was gone before turning to Chad and saying, "Looks like big brother met his match. I don't know if he's damn fortunate or the unluckiest man alive."

Zoey found the Rocking D ranch with little trouble. She tried to ignore the hands who stopped their work to leer at her as she rode into the yard and dismounted. They seemed a lazy lot, more prone to rest against a fence than to repair it. The ranch and outbuildings were in dire need of repairs, much like her own ranch until Pierce changed things.

Gathering her courage, Zoey marched up the front steps and knocked on the door. Nothing. She rapped a second time and was about to knock a third when the door was opened by a striking blonde with chocolate brown eyes and a peaches-and-cream complexion. She looked small and fragile and . . . pregnant.

"What do you want?" Cora Lee asked nervously. She seemed frightened of something, and Zoey wondered who or what had made her so jittery. "Who are you?"

"May I come in?"

"I don't know. I'm alone."

"I just want to talk." She brushed past Cora Lee and found herself in a comfortably furnished parlor dominated by a huge fireplace.

Cora Lee closed the door and followed Zoey into the parlor. "Who are you?" she repeated.

"May I sit down?" Zoey asked, not waiting for an answer as she perched on the edge of the sofa and patted the seat beside her.

Stunned by her visitor's rather presumptuous manner, Cora Lee sat down, her eyes settling disconcertingly on Zoey's trouser-clad legs. "I've never seen a woman wearing men's britches before. Are you a friend of Hal's?"

Zoey managed a taut smile. "Hardly. I'm Zoey, Pierce Delaney's wife."

A mask slid over Cora Lee's features and she leapt to her feet. "Do you know what you've done? You spoiled everything! How dare you show up on my doorstep like this."

"I'm sorry, Cora Lee, but I had to know what really went on between you and Pierce. I've come to know Pierce well, and I don't believe he'd do the terrible things you accused him of."

Cora Lee's lower lip quivered, and Zoey feared the woman was going to burst into tears. "I don't want to upset you. It's not good for a woman in your condition to become emotional. Tell me in your own words what happened between you and Pierce."

"What did Pierce tell you?"

"He denied he did anything to . . . hurt you."

Cora Lee's eyes shifted furtively. "Yes, well . . ."

"Tell the bitch the truth, Cora Lee!"

Zoey jumped nearly as high as Cora Lee when Hal Doolittle strode into the room, his face a mask of rage.

"Hal, I thought you went to town."

Zoey had never seen such naked fear on a woman's face. Cora Lee appeared petrified of her brother.

265

"I did leave, but my horse went lame and I returned for another mount. The hands told me you had a visitor, and I thought I would find out who'd come calling. I see I'm just in time. Go on, Cora Lee, tell Delaney's wife what her husband did to you."

Two huge tears appeared at the corners of Cora Lee's eyes. "Do I have to, Hal? I've already told the doctor, the Delaney boys, and Riley Reed. I don't think . . ."

Hal took a menacing step toward his sister, brandishing a meaty fist in her face. "You'll tell it again and again, as many times as is necessary. We're a proud family. Pierce Delaney isn't going to get away with flaunting the rules of society. The townspeople are clamoring for a lynching. Tell her, Cora Lee, tell her."

Zoey watched in dismay as Cora Lee recoiled in fear. Something was wrong here. Why was Cora Lee so terrified of her brother?

Cora Lee's voice was so low, Zoey had to strain to hear her. "P-Pierce used to visit Papa every week. After a while he began drawing out his visits. He was very kind and supportive of me. Hal wasn't home much, and I cared for Papa the best I could without help. As you can see, the

266

ranch isn't prospering. Pierce was attentive to my needs, and I . . . I believed he cared for me." She looked at Hal, her eyes moist and pleading. "Do I have to continue?"

"Tell her everything," Hal said, his voice low and menacing.

Cora Lee licked moisture onto her dry lips and said, "One day Pierce started kissing me. He wouldn't stop when I asked him to. I grew frightened and pushed him away, but he just laughed at me. I wanted to scream, but he kept kissing me and telling me how much he wanted me." She started crying in earnest, big, tearing sobs, as if remembering the horror. "After a while I would have done anything he said."

Zoey knew the feeling. Pierce had but to touch her and she melted in his arms.

"Did Pierce rape you?" Zoey asked, choking over the word.

"Not . . . not exactly. He said things to me. Did things that made me want him in that way. He seduced me, and I was naive enough to believe he really cared for me." Cora Lee hesitated, sending Hal a pleading look.

"Go on," Hal said remorselessly.

"We . . . Pierce and I . . . made love many times after that. Then one day I realized I was pregnant. I couldn't wait to tell

Pierce. I fancied myself in love with him. We'd marry and live happily ever after with our child."

"What did Pierce say when you told him?" Zoey asked, as almost afraid to hear the answer. Cora Lee was so naive, so sincere, it was difficult not to believe her.

"Pierce changed when I told him about our baby," Cora Lee continued. "He turned into a monster. He said I was a gullible little fool who was good for only one thing."

"No! Pierce would never say anything like that," Zoey denied, unable to reconcile Cora Lee's words with the Pierce she knew and loved.

"When I asked Pierce to marry me and give our child a name, he slapped me. Suddenly he turned on me like a madman, battering me with his fists. My face, my stomach, he didn't care where his punches landed, he must have beaten me long after I passed out, for the doctor told me I was lucky to be alive. And so was my baby."

Zoey sat like a statue throughout the telling. She didn't want to believe Cora Lee, and yet . . .

"Have you heard enough?" Hal asked nastily. "Your husband put my sister through hell, and he's gonna pay. He could have been Cora Lee's husband if you hadn't snagged him first."

"Why would you want your sister to marry a man who had beaten her senseless?" Zoey asked, finally finding her voice.

"Once he was Cora Lee's husband, I'd make certain he toed the line," Hal sneered. "We've never had a bastard in the family before. It's damn humiliating."

Cora Lee cried out in distress. "Oh, Hal, how can you say such a thing when —"

Hal grasped Cora Lee's arm in a hurtful grasp. "Shut up!" he demanded.

Cora Lee's lips whitened as she clamped them tightly together.

"Since Pierce is already married, why not demand that he pay a monetary fee for damages," Zoey suggested, "and drop the charges against him? He's not doing anyone any good locked up in jail."

Hal gave Zoey a truly evil smile. "He's not going to get off that easily. Cora Lee has her heart set on marrying into the Delaney family, and I don't like to see my little sister disappointed."

"Are you suggesting that I divorce my husband?" Zoey asked quietly.

"I ain't suggesting a damn thing. When I'm ready to tell the high-and-mighty Delaneys what I want, I'll let them know.

I've been thinking on this ever since I learned Pierce already had a wife. And don't think for a minute I don't know why Pierce married you."

Zoey didn't want to hear Hal's opinion of her marriage. The man was disgusting; big, brash, and demanding. Zoey had met his kind before. He was possessed of passing good looks, with blond hair and brown eyes like his sister, but Zoey knew him for the bully he was. What had he done to make his sister so terrified of him? she wondered. She rose to leave, having heard more than she wanted to about the alleged affair between Cora Lee and Pierce.

"Have you heard enough?" Hal goaded mercilessly as Zoey prepared to leave. "Maybe you should stick around and compare notes with Cora Lee about Pierce's bed manners."

"Hal, please!" Cora Lee's face turned beet red.

"There's still time to recant your story," Zoey told Cora Lee. "Pierce couldn't have done the things you said. He'd never hurt a woman. Please, tell the truth before it's too late. Are you frightened of your brother? Is that why —"

"Get out!" Hal shouted, shaking his fist at Zoey. "You're upsetting my sister."

Zoey didn't argue. She couldn't wait to leave. Hal Doolittle was a heartless bully who obviously terrorized his sister. "I'm going," she said, sending Cora Lee a pitying look. "You can reach me at the Delaney ranch if you decide to tell the truth."

No matter what she thought of Cora Lee and the lies the woman told about Pierce, Zoey still felt sorry for her. Living with a brother like Hal must be pure hell.

The ride back to the Delaney ranch gave Zoey ample time to review every word of her conversation with Hal and Cora Lee. Cora Lee had sounded so earnest, it was difficult to discount her story. No wonder the townspeople were up in arms about the terrible thing done to Cora Lee. The petite blonde was a victim, all right, but of whom?

The incongruity of the situation was puzzling as well as disheartening. Were there two Pierce Delaneys? The one she knew and the one who got Cora Lee with child? The longer she thought about it, the more she became convinced that she had missed something important during her visit with Cora Lee. Cora Lee's fear, Hal's odd behavior, nothing made sense. And what kind of retribution did Hal have in

271

mind? Whatever it was couldn't be good for the Delaneys. By the time she reached the ranch she was no less confused than before she left.

Chad and Ryan met Zoey as she rode into the yard. They were both mounted, and she looked at them askance.

"We were just on our way to visit Pierce," Chad informed her. "Want to come along?"

Zoey nodded. There were things she needed to ask Pierce.

"How did it go with Cora Lee?" Ryan asked.

"Hal was home," Zoey said. "Cora Lee seems terrified of her brother."

Ryan spit out a curse. "Hal can be a real bastard. He didn't hurt you, did he?"

"No, nothing like that. I listened to everything Cora Lee had to say about Pierce, and it didn't make sense. Pierce isn't anything like she described. Yet she seemed so sincere. I need to talk to Pierce."

"Let's ride then," Chad said. "Bill returned from town while you were gone and said the mood there was ugly. Ryan and I want to make damn sure there won't be a lynching."

Chad and Ryan spoke with Pierce first

272

when they reached the jailhouse. They weren't allowed inside the cramped shed, so they conversed through the single barred window. While they spoke in low tones, Zoey kept close tabs on the crowd milling around the jailhouse. The crowd ebbed and flowed, but the mood remained the same. Surly and hostile. Zoey stiffened when she saw Hal Doolittle join a group of people and speak furtively. His words seemed to rile the crowd and they surged forward. Zoey grew frightened and alerted Pierce's brothers.

"Go talk to Pierce, Zoey. Ryan and I will take care of things here," Chad said, pulling away his jacket to expose the lethal-looking gun riding on his hip.

Zoey peered through the narrow window with misgivings. She had no idea how Pierce would greet her, or if he'd acknowledge her at all. She saw him sitting on a bench, his expression etched into a scowl. When he saw her his scowl grew even more fierce.

"I thought I told you to go home."

"I will . . . soon."

He unwound his long frame and walked to the window. "You know what's going to happen. Why are you still here? Listen to those bloodthirsty fools outside. Hal

Doolittle has done his worst to see me in hell. He couldn't wait to get his hands on my share of the Delaney money, but it seems our marriage has foiled his well-laid plans.

"What a damn shame. Little did Hal know I wouldn't marry his sister under any circumstances. Unfortunately, both he and Riley Reed will probably have their way."

"They can't hang you," Zoey said fiercely. "They have no legal right."

"Do you see the regular law around here?"

"Your brothers . . ."

"Zoey, I'm going to tell you one last time. Go home to your ranch. I don't need you here. I don't *want* you here. Everything has been settled between us. We're even. Our 'arrangement' has served its purpose."

"Why are you being so hateful?"

Something flickered in Pierce's eyes but was quickly gone. "I'm not being hateful. Merely practical. We married for reasons of which you are well aware. It's over, Zoey." He turned away.

Zoey tried to summon anger but couldn't. Pierce's words may be true, but she wasn't going to let them drive her away.

"Don't you dare walk away from me,

Pierce." Her strident words brought his head spinning around in her direction. "I want to know the truth. Did you seduce Cora Lee? Did you get her with child? I'm not going to ask if you beat her, because I don't believe you're capable of that kind of brutality."

Zoey clearly had his undivided attention now. A tense silence stretched between them. Finally he said, "Maybe I did and maybe I didn't. What does it matter? Believe what you want." He shrugged. "If you believe I seduced Cora Lee . . ."

Her voice was scarcely louder than a whisper when she said, "You had no problem seducing me."

A long silence ensued as the air thickened around them. "You were ripe," he said simply.

Zoey tried to tell herself that Pierce was speaking out of hurt and anger. People often said hurtful things when they were under great stress.

She stifled a sob, raising her chin in defiance. "Getting a woman with child isn't a hanging offense. I'm not leaving."

Pierce watched Zoey walk away with mixed feelings. He had no earthly idea why she remained loyal to him when he'd done his damnedest to send her packing. He'd gone so far as to put doubts in her head about his guilt.

Zoey had ridden after him, saved him from the hangman, and done more than was required of a wife. And he had repaid her by acting like a surly bastard and ordering her home.

She'd refused.

Stubborn little witch.

A smile hung on his lips as he returned to the bench to contemplate his fascination with fierce blue eyes, hair the color of ripe wheat, and lush red lips that begged for his kisses.

Chapter 12

Zoey felt utterly defeated after returning from her visit with Cora Lee. She had gained nothing for her trouble but Hal Doolittle's animosity. Zoey could tell that Chad and Ryan were just as worried as she. The mood around the supper table that night was glum.

Just that day Chad had heard in town that Judge Walters was expected in a few days. He shared that bit of depressing news with both Ryan and Zoey at the supper table that night.

"I hope the judge is in a good mood," Ryan grumbled into his plate. "Judge Walters may be fair, but he earned his name legitimately."

Zoey looked at him askance. "What name is that, Ryan?"

"People hereabouts call him the 'hanging judge.' "

"Dammit, Ryan, why did you have to go and say that?" Chad chided.

Ryan sent Zoey a sheepish look. "Sorry."

"The charge against Pierce isn't a hanging offense," Zoey contended.

"It is if the judge says so," Ryan countered. "But I don't think it will come to that. Pierce has done nothing to deserve hanging, and I think the judge will agree."

Zoey rose abruptly from the table, her expression grim. "Please excuse me."

"You did it now, Ryan," Chad said.

"Zoey should know what to expect in case the judge decides against Pierce. What are we going to do if it comes to that?"

"I've been thinking," Chad said confidentially. "If the judge comes down hard on Pierce, we'll break him out of that pesthole they call a jail."

"I hope it won't be necessary. We'll all be on the run if we're forced to break the law."

Ryan and Chad exchanged worried glances, but each man knew he would do just about anything to save Pierce.

Zoey visited Pierce at the jailhouse the following day. For his sake she tried to maintain a cheerful facade. She brought a tempting array of food prepared by the Delaney cook and passed it to him through the barred window. Pierce didn't seem much interested in food and set it down without tasting it.

"Why are you still here, Zoey?"

Zoey gave him an exasperated look. If he didn't know, she certainly wasn't going to tell him. "I'm your wife."

"You may be a widow soon."

"Don't talk like that!"

"You've probably heard by now that Judge Walters is called the 'hanging judge.'"

"I heard. He can't hang an innocent man."

"I'm sorry it turned out like this."

"No judge is going to hang you for so minor an offense," Zoey insisted.

"Does that mean you're not returning home?"

"Damn right it does!"

He stared at her through the bars. The heat of his look warmed her bones. He reached out and ran the back of his hand along her cheek and down her neck.

"You're a stubborn woman, Zoey Delaney. And a hard woman to forget. You're passionate and loyal . . . but dare I trust you? If I surrendered to my feelings, it would be a sure passage to pain. Disaster waiting to happen. Once a woman gets her clutches into a man, once she has him reeled in, she uses him, then discards him for the next victim. I couldn't go through that with you."

Pierce's twisted opinion of women left Zoey speechless. But she couldn't really blame him. His past experiences had left him scarred. Both his mother and his wife had betrayed him. Then Cora Lee had committed the final offense. No wonder he feared involvement with a woman. But Zoey wasn't just any woman. She was a woman who truly loved him.

"I'm sorry you feel that way, Pierce. I'm not like those other women you've encountered in your life. I know I've done nothing to earn your trust, but I assure you I'm here simply to help you. If it will make you feel better, I'll see that lawyer today about a divorce."

The note of finality in her words made Pierce wince. It was what he wanted, wasn't it? He closed his eyes, picturing her sweet body pressed against his, naked, wet for him, responding to his loving with an eager innocence that drove him wild to possess her. He had set out to seduce her, but she had given herself to him willingly, generously, and he had taken.

Zoey had forced him to marry her, the hard place inside him argued.

"Pierce, are you all right?" His eyes were closed so long, Zoey began to worry.

His eyes shot open. "I'm fine. The lawyer's name is Chambers. Just tell him the truth and he'll do the rest."

Swallowing the lump in her throat, Zoey nodded and walked away. She didn't want Pierce to see how deeply his words had hurt her. He wanted to be free, and if it eased his mind, she would give him what he wanted.

A pair of visitors arrived at the Delaney ranch the next morning while they were eating breakfast and discussing their plans for the day. They were the last people Zoey would have expected to come calling.

The loud racket at the front door brought Ryan to his feet. "I'll get it," he said, scraping back his chair.

Both Zoey and Chad were startled, and none too pleased, when Ryan ushered their visitors into the kitchen.

"What are you doing here?" Chad asked crossly. "Haven't you done enough to hurt my family?"

"Don't get your dander up," Hal Doolittle said as he seated his sister in an empty chair without waiting for an invitation. "Cora Lee and I are here to present

281

you with a proposition."

"We don't want to hear it," Ryan grouched.

"Let him talk," Zoey argued. "I'm interested to hear what he has to say."

"Listen to the little lady, Delaney. You want to get your brother off the hook, don't you?"

Chad's gaze settled disconcertingly on Cora Lee. "Has your sister come to her senses? Is she ready to tell the truth?"

Something flickered in the depths of Cora Lee's eyes before her lids fell to hide them.

"Don't jump to conclusions," Hal warned. "Cora Lee didn't lie. But she's willing to change her story to save your brother. Let's say she just forgot what really happened. You know how fanciful women can be. She's always had this hankering to be married to a Delaney."

"And my brother was made the scapegoat," Chad observed dryly. "State your proposition, Doolittle."

Hal sent Zoey a disgruntled look as he said, "Since Pierce is already married, there ain't no use in expecting a marriage between him and Cora Lee." He searched Chad's face, a guileless smile curving his lips. "Cora Lee has set her heart on marrying a Delaney, so I convinced her to settle on one of the two remaining brothers." He didn't wait to ascertain the shock value his words had on the brothers before saying, "Ryan is a mite young, but Chad is just about the right age to take a wife."

Since both the Delaneys were too stunned to speak, Zoey rounded on Hal. "You're mad! Chad would never consent to such an idiotic proposal."

"It's not your decision, lady. Cora Lee is willing to tell both Riley Reed and the judge that Pierce is innocent. That she was confused because of what was done to her. She remembers that a stranger came around looking for work one day when I was out. When he noticed that Cora Lee was alone, he attacked and raped her. When she threatened to set the vigilantes on him, he beat her viciously. She made up that story about Pierce because she was too ashamed to admit what really happened. That's the story she'll stick to if Chad agrees to marry her."

Chad glanced at Cora Lee, who still refused to look anyone in the eye. She sat dry-eyed and stoic, twisting her handkerchief in her hands. "Is that true, Cora Lee?"

Still keeping her eyes downcast, Cora Lee said, "Whatever Hal says is the truth."

"The truth is that Pierce seduced my sister, got her with child, and beat her when she asked him to marry her," Hal said pugnaciously. "But Cora Lee is willing to lie as long as one of the Delaneys gives her baby their name. Don't matter which brother. Since Pierce is unavailable, Chad will do."

"What if I tell the judge what you've just told me," Chad demanded.

Hal seemed unconcerned. "Cora Lee will deny it, of course, holding to her original story. Think about it, Chad, but not too long. Agree to a marriage between you and my sister, and Pierce will go free. But not before a legal marriage is performed."

"What a fiendish mind you have," Ryan charged. His fists curled at his sides as he fought the obvious urge to slam them into Hal's mouth. "What do you hope to gain personally? I know there's something diabolical brewing in your mind."

"Why, I expect Chad to share some of the Delaney wealth with my sister. Which, of course, she'll share with her loving brother." Suddenly his expression changed from pleasant to downright nasty. "I need five thousand dollars immediately to repay gambling debts."

"So," Chad sneered, "it's down to money, is it? Say I give you the money but refuse to marry Cora Lee. Will that make you happy?"

Hal scowled. "Not on your life. My sister needs a papa for her bastard. Nothing but the Delaney name will make her happy."

"You can't agree to this farce, Chad!" Zoey cried indignantly. "It's blackmail."

The accusation brought a guilty flush to Zoey's face. It was too close to what she'd done to Pierce. She had acted out of desperation, but it placed her in the same class with the Doolittles. What Hal demanded of Chad was no worse than what she'd demanded of Pierce. That singular thought made her understand more clearly why Pierce hated the thought of remaining married to her. She had blackmailed him into a situation he could not tolerate.

"Do you swear Pierce will go free if I marry Cora Lee?" Chad asked. His voice was far too calm and controlled for such a reputedly volatile man, and Zoey waited for the explosion.

"Dammit, Chad, use your head!" Ryan blasted. "Pierce wouldn't want you to sacrifice yourself for his sake. He'd hate the idea and you know it."

"Pierce has no say in this," Chad said tightly.

"You're a smart man, Delaney," Hal said, sending Chad a mocking smile.

"How long would I have to stay in this marriage?" Chad wanted to know.

"Forever, if I had my way. But being realistic, I'd say you should remain married at least until Cora Lee delivers her child. There are no bastards in the Doolittle family, and there ain't gonna be none if I have my way. If and when you divorce, Cora Lee will expect a generous settlement, of course."

"You're wrong, Doolittle," Ryan spat. "There already is a bastard in the Doolittle family. His name is Hal."

Hal appeared unfazed by Ryan's insult.

Zoey glanced at Cora Lee and decided to attack the problem from another angle. Cora Lee had remained quietly submissive through all this, saying little beyond agreeing with her brother. Zoey decided to appeal to Cora Lee's sense of right and wrong.

"Don't you have anything to say, Cora Lee?" Zoey asked, hunkering down to confront the pale woman. "Do you really want a husband who doesn't want you?"

"My baby needs a name," she said in a

low voice. She sent a wary glance at her brother before continuing. "Hal loves me, he wants what's best for me."

"You really were raped and beaten by a stranger, weren't you?" Zoey challenged, going directly to the heart of the matter.

"I . . . I . . . No, it didn't happen like that. Please, don't ask me any more questions."

"Coward!" Zoey hissed.

"Quit harassing my sister," Hal warned. "Can't you see she's in a delicate condition?" He turned back to Chad. "Well, Delaney, do we have a deal?"

"Pierce wouldn't condone this," Zoey reminded him.

Ryan was more forceful in his objection. "Don't do it, Chad! The bastard thinks he has us over a barrel, but he doesn't. It's all up to the judge."

"No, it ain't," Hal hinted slyly. "Rumor has it Riley Reed has convinced the vigilantes to lynch Pierce before the judge gets here. They're gonna take him out of the jail tomorrow night."

Zoey cried out in dismay. "We've got to do something!"

"You can't do a damn thing," Hal contended. "The townspeople are with Reed. You don't have enough hands on the ranch to stop the whole town."

"He's right," Ryan admitted grudgingly. "Reed hates Pierce. Ever since Polly . . ." He sent an apologetic look at Zoey. "Ever since Pierce took Polly away from him. Reed knows the judge is just as likely to fine Pierce or give him a light sentence as he is to hang him, and he can't accept that. Judge Walters may have earned his reputation as the hanging judge, but he's not going to hang an innocent man."

"You mean there's nothing you can do to stop an illegal lynching? It's a travesty of justice!" Zoey's voice was shaking so, she could barely speak.

"There is something *I* can do," Chad said, his voice dull with resignation. "Ryan, go into town for the preacher."

Ryan paled. "You can't!"

"Do — as — I — say, Ryan." The words were drawn out, hard and distinct.

Ryan could tell from Chad's implacable tone and hardened features that his brother was utterly committed to this folly. Nothing he could do or say would change Chad's mind. Still, he had to try. "Are you sure, Chad?"

"Get going, Ryan."

Ryan slammed out the door. Chad waited until Ryan was on his way to the barn for his horse before saying, "Don't expect me to live with my little bride, Doolittle. I wouldn't insult my brothers by bringing her into our home. I'll give her my name and the money you want, but nothing else. If you don't agree to my terms, then the hell with you both."

Hal eyed Chad narrowly, then turned to his sister. "Is that agreeable to you, Cora Lee?"

As if she was startled to be included in the decision, Cora Lee's head rose sharply. "Is it my choice to make, Hal?"

"Of course, dear." His voice held a hint of menace. "Just make sure you say the right thing. You can't have Pierce. But Chad is a Delaney, too. And a better choice in some ways. Your baby will still be a Delaney."

"You're as corrupt as your brother, Cora Lee," Zoey charged. "Everyone in this room knows Pierce would never beat a woman." What she didn't say was that there was a very real possibility that Pierce was the father of Cora Lee's baby. Try as she might, Zoey couldn't help thinking that Pierce could have seduced Cora Lee. He was so good at it.

"Well, sister," Hal prodded, "will you accept Chad's terms and have him in place of Pierce?"

Cora Lee peeped at Chad through lowered lids. His fierce visage frightened her. She'd be perfectly happy not to have to live with such an angry man, not that she could blame Chad for being angry. Hal was like that sometimes, but he kept his brutality under control, except when . . . She shook her head, fearing to allow those unpleasant thoughts into her mind. If she refused to acknowledge them, she could almost believe Pierce Delaney really was the father of her child.

"I don't mind if Chad doesn't want to live with me. My baby will still have the Delaney name." She looked hopefully at Hal, as if seeking his approval. He gave it to her, blessing her with his smile.

"Very well, we'll just all sit here and wait for the preacher. Miz Delaney and Ryan can act as witnesses, and I'll give my sister away in Pa's absence."

"What does your father think about this mess?" Chad asked curiously. "He can't help but notice Cora Lee is increasing."

"The old man is too feeble to think anything," Hal sneered. "He believes what we tell him. I mentioned today before we left that Cora Lee will soon have a husband for her child, and that seemed to satisfy him."

"Pretty sure of yourself, weren't you?"

"Damn right! I know how you Delaneys stick together. One way or another, Cora Lee was going to bear the Delaney name. And you'd be wise to let her keep it. Once Cora Lee drops her brat, you might find some use for her."

"If Pierce's life didn't hang in the balance, I'd throw you both out of here," Chad growled. His temper dangled by a slim thread. He was nearly driven to madness and didn't know how long he could keep his fists out of Hal's face.

Trying to defuse the explosive atmosphere, Zoey urged Chad to sit down and relax. It would be a good two hours or better before Ryan returned with the preacher.

"Chores waiting for me," Chad said, heading for the door. "See to our guests, Zoey."

"Don't get no ideas about lighting out of here," Hal called after him.

"He's not going anywhere as long as his brother's life is at stake," Zoey said. "I'll get us some coffee while we're waiting."

Two hours later, Ryan returned with Reverend Purdy, a short, balding man with small, beady eyes and a bulbous nose. They were accompanied by another man.

291

Reverend Purdy was expected, Riley Reed was not.

"I wanted Reed to hear the truth about Pierce, so I brought him along to hear what Cora Lee had to say," Ryan said as he ushered the men into the house.

"Not until after the wedding," Hal reminded him. "Shall we get on with it, Reverend?"

"Where's the groom?" Reverend Purdy asked, casting about anxiously. Ryan Delaney had paid him hard cash to comply with his odd request, and he wasn't about to lose more money than he'd seen in a good long time. He had no idea why Cora Lee was changing brothers in midstream, so to speak, but he wasn't being paid to ask questions. His job was saving souls, even if in his estimation those souls were beyond redemption.

"Right here, Reverend," Chad said, stepping into the parlor. "Shall we begin?"

Reverend Purdy took one look at Chad's fierce countenance and the color drained from his face. He cleared his throat noisily. "If you and your bride will step in front of the fireplace, I'll begin immediately. Who are the witnesses?"

"Here," Ryan said, stepping forward. "Zoey and I will act as witnesses."

"And I'll give the bride away," Hal added.

It was over in five minutes. Chad repeated his vows in cold, clipped words. Cora Lee's voice trembled but didn't falter as she spoke her vows.

The papers were duly signed and witnessed. Reverend Purdy made a hasty departure, richer by a hundred dollars.

"Now that the wedding is over, what in the hell is this all about?" Reed asked. "I know I wasn't dragged out here for a celebration. This has all the makings of a shotgun wedding. Do I have the wrong brother in jail?"

"Sit down, Reed," Chad invited. "My little *bride* has something she wants to get off her chest. Go ahead and tell him, *darling.*"

Cora Lee sent a look of such terror at Chad that Zoey almost felt sorry for her.

"Go ahead, Cora Lee," Hal urged, "you're married now. It's all right to tell the truth."

For a moment Cora Lee looked confused. "The truth, Hal?"

"You know," Hal rasped. "Just tell Reed what we talked about earlier. Just before Chad so gallantly offered for your hand."

Chad gave an inelegant snort.

"Pierce didn't do those things I accused him of," Cora Lee said, looking to Hal for support. Then she proceeded to tell Reed the story Hal had concocted about the man who raped and beat her, and why she'd made up the story about Pierce. "I was so ashamed," she said as she ended her fabrication. "Being raped and beaten by a strange man must have done something to my mind. And . . . and I fancied Pierce."

Hal added, "We came here to tell Chad and Ryan about Cora Lee's mistake, and Chad admitted to having a fondness for Cora Lee. He asked her to marry him and she accepted."

"If you think I believe that cock-and-bull story, you're crazier than I thought," Reed hooted.

"You have no choice," Ryan said. "Cora Lee will tell her story before the judge if she has to. Hanging judge or not, Judge Walters won't hang an innocent man, and you know it. We'll all go to town together and set Pierce free."

"The townspeople ain't gonna like it," Reed warned. "Hell, I don't like it. I've waited a long time to bring Pierce Delaney down."

"You and Hal are the ones who riled the townspeople," Chad charged. "Their attitude will change once Cora Lee recants her story."

Cora Lee paled. "Do I have to?"

"Yes," Zoey said remorselessly. "If it comes to that."

Reed fumed in impotent rage. He shouldn't have waited so long to lynch Pierce. Unfortunately some of his own men had balked at hanging him. And the townspeople were beginning to tire of hearing Hal rant on and on about how Pierce had seduced Cora Lee. Hell, some of the same men who had raised a ruckus about the affair had done their own share of seducing and beating in their time. That's why he'd planned on having a secret lynching tonight. Nothing had happened the way it was supposed to. If he didn't know better, he'd think Delaney was in cahoots with the Devil.

"Are you ready to ride, Reed?" Chad asked. The harshness of his voice warned Reed to do as Chad ordered or suffer the consequences. The Delaney boys weren't to be fooled around with when their dander was up.

Zoey's heart sang with joy as she rode to town. *Pierce is free, Pierce is free,* over and over the refrain repeated itself in her head and heart. She lamented the method by which his freedom had been gained, and Chad had her full sympathy. But she still couldn't help rejoicing. Even if it meant she'd no longer have a reason to remain in Dry Gulch.

Pierce didn't want a wife, and she wouldn't burden him with one. She had spoken with the lawyer the day before, and after listening to her rather unusual story, he had agreed to prepare divorce papers to present to the judge. This surprising turn of events convinced Zoey to submit to Pierce's wishes and leave within the next day or two. Since Pierce wanted the divorce so badly, he could deal with it himself.

Zoey's thoughts were still in a turmoil when they reached town. They rode directly to the jailhouse and waited for Reed to produce the key that would release Pierce.

Pierce looked out the barred window of the jail, and a frisson of apprehension slid down his spine when he saw his family gathered outside the jailhouse. "What is this all about?" he asked, his eyes finding Zoey among the strange assortment of people that included the Doolittles and Riley Reed. "Has the judge arrived? Or is this a lynching party?"

Zoey gave him a brilliant smile, and Pierce was astounded by the inner radiance flowing through her. Something had happened. Something that made Zoey beam with happiness. Then his gaze sought Chad's and his heart plummeted to his feet. Pierce knew his brother as well as he knew himself, and Chad's expression wasn't one that gave him a great deal of confidence. He looked at Ryan and thought it strange that both his brothers were scowling at a time when Zoey appeared nearly overcome with joy.

"You're free, Pierce," Chad said as he waited for Reed to unlock the door. When Reed appeared reluctant to put the key to the lock, Chad shoved him aside, placed the key into the rusty padlock, and turned it himself.

Pierce stepped through the door, blinking in the bright sunlight. "Will someone explain what's going on?"

Hoping to avoid a nasty scene when Pierce learned what Chad had done, Zoey stepped forward and pulled him toward the horse they had brought for him. A crowd of curious bystanders had already begun to gather around the jailhouse.

"Wait until we get home," Zoey said,

eyeing the crowd nervously.

Pierce balked. He didn't like being put off. Something was afoot and he wasn't sure he was going to like it. His gaze fell on Hal and Cora Lee, and he pulled from Zoey's grasp. "What are they doing here?"

Hal shoved through the crowd, dragging his sister with him. He stopped when he reached Pierce. "Congratulate my sister, Pierce," he said, clearly gloating. "She and your brother Chad were married today. Cora Lee was so happy she suddenly recalled that you weren't responsible for her condition. You can thank her for your freedom."

Pierce whirled on Chad, his face a mask of rage. "Are you crazy? What made you do such a damnfool thing?"

Chad faced his furious brother squarely. "I did it for you. They were planning to lynch you before the judge arrived, and I couldn't stand by and do nothing."

"So you married a scheming bitch in exchange for my life."

"You would have done the same for me."

"Is there nothing a woman won't do to get what she wants?" Pierce charged harshly. He looked directly at Zoey, including her in his condemnation of the fair sex.

With sinking heart, Zoey felt the searing heat of his gaze and the animosity it reflected. It was almost as if Pierce blamed her for Chad's unfortunate predicament.

Stifling a sob, she turned away from the dark hostility of Pierce's resentment. Without uttering a word in her defense, she mounted up and rode off toward the Delaney ranch. Perhaps she could pack and be gone before Pierce arrived home, saving him the trouble of throwing her out.

Chapter 13

Pierce watched Zoey leave but made no move to follow. He was surrounded by people. People who two days ago were clamoring for his death were now congratulating him for escaping the hangman. Through it all Pierce remained unresponsive, his fists clenched at his sides, skewering the Doolittles with a look so filled with animosity that Hal instantly bit off his taunting words.

Finally Ryan worked his way to Pierce. "Let's go home, Pierce."

"What about Chad? He isn't planning to honeymoon with Cora Lee, is he?" His words were cold, clipped, mocking. "I hope he doesn't think he's going to escape my wrath. You're as crazy as he is for letting him sacrifice himself for me."

"I couldn't stop him, Pierce. You know Chad. Once he makes his mind up about something, nothing is going to change it.

Chad will be along soon. He has some business to conduct with Hal Doolittle. As for Cora Lee, her living arrangements will remain the same. Everyone knows the marriage is a farce. She'll continue to live at her place, and Chad will remain home with us."

"All marriages are a farce," Pierce claimed. "Nothing in life so far has shown me differently. Let's get the hell out of here. I'm dirty, hungry, and . . ."

"You want to see Zoey," Ryan supplied. "Wonder why she took off like she did. Did you say something to upset her?"

"You don't know a damn thing about my marriage," Pierce said as he and Ryan walked to where their horses were tethered.

"Zoey told us everything. Chad questioned her when she arrived at the house. She must love you a great deal to follow you like she did. She saved your life, brother."

Both men mounted up. "She's been amply repaid," Pierce bit out as he put his heels to his horse's flanks. "Love has nothing to do with Zoey and me."

Ryan wasn't so sure. He wasn't given to maudlin sentiments, but in his opinion Zoey had displayed more than normal concern for Pierce. She had gone out of her way to help him, and when pushed, had admitted she loved him. He wondered if his brother had considered the possibility that Zoey could be carrying his child.

Pierce's thoughts ran the gamut of his emotions. He was angry at Chad and enraged at Cora Lee. The entire female population consisted of connivers and schemers. Cora Lee had tried to seduce him before but he had ignored her. He'd always considered her a bitch, but he never would have suspected her of the kind of duplicity in which she was involved. Cora Lee wasn't smart, or sly enough to hatch this kind of plot on her own. But Hal was. Suddenly Pierce reined in sharply.

"What is it?" Ryan asked, reining in beside Pierce. "Why did you stop?"

"How much money did Doolittle demand from Chad? Marrying off his pregnant sister to a Delaney wouldn't be enough for him. How much, Ryan?"

Pierce was too perceptive by half, Ryan reflected. He'd dig and dig until he had every last detail. "Five thousand dollars. That's why Chad stayed in town, to get the money for Hal."

Pierce said nothing; his expression spoke for him. Kneeing his horse, he sped off down the road, leaving Ryan in his dust.

Riding at breakneck speed, Pierce cursed at the pace at which his life was unraveling. It wasn't enough that his own life had become a living hell, he had to drag Chad down with him. He blamed himself for Chad's marriage to a woman carrying another man's child. A woman Chad didn't love, didn't even like.

That thought brought another. Zoey wasn't like Cora Lee, or any of the other women in his past. He actually *liked* Zoey. He had come to understand and even to sympathize with Zoey's need for a husband. Zoey loved her land as fiercely as he loved his. Despite being coerced into an unwanted marriage, he felt he had repaid his debt above and beyond the call of duty. Then she had followed him and risked her life to prevent the vigilantes from lynching him. If he had to trust one woman, it would be Zoey.

In a roundabout way, Chad's forced marriage to Cora Lee had reaffirmed for Pierce what women were capable of and all but destroyed the fragile trust that had been building between himself and Zoey. Once again he'd learned that no woman was worthy of trust. Yet he couldn't deny that he'd wanted Zoey from the moment he'd awakened in her house and seen her bending over him. He'd vowed then he'd have her, and on his terms.

God, he could almost feel her sweet breasts in his hands, her body undulating against his, her moist lips begging for his kisses. He loved the way her denims hugged her sweet little bottom, her long, long legs, and her rounded hips. She had given him her virginity and asked nothing in return. But not even all those inducements could hold him in a marriage he didn't want.

Perhaps Zoey would remarry once their divorce was granted, he reflected, grimacing at the thought. Zoey was a beautiful, giving woman, one whom any man would consider a prize. Any man but Pierce Delaney.

Pierce reached the ranch house, bringing his mount to a prancing halt at the front door. He was immediately surrounded by a dozen hands, all talking at once, offering their congratulations and slapping him on the back. No one made mention of the wedding that took place that day, but everyone was aware that one had occurred. Ryan reined in beside Pierce and sent the hands about their chores. The brothers walked into the house together and headed for the kitchen.

Zoey heard the door slam and a shudder went through her. Pierce was home. She wanted to run downstairs and throw herself into his arms, but instead continued folding and packing her meager belongings into her saddlebags. It was time for her to leave. But oh, how she hated to leave with Chad's life in such a muddle. She knew Pierce would hold himself responsible for Chad's predicament, and she wanted to be here to offer comfort. But Pierce didn't want her and she wouldn't add to his woes by staying where she wasn't wanted. She wasn't part of this family and never would be.

Hefting her saddlebags over her arm, Zoey left her room and walked down the stairs. No one was around. She supposed she should tell someone she was leaving, and headed for the kitchen. She opened the kitchen door and stopped dead in her tracks. Pierce sat in a huge wooden tub that had been placed beside the big cookstove. His eyes were closed, his head resting against the rim.

"There's a kettle of hot water on the stove, Ryan. Pour it into the tub, will you? God, this feels good. I feel almost human again."

Zoey set her saddlebags on the floor,

walked to the stove, and picked up the kettle. She poured it into the tub, then set it back on the stove. Pierce's eyes were still closed and he heaved a tremendous sigh as he settled deeper into the hot water.

"Has Chad returned from town yet?" Pierce asked.

Zoey remained mute as she tiptoed around the tub, retrieved her saddlebags, and headed for the back door. As he sensed her presence, Pierce's eyes flew open. He saw the saddlebags slung over her arm and all but leaped from the tub. Water sprayed out around his naked body as he reached for Zoey.

"Where in the hell do you think you're going?"

Zoey's gaze slid over his glistening nude form, and she felt her cheeks heating. Awareness flew between them. She shuddered, then forced a taut smile to her lips. "I'm going home. I don't want Cully to worry about me any longer."

"You're not going anywhere. Not today," he qualified.

"I'm merely following your orders," Zoey charged, keeping her gaze upon his face. If she let it stray, she wouldn't be able to leave this room, this man, this marriage.

"It's late," Pierce said. "I won't let you

leave without a proper escort. It's a long way to Rolling Prairie, and anything could happen on the road."

Zoey's heart sank. In a moment of bittersweet clarity she realized that Pierce was asking her to remain only until he could arrange an escort, not because he really wanted her to stay.

"Don't worry about me. I can take care of myself. If you're concerned about the divorce, it's been taken care of. I left everything up to Lawyer Chambers. He'll present the petition to the judge when he comes through."

"I'm not worried about the divorce," Pierce said, making an impatient motion with his hand. "I'm concerned more about your safety. You're not going anywhere until I say so."

They stood nose to nose, neither willing to give an inch. Suddenly the back door opened and Ryan stepped inside. He took one look at Pierce, naked and sporting an erection, and at Zoey, standing close enough to feel his response to her, and turned beet red.

"Sorry," Ryan said as he spun on his heel and left as abruptly as he had appeared.

Upset and embarrassed, Zoey said, "He shouldn't have seen us like this."

"You're right. We shouldn't be standing in the middle of the kitchen, not while I'm in this condition."

Zoey pounded his chest in protest as Pierce scooped her up in his arms and carried her up the stairs to his room. He dropped her in the center of his bed and stood over her, his green eyes dark and unfathomable. She sat up immediately, chin raised, glaring at him.

"What do you think you're doing?"

He sat down on the bed, making no move to dress. "We need to talk before you leave. This is the only place we can have privacy."

"Get dressed, then we'll talk. I'm not going to . . . That is, we aren't going to make love."

"Did I ask it of you?"

Her gaze dropped to his arousal. He might not ask, but it was all *she* could think of. "Please, Pierce, put on some clothes."

He laughed, clearly aware of the effect he was having on her. But to please her he pulled the bedcover over his loins. "Satisfied?"

"Yes. What is it you wished to talk about?"

"I want you to remain here a few days longer. When things are more settled I'll have Ryan see you home to the Circle F."

"I told you —"

"I insist. There's one other thing." He cleared his throat. "I wrote a will when I thought Reed was going to lynch me."

She stared at him curiously.

"I left my share of the ranch and its profits to you."

Zoey went still. "Why did you do that?"

Pierce shrugged. "It seemed right at the time."

"There's no need for that now. You're hale and hardy and not likely to leave this earth any time soon."

"I want you to have it," Pierce said, surprising her. "It seems right somehow. My brothers have no need of my money. I'm going to have Chambers draw up a legal document. I just wanted you to know."

Zoey's eyes grew large and liquid. She didn't want Pierce's money, she wanted him. "I wish you wouldn't do that."

He was looking at her so strangely, she felt drawn to him by strong emotional ties. Did Pierce feel it, also? she wondered, suddenly finding herself growing breathless in his daunting presence. Of course not, she chided herself. Pierce was a hardheaded cynic, inured to love. His distrust of women made it impossible for him to love her.

"Why are you looking at me like that?" she asked.

Because I want to be inside you, he thought but left unsaid. *I want to thrust myself to the hilt into your hot center. I want to feel you close around me, squeezing me, taking me to Paradise. And when I am spent inside you, I want to hear my name on your lips.*

"Pierce, what is it? You've got a strange look on your face."

She was startled by his unexpected move. He reached for her, dragging her hard against him. "I have this unaccountable urge to kiss you," he said. There was a huskiness in his voice that she recognized and responded to. Her mouth was tipped up to his, moist and slightly open. Until she realized what kissing him would lead to and deftly turned her head aside so that his kiss lit at the corner of her mouth.

"I won't allow you to use me again, Pierce."

He touched her cheek, turning her face toward him. "I thought we agreed that we had used one another. I can't think of another woman I'd rather bed."

"And I can't think of another man I'd rather bed."

"We're still married," he reminded her.

"Not for long."

"Zoey, I know this sounds strange in light of my aversion to marriage, but you are the only woman I'd even consider marrying if I was a marrying man. But I wouldn't make you happy. I'd be a jealous, suspicious husband, always waiting for you to find someone else and leave me."

"I'm not asking for a commitment," Zoey said. "I do have some pride left. Besides, permanency was not part of our arrangement." He couldn't know how dearly those words cost her.

"Neither was making love, which we did freely and joyously," Pierce reminded her. "I deliberately set out to seduce you, you know. You should hate me for taking your virginity."

"I've told you before, you took nothing from me!" Zoey bristled angrily. "I gave my virginity to you because I wanted to. It was my choice. You don't owe me a damn thing. I forced you into marriage, remember?" She rose from the bed. "We both have much to forgive the other for," she said in parting.

She heard Pierce groan and then he was pulling her back on the bed, bringing his mouth down on hers, savoring her with the sweep of his tongue, stealing her breath and her senses. He groaned again, and she tasted it on his lips and caught it in her throat. As if under a sorcerer's spell, she yielded to the gentle coaxing of his mouth, opening to him, welcoming him.

Then she felt his hands, warm and slightly callused, opening her blouse and cradling her breasts, holding them in his palms as if they were something precious.

"Let me love you," he said, breaking off the kiss and staring at her. His green eyes gleamed with undisguised hunger as his thumbs grazed lightly over her raised nipples.

She shivered with delight, and a sharp shaft of longing jolted through her at his touch. "We . . . shouldn't."

His captivating smile made her forget why they shouldn't.

She stared at his mouth, wanting him to kiss her again, unaware that he had removed her shirt and was now ridding her of her camisole.

"Your body is so beautiful," he said. "All soft and smooth. Your breasts are two mouth-watering morsels, begging to be tasted."

His dark head lowered, his lips closing moistly over one coral peak. His tongue flicked at it in sensual strokes, and Zoey felt her insides bubbling to a boil. He sucked deeply, and she felt hot, damp moisture gathering between her legs. By the time he moved to the other breast, she was pulsing with an insistent ache. She moaned, her hands clasping his head to hold him in place against her breast.

Pierce skillfully unfastened the front of her denims, running his hand beneath the material, lower. Zoey lurched against him, murmuring a protest that had no substance.

"Let me touch you, love," Pierce whispered against her lips. "Let me make you feel good again. This might be the last time for us."

Zoey wanted to deny him, truly she did, but the words would not come. She wanted Pierce as badly as he seemed to want her. Then his hand found her and she lost the ability to think.

"It's always been good between us," Pierce said as he skimmed her denims down her legs. Then he removed her boots and denims and tossed them aside.

It was too late for Zoey to protest as Pierce kissed her again, one hand kneading her breasts, the other intimately cupping her between the legs, his knowing fingers delving through the down sheltering her to caress the soft, dewy cleft hidden there. He rotated the heel of his hand against the tender bud where passion dwelled, so sensitive that Zoey jerked wildly, drawing in an explosive gasp.

"Pierce! It's too much!"

"It's not nearly enough. Take a deep breath, relax, and let me love you the way you deserve."

He eased his finger inside her, gliding on the slick moisture, and she arched up against the pressure of it.

As his fingers stroked and prodded, every nerve in Zoey's body drew tight as a bowstring, centering upon that place where he was touching her. Desire spiraled through her and she felt as if she'd break in two if Pierce didn't give her that final release. But Pierce had just begun.

Rising slightly, he slid down her body and placed his mouth where his fingers had just been. His tongue parted and teased, laved and stroked, a firebrand that ignited her flesh. Zoey tingled, she burned, flames licked along her flesh, consuming her in their inferno. It could end no other way but explosively. With a hoarse cry, she found that final, mindless release as incredible waves of ecstasy rippled through her.

"Now it's my turn," Pierce gasped, his

blood clamoring for release. "Concentrate, love. Come with me again."

Raising her hips, he positioned himself between her thighs and thrust inside her. He shuddered. The pleasure of sheathing himself in her tight, warm passage nearly brought him to the pinnacle. Clenching his teeth against the need to spill himself, he held very still inside her until his control returned. Then he flexed his hips and thrust himself to the hilt, withdrew and thrust again. Thrust and withdrew, until his hips were pistoning into her, against her.

She arched up to meet his thrusts, grasping his shoulders as if to stop the world from spinning. Then she cried out and convulsed as Pierce took her along with him to blissful completion. He shouted her name, shuddered, then went still with contentment.

Zoey sighed and opened her eyes. Pierce was grinning down at her. She grinned back. Pierce's loving always seemed to do that to her. It was almost like dying a little.

"No other woman has ever done that to me," Pierce confessed.

"Do what?"

"Made me feel . . . I don't know, it's an extraordinary feeling."

"I can't even begin to describe how you make me feel," Zoey said. "I'm not an authority on this sort of thing, but you seem to be awfully good at it."

Pierce gave her a cheeky grin. Zoey thought he should smile more often; it made him look young and wonderfully appealing. "You're not so bad yourself for a beginner."

Zoey flushed. "We should get up. It's growing late and I wanted to be on my way before dark."

Pierce scowled. "You're not going anywhere until I can provide you with an escort. It may be a few days before someone is available."

"Why are you doing this? I just don't understand you. You want me, yet you don't want me. Make up your mind."

Pierce stared at the ceiling. "I've been thinking. Maybe you shouldn't return home at all. My brothers seem to like you, and I . . . well, you know how explosive we are together. Besides, it will be a while before our divorce is granted."

"Let me get this straight. You want me to stay because we're good in bed, is that it?" Zoey asked evenly.

Pierce wasn't sure what he meant. He was confused. For some reason he was loath to let Zoey leave, even though common sense told him he was asking for more heartache than he could bear.

"Isn't that a good enough reason?"

"I repeat," Zoey said quietly. "You want us to share a bed until our divorce is granted."

"Or until we tire of one another." Lord, what made him put things so crudely? Each time he opened his mouth he seemed to put his foot into it. "I won't lie to you, Zoey. I don't want a permanent relationship. I'm just saying that we're not ready to part yet. What just happened between us proves it."

"In other words," she enunciated slowly, "you want to keep me as your whore until you tire of me."

"Don't put words in my mouth. You're my wife, not my whore. You could never be that."

"Explain the difference, please. The only reason you want me to stay is so you'll have a bed partner for as long as I continue to please you. Thank you, but no thank you."

"I'm not presenting this well, am I?"

Zoey gave an inelegant snort. "I understand you perfectly. Forget it, Pierce. You're making a mockery of marriage."

Pierce's answer was forestalled when someone knocked on the door.

"Pierce, are you in there?" Ryan called through the door. "Chad is home. If you want to talk to him, you'd better come quickly."

"I'll be down in a minute, Ryan," Pierce replied. "Tell Chad not to go anywhere until I speak to him."

"What are you going to say to Chad?" Zoey asked as she slid out of bed and gathered her discarded clothing.

Pierce scrambled for a pair of pants. "I've got plenty to say to him."

"Chad did it for you, you know."

"Not for me. I never would have asked this of him. Dammit, Zoey, now Cora Lee's bastard will carry the Delaney name."

"Don't be too hard on him," Zoey said as she pulled on her shirt and buttoned it across her breasts.

Finished with his own dressing, Pierce picked up Zoey's boots and handed them to her. "Tell me later what you decide about us. If you still want to leave, at least wait until things are settled here and someone can escort you home."

"I'll wait a few days, but nothing will change my mind about leaving."

318

★ ★ ★

Pierce faced Chad across the table, his anger palpable. "I don't care why you married Cora Lee, Chad. Your intentions may have been good, but your sacrifice was uncalled-for."

"They were going to lynch you," Chad said defensively.

"I doubt it," Pierce replied. "Riley Reed was the only one who really wanted to see me swing at the end of a rope. The townspeople were becoming bored with the whole affair. Reed and Doolittle were the ones keeping it alive. I think they were afraid Judge Walters would let me off lightly. You got yourself a wife for all the wrong reasons, Chad."

Chad's lips thinned. "You're a fine one to talk! Look how easily you got railroaded into marriage."

Zoey gave a strangled gasp.

"Dammit, Chad, watch your tongue!" Ryan snapped.

Chad sent Zoey a sheepish look. "Sorry, Zoey."

"There's nothing to be sorry about. You didn't lie," Zoey said. She scraped her chair back. "If you gentlemen will excuse me, I think I'll take a walk."

"Go after her," Chad said after Zoey left.

"Later. I'm not finished with you yet."

"As far as I'm concerned, you are. What's done is done. I did what I thought was necessary at the time. I don't intend to live with Cora Lee, or bring her here. In a few days, once I can face that little bitch again, I'm going over there to talk with her father. I'd appreciate it if you came along. Old Ed Doolittle always liked you better than any of us. I'm going to explain just how I ended up married to Cora Lee."

"I'm not sure he'll understand," Pierce said. "He's in pretty bad shape."

Chad's expression hardened. "I'll make him understand. Will you come with me? We're a family, Pierce. We have to stick together. It's not going to do a damn bit of good to stay mad at me. What's done is done."

Pierce stared at Chad, realizing that everything his brother said was true. Chad wasn't a naughty child he could punish at will. He was a man, one who must live with his mistakes. Chad's motives had been unselfish; he'd only wanted to save his brother's life. Pierce would have done the same.

"Very well, Chad, you've made your point. You'll have to live with your mistake until we can do something about it. We're brothers. Pa taught us to stick together through thick and thin. I may not like what you did, but I respect your right to make the decision you did. I blame myself for the mess we're in."

"Let's just try to forget this episode in our lives," Chad suggested. "Marriage isn't all that final. We'll work this out like we've done everything else. One day we'll both be free of entanglements."

Pierce suffered a pang of disquiet. To be honest, life without Zoey would be damn dull. He glanced at the door and had to forcibly prevent himself from going after her, taking her in his arms, and making sweet, passionate love to her. He could almost taste her sweet kisses, feel the heat of her body moving against his as he thrust into her, hear her breathless little cries of ecstasy. Stifling a groan, he wielded his fork with angry dexterity, chewing and swallowing food that tasted like sawdust.

He regretted the way he'd suggested to Zoey that she remain at the ranch and occupy his bed until they tired of one another. In retrospect it sounded cold and demeaning. Some part of him wanted Zoey to stay with him. Some soft place he neither recognized nor welcomed. A place that he feared.

Chapter 14

Zoey locked her bedroom door against Pierce that night. And each night for the next three nights.

On the morning of the fourth day Zoey confronted Pierce, inquiring about his plans to provide her with an escort. "There must be someone on this ranch who can escort me home," she charged after Chad and Ryan left the breakfast table.

"I prefer to keep Chad close by right now. His mood isn't the best and he'd make a surly companion. Both Ryan and I are needed for roundup. It shouldn't be much longer," he hedged.

"You're stalling, Pierce. Why?"

He ignored her question and posed one of his own. "Why have you locked me out of your room?"

Because if I let you make love to me one more time, I'll never be able to leave, and that isn't what you want. "It's for the best."

"For who?"

"Both of us."

"Zoey, I —"

Chad entered through the back door, halting Pierce in midsentence. "Pierce, I'm going over to the Doolittle place to talk to Ed. Would you ride over there with me?"

"You're going now?"

"Right after the chores are finished."

"Sure, I'll tag along if that's what you want."

"I need your support. I don't want to be alone with Cora Lee. I'm afraid I might wring her pretty little neck. If Hal runs true to form, he'll be in town spending his newly acquired windfall at the poker table."

"Can I come?" Zoey asked. She was bored with nothing to do. If this were her own ranch, she'd be out with the hands tending to the chores.

Chad shot Pierce a questioning look. Pierce answered with a shrug, indicating his indifference to Zoey's request. "Sure, if you want to," Chad said. "You can keep Cora Lee occupied while Pierce and I talk to her father."

Shortly after lunch, Zoey, Pierce, and Chad saddled up and rode to the Doolittle ranch. The place gave every indication of being deserted as they rode through the front gate.

"I wonder what happened to the hands," Chad said, seeing signs of gross neglect.

"There weren't many left," Pierce replied. "Those who remained after Ed took sick probably got tired of working without wages and took paying jobs. Hal never did care for the ranch, even though it provided him with his livelihood."

They dismounted close to the house, tethered their horses to the porch rail, and climbed the three front steps to the door. They found the door open to the breeze, and Chad rapped on the screen door. No one answered. He rapped again. Still no answer.

"Strange," Pierce mused. "Someone should be home. Ed can't be left alone for long."

"Maybe Cora Lee is in the vegetable garden out back," Zoey suggested. "I'll go take a look."

"I'm going in," Chad said as he opened the screen door and stepped inside. Pierce followed.

They wandered through the downstairs, finding the rooms unoccupied. "Reckon I'll check on Ed," Chad said, looking as though climbing those stairs was the very last thing he wanted to do. He felt an odd prickling at the back of his neck. Usually more practical than fanciful, Chad couldn't quell the premonition that something disastrous waited for him.

Shaking his head to clear it of the dark thoughts swirling inside him, Chad paused at the foot of the stairs. "I'm going up," he said to Pierce. "Give me a few minutes alone with Ed, then come on up."

Pierce watched Chad walk up the staircase. He could tell by the set of his shoulders that his brother's nerves were stretched taut. Something was wrong; Pierce could feel it in his bones, smell it in the air. He began to pace, wondering how much time he should allow before following Chad.

From previous visits he'd made to Ed Doolittle's sickroom, Chad knew where to find it. Ed's door was ajar and he peered inside. The old man appeared to be sleeping soundly. Chad stood in the doorway, watching Ed's thin chest rise and fall with each shallow breath he took. The steady cadence reassured Chad and he tiptoed from the room, intending to join Pierce downstairs and wait until Ed awakened. As he passed a closed door at the top of the stairs, he heard noises coming from inside. Grunts, sobs, garbled phrases he couldn't understand. He paused with his hand on the doorknob, recognizing the sounds but not wanting to believe them.

Pierce continued to pace the narrow space at the foot of the stairs until curiosity got the best of him. Muttering an oath, he started up the stairs. Suddenly the screen door behind him banged shut and Pierce spun around.

"Pierce Delaney, what in the hell are you doing here?"

Pierce's eyes narrowed; he was surprised to see Riley Reed. "I might ask the same of you."

"Hal didn't come to town today. He owes me money. Thought I'd ride out here and collect it."

"Hal isn't home. No one appears to be home," Pierce said. "Chad is upstairs talking to Ed. I'm on my way to join him."

"If Hal isn't home, where in the hell is he?" Reed wondered, clearly upset over Hal's failure to pay his debt. "He promised to pay up today."

"I don't know and I don't care," Pierce muttered, continuing up the stairs. Reed followed.

Chad turned the doorknob slowly and

pushed the panel inward. It opened on silent hinges. A scene straight from the darkest hell stopped him in his tracks.

Hal Doolittle's naked rump rose and fell as he vigorously pumped away into his sister's swollen body. Chad could see Cora Lee's protruding belly quiver and hear her tiny sobs as she tried to push Hal off her.

"You're going to hurt the baby, Hal," Cora Lee said in a small voice that was barely discernible over her brother's coarse grunting.

"It's all your fault, Cora Lee," Hal said between gasps. "You weren't supposed to grow a baby. You went and ruined everything. We could have kept on doing this for a long time without anyone the wiser."

Chad exploded with rage. He wasn't easily shocked, but what Hal was doing was obscene. "My God! Your own sister! You rotten, rutting bastard!"

"What!" Hal lifted his head and glared at Chad over his shoulder. "What are you doing here? How dare you interrupt a private moment between brother and sister."

"Get off her," Chad ordered. He was deadly calm now, his voice hard, his eyes glittering dangerously.

"I can see you're going to be trouble in the future," Hal said ominously. "I don't like trouble, Delaney."

He was fast, so fast Chad almost didn't see him reach for his gun on the nightstand. But Chad was faster. Hal swung around and aimed at Chad. Chad drew his own weapon and fired before the bullet left Hal's gun. Hal fell sideways, rolling off the bed and onto the floor, blood streaming from the hole in his forehead. As they stood on the landing behind Chad, witnessing the whole sordid affair, the gunfire released Pierce and Reed from their frozen stance.

Wild-eyed with shock, Cora Lee sat up in bed and screamed as Pierce pushed past Chad to check Hal for a heartbeat. She screamed even louder when Pierce shook his head and said, "He's dead."

Zoey, having searched the garden and barn without finding Cora Lee, had returned to the house. She'd heard the gunshot and taken the stairs two at a time. She came to a skidding halt when she saw Pierce and Chad leaning over a dead man in Cora Lee's bedroom, and a naked Cora Lee sitting up in bed screaming.

"What happened?" Zoey asked as she took a closer look at the body on the floor and recognized Hal Doolittle.

Riley Reed came up behind her. "Hal Doolittle was rutting with his own sister.

Chad caught them in the act. I seen it all."

"See if you can quiet Cora Lee, Zoey," Pierce said as he led Chad aside to talk to him.

Zoey hurried to Cora Lee's side, tossing a sheet over her and attempting to help her up from the bed, while Pierce spoke earnestly to Chad. Zoey thought Chad looked dreadful. His complexion had turned pasty and he looked as if he wanted to spew out his guts. Whatever Pierce was saying to him didn't seem to register; Chad kept shaking his head.

Suddenly Cora Lee cried out and doubled over, clutching her stomach.

"Cora Lee, what is it?" Zoey asked anxiously.

"Something's happening! It's too early." Moaning, she rolled from side to side as if trying to ease the pain.

Zoey had no idea what to do. She'd seen animals give birth, but never a human. Then she spied a wide red stain pooling beneath Cora Lee, and panicked.

"Pierce! Come quick!"

Pierce was beside her in two strides. "What is it?"

"It's Cora Lee. I think she's in trouble." She pointed to Cora Lee's bloodstained sheets.

Pierce dragged her aside, where Cora

Lee couldn't hear them speaking. "Do you know what to do?"

Zoey shook her head. "If it was a simple birth, maybe, but this is serious. I've never seen so much blood. Cora Lee's as white as a sheet. Someone better ride into town for the doctor."

"Is she going to die?" Chad asked dully. He appeared to be in shock. "Am I going to be responsible for her death, too?"

"You're not responsible for a damn thing, Chad," Pierce snarled.

A commotion near the bedroom door turned their gazes in that direction.

"Holy shit!" Reed said on a sudden intake of breath. "It's old man Doolittle."

Ed Doolittle, having heard the shot and screaming that followed, had crawled from his bed and hobbled down the hall to Cora Lee's bedroom. Though his eyes were dimmed from age and illness, he saw the body of his son lying on the floor in a pool of blood, and his daughter writhing on her bed, her face contorted with pain.

"Hal!" he gasped, clutching his chest as he tottered into the room. "Is he dead?"

Pierce stepped forward to steady the old man. "I'm sorry, Ed." He would have given anything not to have to tell the old man what had taken place in this room.

"Dead," Ed repeated, hearing his worst fears confirmed. Then his eyes rolled back in his head, the breath rattled in his throat, and he collapsed in Pierce's arms. Pierce lowered him to the floor beside his son as the old man breathed his last.

"He's gone," Pierce said tonelessly.

"Papa!" Cora Lee screamed. Then she doubled over, seized by another pain. "I'm going to die, just like Papa and Hal."

"You're not going to die, Cora Lee," Pierce soothed, exchanging a look with Zoey that belied his words.

"Someone should go to town for a doctor," Zoey said shakily.

"No time," Pierce replied. Suddenly he remembered that Reed was still here. "The Zigler ranch is not far. Mrs. Zigler has borne several children, she'll know what to do. Get her, Reed. And hurry."

Reed looked as if he wanted to refuse, but Pierce's fierce scowl convinced him otherwise. He left immediately.

"Try to keep her calm," Pierce told Zoey as he returned to his brother's side. Truth to tell, he was damn worried about Chad. His brother appeared to be in a state of shock as he stared at the corpses of the Doolittle father and son. He gave Chad a rough shake. "Snap out of it, Chad! Ed was on his deathbed. He couldn't have lasted much longer."

Chad looked at Pierce through hollow eyes. "Nothing will ever be the same for me, Pierce. The Chad Delaney you knew no longer exists. My life has been torn apart."

Pierce cursed beneath his breath. The situation had gotten completely out of control. Chad wasn't thinking clearly, and Cora Lee's moans were growing weaker, adding to Chad's distress. If she died, Chad would hold himself responsible for the tragic deaths of so many people, even though he was blameless. What a tangle.

"Reed will return with Mrs. Zigler soon. Help me get these bodies out of here," Pierce said, forcing Chad to move despite his apathy. "Take Hal's feet. We'll put him and then Ed in another room."

Chad and Pierce moved the Doolittle father and son into the older man's bedroom and closed the door. When they returned to Cora Lee's room, they could tell by Zoey's expression that the situation was growing desperate.

"She's unconscious. I don't think she'll make it."

The sound of footsteps pounding up the stairs brought a collective sigh of relief. Seconds later Mrs. Zigler burst into the

332

room, took one look at Cora Lee, and began issuing orders. "Bring hot water and plenty of towels! The rest of you get out of here, except for the woman. I'll need her."

She was obeyed instantly. Stern of countenance, tall and thin, her hair skinned back on her small head, Naomi Zigler looked capable of handling any situation.

After putting a kettle on to boil, the three men sat down at the kitchen table to wait. The uneasy silence was broken when Reed said, "I never would have thought it of Hal. I'm not a prudish man, or even a squeamish one, but there is something sickening about using your own sister as your whore."

Chad's expression didn't change. He was totally immersed in the dark abyss of misery.

"You saw what happened, Reed," Pierce said, challenging Reed to deny it. "Chad's not to blame for what happened. Hal drew his gun on Chad; Chad was faster. What followed was tragic but accidental."

Reed was silent a long time, staring glumly at Pierce. Pierce could tell Reed begrudged having to agree with him on anything. Fortunately, the sight of Hal humping his own sister had obviously disgusted Reed so thoroughly, he was forced to agree.

"Yeah, as much as it wounds me to agree with a Delaney, none of what happened here was Chad's fault."

They looked up as Zoey walked into the kitchen to fetch the kettle of hot water.

"What's happening?" Pierce asked.

Zoey swallowed hard and shook her head. "It's bad." Then she turned and hurried upstairs, leaving the men to wait and worry.

Cora Lee's body had expelled the dead fetus, but she still continued to bleed profusely. Mrs. Zigler had tried packing her with towels, but nothing seemed to help. Zoey feared for Chad's sanity if Cora Lee died too. Not that Chad loved Cora Lee, but Zoey knew guilt over these senseless deaths was nearly killing him.

Pierce found coffee on the stove and poured them each a mug. It tasted like mud, but Pierce welcomed the bitterness; for Chad's sake he needed to keep a clear head. No matter what happened, Chad would need him when this was over. Delaneys always stuck together.

Chad merely stared into his cup, bile rising in his throat. Nothing would ever taste good to him again. He wanted to get on his horse and ride. Ride away from the ranch, away from the tragedy he'd witnessed today, and away from everything and everyone that reminded him of Dry Gulch and the Doolittles. One might say that today he'd lost his innocence, though Lord knew he was far from innocent. What a naive, arrogant man he had been. What a foolish, noble fool! Never again, he vowed. Never again would he act the gullible fool. He'd always suspected the Devil really existed, and today he'd witnessed his evil. Though not entirely her doing, Cora Lee had committed an unpardonable sin with her own brother. He'd never again underestimate a woman, Chad vowed. Or a man, for that matter. If he could, he'd live his life as a hermit.

Time passed. When Zoey returned to the kitchen, her face was pale and drawn. Pierce leaped from his chair. "How is she?"

"She's dead," Zoey said, more shaken than she cared to admit. She and Cora Lee weren't friends, and she didn't condone the horrible sin she had committed with her own brother, but the life of an innocent child had been lost. The loss had hit Zoey hard, for she suspected she carried Pierce's child and would die if anything happened to it.

Reed pushed his hat to the back of his head and cleared his throat. "I reckon I'll get on back to town. Don't look like Hal is gonna repay his debt to me." He made a sweeping motion with his hand. "This all belongs to Chad now. He's Cora Lee's legal husband and the only survivor, far as I know. I'll stop by the undertaker and have him bring out three pine boxes. When's the funeral?"

"Tomorrow," Pierce said when Chad appeared beyond speech. "I'd advise you to keep what you saw here today under your hat. Contact the preacher, ask him to be here at two o'clock tomorrow to conduct the funeral."

Reed sent Pierce a mutinous look. "I don't like you, Delaney. Never did. Don't like your brothers, either. People are gonna wonder what happened here today, and I'm gonna tell them. The truth might be humiliating to Chad, but that's the breaks. He got a ranch out of the bargain. That's more than he deserves."

Chad looked up at Reed through eyes as cold and bitter as sin. "I want nothing to do with the Doolittle ranch. I never want to hear that name again."

Reed sent Chad a mocking grin. "Too bad. It's yours now." Turning on his heel, he left through the back door, slamming it behind him.

"Reed is right in that respect," Pierce contended. "The ranch is yours now."

Chad's green eyes burned with unholy light. "Didn't you hear me? I don't want it! Sell it, burn it down, do whatever you please with it. I won't be around, whatever you do."

"What the hell does that mean?"

"I'm leaving."

"Leaving? Where will you go?"

"Anywhere, as long as it's far away from here."

"You're not thinking straight, Chad. None of this is your fault."

"Isn't it? I killed Hal, and that makes me responsible for everything that happened after that."

Pierce knew he couldn't stop Chad from leaving, and it made him mad as hell. From the corner of his eye he saw Zoey standing in the doorway. He turned and faced her squarely, his anger palpable.

"Are you satisfied now?" he charged. "No woman is worth the kind of anguish my brother is suffering now."

His expression was so fierce, Zoey recoiled in horror. His rejection struck her like a physical blow. She knew he spoke from concern for his brother, but that didn't make the hurt any less intense. She was a woman, thus he despised her. Cora Lee and her despicable brother had hatched this plot against the Delaneys, but Pierce was making her take the brunt of his hatred. He blamed her for meddling in his life. Everything that had happened from the day of their wedding to this tragic event was the direct result of their forced marriage.

"I don't want to intrude on your privacy, but I thought you'd like to hear what Cora Lee told me before she died," Zoey mumbled.

Pierce preferred not to listen, but realized it was something that had to be brought into the open. "Very well, what did she tell you?"

"She said the baby she carried belonged to her brother. That they had been . . . been intimate since she was fourteen. When she conceived, Hal told her to get you into bed and convince you that the baby belonged to you. When that didn't work, Hal became enraged and beat Cora Lee. She was so frightened of him that when he suggested Cora Lee blame Pierce for the beating, she went along with him. If you need a witness, Mrs. Zigler heard everything and can verify Cora Lee's dying words." She turned away. "Oh, one more thing," she threw over her shoulder. "Cora Lee said she's sorry. Good-bye, Pierce."

Pierce laughed harshly, her good-bye all but lost on him. "Sorry! What good does that do now?" He didn't try to stop Zoey when she left the kitchen. He was still upset over Chad's decision to leave. Whatever was between him and Zoey could be settled later, after he had time to cool down. At this moment he regretted his marriage to Zoey more than he'd regretted anything in his life. Unfortunately, for the majority of men, women were a necessary evil. There were times when his need for Zoey was obsessive. When that happened he felt as if he'd compromised everything he knew and believed in.

"Aren't you going after her?" Chad asked when Pierce made no move to follow Zoey. "You know you don't want her to leave."

"She's not leaving," Pierce said. "I'll see her back at the house. Someone has to wait for the undertaker. Go on home, Chad. I'll take care of things here."

"I'm not going home, Pierce." Chad's calmness betrayed nothing of the turmoil roiling inside him. "I'm leaving . . . now. Tell Ryan good-bye for me."

"You can't do this!" Pierce shouted, desperate to change Chad's mind.

"Good-bye, Pierce."

Chad slammed out the door; Pierce followed. "When will you be back?"

"Maybe never. Don't you understand? I killed four people. It's going to be damn hard to live with myself after today. I'm going to ride as hard and far as I can."

He mounted up.

"Chad, wait! Don't go like this. Stick around. You're bound to feel different tomorrow."

Chad gave Pierce a look that made his blood congeal. "I'm not the same man who arrived here a few hours ago. I'm a killer of women and babies."

Before Pierce could form a reply, Chad dug his heels into his mount and thundered off, raising a cloud of dust behind him.

Zoey left the Doolittle ranch, her heart aching. She knew what she had to do. Pierce didn't want her, could barely stand the sight of her. He had no need of a wife, and she'd known it from the beginning. She never expected to fall in love with the stranger who had appeared in her root cellar, clinging to life by a slim thread. She had forced the marriage between them, and now must pay the consequences for her rash act. Pierce had too many things to contend with now; he didn't need her around to reinforce his low opinion of women.

When she reached the Delaney ranch, Ryan came out of the barn to meet Zoey. He waited for her to dismount before asking, "Where are Chad and Pierce? They should have returned hours ago. What happened at the Doolittles'?"

Zoey hated to be the bearer of tragic news, but there was no help for it. Ryan had to be told about the tragedy that had taken place at the Doolittle ranch.

"The worst thing imaginable happened, Ryan." Then she proceeded to tell him everything that had taken place as succinctly as possible. By the time she finished, Ryan's face was ashen and he appeared visibly shaken.

"My God! Poor Chad."

"There's more," Zoey said. "Chad's leaving. He's upset and devastated and not thinking clearly. He's taking full responsibility for all four deaths."

"Maybe I can change his mind," Ryan said as he hurried away. "I'm going to the Rocking D."

"Ryan, tell Pierce good-bye for me, will you?"

"Sure," Ryan agreed, absently.

Zoey watched as he stopped to speak briefly to one of the hands before riding off. She fervently prayed he wasn't too late to stop Chad from ruining his life. When Ryan had ridden out of sight, she headed toward the house. She couldn't remain here. Not now, not the way Pierce felt about her. It was time she went home to the Circle F.

A handful of neighbors showed up the following day for the funeral. All three Doolittles were buried in a plot behind the house. If people thought it strange that Cora Lee's husband wasn't present, no one mentioned it. After the preacher prayed over the pine boxes, no one returned to the house for refreshments, which was the usual custom. They drifted back to their homes, and the preacher returned to town immediately. Only Otto Zigler and his wife remained to speak with Pierce.

"What does Chad intend to do with the ranch?" Otto asked, gripping his hat in his sweaty hands.

"Sell it, I suppose," Pierce said. He didn't care what happened to the place. He hadn't been home since the deaths and was anxious to leave this accursed place.

Otto cleared his throat. "I'd like to lease it. I know the land and ranch house have been neglected since Ed fell ill, but I have several sons, any one of whom can work the land and make it productive again. I'm not rich, you understand, but perhaps we can work something out."

"Come see me in a few days, Otto, and we'll discuss it. Chad gave me permission to handle things in his absence."

The Ziglers left a few minutes later. Ryan approached, leading both his horse and Pierce's. "Let's go home, Pierce. Maybe Chad changed his mind and is waiting for us at the ranch."

Pierce shook his head. "That won't happen, Ryan. You didn't see Chad. He was profoundly shaken by what had taken place here."

"I wish I'd gotten here in time. Maybe I could have changed his mind."

"There's nothing you could have done. All we can do now is pray that he comes to his senses soon. I hate to think of him wandering around the country in the frame of mind he's in." He sighed regretfully. "I couldn't reach him, Ryan."

They rode home in silence. When they reached the ranch, Pierce's thoughts turned to Zoey. Vaguely he wondered why she hadn't shown up for the funeral. Not that he blamed her. The funeral had been an ordeal from start to finish. Throughout the brief service Pierce could sense the unspoken questions hanging in the air, the accusatory looks, the curious stares.

They rode into the barn. One of the hands came up and took their mounts. From the corner of his eye Pierce noted an empty stall, and something cold slid down his spine. "Where's Zoey's horse?"

The hand, Rick Bowman, shrugged his shoulders. "She lit out of here yesterday, boss."

Pierce went still. "She left? Did you see in which direction she rode?"

"No, can't say as I noticed. Maybe she went into town. I figured she was going to join you and Ryan at the Doolittles'. Terrible thing," Bowman said, shaking his head. "Ryan told me what happened before he left yesterday."

"A real tragedy," Pierce agreed. "Did you notice if my wife's saddlebags were packed when she left?"

"Sorry, boss, can't rightly say." Having nothing more to add, he walked away.

"Wait a minute!" Ryan said, slapping his forehead. "In all the excitement I forgot. I don't know if it means anything, but Zoey told me to tell you good-bye."

Pierce was more shaken than he let on, and couldn't understand why. He hadn't made a secret of the fact that he didn't want a wife. Everyone knew he wasn't a marrying man. What happened at the Doolittle ranch had been a grim reminder of the trouble women could bring into a man's life. It was inevitable that he and Zoey would part one day. He had neither the time nor the inclination to complicate his life with a permanent relationship. Without Chad pulling his weight with the chores, the ranch needed him, and that was what was important to him now. When Chad returned . . . if he returned . . . he would need the support of both his brothers, and Pierce intended to be here for him.

"Sorry I didn't tell you sooner, Pierce," Ryan continued, "but I was so worried about Chad, I couldn't think straight."

"It's all right, Ryan. I knew Zoey was going to leave. It's not as if this comes as a surprise."

"Go after her, Pierce."

Pierce shook his head. "No, this is what Zoey wants. Her land and ranch mean as much to her as our land means to us."

"She loves you. She confessed as much

to both me and Chad."

Pierce gave a derisive laugh. "Love? It doesn't exist. Zoey used me. We used one another. She saved my life, and in return I made it possible for her to keep her land."

"Don't tell me she wasn't a real wife to you, because I don't believe that. I heard the noises coming from your room."

Pierce flushed. "I don't deny it. That's the only part of our marriage that was real."

"Look, Pierce, you know I'd never try to tell you what to do, and Lord knows I'm never going to be saddled with a wife myself, but dammit, man, I think you should go after Zoey. What if the 'real' part of your marriage produces a child?"

A coldness crept over Pierce. "Did Zoey tell you there was going to be a child?"

"No, but it's a possibility, isn't it?"

"I reckon," Pierce admitted. "I wasn't as careful as I should have been. I'm going up to my room. I'm beat."

A child, Pierce reflected as he lay on his bed, staring at the ceiling. Was it possible? Would Zoey leave him if she was carrying his child?

Chapter 15

Zoey swayed in her saddle as she rode through the entrance to the Circle F. She was exhausted, dirty, and depressed. Fortunately, she had encountered no problems on the trip. She had sought cover in a fringe of trees a short distance from the road and passed an uneasy night. Not wanting to attract attention, she had eschewed a fire, munched on dry biscuits and cheese she had taken from the Delaney kitchen, curled up in her blanket, and tried not to think of Pierce.

She would never forget the way Pierce had looked at her that tragic day at the Doolittles'. That one feral look spoke volumes about his feelings. He didn't want her, didn't want any wife. The least she could do was honor his wishes and leave.

Zoey spied Cully working near the corral and hailed him. Cully saw her, gave a whoop, and trotted over to meet her. He appeared upset, and a frisson of fear slid down her spine. *What now?* she wondered, hoping nothing had gone wrong with the cattle drive.

"Miz Zoey, thank God you're home! Is Delaney with you? They didn't hang him, did they? We heard all about it when we returned from the fort. It was the talk of the town for days."

Zoey dismounted. "I'm alone," she said crisply. "Pierce is well. He's been cleared of all charges. Was the cattle drive successful? Was the army pleased with the delivery?"

Cully nodded. "Got them there in good shape. Me and the boys spent the night at the fort and started for home the next morning. We weren't expecting trouble."

Zoey shivered. Days were getting cooler now and a cold wind blew down from the mountains. But it was Cully's expression that both chilled and frightened her.

"Come inside where it's warm and I'll explain everything. You look plum beat. I can't believe your husband let you travel all this way by yourself."

Cully put the coffeepot on to boil while Zoey dropped down into the nearest chair. "I am beat, Cully. These past weeks have been exhausting. You can't imagine the things that went on in Dry Gulch. I'll explain after you tell me what's wrong. I know you, Cully, and something tells me I'm not going to like what you're going to say."

"You're right," Cully said, easing his spare frame into the chair across from Zoey. "We were robbed on the way home from the fort. A dozen masked men attacked us one night after we'd bedded down. We were overpowered before we even knew they were in our camp. Took every last dime the army paid for the steers, and then some. Stole my watch and other valuables me and the boys had on us. Weren't much, but it's all we had."

Zoey stared at Cully; she was absolutely horrified. "Stolen? Everything? Oh, God." She dropped her head in her hands and sobbed. This on top of everything else was just too much. With the taxes due this fall and no money with which to pay them, the Circle F was no better off than it had been before Pierce had arrived and changed their fortune.

"This was Willoughby's doing!" Zoey blasted. "That man just won't give up. Whatever are we going to do? There's enough money in the bank to pay the hands, thank God. But what then?"

"Winter's coming on," Cully said. "We won't need help till spring, when the cows start calving and we rebuild our herd."

Zoey gave a harsh laugh. "How are we going to buy feed and supplies for the winter and pay the taxes?"

"Ask Delaney for money," Cully suggested. "He'd help, I know he would."

Zoey sighed wearily. "Pierce and I are no longer married. The divorce decree is with Pierce. Once the judge signs it, it's all over. I suspect I'm already a divorced woman. Pierce doesn't owe me a thing. He upheld his part of our arrangement. More than upheld it, and we all know it. He earned his freedom."

"But he don't know about this, Miz Zoey. I could go to Dry Gulch, explain —"

"No! Pierce is no longer responsible for me or my problems. He has enough problems of his own."

"I ain't prying, but it might help if you told me about it, Miz Zoey."

"It's . . . difficult to explain, but I'll try. After they took Pierce away, I followed. I feared the vigilantes would hang him before he reached Dry Gulch. As it turned out, I was right. When I caught up with them, the rope was already around Pierce's neck."

Cully gave a low whistle. "How did you stop the lynching? Did Pierce do all them things he was accused of?"

"No, Pierce was innocent of all charges. I never doubted it for a minute. I was able to interrupt the lynching long enough for his brothers and the hands from the Delaney ranch to stop it. Pierce did spend a few days in jail before things took a turn none of us expected."

Her voice faltered; she girded herself for the retelling of the tragedy that followed.

"You might as well tell me everything," Cully said, giving her hand a sympathetic pat.

Swallowing the lump in her throat, Zoey took a deep breath and related the events that led to the deaths of the entire Doolittle family. She held nothing back, even revealing how Pierce had looked at her after Chad left. When she finished, her mouth was so dry it felt as if she were talking around cotton. Cully poured her a cup of coffee and she gulped it down, welcoming the burning trail it left in her mouth.

"That's some story," Cully said, shaking his head in commiseration. "Can't rightly say I blame Pierce for being upset. You should have stuck around, given him time to work through this. I could of sworn he cared for you."

He started to say something else, then flushed and looked away.

"Go ahead and say it, Cully. You're more like a father to me than a hired hand. You know me better than anyone alive."

"It ain't my place."

"You were going to say that Pierce and I shared a bed," Zoey said, sparing herself nothing. "Pierce didn't take advantage of me, if that's what you're thinking. It's true he tried to seduce me, but I was willing to be seduced. I don't regret a thing."

"I reckon he'd help if you were to ask him," Cully suggested hopefully.

"I . . . can't. We'll just have to let the hands go for the winter and get by as best we can. As for the taxes, I'll borrow the money from the bank."

Cully looked aghast. "From Willoughby's bank?"

"Is there another bank in town?"

"You know right well there ain't."

"I still have the confession Willoughby wrote. He won't dare refuse to loan me the money I need."

"We'll see," Cully muttered. He didn't trust Willoughby any farther than he could toss him.

Zoey rose tiredly. "I'd appreciate it if you'd put some water on the stove to boil. I

352

need to soak in a hot tub and think. I'll wait until I have my wits about me before going to town to apply for a loan."

Cully nodded and left the kitchen. It was a damn shame Pierce and Zoey were no longer a couple, he mumbled to himself. They suited each other so well. But more to the point, Zoey needed Pierce.

Dry Gulch

Pierce threw himself into his work, prowling around the ranch like a caged tiger. Angry, edgy, spoiling for a fight. The hands made sure they kept their distance, skirting around him on tiptoes, so to speak.

Pierce blamed his glum mood on Chad's continued absence, but Ryan and the hands knew better. Arising at dawn, Pierce drove himself relentlessly until dusk. He took supper with Ryan and retired early. Ryan was so disgusted by Pierce's short temper and taciturn manner that he accused Pierce of alienating everyone on the ranch.

"Go to town and get yourself a woman," Ryan suggested after he'd taken all he could of Pierce's foul temper. "Dinah down at the saloon always had a soft spot for you. Take her to bed, work out your frustrations. Brooding isn't going to bring Chad back. And it won't make you miss Zoey any less."

Pierce's head shot up. "Who says I miss Zoey?"

"I do!" Ryan shot back. "Don't deny it, brother. I know you too well."

"You don't know me at all. A wife is the last thing I need right now. As for bedding a woman, you might have something there. If I recall, Dinah is obliging as well as accomplished. Want to come to town with me tonight?"

Ryan gave him a cocky grin. "Sure! Just like old times. There's a girl named Tess working for Jake I'd like to get to know better. While we're there, maybe we can find a fight."

They parted company. Ryan headed to the barn, and Pierce to the corral to break a horse. He decided the hands would like him better if he took his frustrations out on an animal. He was half out of his mind with worry and couldn't help his dark mood. Where was Chad now? Pierce wondered. Was he in trouble? In need of money? Hungry?

But mostly he couldn't stop thinking

about Zoey. Had she reached the Circle F without mishap? Did she miss him? Was she happy to be home? There were so many questions and so few answers where Zoey was concerned. He'd never forget the first time he saw her, dressed in denim pants and flannel shirt. Her taut little bottom and bouncing breasts had enticed and beguiled him. He had set out to seduce her and succeeded beyond his wildest dreams. Once stripped of her virginity, Zoey had turned to living flame in his arms.

One by one he withdrew his private memories, examining each treasure jealously before sending it back into the dark recesses of his mind where he could draw on them whenever he dared to remember. He groaned aloud, then looked around sheepishly to see if anyone had heard. Ryan was right, he decided, a woman was exactly what he needed.

Pierce glanced out over the corral fence and saw a horse and buggy coming down the road. The driver of the rig saw Pierce and swung around in his direction. Pierce waved to Warren Chambers, his lawyer, and waited with no small amount of curiosity.

"Howdy, Pierce," Chambers said as he

pulled up and climbed down from the buggy. "You didn't come to town to see me, so I came out here to see you."

Pierce gave him a puzzled look. "Did we have an appointment?"

"Not exactly. Judge Walters arrived in town the day before yesterday, and he's agreed to see us tomorrow at two o'clock."

"For what reason?" Pierce asked, still clueless. "Are there still charges pending against me? I thought that was all cleared up."

Chambers reached into the buggy and pulled a sheaf of papers from a portfolio he'd left on the seat. "No, no, nothing like that. It's about your divorce. The papers are all drawn up and awaiting your signature." He handed them to Pierce. "Just see that they're signed before you appear before the judge tomorrow. Given the circumstances of your marriage, there should be no difficulty. Tell the judge the truth. Your wife already explained it all to me."

Dumbfounded, Pierce merely stared at Chambers.

"Is something wrong, Pierce? This is what you wanted, isn't it?"

Pierce's mouth snapped shut. "Of course it's what I want. You just took me by surprise. My wife left several days ago, and with Chad gone, the work has piled up. I've had damn little time to think of the future. What did Zoey say?"

"Read the divorce decree. I think you'll find everything in order. Your wife was surprisingly candid. See you tomorrow. The judge is holding court in the new courthouse on Second Street."

"I know where it is."

Chambers climbed back into the buggy and picked up the reins. "Oh, by the way, Chad stopped by before he left town and signed a power of attorney so you can conduct business on his behalf during his absence."

Pierce was stunned. He didn't think Chad was thinking all that clearly when he lit out of town. "Thanks for telling me. How did Chad look to you?"

"Upset, but who can blame him? I wouldn't worry about Chad. He's got a good head on his shoulders."

"Is it true that the Doolittle ranch belongs to Chad now?" Pierce asked.

"To my knowledge, the Doolittles had no relatives. None have stepped forward yet. I was told that Cora Lee was the last to die. Chad was her legal husband at the time, so it would seem the ranch belongs to Chad."

"Since Chad gave me power of attorney, I'd like to lease the ranch to Otto Zigler for the time being. Chad gave me permission to handle the property in any way I thought best. Will you draw up the papers?"

"Sure thing, Pierce. I'd best be getting along. See you in town tomorrow."

"Yeah," Pierce muttered, scowling at the divorce document as if he expected it to bite him. "Tomorrow."

Pierce and Ryan rode into town right after supper that night. They ambled into Jake's Saloon and looked around, spoiling for trouble. The fierce look on Pierce's face gave ample proof of his mood, and most of Jake's customers gave him a wide berth. Few men in Dry Gulch were willing to tangle with the Delaneys when they were in a fighting mood.

"There's Dinah by the bar, Pierce," Ryan said, calling Pierce's attention to a pert redhead with a wide mouth, sharp blue eyes, and a voluptuous figure. "Go on over and talk to her. She's looking at you like she'd like to have you for dinner."

Pierce had little inclination to bed the beautiful whore, but he'd never admit it to Ryan. Though he'd bought Dinah's favors many times in the past and had no complaints, she suddenly looked coarse and unappetizing to him.

"Go on," Ryan urged, giving Pierce a nudge. "I see Tess by the poker table. I hope she's not already engaged for the night." He wandered off to pursue his own interests.

Pierce's feet refused to move in Dinah's direction. Instead, he bellied up to the bar and ordered a whiskey. He gulped it down and motioned for another.

"Trying to tie one on, cowboy?"

Dinah stood at his elbow, smiling up at him in blatant invitation. "You gonna buy me a drink?"

Pierce nodded at the bartender, who poured Dinah a drink. She sipped it, gazing at Pierce through long, feathery lashes.

"How are you, Dinah?"

"How do I look?" She spun on her heel for his benefit, her short skirt swirling around her legs to reveal smooth white thighs.

Pierce gave her a leering grin. "Damn good."

"Haven't seen you around town in a coon's age. Heard you got yourself hitched."

"It was a mistake. Won't be hitched after tomorrow."

Dinah lifted her drink in salute, her eyes sparkling. "Congratulations. Shall we celebrate your freedom up in my room?"

Five girls made their living at Jake's Saloon. All were professional whores who paid a portion of their earnings to Jake for the use of the rooms abovestairs. Dinah and Tess were the most popular because they were still young and attractive. They were also the most expensive. But expense meant nothing to Pierce. He needed to purge Zoey from his system, to prove to himself that Zoey wasn't the only woman who could please him. Why did he need a wife when he could have Dinah any time he wanted her, with none of the responsibility or permanency that went along with marriage?

"Are you free?" Pierce asked.

"I'm always free for you." She took his arm and led him toward the stairs. "You're the best, Pierce. You know how to please a lady."

Pierce tried to summon passion as they ascended the stairs to Dinah's room. God knew he wanted to experience that special rush he'd always felt just thinking about making love to Zoey. Unfortunately it didn't come. He felt dull and listless. To his embarrassment, he remained un-aroused as Dinah slowly stripped and pushed him down onto the bed.

She has a nice body, Pierce thought dis-passionately. Not as good as Zoey's firm young curves, but fully capable of arousing most men. And Dinah was experienced. As she undressed him she used her hands and mouth with expertise and cunning. When Pierce remained unmoved by her ministra-tions, she looked at him curiously.

"What's the matter, Pierce? Have I done something wrong?"

"You've done everything right," Pierce said, removing her hands from his body. "It's just me. I reckon I'm not in the mood. How about another time?"

"Sure, honey, but I don't think that's necessary. Just lie back and let me work on you. I'll have you up and running in no time at all." Her mouth descended on him, her lips ripe and red and willing.

Suddenly Pierce shoved her away. "No! I'm sorry," he said, his tone gentling, "not tonight." He rose from bed and gathered up his clothing. When he was fully dressed he pulled a small wad of bills from his pocket and peeled off a ten-dollar bill. "This should more than cover the time we spent together."

Dinah stared at the money, then at Pierce. "I didn't earn this."

"I want you to have it."

"Thanks." She planted a wet kiss on his lips. "The next time is on me. Come back when you're feeling better. I'll make it up to you."

"Sure, Dinah," Pierce said, anxious now to leave. He couldn't believe what had just happened to him. It had never happened before and it frightened the hell out of him. In the past his body had never failed him. Sometimes a woman's smile was all it took to get a rise out of him.

This was all Zoey's fault, Pierce thought as his mood turned from bad to worse. Maybe after tomorrow, things would change. Once he and Zoey were no longer husband and wife, he could forget she ever existed. He almost laughed out loud at that thought. He would probably remember that phase of his life forever.

Pierce was feeling so disgruntled over his failure with a woman that he marched right over to the bar and ordered another whiskey. And another after that. After several more, his problems no longer seemed significant. What he needed now was a good fight to work off his excess energy.

He found the excuse when the man next to him jostled him, making him spill good whiskey down the front of his vest.

What happened next was inevitable. The fight that ensued soon attracted others, who squared off against one another merely for the pure joy of engaging in fisticuffs. When Ryan came downstairs a few minutes later and saw his brother about to be bashed over the head with a bottle, he eagerly joined the fray. When the time seemed right to duck out, Ryan shoved Pierce through a broken front window.

"What in hell was that all about?" Ryan groused, nursing his scraped knuckles.

Pierce gave a careless shrug. "Felt good. It's been a long time since the Delaney brothers got into a good scrap." His words were slurred as he staggered to his horse.

"You're drunk!" Ryan accused. "Say, what happened upstairs between you and Dinah? Was she already booked for the night?"

"I don't want to talk about it," Pierce growled as he tried to mount his horse. Ryan took note of his clumsy efforts and gave him a boost up.

Ryan shook his head in consternation. "You got it bad, brother. Why don't you just admit it and forget about that divorce?"

"Admit what?" Pierce mumbled. "Are you trying to saddle me with a wife I don't want? Have you forgotten the lesson we learned at Pa's knee? A woman has accomplished what no man had been able to do. She broke up our family. Lord knows where Chad is now, or what kind of trouble he's in."

"I haven't forgotten a damn thing. But I think you ought to consider carefully before signing those divorce papers. There comes a time in every man's life when he has to make a decision that's right for him without outside influence."

"Who in the hell made you my conscience?" Pierce muttered crossly. "I've already made my decision. You don't know what it's like being forced into marriage. I have an appointment with the judge tomorrow at two o'clock, and I aim to keep it."

"Suit yourself, Pierce. If it was me, I'd want to know if my wife was carrying my child."

Pierce had listened to all he cared to on the subject. Digging his heels into his horse's rump, he shot past Ryan and rode hell for leather back to the ranch.

Zoey had been home one week. Most of the hands had already taken their pay and left. Only Cully remained. All had expressed the desire to return in the spring should Zoey need them.

Zoey had put off her visit to Willoughby as long as she could, but now the money situation was pressing. The taxes were due and no money remained in the bank. Winter was coming and she needed to buy feed for the animals and sufficient supplies to last during those days when making the trip to town would be dangerous. Montana winters were hard, with few breaks in the weather to allow for safe travel.

Zoey asked Cully to saddle her horse and bring it around to the front for her. "You want me to go with you, Miz Zoey?"

"No, Cully, that won't be necessary."

"I don't trust that banker, not after the way he tried to cheat you."

"I'll be fine. I still have the confession Willoughby signed in the desk drawer. The contents would make for juicy reading should the newspaper print it. Willoughby's reputation would be ruined once the townspeople read it."

"I reckon you're right," Cully said,

doubtfully. "Do you think he'll give you the loan?"

"I'm sure of it."

Zoey should have known Samson Willoughby wasn't a man to give up easily. The moment she was shown into his office, she realized things weren't going to go as she'd expected.

"Sit down, Zoey. It's good to see you again. I heard you were out of town. Why aren't you wearing widow's weeds?"

"I hate to disappoint you, but Pierce was cleared of all charges. He's still hale and hardy."

"Pity. I got the impression that the vigilantes were eager to lynch your husband. By the way, where *is* Delaney?"

"Back in Dry Gulch, taking care of his ranch."

Willoughby's eyes gleamed. "Oh? Have you separated, then? I didn't expect the marriage to last. I knew immediately Delaney wasn't a marrying man. You lied to me about Delaney being your fiancé of long standing, didn't you? You never intended for your marriage to last, did you? It was just a ploy to thwart me."

"I don't wish to talk about my marriage, Mr. Willoughby. I'd like to apply for a loan. The money I was expecting from the sale of my steers to the army was stolen from Cully and the boys on their way home from the fort."

"Really?" His gaze slid away from hers. "That's a shame. Do they know who did it?"

"No, the men were masked. I need a loan to see me through the winter and pay the taxes. Since yours is the only bank in town . . ."

"So you finally admit to needing me," Willoughby crowed. "A loan, eh? Well, now, why don't you ask Delaney for a loan? Or has he washed his hands of you? Has the marriage been dissolved already?"

"I'm not here to discuss my personal life, Mr. Willoughby. Will your bank give me a loan or won't it? I'd think carefully before answering if I were you. I still have your signed confession in my possession. Making it public could ruin you."

Willoughby smirked. "Confession? Are you certain you still have it?" He opened his drawer, withdrew a sheet of paper, and dangled it before Zoey's eyes. "Is this the confession you're talking about?"

Zoey made a desperate grab for the paper. "How did you get that?" Lord, why hadn't she thought to check to see if it was still in the drawer before approaching Willoughby? How could such a thing happen twice?

He made a show of tearing it into little pieces and letting them drift down to his desk. "You *did* have a confession. You went away and left your house unguarded. It was easy for one of my men to break in and find this incriminating piece of paper." He leaned back in his chair and tented his fingers. "Now, shall we talk about a loan?"

"You corrupt bastard! What is it you want from me?"

"The same thing I've always wanted, my dear. You no longer have a husband to keep me from taking what I want. I know you bedded Delaney, and I don't intend to hold it against you. Virgins are boring. I thanked Delaney for breaking you in for me. You have fire in you, Zoey, and I'm going to explore it fully."

Zoey leaped to her feet. "I'm leaving. I won't listen to this . . . this nonsense. I . . . I still have a husband," she lied.

"Sit down, Zoey," Willoughby said calmly. "You need a loan, don't you? You may as well admit your marriage is over. Is Delaney the one getting the divorce?"

"How did you —"

"I have ways. You're a free woman now,

or will be in a day or two."

"What do you want?"

"Just this. You've already had a man, so you can't be frightened." His gaze flicked over her insultingly. "By now you're probably needing what I can give you, and I'm not just talking about money. Once you've had it, it's sometimes painful to be cut off abruptly."

"What are you suggesting?" Zoey asked evenly.

"What I'm suggesting is that we continue where we left off before Delaney interfered in our lives. Set a date for our wedding and my bank will loan you all the money you need."

Zoey stared at him in disbelief. The gall of the man! "I can go to another town for the loan. Yours isn't the only bank in Montana."

"It is as far as you're concerned. Bankers stick together. All I have to do is wire the bank and tell them you're a bad risk. You need me, Zoey. I won't be a harsh husband, if that's what you're worried about. You know I've always wanted you."

Zoey gave an inelegant snort. "You wanted my land."

"That, too," he admitted. "You've got no choice this time, Zoey. All those stray steers Delaney rounded up to sell to the army were your last hope of hanging on to your ranch. Obviously Delaney doesn't care what happens to you or he wouldn't have let you go so easily. Your marriage *is* over, isn't it?"

"Yes, damn you!" Zoey bit out, though it nearly killed her to do so.

"Then set a date, Zoey. I've always wanted you. I have money. You can rehire your hands, spruce up your house, buy brood cows, do whatever you like. I'm not a bad catch. You could do a lot worse."

Zoey's mind worked furiously. How could she marry Willoughby when she was carrying Pierce's child? What was she to do? Asking Pierce for money was out of the question. She'd already upset his life and didn't have the nerve to turn to him again in her time of need. This time she was well and truly on her own.

"Well, Zoey, what do you say?"

If she agreed, perhaps she could buy precious time to think of a way to hold Willoughby off indefinitely. She needed that loan and saw no other way to get it.

"Very well," Zoey agreed. "Give me the loan I need and I'll set a date for our wedding."

"Done!" Willoughby said, leaping from his chair. "You won't regret it, my dear.

How much do you need?"

"Two thousand dollars," Zoey said without pause. "And I need it today."

"We will be married two weeks from Saturday. I'll arrange everything."

"No! That's too soon. A month. Give me a month."

He raked her with a hungry gaze. "I don't know if I can wait that long."

"A month or the deal's off," Zoey insisted. Surely she'd think of something before then. Lying came easily when her adversary was Samson Willoughby, the king of all liars.

Willoughby gave her a narrow-eyed look. "A month. I'll make the arrangements. I'll ride out to the ranch tomorrow to discuss the details with you. You can have your money today, but I warn you, don't try to double-cross me. I always win. And one more thing. Call me Samson. 'Mr. Willoughby' isn't seemly for one's fiancé."

Zoey bit down hard on the inside of her lip to keep from spewing out hateful words. "Very well, Samson. But it isn't really necessary to come out to the ranch tomorrow."

His eyes gleamed darkly. "Oh, yes it is, Zoey, my dear, very necessary."

Chapter 16

"You what!" Cully shouted, aghast. "Are you loco, Miz Zoey? You can't marry Samson Willoughby."

"I said that I promised to marry him, not that I would," Zoey clarified. "I signed papers and he gave me the money I needed to pay the taxes. That's all I really wanted. I settled the taxes before I left town. That's one less thing to worry about."

"You better worry about Willoughby," Cully warned. "I thought you said he couldn't hurt you as long as you had his signed confession."

"I *did* have it, Cully," Zoey corrected. "I put the confession in the desk drawer and forgot about it. I never figured to leave the ranch quite so suddenly. I was too worried about Pierce to think clearly. I would have hidden the confession in a safe place had I not been in such a hurry. It's entirely my fault, and I have no excuse for leaving such a valuable document where it could be stolen."

"It was stolen?"

"Exactly. The house was left unguarded. Willoughby must have acted as soon as he learned I'd left the ranch. Before you and the hands returned from the fort."

"All the more reason you shouldn't marry a man like Willoughby. He tried to buy the land long before your pa was killed. He even tried to convince your pa to let him marry you. But your pa was a smart man. He knew what Willoughby was after and sent him packing."

"I told you, Cully, I have no intention of marrying Willoughby. I have a month to come up with a plan."

"God help us all if you don't," Cully said, throwing up his hands in dismay.

"Yes, God help us," Zoey concurred as Cully walked away.

Proof that Zoey carried Pierce's child came early the following morning when she got out of bed and promptly lost the contents of her stomach. She was still pale and shaken when she went downstairs to prepare breakfast.

Cully took one look at Zoey and shook his head. "You didn't sleep last night, did you? You look purely awful."

"I'll be fine, Cully, don't worry."

"You need help with the housework. After we lost the money from the sale of the cattle, the Consuelos brothers didn't make that detour to fetch their sister. She would have been a big help with the household chores."

"It's just as well. I wouldn't have been able to pay her." Zoey sighed despondently and grasped Cully's hands. "I don't know what I would do without you, Cully. I've never felt so alone."

"I ain't never leaving, honey. We'll get by, just you wait and see."

Cully had a notion to go to Pierce. He knew Zoey wouldn't like it, but he could see no other solution. Zoey thought she could handle Willoughby, but she was a mere babe in his wicked hands. Having Zoey angry with him was better than letting her ruin her life. He decided to wait and see how things developed, and if he didn't like how they were going, he was definitely going to do something about it.

Smiling smugly, Samson Willoughby approached the Circle F. *Soon,* he thought, as he looked around, enjoying the grand panorama of lush land and snow-topped mountains that would soon be his. The month he'd allowed Zoey was half-over. In two short weeks he'd own every acre of land he'd coveted all these years. And he'd have Zoey, too. This time there was no Pierce Delaney to stop him. His dream had been to own the largest spread in Montana. He'd had his eye on the Circle F long before he'd opened the bank. It was prime acreage, the best in the area. By the time he rode through the front gate, he was picturing cattle, sporting his brand, growing fat on his land.

Zoey had remained close to the house all day, catching up on household chores. She was hanging clothes on the line when Willoughby rode up.

"You won't have to do that after we're married. There will be servants to do the work. And enough hands to make this fertile land profitable," he told Zoey as he dismounted.

"We're not married yet," Zoey muttered. "What brings you out here, Mr. . . . er . . . Samson?"

"You, of course. Shall we go inside? The wind is brisk today. You'll catch pneumonia out here handling wet clothing."

Zoey shrugged. "Someone has to do it."

"I'll send my laundress out to pick up your clothes each week."

"There's no need . . ."

"Of course there is. You're going to be my wife," he said pompously. He took her arm, dragging her away from the clothesline. "Come along inside. The ride out here made my throat dry. I'll bet your pa left some whiskey around somewhere."

Zoey pulled out of his grasp and walked ahead of him. They entered the house, and she showed him into the parlor.

"I'll see about that whiskey."

Willoughby watched her leave, admiring the sway of her shapely hips beneath her denims. *She won't wear pants after we're married,* he thought. No, sir, he was going to be the only one privy to his future wife's charms. It made him angry to think that Delaney had sampled her first, but he'd told the truth when he said he didn't enjoy virgins. Zoey was a woman now, and he intended to savor every nuance of her awakened sexuality.

"I hope you like this brand," Zoey said, returning to the parlor with a bottle and glass. "It's all I have. Pa wasn't a drinking man."

"It will do just fine. Sit down and share it with me."

"I . . . I don't drink." She poured his drink and set both the glass and bottle on the table beside him.

"Just as well." Suddenly Willoughby reached out and pulled her into his lap. Zoey tried to break free, but he was too strong and too determined. "Here's where you belong."

"Please release me."

He laughed. "A man should be allowed some privileges with his fiancée. Why are you so skittish, my dear? I'm not too hard to look at, and I've already said I won't hold your disastrous marriage against you. Accept the inevitable. Once we're married, I'm going to do a lot more than this. In fact," he said, his eyes glowing hungrily, "I don't think I can wait until we're married."

His hands skimmed her shoulders and arms, settling on her rib cage, dangerously close to her breasts. "You have a beautiful body, Zoey. I never realized your breasts were so full and rounded. They don't belong hidden beneath baggy shirts." His hands rose up to cup her breasts, as if weighing them in his palms.

"Stop it!" Zoey was frantic. What would she do if he tried to bed her? Was she strong enough to stop him? Where was Cully when she needed him?

Willoughby's expression hardened into a mask of ugliness. "Don't deny me, my dear. I've waited a long time to possess you."

"So wait a little longer, until we're married." Zoey cajoled. "I'll come to you willingly in less than two weeks. If you took me now, it would be by force."

"Just this once, as a show of good faith. Then I'll contain my passion until after we're wed."

"No! I —"

His mouth slammed down on hers, hard, angry, hungry. Zoey whimpered, but her protests served only to spur his ardor. She was going to be sick, she knew it! She felt gorge rising in her throat, and in another minute she'd —

"Miz Zoey, where are you?"

Willoughby released her mouth but kept his hands possessively on her waist. "Who is that?"

"It's Cully." She leaped off Willoughby's lap, and he let her go. "I'm in the parlor, Cully!"

"Damn you! Why did you call him?"

"He has the run of the house. He'd find me anyway."

"That old bastard's got to go. You don't need a keeper. I want him out of here before our wedding. Is that clear?"

"There you are, Miz Zoey," Cully said,

walking into the parlor. His eyes narrowed when he saw Zoey's flushed face and Willoughby's stiff demeanor. He glared at the banker, his eyes bright with hatred.

"Are you all right, Miz Zoey? The banker ain't bothering you, is he?"

"Mind your own business, old man," Willoughby retorted. "Go on with your chores. You're not needed here."

"Do you want me to go, Miz Zoey?"

"Wait for me outside. I'll be out directly. Mr. Willoughby was just leaving."

Cully left the parlor.

"I wasn't going anywhere, and you know it," Willoughby said, glaring at her. "Except up to your bed, maybe."

"Not until we're married," Zoey insisted.

"I'll not be put off, Zoey. After we're married you'll bed me or else. I'm willing to treat you right, but there are limits to my patience. You don't want to see the vindictive side of me."

"I've already seen it," Zoey muttered, feeling as if time were slipping through her fingers.

Willoughby merely smiled. "The arrangements are all made. The preacher will marry us in church two weeks from last Saturday, at two o'clock in the afternoon. See that you're there on time. I'll stop by again in a day or two. Perhaps you'll be more amenable next time I come calling. And get rid of that saddle tramp before I do it for you."

Willoughby strode out the door, feeling more than a little frustrated. If that old codger hadn't interfered, he would have taken Zoey to bed whether she liked it or not. He was still scowling when he ran into Cully outside.

"Get out of my way, old man. Have you been waiting for me?"

"I ain't going nowhere until I've said my piece, Willoughby. I ain't afeared of you."

"You should be," Willoughby said as he prepared to mount. "Have your say, not that it will make any difference."

"I want you to leave Miz Zoey alone. You've caused her enough grief as it is."

"I'm going to marry Zoey. You're not her pa, you have no say in the matter. I've waited a long time for this."

"It ain't gonna happen. I won't let it."

Willoughby gave a shout of laughter. "You and who else is going to stop me? I could crush you with my bare fists."

"I wouldn't try it," Cully threatened.

"Move, old man," Willoughby said, giving Cully a vicious shove. "I want you off this land before the wedding."

"I don't scare easily," Cully said as Willoughby put his spurs to his mount.

Willoughby fumed all the way back to town. He wasn't going to let an old man with one foot in the grave dictate to him. Cully was too damn protective of Zoey, and Zoey cared about him too much to suit Willoughby. He had to do something about it before Cully went and spoiled everything. He had both Zoey and her land within reach, and nothing was going to ruin his plans now.

Upon reaching town, Willoughby put out the word that he wanted to see Pete Crowley. Pete arrived in Willoughby's office a short time later.

"You wanted to see me, boss?"

"I've got a job for you, Pete. I want you to keep an old man in a safe place for a week or two."

"I can handle that. Who is the old man and where do you want me to keep him?"

"The man is Cully, from the Circle F. There's an old deserted mine east of town with a run-down shack on it. No one ever goes there. Stock the shack with enough supplies to keep him from starving before you lock him in."

"Why not just kill him? He's a worthless

old codger. No one will miss him."

"No one except my future wife. He has to stay alive until after the wedding. Zoey won't marry me if she thinks I've harmed him. After the wedding you can dispatch him to Hades. I'm not going to let Zoey back out of this wedding. If forcing her to comply is the only way to do it, then so be it. She's fond of that old man, she'd do anything to keep him safe, even marry me."

"Smart move, boss." Pete grinned. "Real smart. How soon do you want Cully to drop out of sight?"

"Do whatever it takes to make that old shack escape-proof before you take him out there. You'll be amply paid for keeping the old man out of sight until after the wedding. You can kill him any time after a week from Saturday."

"You can count on me, boss."

A few days later Cully disappeared into thin air. Zoey couldn't find him anywhere. She was worried half out of her mind. It wasn't like Cully to up and leave without checking with her first. He didn't scare easily, so she didn't think he'd taken Willoughby's threat seriously. She couldn't help but think, fearfully, that Willoughby might have had something to do with Cully's disappearance.

To add to Zoey's distress, Samson Willoughby showed up shortly after Cully went missing. Refusing to allow him into the house, Zoey spoke with him on the doorstep.

"That old cowpoke must have taken my advice and lit out of here," Willoughby said. "I didn't see him around when I rode in."

Zoey gave him a baleful look. "You didn't scare Cully. He's around here somewhere."

"I doubt that, my dear. I'm willing to bet he lit out for healthier territory."

Zoey inhaled sharply. "What have you done to Cully?"

"You're fond of that old codger, aren't you? I predict he'll be fine as long as you show up at the church on time."

"You *have* done something to Cully!" Zoey cried. Rage slammed through her. "How dare you! If you've hurt him, I'll . . ."

"You'll what? You're in no position to do anything but what I want."

Never had Zoey felt such hatred for another human being. The urge to pull her gun and shoot Willoughby between the eyes was overwhelming.

"Let Cully go," Zoey demanded.

Willoughby laughed. "In my own good time. Perhaps after the wedding."

"You low-down dirty skunk," Zoey snarled from between clenched teeth.

"I'm just being cautious, my dear. I don't trust you. You already have your bank loan, but I had no assurances that you'll show up for our wedding. Now I do. Clever of me, wasn't it?"

Zoey tried to quell the sinking feeling in the pit of her stomach. She began to realize just how hopeless her situation was. She was trapped, with no one to turn to and nowhere to go. Unless she married Willoughby on the appointed day, he'd harm Cully, and she couldn't let that happen.

"You win, damn you! You can rest assured I'll be at the church on time."

He grasped her arm and turned her toward the house. "I knew you'd see it my way. Shall we go up to your bedroom and find out how compatible we are in bed? I've been looking forward to this for a long time."

Zoey refused to budge, bracing her arms and legs against the doorway as Willoughby tried to steer her into the house. "I'm afraid you'll have to wait a while longer. It . . . it's not the right time."

Willoughby's eyes narrowed dangerously. "What are you saying? It's the right time if I say it is."

"You . . . you don't understand," Zoey stammered. "I . . . It's a woman's thing."

"Do you take me for a fool? You've put me off one time too many." He pulled her against him, claiming her mouth with fierce possession. His kiss was harsh, his tongue demanding as he tried to pry her mouth open.

Summoning all her strength, Zoey pulled from his grasp, shaking in impotent rage as she wiped her mouth with the back of her hand. "I told you the truth! It's not the right time. If you want me to come to you willingly, you have to wait until we're married."

"Little bitch!" Willoughby cursed, shoving her violently away. "Have it your way . . . for now. But once we're wed you'll spread your legs for me whenever I want you, and I'll expect you to comply with my wishes. You'll be the kind of wife an important man like myself demands. You'll wear dresses and act the proper lady. You'll give tea parties to entertain my friends and bear my children willingly.

"I'll do whatever it takes to make you

docile, even if it means putting a child in your belly every year." He grinned, eyeing her with relish. "Keeping you pregnant is a chore I'm going to enjoy."

He kissed her on the lips again, hard, then turned and strode away.

"Don't you dare hurt Cully," Zoey hissed after him.

"Just show up on time to the church," Willoughby returned over his shoulder. "You'll have to take my word that he's alive and well, for you'll not see him until after the ceremony."

Zoey caught hold of the porch railing to keep from collapsing as Willoughby rode away. He had won, she thought disconsolately. There was nothing more she could do now to keep from marrying the greedy banker. She had to endure his mouth and hands on her and somehow survive being bedded by a man she despised. For Cully's sake she'd do whatever was required of her.

Her hands spanned her still flat stomach as she shed silent tears for her unborn child. Pierce's child. Vaguely she wondered if things might have turned out differently had she told Pierce she suspected she carried his child. She supposed nothing would have changed. Pierce never wanted a wife, and a child would only complicate his life and make him hate her for tying him down even more. By now Pierce had obtained his divorce and forgotten all about her. Had he wanted her, he would have come after her long before now.

Frustrated beyond human endurance, Zoey feared there was no way out of this marriage to Samson Willoughby. But once she knew for sure that Cully was free, Willoughby wouldn't find her the obliging wife he expected. She would have to find a way to escape before Willoughby found out she carried Pierce's child.

Cully groaned and opened his eyes. The last thing he remembered was walking into the bunkhouse, then his head exploded and everything went black. He slowly pushed himself upright, holding his head until the world stopped spinning. When he finally felt strong enough to open his eyes, he saw nothing familiar. He was sitting on a bunk inside a small, dark room whose only light seeped in from between the cracks of the boarded window and from underneath the door.

Staggering to his feet, he went to the door and tried the latch. Locked. Mustering his strength, he pounded on the door until he heard a voice on the other side advising him to stop.

"Where am I?" Cully asked through the panel.

"None of your business. You're still alive, ain't ya? There's food and water, all the comforts of home. I'll bring more when that runs out."

Cully recognized the voice of his captor. "Pete? Is that you? What's going on? Let me out."

"You ain't going nowhere, Cully. Not until the boss says so."

"You're working for Willoughby! Damn your soul! He better not hurt Miz Zoey."

Pete gave a nasty laugh. "Don't worry about the woman, worry about your own future. Willoughby is gonna take good care of Zoey Fuller."

Cully cursed long and fluently as he turned back to the bunk to take stock of his surroundings and to think. His prison was an ancient one-room shack that had been hastily repaired to keep him from escaping. A bare bunk, a lopsided table, and two rickety chairs were the only furnishings. A sack of nonperishable food rested upon the table beside a canteen of water. A bucket for waste sat in another corner.

Boards were nailed across the one

window, and the door was barred on the outside. Cully stared at the light that spilled through the numerous cracks in the walls and began to entertain a slim hope of escape. He hadn't lived all these years without learning a thing or two.

Before darkness brought an end to his observations, Cully had located two weak places in the walls that had been hastily repaired, places that demanded further investigation. As he munched on jerky and hardtack and drank from the canteen, he decided to tackle the walls in the morning, when he could see what he was doing.

Cully awoke at daybreak and went immediately to the planked wall to study the situation. He realized it would take a great deal of time and patience to break through the large hole that Pete had repaired by nailing a board over the opening. Unfortunately his efforts would produce enough noise to alert even a deaf man. Dejected, Cully sank down on his haunches to rethink the situation.

Four days later Cully was no closer to escaping than he had been the first day. He could hear Pete moving around outside and tried talking him into letting him go, to no avail. A welcome break came when Pete told Cully he was returning to town for instructions and supplies. Cully almost shouted aloud for joy. If Pete stayed away long enough, he was positive he could gain his freedom.

Cully set to work the moment he heard Pete ride away. He'd already searched the small room for weapons or tools and found nothing. But he didn't let that stop him. Finding the weak place in the hastily patched wall, Cully began kicking the board with his booted foot. He worked a long time, tiring both legs before realizing it was going to take more than a few well-aimed kicks to knock loose the board. Thoroughly winded, he sat down to take stock of the situation.

His gaze fell on one of the chairs, specifically on the one with wobbly legs. Realizing it wouldn't take much to wrest one leg free, he soon had the sturdy chair leg in his hands and began to batter it against the board. Unfortunately the nails held. Cully had no idea how much time had passed until he heard Pete hollering at him through the door.

"What in the hell are ya doing, Cully?"

"Beating out my brains," Cully yelled back.

"Stand back, I'm coming in with fresh water and food. The boss says you're to live a few more days. Don't try anything funny, I've got my gun out."

"What do ya think I'm gonna do?" Cully retorted, clutching the chair leg and pressing himself against the wall behind the door. "I'm unarmed."

The bar made a scraping sound against the door, and Cully smiled in anticipation. As the door inched open he gripped the chair leg and raised it over his head. When Pete stepped inside, Cully brought the club crashing down on Pete's head. Pete went down, but the blow didn't completely knock him out. He had the wherewithal to send off a wild shot. The bullet caught Cully in the thigh. Cully grunted, staggered, then brought the club down again and again, until Pete lay still as death.

Pete's horse was tethered nearby. With difficulty Cully limped to the animal and pulled himself onto its broad back. Before riding off, he bound his bleeding wound with his bandanna, hoping he wouldn't bleed to death before reaching his destination, and praying he'd be in time to help Zoey.

Cully didn't dare ride to the Circle F, or even into town. He knew Willoughby wouldn't hesitate to do away with him if he showed his face in town, and that would leave Zoey without protection. There was only one place Cully could go, one person he could confide in. And the good Lord help them all if he failed.

No matter how long or hard Pierce drove himself, he could not forget Zoey. He recalled every tantalizing inch of her. The softness of her skin, the sweet taste of her, her taut, athletic body, the firmness of her breasts. He had initiated her in the ways of love and she had been an apt pupil, turning to wildfire in his arms, branding him with her passion. Indeed, the physical part of their short-lived marriage had been very real and intensely satisfying.

Despite all those wonderful things about Zoey, he knew she would be better off without him. His deep-rooted fear of intimacy made him terrible husband material. Zoey was loyal and loving and much too good for him.

Ryan's voice interrupted his reverie. "Are you coming, Pierce? Those cows in the west pasture won't wait for branding."

"Be right with you," Pierce said, striding toward his horse in angry steps that matched his mood.

He paused with one foot in the stirrups when he noticed one of the hands riding in, leading a horse that appeared riderless. Then he saw a man slumped over the saddle, and a frisson of foreboding slid down his spine.

"Looks like Red riding in, Pierce," Ryan called as he spurred his horse to meet the riders. Pierce mounted quickly and followed.

From a distance Pierce couldn't tell whether the man slumped in the saddle was alive or dead. His right pant leg was blood-soaked, and a bandanna was wrapped around his thigh.

"What happened?" Pierce asked as he and Ryan met the riders.

"Don't know, boss." Red nodded toward the wounded man. "Found him lying on the ground in the south pasture. His horse was grazing nearby. Had to tie him to the saddle to get him here."

"He's still alive, then?" Ryan asked.

"He was. Lost a lot of blood, though. Appears to have a gunshot wound."

"We'll take it from here, Red. Go on back to your duties," Pierce said, taking the leading reins from Red's hands. "Go fetch the doctor, Ryan. The poor bastard's in bad shape."

It wasn't until Pierce reached the house and carefully lowered the wounded man from the saddle that he recognized Cully.

The breath caught in his throat as he imagined the desperate circumstances involving Zoey that must have brought Cully to his door in such sad shape.

Pierce's worst fears were realized when Cully regained consciousness briefly and recognized Pierce.

"Thank God," Cully gasped, as if the effort to speak was too much for him.

"What is it, Cully? Who shot you? Is something wrong at the Circle F?"

It took several agonizing moments for Cully to gather his wits. "Zoey needs you. Willoughby . . ." Words failed as Cully sank into a pit of blackness.

"Cully, what about Zoey? What happened? Did she send you? What about Willoughby?"

To Pierce's chagrin, Cully had passed out, leaving him with a million questions and more fear than he'd ever known.

Chapter 17

Cully didn't regain consciousness immediately. The doctor had arrived, treated the wound, and said the old man was in serious condition. Infection raged throughout his body, and Cully thrashed feverishly about in the bed. Pierce could make little out of the old man's wild ravings, except for Zoey's name, which he muttered repeatedly.

Fear raged through Pierce. He didn't know what had happened at the Circle F, and Cully couldn't tell him. What could have possibly happened to bring Cully here, wounded and near death?

Pierce didn't see how it could involve Willoughby. Zoey held the confession that could ruin the banker, and he wouldn't dare do anything to risk his reputation. Pierce would never have let her leave Dry Gulch had he thought she'd be in danger. If Zoey were safe, however, Cully wouldn't be here now, fighting for his life.

"Has Cully said anything yet?" Ryan

asked as he walked into the room.

"He's still unconscious," Pierce replied. "His fever is down some. I hope to God he makes it."

"Only one thing would bring him here, Pierce. Zoey is in trouble."

"I can't wait around here any longer. I'm going to ride to the Circle F and find out for myself. Everything was going well before I left. Damn, not knowing is driving me crazy."

"Don't you think it's time to admit you love Zoey? I've seen how you've been these last few weeks. You're not yourself, brother. You miss Zoey and you know it. Why fight it?"

"You know why as well as I."

"Then why did you refuse to —"

Just then Cully groaned and said something, halting Ryan in midsentence. Pierce bent over Cully, encouraged when the old man opened his eyes and seemed to recognize him.

"Cully, it's Pierce. Can you tell me what happened?"

Cully wet his lips and tried to focus his gaze on Pierce. His voice came out thin and raspy. "Pierce? That you? I made it?"

"You were brought in by one of the hands earlier today. I won't lie to you.

You're in bad shape, Cully. Your wound was left untreated too long. Who shot you? Why didn't you seek help right away?"

"No time," Cully gasped. "Willoughby . . ."

"What about Willoughby? Did Willoughby shoot you?"

"His man did."

"Why?"

"I was being held prisoner at an old mine. I reckon Miz Zoey was balking at marrying Willoughby, and the only way he could force her to comply was to make threats against my life. I was shot as I escaped. All I could think of was getting to you."

Dismayed, Pierce gaped at him. "What! How could Willoughby force Zoey into anything when Zoey held Willoughby's confession? She could have ruined him had she chosen to do so."

"The confession was stolen," Cully muttered. "There was no one left to guard the ranch when Miz Zoey left suddenly to follow you. To make matters worse, the money from the sale of the cattle was stolen before we returned to the Circle F. Miz Zoey needed that money to pay the taxes. Willoughby loaned her the cash, but she had to agree to marry the bastard to get it."

Cully began coughing. Pierce held a cup of water to the crusty old cowhand's lips and he drank greedily, but it did little to revive him. Cully lay back and closed his eyes.

"What do you make of it, Pierce?" Ryan asked.

Though Cully's explanation left much to the imagination, Pierce had gotten the frightening message, and the urgency of Cully's words.

"Zoey can't marry Willoughby," Pierce said, his voice low and strident.

"You and I know that, but looks like Zoey and Willoughby don't," Ryan said. "Did you ever let Zoey know that you didn't —"

"No, and I know what you're going to say. I'm a stubborn fool who can't let go of the past to make a future with Zoey. Don't lecture me, Ryan, I'm in no mood."

"So what are you going to do about it? Let Willoughby bully Zoey into marriage?"

"I'm riding to the Circle F."

"I'll go with you."

"No. Someone has to stay behind to run the ranch and look after Cully. He's not out of danger yet. I can take care of Willoughby on my own."

"Good luck," Ryan called as Pierce strode from the room.

Thirty minutes later Pierce had packed his saddlebags with supplies and ammunition, strapped on his guns, and was ready to leave.

"Tell Cully not to worry," he told Ryan in parting. "I'll set things right with Zoey. Tell him to concentrate on getting well."

Ryan watched Pierce ride away, hoping his brother hadn't bitten off more than he could chew. Willoughby sounded like a wily bastard who would stop at nothing to get what he wanted.

Zoey's wedding day dawned clear and bright. There was a nip of frost in the air, surpassed only by the coldness of her heart. Cully was still missing, and Zoey had no idea whether he was dead or alive. She had only Willoughby's word, and he wasn't to be trusted.

For her wedding day, Zoey donned a plain blue serge dress with a cape and fashioned her wheat-colored hair into a severe bun at the nape of her neck. After pinning a hat into place, she was ready to leave. At the last minute she took her gun from a drawer, loaded the chambers, and slid it into the pocket of her cape. Willoughby arrived a few minutes later to fetch her in his buggy.

"I wasn't expecting you," Zoey said, eyeing him coldly.

"I don't trust you. I decided to fetch you myself to make sure you didn't back out."

"You hold Cully as insurance, remember? When can I see him?"

"Later," he hedged. "The whole town is waiting at the church for us. I came a little early to tell you to pack a bag. We're leaving on a honeymoon immediately following the ceremony."

"Honeymoon?" Zoey parroted dully. She was living her worst nightmare.

"I thought you'd like to get away for a while. I've hired men to run the Circle F in our absence."

"Where are we going?"

"We're taking the stage to Butte. I've wired ahead for the best room at the Claymore Hotel. I want you all to myself, Zoey. I fully intend to plant our first child in you while on our honeymoon."

If you only knew I already have a child inside me, Zoey thought bleakly. But Willoughby's surprise honeymoon was a welcome reprieve. Butte was several days journey by stagecoach, days in which she'd have time to think of ways to evade her husband's lovemaking. She almost cried with relief.

"When am I going to see Cully?" Zoey wanted to know.

"You're going to have to trust me," Willoughby said. "Cully won't be harmed as long as you do what's expected of you."

"I want to see him now," Zoey persisted.

Willoughby had no intention of telling Zoey that Cully was no longer at the old mine. When he'd ridden out there to see why Pete hadn't checked in with him, he'd found Pete dead and Cully missing. There'd been enough blood around to indicate that Cully had been wounded. For all Willoughby knew, Cully was lying dead someplace in this vast territory.

"You can't see him."

"But —"

"No buts, Zoey. His life lies within my hands. Thwart me on this and you'll never see Cully again. The moment you step aboard the stage with me, he'll be set free. Do I make myself clear?"

"Perfectly," Zoey bit out. There was no justice. Willoughby held all the cards.

"Go pack your bag. The reverend is waiting."

The wedding went off without a hitch. Willoughby was all smiles. Zoey felt the cold hand of doom guiding her through the entire ordeal. Even as she spoke her vows, her heart cried silent tears for Pierce and what could have been. She had truly loved him, but losing him had been inevitable, considering the circumstances of their marriage. At least she had his child, she thought as the preacher intoned his final blessing.

Zoey was numb when it came time for the bride and groom to kiss. She stared at Willoughby dumbly, refusing to participate in the kiss that would seal their vows.

Unperturbed by her listlessness, Willoughby pulled her into his arms and kissed her possessively, his hard lips telling her that she now belonged to him.

In a daze, Zoey accepted the congratulations of the townspeople as Willoughby led her through the throng of well-wishers to the stagecoach, which had pulled into town during the ceremony and was now loading passengers. Willoughby had timed everything to coincide perfectly. He hustled her aboard the stage, and within minutes they were hurtling down the road toward Butte.

Pierce hit town two days later. He stopped first at the Circle F and found the place overrun with Willoughby's hirelings.

When he visited the bank he was told that Mr. and Mrs. Willoughby were on their honeymoon. Cursing violently, Pierce headed for the saloon. He'd been too late to stop the wedding, and if he didn't have a drink to calm himself, he feared he'd kill someone. He'd ridden night and day to reach Rolling Prairie, but he still hadn't arrived in time.

Duke, the bartender, seemed surprised to see Pierce. "What are you doing in town, Delaney? We heard you and Miss Zoey were divorced. She married Samson Willoughby two days ago."

"So I heard," Pierce muttered. He ordered whiskey and tossed it back in one gulp.

"Sorry it didn't work out between you and Miss Zoey," Duke commiserated. "Samson Willoughby always did have a hankering for her. Seems he finally got what he wanted."

"Don't count on it," Pierce muttered darkly.

"What did you say?"

"Nothing important. I heard the newlyweds are on their honeymoon."

"That's right. They boarded the stage immediately after the ceremony. Heard Willoughby say they're going to Butte."

"Butte," Pierce repeated, slapping a coin down on the counter. "Thanks, Duke."

"Something wrong, Delaney?"

"Everything is wrong, Duke, including the marriage between Zoey and Samson Willoughby."

Zoey was grateful for the other passengers traveling on the stage with them. Having fellow travelers kept her husband in line. She could tell by the lustful looks he gave her that he was eager to consummate their marriage. They stopped at a way station each night, and Zoey was only too happy to share a room with the other female passengers while Willoughby slept in the room set aside for the men. The accommodations were very much to her liking.

Zoey had been nauseous during most of the trip. She knew it was the baby giving her fits and wondered what Willoughby would do if she told him she carried Pierce's child. She would tell him in a minute if she didn't think he'd try to harm her and her baby. In fact, she was seriously considering telling him in hopes that he wouldn't want her under those circumstances. It was a long shot, but one worth taking if things got out of hand. Never would she let him in her bed!

Zoey tried to doze as the scenery sped by. Unfortunately Willoughby's daunting presence beside her, touching her possessively from time to time to remind her that she belonged to him, kept her alert and watchful.

Pierce wasn't far behind the stagecoach. He had inquired at the last stop and learned that the Willoughbys were still aboard. A smile kicked up the corner of Pierce's mouth. If he had his way, Willoughby's final destination would be in hell. Zoey belonged to him, Pierce. No other man had a right to her. The revolting image of Willoughby's hands on Zoey made him physically ill and angry enough to kill.

Pierce couldn't ever recall feeling this strongly about a woman. His damn pride had kept him from following Zoey after she left Dry Gulch. There were just too damn many reasons why they couldn't find happiness together. His family was falling apart and he couldn't seem to think straight. Now, when he'd finally realized he needed Zoey to make his life complete, he might lose her.

Chad Delaney rested his lanky frame against the saloon from which he had just exited and lit a cigarette. He watched with bored disinterest as the stagecoach pulled into town and discharged its passengers. What he saw jerked him to attention. Flinging his cigarette to the ground, he settled his hat farther down on his forehead and stared with disbelief at the couple who had just piled out of the stage.

It was Zoey, all right. Accompanied by a man he'd never seen before. He waited for Pierce to appear, and when he didn't, Chad spit out a curse. It was just like a woman to pull a dirty trick like that on a man. He had no idea what was going on, but he sure as hell was going to find out. Chad followed the couple to the Claymore Hotel, watching from the front window as the man signed the hotel register and turned to speak to Zoey. He couldn't hear what the man said, but he could tell Zoey wasn't happy about it.

"Go upstairs with the bellhop, my dear," Willoughby said, sliding his hand down Zoey's arm in a possessive manner. "Prepare yourself for me. I'll give you time to . . . do something more appropriate for our first night together. Meanwhile, I'll arrange for an intimate supper to be served in our room."

When Zoey balked, Willoughby closed brutal fingers around her arm and turned her toward the stairs. "Go!"

Giving Willoughby a hateful look, Zoey followed the bellhop up the stairs to the second floor, unaware that Chad had entered the hotel right behind her and Willoughby. Chad waited around until they had gone their separate ways before approaching the clerk.

"Who is that couple that just signed in?" Chad asked.

"We're not allowed to give out that information," the clerk said, looking down his long nose at Chad.

Chad dug in his pocket and pulled out a ten-dollar bill. "Are you sure?" he asked, sliding the money toward the clerk.

The money disappeared into the clerk's palm. "I can't tell you anything." Then in a low voice he said, "The register is on the counter." He deliberately turned his back while Chad availed himself of the hotel register.

"Mr. and Mrs. Samson Willoughby." Chad muttered something vile beneath his breath. What in the hell was going on? He knew Willoughby to be the man who had given Zoey so much grief. Why would she marry a man she despised? And what had happened to Pierce? How could Zoey be married to two men? The answers lay with Zoey, and Chad intended to get them. He took note of the room number and made for the stairs.

Zoey stared out the window, gathering her courage for what was certain to be a nasty confrontation with Willoughby. There was no way she was going to let Willoughby bed her. If he so much as touched her, she'd make him sorry. He'd promised she could see Cully after the wedding ceremony, but she knew now he never intended to keep his word. Willoughby was a heartless, lying bastard; Cully could already be dead.

The weight of the gun in her pocket lent her courage. She'd carried it since departing Rolling Prairie, and she wasn't afraid to use it. She'd give Willoughby a dose of lead poisoning if he tried to force her, and she'd feel no remorse for shooting a man like Willoughby. Jail held little appeal, but neither did bedding Willoughby.

A furtive knock on the door brought Zoey's thoughts to a skidding halt. *He's here!* Expecting her to act the dutiful wife. Her hand slid into her pocket as she walked to the door and flung it open. Her hands were shaking, but her resolve was firm. The last person she expected to find outside her door was Chad Delaney.

"Dear God, it can't be! Chad! Is it really you?"

His gaze slid over Zoey, his eyes hard and relentless. "In the flesh, Zoey, and demanding answers. What in the hell are you doing with Willoughby? Where is my brother?"

"It's a long story, one I don't have time for now." She caught his arm. Her voice rose on a note of desperation. "Oh, Chad, you're the answer to my prayer! Will you help me? I'll explain everything, but please, take me away from here."

Chad caught her shoulders in his strong hands, holding her away from him while he searched her face. "Are you in danger, Zoey?"

"Please, Chad, later. Just get me away from here before Willoughby returns. I'm not here by choice."

That was all Chad needed to hear. He grasped Zoey's hand and pulled her from the room. Going down the front stairs was out of the question, so he looked for a back exit and found it.

"This way," he urged, pulling Zoey to the end of the hallway with him. In minutes they had negotiated the back stairs and were standing in the alley behind the hotel.

Zoey was out of breath but exultant. Having Chad appear when she needed someone was a miracle. "Where to now?" she asked, casting furtive glances over her shoulder.

"I'm taking you to my lodging. You'll be safe there until I hear an explanation and determine what course to take. My hotel isn't as grand as yours, but no one will ask questions when I bring you upstairs with me."

They turned down a side street to a seedier part of town and entered the run-down lobby of an establishment calling itself the Cow Town Hotel. A couple of cowhands standing around shooting the breeze took scant interest as Chad led Zoey down the hall to his room. Zoey nearly collapsed with relief when Chad closed and locked the door behind them.

"You're safe here, Zoey. Sit down and tell me how you ended up in a hotel room with Samson Willoughby when you're married to my brother."

Zoey perched on the edge of the sagging bed, wondering how and where to start. Finally she said, "Much has happened since you left Dry Gulch, Chad. I returned to the Circle F . . . alone, and Pierce and I divorced."

"Divorced! I thought you and Pierce . . . That is, I could have sworn you really cared for one another."

"You're half-right. I care for Pierce, but he doesn't return my feelings. He can't get past the fact that I forced him into marriage. He also holds me responsible for driving you away."

"Now, that's plain dumb. You didn't drive me away. I left of my own free will."

"But everything that's happened started with my forcing Pierce to marry me."

"You're wrong, Zoey. Cora Lee started the whole thing when she said Pierce got her with child and beat her."

"Pierce doesn't see it that way. If he wanted me, he would have come to the Circle F after me. He let me leave because he didn't want me."

"Damn him! Didn't he realize how vulnerable you'd be to Willoughby without him to protect you?"

"Not really. Pierce believed I was safe from Willoughby. Everything would have been fine if I'd taken the time to hide the confession Willoughby signed before I left. He had it stolen while I was with Pierce in

411

Dry Gulch and the hands were on a trail drive."

"Why did you marry Willoughby?"

"I needed money to pay the taxes. He knew Pierce and I were . . . no longer together. I agreed to marry him in return for the loan, but I never intended to go through with it once the taxes were paid. He suspected I wouldn't keep my word and had Cully kidnapped. He threatened to kill Cully unless I married him. Cully is like my own family. I couldn't let him be hurt."

"The bastard," Chad snarled. "Why didn't you ask Pierce for the money? He wouldn't have refused you."

"Pierce made it perfectly clear that he wanted nothing to do with me. My pride wouldn't allow me to ask him for money." She twisted her hands in her skirt. "I vowed to stay out of his life no matter what. I can raise my baby —" She clamped a hand over her mouth, realizing what she had just said.

Chad's eyes narrowed. "You're expecting Pierce's child and you married Willoughby?" His voice held a wealth of contempt. "What kind of woman are you? What would you have done had I not come along when I did?"

Zoey reached in her pocket for her gun. "I had this. I would have killed Willoughby before I let him touch me."

"Wouldn't it have been easier to ask Pierce for help?"

Her chin tilted defiantly. "I am fully prepared to take care of myself, and that includes raising my child. I forced Pierce once, I won't do it again."

Disgusted, Chad shook his head. "You would rather have gone to jail for shooting Willoughby? Women, they're more bother than they're worth," he muttered. "I take it my brother doesn't know he's going to be a father. Never mind, I already know the answer."

Suddenly Zoey looked so dejected, so utterly defeated, that Chad thought it best to save further questions for later. "Tell you what. I'll move my things from the room and find some other place to sleep. We'll finish this discussion tomorrow. I'll arrange to have food sent up to you so you won't have to leave the room. You'll be safe here."

He picked up his saddlebags and turned to go. "Don't open the door to anyone but the maid until I return tomorrow."

"It isn't right to turn you out of your room."

"I can sleep anywhere. Besides, I need to make arrangements to send you back to Pierce."

Zoey bristled indignantly. "Sending me back to Pierce will solve nothing. He's going to resent me for trapping him."

"Perhaps, but that's my brother's child you're carrying. Get some rest. I'll return in the morning." He opened the door, stepped out into the hall, and pulled the door shut behind him.

Zoey stared at the closed door. She knew Chad was angry with her. He didn't seem happy about getting involved in her problems. She couldn't blame him. Nothing could change the fact that she was Willoughby's wife. He had every right to demand that she return to him, and the law would back him up.

Sighing dejectedly, she lay down on the bed and closed her eyes. She wanted Pierce, desperately, and it hurt to know he didn't want her. She would love him always; that would never change. She regretted mentioning the baby to Chad, but it had been a slip of the tongue. She hadn't wanted any of the Delaneys to know. As much as she loved Pierce, she wanted him to want her for herself. Exhausted from the long days of travel, Zoey fell into a fitful sleep.

★ ★ ★

Pierce rode into Butte several hours behind the stage. He was dirty, tired, and hungry. Putting physical comfort aside, he wanted to begin his search for Zoey immediately. Common sense told him Willoughby would stay at the best hotel in town, and that sounded like a good place to start.

Chad flung his saddlebags across his horse's withers and walked him to the Claymore Hotel. He wanted to keep tabs on Willoughby, to see what he would do when he found Zoey missing. He could summon the law, and that could present problems. Chad had no idea how all this would be resolved, but he knew he couldn't abandon Zoey to Willoughby. Not while she carried Pierce's child.

Lost in thought, Chad accidentally bumped into a man who attempted to enter the hotel at the same time he did.

"Sorry, mister," Chad said, giving the man a brief glance.

The man merely grunted, but something about the set of his shoulders made Chad turn and give him a hard look.

"Pierce?! My God, man, you couldn't have turned up at a better time."

Pierce straightened his weary form and stared with disbelief at his brother. "Chad? You're a sight for sore eyes, brother. What are you doing in Butte?"

They clapped one another on the back and then exchanged a hearty bear hug.

"I've been in a lot of places since I left the ranch. Butte is just one of them. We need to talk, Pierce. There's a saloon around the corner. We can talk privately there."

Pierce followed Chad to the saloon, more than a little confused by the surprising turn of events. They found a table in the rear of the room and ordered drinks.

Chad waited until after their drinks arrived to ask, "What brings you to Butte, Pierce? You're a long way from home."

"I'm looking for my wife. Zoey and Willoughby left Rolling Prairie together, and I want my wife back."

"It's taken you a long time to decide that."

"I admit I've been a stubborn idiot, but I've finally come to my senses. Zoey belongs to me. I've got to find her before . . ." His sentence fell off and he stared moodily into his drink.

Chad knew exactly what Pierce was thinking. "Willoughby hasn't touched her."

Pierce's head jerked up. "What? How do you know?"

"Because I just left Zoey. She's stashed away where Willoughby can't find her."

Pierce shot to his feet. "How? Where?"

"Keep your pants on, brother. Zoey is married to Willoughby. Did you know that? I saw them getting off the stage and followed them to the hotel. I managed a moment alone with Zoey and she asked me for help."

"Of course I know Zoey married Willoughby, but it isn't legal. I never signed our divorce papers. Zoey is still my wife and she's going to remain my wife."

A cynical smile spread over Chad's handsome features. "Changed your mind about women, huh? Zoey is your problem now, Pierce. I'll tell you where to find her, and you can take her home where she belongs."

Pierce's relief was so profound that at first he failed to comprehend everything Chad had said. Then it dawned on him. "Aren't you coming back with us? Let the past go, Chad. It's time to return home."

Chad's mouth thinned and his eyes reflected a soul-deep bitterness. "I'm not coming home. I can't forget what happened there. I was responsible for four deaths, Pierce, and I can't seem to run fast enough to escape it. I'll tell you where to find your wife, then I'm heading out of town."

"Dammit, Chad, listen to reason."

"Forget reason. It's too late for that. Do you want to know where to find Zoey or not?"

"You know I do."

"Then go to her. She needs you. You're going to be surprised by what she has to tell you."

"What are you talking about?"

"It's best if it comes from Zoey. You'll find her at the Cow Town Hotel, Room 129. It's just around the corner. Get her out of town before Willoughby turns the city upside down to find her."

"I don't know how you managed this, Chad, but I'm damn grateful. Are you sure I can't convince you to come back to the ranch with us?"

"Positive." He dipped a hand into his pocket. "Here's the key. You'll probably find her sleeping. The room's paid for."

Pierce swallowed the rest of his whiskey and pocketed the key. "Keep in touch, Chad. Let us hear from you from time to time."

Chad nodded curtly and rose to leave. "One more thing, Pierce, take a bath before you go to Zoey. You stink." His laughter followed Pierce out the door.

Pierce took Chad's advice. He visited a bathhouse, shaved, and changed his clothing before heading over to the hotel. He found his way to Room 129 with no difficulty or interference. He stared at the door for several moments before fitting the key into the lock and turning the knob. The door opened noiselessly and he slipped inside. A single lamp cast a nimbus of light throughout the room.

Pierce softly closed the door, turned the key in the lock, and tiptoed across the room. He noticed the tray of half-eaten food first, then her dress, which lay neatly folded across the arm of a chair. Finally his gaze settled on Zoey. She was curled up on the bed, sleeping soundly. She didn't awaken when he shed his clothing and slid into bed beside her. When he took her into his arms, she murmured his name and slid naturally into his embrace.

Zoey felt his warmth beside her and thought she was dreaming again of Pierce. Wanting him so desperately always produced dreams that shattered before the light of morning. But when she felt his lips upon hers, drawing her into his heat, she knew this was no dream. She opened her eyes and whispered his name.

Pierce . . .

Chapter 18

Zoey jerked upright, reaching out to touch Pierce before he disappeared into the land of unfulfilled dreams. "What . . . How . . . Dear God, am I dreaming?"

"Not dreaming, love. It's really me."

"What are you doing in Butte?"

"Looking for you. It's a small city, after all. I just bumped into Chad."

Zoey's vision blurred, but her gaze remained intent upon Pierce's face. "Then you know I married Samson Willoughby. But I couldn't . . . couldn't let him . . . Not after being loved by you."

"You don't have to explain, love. Cully told me everything."

"Cully? You've seen Cully?" Excitement colored her words. "Is he all right?"

Pierce pulled her into his arms, stroking her back to calm her. "Cully was wounded while trying to escape Willoughby's man. By some miracle he made it to Delaney land. He was recuperating when I left. I have every reason to believe he'll make a complete recovery."

Relief shuddered through Zoey. "Thank God. I've been so worried. Willoughby wouldn't let me see Cully after the wedding. The only reason I married him was because he said he'd hurt Cully if I didn't."

"I know. Can you forgive me, love?" Pierce asked, tilting her chin so he could look into her eyes. "I've been such a fool."

"I'm the fool, Pierce, but it's too late for regrets. I'm married to a man I despise."

"It's not too late, love. I never signed the divorce papers. I destroyed them. Your marriage to Willoughby isn't legal. You're still my wife."

Numb with disbelief, Zoey stared at Pierce. "You destroyed them? I . . . I don't understand. Why didn't you let me know? Why did you go on letting me think we were no longer married?"

"You have every right to be angry. It was difficult to toss aside old prejudices. Once I came to grips with my feelings for you, I realized how much I needed you. I wanted to come for you, but didn't know how you felt about me. Had I any idea Willoughby was causing you trouble, I would have come to your aid immediately. If you needed money for the taxes, you should have asked me."

"I guess we both acted stupidly," Zoey confessed. "I didn't want to burden you. I promised myself I'd never force you into anything again."

Her head rested against his chest as he held her tightly against him, savoring her warmth, her special scent, the way her body fit his so perfectly. Zoey was his; he was never going to let her out of his sight again. When she lifted her head to smile at him, her lush lips were too great a temptation. Too many weeks had passed since he'd held Zoey in his arms like this.

Zoey snuggled against the heat radiating from his body. His eyes were darkly brilliant as she lifted her face for his kiss. Then she tumbled into the promise in his passion as his mouth claimed hers. She clung to him, consumed by the hunger of his kiss, by the hardness of his body, his strength, the way his hands were skimming over her body, possessing her utterly by touch alone.

She felt her nipples pucker under his expert touch, felt swirling pleasure begin in the pit of her stomach as he pulled her shift over her head and stroked the hardened tips. When he sucked and licked the aching peaks, she whimpered and arched into the molten heat of his mouth.

"You're mine, Zoey," he whispered raggedly. "You never belonged to Willoughby. I was mad to let you go. I want you, Zoey. I want to love you until neither of us has energy left to move."

Pierce stroked and caressed her gently. The feel of her skin, so hot and smooth and flawless, made him shudder with desire. He buried his face in the crook of her neck, inhaled her sweet scent, and let the pleasure of having her in his arms consume him.

He spread wet kisses along the side of her neck, teased her earlobe with his tongue, and whispered words as arousing to her as the magic of his touch.

Zoey moaned as she reached out to caress him, needing to touch him everywhere. She stroked his chest, his shoulders, his neck, loving the play of rippling muscles beneath her fingertips. She moved restlessly against him, needing to get closer to his incredible heat. Then slowly she blazed a trail of fire with her lips across his chest, continuing downward to his stomach. She heard him take a deep breath and hold it, enormously pleased by his response to her mouth and hands on his flesh.

Then she found him, cupping his erection in her hand and rubbing the warm crown of his thick shaft against her cheek, thrilled by the strength of his need for her. She ran her mouth over his hard length, felt him shudder and saw his stomach muscles jerk spasmodically. Then her lips parted over him, her tongue flicking out to sample the smooth, velvety texture.

Pierce howled with pleasure, then gnashed his teeth to keep from spilling immediately. He wanted to love her slow and easy, but Zoey was making it difficult for him to control his raging hunger. The uninhibited way she responded to him aroused a fever of passion inside him. He shook with the need to thrust inside her, to feel her heat close around him, to have her take him high inside her. And once he was as far as he could go, he wanted to bring them both to shuddering release.

"No more, love," he said, disengaging her mouth. "We don't want to end this too soon."

As he crawled over her, his mouth took possession of hers. He kissed her endlessly, using his tongue, lips, and teeth to nip and tease. She was gasping from lack of air when Pierce's mouth left hers and roamed lower, licking and sucking her nipples into stiff peaks. Zoey responded with a driving ardor that matched his own, moaning and twisting beneath him. Then his mouth took a downward path, across the ivory softness of her belly, hovering over the tight nest of curls at the top of her thighs.

He nudged her legs apart, his mouth finding the sweet moistness there as he thrust his tongue inside and tasted her. He heard her breathless cry of ecstasy, heard her call his name as he lifted her buttocks, raising her up so he could push his tongue even more deeply inside her.

Pierce felt a surge of hot blood lengthen his staff. He was swollen, hard, painfully full, and he couldn't wait. Rising, he slid upward along the length of her body.

"Open for me, love," he whispered against her lips. "I'm coming home."

Zoey gave a glad cry as Pierce flexed his hips and thrust into her. He worked her gently at first, trying to go slowly, but with her tight, hot sheath squeezing him, his good intentions flew out the window. When her knees came up to give him fur-ther access, the banked hunger in him erupted. He pumped his hips with in-creasing vigor, each deep penetration sending scorching flames through her body. Zoey rocked beneath him, taking him inside her to the hilt. Mouths clinging, loins meshed in violent rhythm, they reached for ecstasy.

Zoey felt the blood hammering through her veins, exhilarated by the incredible passion they were sharing. Her face blazed with fierce joy as she wrapped her arms around him and crushed her breasts against him. Heat was building, fire blazed through her, searing her with shattering force. She was dying the sweetest death possible. He locked his arms around her and yelled his release, draining himself inside her as she pulled his hips to hers and exploded around him.

"If that doesn't make a baby, I don't know what will," Pierce gasped. "That was worth waiting for, love."

"A baby," Zoey repeated dazedly. There was something she wanted to tell Pierce, something about a baby, but she was too tired right now to think. The long journey from Montana and living in turmoil since marrying Willoughby had left her drained. When she woke up she'd tell Pierce he was going to be a father.

"I love you, Zoey," Pierce whispered as she drifted off to sleep. "I know it's love because nothing could hurt so much yet feel so wonderful."

Zoey heard and smiled dreamily. "I've always loved you, Pierce."

"Sleep, love. We'll talk in the morning."

Settling snugly into the curve of his body, Zoey let sleep claim her.

Zoey opened her eyes and smiled sleepily. Sunlight flooded into the room, revealing a drabness that she hadn't noticed the night before. But to her it was the most beautiful room in the world. Pierce had found her in this room, made love to her here, and told her he loved her. They were the sweetest words she'd ever heard.

"I've been waiting for you to wake up," Pierce said, pulling the blanket from her body. "I want to make love to you in the light of day. I want to see all of you. I want to watch your face when I bring you to pleasure."

"Do we have time for this? Shouldn't we —"

"We have time." His eyes darkened with desire as he stared at her breasts.

"There's something I want to tell you."

"It can wait."

With an efficiency of motion he lifted her atop him, settling her across his loins. He was already swollen and hard. He kissed her as he reached between them and touched her, delving his fingers inside her. She was wet and hot, and as ready as he.

"You want me as much as I want you. The proof of your need is at my fingertips."

Zoey blushed but could not deny it. Wanting Pierce was as elemental to her as breathing.

"Take me, love. Take me inside you."

Grasping his erection, she lowered herself onto him, gasping as he slowly filled her. Spanning her hips with his hands, he drove himself into her, taking them both to Paradise.

Afterward they lay in one another's arms, basking in the aftermath of their love. Zoey smiled dreamily, imagining Pierce's reaction to her pregnancy. She no longer worried about his acceptance of their child. He loved her, therefore he would love the babe he had put inside her. She tried to form the words to tell him, but they never left her mouth. The door crashed open and Samson Willoughby stepped into the room, accompanied by the sheriff and two deputies.

Pierce jerked upright, pulling the blanket around Zoey's shoulders.

"What in the hell is the meaning of this?" Pierce roared. He glanced at his clothing lying in a heap beside the bed and spit out an oath. Being caught naked, without his guns, unable to protect Zoey, left him feeling as vulnerable as a newborn babe.

"You're in bed with my wife, Delaney," Willoughby said from between clenched teeth. He turned to the sheriff. "Do your duty, Sheriff Wilkins, arrest this man. There must be a law against stealing another man's wife."

"I can let him cool his heels in jail awhile," Wilkins said, "but if the woman was willing, there's little I can do to keep him."

"Of course my wife wasn't willing," Willoughby said huffily. "She was kidnapped from our room."

Wilkins cast an inquiring glance at Zoey. She didn't appear at all pleased to see her husband. "What about it, ma'am? Were you taken against your will?"

His question shook Zoey free of her stupor. "No, Sheriff, I went willingly. Pierce Delaney is my legal husband."

"Like hell!" Willoughby thundered. "My wife and Delaney were divorced before I married her. My wife suffers from delusions."

"Wrong," Pierce said. "I never divorced

Zoey. Now, get the hell out of here."

"Arrest this man, Sheriff Wilkins," Willoughby ordered. "Obviously he's lying. I have a marriage license to back up my claim. You have no proof Delaney is other than a no-account drifter, while my reputation is without blemish. Delaney was the object of a manhunt after he beat a poor defenseless woman in Dry Gulch, Montana."

The sheriff appeared confused. "Are Mr. Willoughby's claims true, Mr. Delaney?"

"Those charges were false, and Willoughby knows it," Pierce said. "I've been cleared of any wrongdoing."

Willoughby smiled blandly. "So he says." He removed a document from his vest pocket and offered it for the sheriff's inspection. "I have my marriage license as proof of my marriage."

"These look legal to me," Wilkins said, handing them back to Willoughby. "Do you have your marriage papers, Mr. Delaney?"

"Not many men carry their marriage license with them," Pierce contended.

"Mr. Willoughby does," the sheriff said. "Until I learn differently, you'd best come with me, Mr. Delaney. And you, Mrs. Willoughby, should return to your husband. Get dressed, Delaney." He strode deliberately over to Pierce's discarded clothing and picked up his gun belt. "You won't be needing this."

"You're making a big mistake, Sheriff," Pierce said, reaching for his clothes.

"That remains to be seen. You can cool your heels in jail while I send out a few telegrams and go through my wanted posters."

"The Delaneys are well known in Montana. My brothers and I own one of the biggest spreads in the state," Pierce said as he pulled on his clothes.

"Pierce is telling the truth, Sheriff," Zoey said, growing frantic. How could this be happening to her? "We're not divorced. My marriage to Samson Willoughby isn't legal."

"Don't listen to her," Willoughby said. "My wife is slightly confused. It's a condition from which she suffers from time to time. The doctors suggested a sanatorium, but I can't bear to part with her." He sent her a sympathetic smile.

Fully dressed now, Pierce lunged at Willoughby. "You lying bastard! You're going to pay for the grief you've caused Zoey."

It took the combined strength of both deputies to subdue Pierce and drag him from the room. The words he flung over his shoulder were those of encouragement to Zoey. "Don't worry, love, I won't let Willoughby get away with this!"

Zoey wanted to run after Pierce, to try to convince the sheriff that he spoke the truth, but she was naked as a jaybird beneath the blanket Pierce had flung over her.

"Get dressed. We're leaving Butte immediately," Willoughby said. "You've caused me enough embarrassment to last a lifetime."

"I'm not dressing in front of you."

His gaze turned lustful. "I can be persuaded to join you in bed. I'd prefer not to take you in the same bed in which you sported with Delaney, but if you don't move quickly, I'll do what I've been wanting to do for a long time."

Zoey gave him a venomous look and did as he requested. She didn't want him to touch her. Holding the blanket to her naked breasts, she snatched her shift from the floor and pulled it over her head. Feeling less vulnerable, she ignored Willoughby's hot gaze as it followed her across the room. Fuming inwardly, she grabbed her dress from the chair and yanked it over her head. The welcome weight of the gun in her pocket bolstered her courage and gave her a sense of reckless confidence.

"I'm not going anywhere with you," Zoey said, facing him squarely. "You don't frighten me. I'm not married to you. I never was."

"I'm not going to return to Rolling Prairie alone and become the laughingstock of the town. Oh, no, my 'wife' will be with me."

Zoey laughed in his face. "Pierce won't remain in jail for very long. You're a fool if you think he won't follow us."

Willoughby's fingers curled hurtfully around her arm as he pulled her toward the door. "We'll be back in Rolling Prairie before the sheriff releases your lover. I've made arrangements to leave on the afternoon stage. I fully expect Delaney to follow when he's released, but he'll never reach town alive. I fear he's going to meet with an unfortunate 'accident.' My men won't fail me this time."

"You can't make me leave," Zoey said, pulling the gun from her pocket and poking the barrel in Willoughby's gut.

"You're threatening me?" Willoughby said, his voice rough with anger.

"Damn right I am. Cully is out of your reach. He's recuperating at the Delaney ranch. You can no longer bully me."

Willoughby's eyes glinted dangerously, which should have warned Zoey.

"Turn around, Mr. Willoughby. Walk out that door and keep walking."

Willoughby made as if to comply. He placed his hand on the doorknob, but instead of turning it, he whirled abruptly, flinging his arm out at the same time, dealing Zoey a blow to the face that sent her flying. Too stunned to move, she lay at Willoughby's feet as he calmly bent and ripped the gun from her hand.

"What were you saying, my dear?" His face turned hard; his icy gaze impaled her. "Get up. We're both walking out of here and boarding the stagecoach. Before I left the hotel I arranged for our luggage to be delivered to the station."

"How did you know I was with Pierce?" Zoey asked shakily. The left side of her face felt as if it were on fire; her mouth was numb from his cruel blow.

"When I found you missing, I questioned the hotel desk and learned that a man fitting Delaney's description was asking about us. I put two and two together."

Zoey thought it best not to mention that it had been Chad asking questions, not

Pierce. "How did you find me?"

He gave a hoot of laughter. "Easy. I went to the sheriff's office and told him my story. His deputy just happened to see a woman and man fitting the descriptions I gave him enter the Cow Town Hotel while he was making rounds. I remarked to Sheriff Wilkins that Delaney was a dangerous man, so he and his two deputies accompanied me. The clerk verified that a Mr. Delaney was registered and gave us the master key.

"I hated to brand my wife a whore, but I had no choice," he continued. "Fortunately no one in Rolling Prairie is likely to find out about this. You won't be going to town much, anyway."

"Holding me prisoner will solve nothing. If you hurt Pierce, his brothers will come gunning for you. They both know why Pierce went to Butte."

"Without a body, they can prove nothing." He pressed the gun against her ribs beneath her cape. "Open the door and walk down the stairs quietly. Don't try anything funny. The sheriff is already half-convinced your mind is unstable. If you force me to shoot, I'll tell him you tried to kill me and were shot in the scuffle for the gun. Your ranch will be all mine then. So you may as well accept this without making trouble."

He pushed her from the room, grasping her arm with one hand and holding the gun against her ribs with the other. Except for the clerk, the lobby was empty when they walked through the front door. He pushed and pulled her along the street, checking his watch as he crossed the road and headed to the stagecoach station. They arrived just as the stage was loading passengers.

"I'm Samson Willoughby. Has our luggage arrived from the hotel?" Willoughby asked the stationmaster.

"It's being loaded now, sir. You and your wife can climb in and make yourselves comfortable. The stage will leave in about fifteen minutes."

"I need to make a purchase from the drugstore next door. Do I have time?"

"Plenty of time, sir."

"Come along, Zoey." He shoved the gun against her side, forcing her to move with him. Zoey wondered what would happen if she made a break for it and ran. Surely Willoughby wouldn't shoot her in front of all these people, would he?

"Don't even think it," he whispered against her ear as he pulled her toward the store. "I've taken all I'm going to from you."

"Why are we going to the drugstore?" Zoey wanted to know.

"You'll see," he said cryptically. "I don't intend to spend four days trying to subdue you. I'm going to make this easy on myself."

Zoey had no idea what he was talking about . . . until she heard him ask the store clerk for a large bottle of laudanum.

"You wouldn't dare!" she blurted out as he paid the curious clerk for his purchase.

"Here's a little extra for you," Willoughby said expansively as he pocketed the bottle of laudanum and handed the clerk a crisp five-dollar bill.

"No!" Zoey cried, truly frightened now. What would the laudanum do to her baby?

"Come along, my dear," Willoughby said for the clerk's benefit. "You know how excitable you are. Your imagination is working overtime. You're going to make yourself ill. My wife suffers from spells," he said as an aside to the clerk.

Without further ado, Willoughby hustled Zoey through the door and into the street. Before she knew what was happening, he pushed her into the alley between the drugstore and stagecoach station, pressing

438

her against the brick wall with the weight of his body. Carefully opening the bottle of laudanum, he held her face between his hard fingers and forced her mouth open as he poured a generous amount down her throat. He held her in his viselike grip until she swallowed and her wild thrashing subsided.

Zoey fought with all her might to escape Willoughby's hurtful grip on her face. But in the end he had his way. He held her nose until she swallowed. The bitterness made her gag and she tried to vomit but couldn't. Her eyes watered and her mouth went dry. Her head spun dizzily and then her legs turned to rubber beneath her.

Willoughby caught her limp form in his arms and left the alley, noting that the stagecoach was making ready to leave. "I'm sorry we're late," Willoughby told the driver, "but my wife took ill. One of her spells," he apologized for the benefit of the other passengers. "She has them frequently. She's a weak creature and her mind is unstable. But I can't bear to part with her, so I keep her with me and do my best to keep her calm."

"It's a hard ride to Montana, sir. Will your wife be all right?"

"Oh, yes, the doctor prescribed liberal

doses of laudanum when she gets like this. She'll probably sleep during most of the trip. I'd appreciate it if you could make arrangements at the way stations for me to stay with my wife at night. She might become hysterical if she awakens and finds herself with strangers."

"Are you sure she should be traveling?" the driver asked with concern.

"She'll be fine, just as long as I'm here to take care of her. I'll put her inside the coach. I see you're ready to leave."

Zoey's nightmare continued. She was rarely awake long enough to realize what was happening. During the scheduled stops between cities, when passengers took to the woods to relieve themselves, Willoughby carried her to a secluded spot, let her take care of her needs, then incapacitated her again by forcing her to swallow more laudanum. Too groggy to protest and too weak to fight him, she was literally at his mercy.

During one of her more lucid moments, Willoughby said with obvious relish, "Everyone on the stage pities me. They think I'm a saint for putting up with a crazy woman who mutters strange things and makes wild accusations."

Zoey knew it was true but couldn't find a way to combat the effects of the laudanum. At least she had the satisfaction of knowing that Willoughby hadn't touched her physically. She may have slept in the same bed with him, but her clothing was never mussed and she awoke wearing the same clothes in which she had fallen asleep.

Even while under the influence of laudanum, Zoey had tried to convey her desperate situation to her fellow passengers, especially during the few times she'd been able to think and speak coherently. But Willoughby would simply give her a pitying look and shake his head, as if to say his wife wasn't in her right mind.

And then, before she could say anything else, the bottle would be pressed to her mouth and soon afterward she'd fall into a black void.

Rolling Prairie was the last stop on the route. All the passengers except Zoey and Willoughby had gotten off at various stops along the way. Zoey awoke slowly from her stupor, confused and befuddled. She was lying across the seat, trying to focus her eyes, when she saw Willoughby dozing across from her. She pushed herself into a sitting position, trying to gather her wits, when she saw his eyes snap open.

"We're almost home," he said. "Once you're at the ranch where my men can keep an eye on you, you'll no longer be dosed with laudanum. Unless you give me trouble."

"People will wonder what's wrong with me," Zoey said. Her brain was dazed, her eyes glassy.

"You're going to be sick when I carry you off the stage. Sick enough to be confined to the house. Old Doc Tucker will corroborate my diagnosis as long as I keep him supplied with whiskey."

He pulled the bottle of laudanum from his pocket.

"No, please! No more. You'll harm my baby."

Willoughby went still. "Baby? You're expecting your lover's child?" The harshness of his voice, the coldness in his eyes, were intense.

"I'm expecting my *husband's* child," Zoey told him, regaining some of her old spunk. Suddenly it dawned on her that she hadn't told Pierce he was going to be a father. She'd meant to, but passion had taken hold of her, and then it had been too late.

"That changes everything. Your recovery is in grave doubt," Willoughby said, forcing her to swallow the vile concoction despite her vigorous objection. "I haven't decided on your fate yet, but killing you shouldn't be any more difficult than killing your father."

Zoey fought through the fog enveloping her brain, clinging to Willoughby's words with frantic desperation. What had he said? He killed her father? Her silent scream of rage echoed through her mind before she sank into a quagmire of murky darkness.

Chapter 19

Pierce was released from jail on the same day Zoey and Willoughby arrived in Rolling Prairie. Sheriff Wilkins returned Pierce's guns with a curt apology.

"Sorry about this, Delaney, but a sheriff can't be too careful. Strangers in town usually mean trouble. The mayor of Dry Gulch confirmed your identity in answer to my telegram, and I could find no wanted posters out on you."

"I told you, but you didn't believe me," Pierce charged.

"You were caught in bed with another man's wife. In the future I suggest you find a single woman to lavish your attentions upon. The Willoughbys were on their honeymoon, for God's sake."

"Zoey is my wife, not Willoughby's. Mark my words, Sheriff, nothing good will come of this delay. I only hope I'm not too late."

"Too late for what?" Sheriff Wilkins called after Pierce.

Pierce didn't bother to reply as he headed for the livery to get his horse. He figured he could reach Rolling Prairie in three days. That would be seven days from the time Willoughby and Zoey left Butte. He hoped to God he wasn't too late.

Zoey opened her eyes and stared at the ceiling. For the first time in days, her eyes focused and she could think. Not clearly, but at least she could put her thoughts in some kind of order. Her gaze flitted from object to object, settling on the dresser, which held the silver-backed brush and mirror her father had given to her on her sixteenth birthday.

Home. She was home and lying in her own bed.

She rose to her elbows, trembling from the effort and cursing the effects the laudanum had on her system. She was wearing her shift, and the thought that Willoughby, her father's killer, had removed her dress made her shudder with revulsion. She forced herself to sit at the edge of the bed, painfully aware of the pressing need to relieve herself.

Suddenly the door opened. Willoughby stepped into the room and smiled at her. "So you're finally awake. It's about time."

"Where did you sleep?" Zoey asked, eyeing him narrowly. She didn't want him anywhere near her.

"Not with you," he sneered. "Not while you're carrying another man's child. I moved my clothing into the room next to yours."

Zoey's relief was instant and profound. "How did I get home? Who put me to bed?"

"I fear I gave you too large a dose just before we reached town. You've been sleeping for the better part of two days. I put you to bed and assigned my man Tubbs to keep watch should you awaken and try to escape. I'm off to the bank now. I've passed the word in town that you're seriously ill and may or may not recover. Doc Tucker is telling everyone that you picked up some fatal disease on our honeymoon."

"You killed my father!" Zoey accused, suddenly recalling his hasty confession in the stagecoach.

"So you did hear me," Willoughby said. "I wondered about that." He shrugged expansively. "No one will believe you."

"Am I to be confined to this one room?" She had to find a way to escape before Willoughby did away with her, she'd be of no use to Pierce dead. She suspected Willoughby had already dispatched men to intercept and kill Pierce, so she had to act fast.

"You're probably hungry. You may have access to the kitchen until I decide what to do with you. Tubbs will make sure you don't get any ideas about leaving. You'll find little in the way of fresh food in the kitchen. Ask Tubbs to bring you something from the cookhouse pantry. It's been fully provisioned. I don't intend to return tonight. I have a dinner meeting with a business associate from Lewistown. I'm thinking of opening another bank in that city. I'll stay in town tonight and bring out the rest of my belongings tomorrow."

"Don't do me any favors," Zoey said tartly.

"Don't worry, I won't," he returned shortly. His words held a wealth of meaning, none of it good for Zoey.

"Pierce won't let you get away with this."

"Your lover will be of no use to you once he meets up with my men. He won't reach town alive. I'm leaving now. Behave yourself."

Zoey wanted to hurl the water pitcher at Willoughby's skull, but resisted the urge.

She had to keep a level head if she wanted to save Pierce.

She rose slowly, fighting wave after wave of dizziness and nausea. She took care of her most pressing needs, then struggled into her clothing. She chose a pair of denims from her closet, hoping the tight pants would still fit. They did, except for the waist, which came within an inch of closing. To hide the gap, she donned a flannel shirt with long tails. Then she opened the bedroom door and peered into the hall.

A man stood at the top of the stairs, lounging against the wall. He was big, had a smashed-in nose, and looked mean.

"Where do ya think yer goin', Miz Willoughby? I'm Tubbs. The boss told me to keep an eye on ya."

"I'm quite aware of Willoughby's orders," Zoey said, unwilling to show any weakness. "I'm going to the kitchen to fix myself something to eat."

"I reckon I'll just tag along to make sure ya go where yer supposed to," Tubbs said. He fell in behind her, and whistled his appreciation of her form.

Zoey found the kitchen cupboards bereft of everything except coffee, lard, sugar, flour, salt, various spices, a tin of corned beef, and a tin of peaches. She made coffee, opened both tins, and ate hungrily. While under the influence of laudanum, she'd eaten far too little to sustain both herself and her child. Tubbs never took his eyes off her while she ate.

"Would you like some coffee, Mr. Tubbs?" Zoey asked, pretending friendliness.

"Don't mind if I do. Baldy is a lousy cook. Can't even boil water without burning it. I sure hope the boss hires a decent cook soon."

Zoey's attention sharpened as an idea took root in the deep recesses of her mind. The plan she hatched was risky and could work only if all the elements were available.

"I'm a tolerable cook, Mr. Tubbs. I'm accustomed to cooking for hungry ranch hands. Bring me some fresh meat from the cookhouse and I'll fix you and the men a meal tonight you won't forget."

Tubbs was instantly wary. "Why would you do that?"

"I'm not accustomed to sitting around and doing nothing. I can bake biscuits that will melt in your mouth. And pies. I have dried apples, flour, and sugar on hand. I can make stew with the meat you provide," she said with sudden inspiration. "There are potatoes, turnips, carrots, and onions in the root cellar. I put them down there myself before I left. How does that sound?"

Tubbs's mouth began to water. A meal like the one Zoey just described sounded too good to be true, but he wasn't sure the boss would approve. "I don't know. The boss said —"

"Did he say I was to be confined to my room?"

Tubbs scratched his head. "I reckon not."

"Then what can it hurt? You and the hands can enjoy a decent meal for a change. Just bring me the meat and I'll do the rest."

"There's a fresh haunch of venison in the cookhouse," he said after some thought. "One of the boys brought in a buck yesterday. I'd hate to see Baldy ruin it like he does everything else."

"Then it's settled," Zoey said. "Go get the meat and I'll do the rest. How many men will I be cooking for?"

"Seven counting myself. Don't try anything funny while I'm gone," Tubbs warned. "The boss said you might make trouble."

"Do I look capable of making trouble?" Zoey said, batting her long lashes at him.

"I'll be back directly," Tubbs said, eyeing her with distrust. He hesitated for a minute, and then headed for the door.

The moment he stepped out, Zoey rushed upstairs. She had to work fast, before Tubbs returned and became suspicious. How this day ended depended on her ability to find the one vital ingredient that would make her stew an unforgettable meal.

Zoey went directly to the room Willoughby was using. The bed was unmade and his wrinkled suit lay in a heap on the floor. Quickly she searched through the pockets, disappointed when she failed to find what she was looking for. She went to the dresser and saw that Willoughby had already made himself at home, filling the drawers with his clothing and personal belongings. He must have brought them out yesterday while she was sleeping off the effects of laudanum. She rummaged through each drawer carefully and found nothing.

Where is it? Zoey wondered, growing desperate. Surely he wouldn't have taken the bottle of laudanum with him, would he? If he had taken it, her plan was doomed to failure. Moving to the closet, Zoey opened the door and saw a neat row of suits, with shoes and boots lined up beneath them.

Every one of Willoughby's pockets was empty, and Zoey knew true despair. Could he have hidden the laudanum downstairs in one of the cupboards? Not likely, she decided. His mind was too devious. He'd never place it where she could easily find it. Then her gaze fell on the shoes and boots. One by one she picked up each shoe and turned it upside down. Nothing. The first boot she picked up yielded the prize Zoey had sought. She nearly whooped with joy. The bottle of laudanum was nestled in the toe. She held it to the light and was thrilled to find it half-full. More than enough to put seven men to sleep and keep them snoozing all night.

Pierce must be close to Rolling Prairie, she thought as she tucked the bottle into her pocket, riding into an ambush staged by Willoughby's men. Zoey knew she wasn't capable of stopping the men without help, though she was certainly willing to try, but she had to be practical. There was a child growing inside her to protect.

Not long ago, on a trip into town, she recalled hearing that Governor Edgerton had assigned a federal marshal to the town of Roundup, which lay a scant twenty miles east of Rolling Prairie. He'd been placed there to control the Vigilantes of Montana, who were raising havoc in the territory. Zoey figured she could easily make Roundup in three hours. Then all she had to do was convince the marshal to go to Pierce's aid.

Zoey returned to the kitchen scant minutes before Tubbs returned. He placed the haunch of venison he was carrying on the table and sat down to watch her.

"I'll need some wood for the cookstove," Zoey said as she retrieved a huge pot from a storage cabinet. "I'll cut up the meat while you fetch the wood and start a fire in the cookstove."

"I've got a better idea," Tubbs said slyly. "I'll cut the meat while you fetch the firewood and start the fire. I don't trust you with a knife."

"Very well," Zoey said agreeably as she went to the woodbox and removed several sticks of wood. Tubbs wielded the knife with dexterity while Zoey built a fire in the stove.

When all was in readiness, Tubbs sat down to watch while Zoey browned the meat. Zoey's thoughts raced furiously. She knew there was no way she could empty the bottle of laudanum into the pot with Tubbs watching.

"I'll need potatoes, carrots, turnips, and onions from the root cellar. Shall I get them or will you? And water. I'll need fresh water."

"I'll get them. You stay here and see to the meat." He walked away, complaining to himself, "I didn't sign on to be a cook's helper."

The moment he left the room, Zoey pulled the laudanum from her pocket, unscrewed the cap, and poured the entire contents into the kettle with the meat. Then she hid the empty bottle in the bottom of the woodbox.

Tubbs returned directly with the ingredients Zoey had asked for. "I hope that's all."

"That will do, thank you."

She peeled the vegetables, dropped them into the kettle, and moved it over the burner to cook. Then she searched through her supply of spices, hoping to find something strong enough to disguise the bitter taste of laudanum. Salt and pepper went into the kettle . . . a lot of pepper. Along with cinnamon, bay leaf, and a pinch of two or three other spices she had on hand.

"There," she said, placing the cover on

the kettle. "It will take several hours to cook and meld the flavors. Meanwhile, I'll start on the pies and mix the biscuit dough."

By six o'clock the kitchen was redolent with spices and mouth-watering aromas.

"Smells good," Tubbs said grudgingly. "Never seen biscuits that high before."

"You'll be surprised at how good everything tastes," Zoey said with confidence. "You can carry the food out to the cookhouse, and I'll do the serving. You did tell the cook not to prepare the evening meal, didn't you?"

"He knows. So do the hands. They're probably all in the cookhouse now, waitin' fer the grub. Except for the man on guard duty. He'll eat later, if there's anything left."

"I'll make sure there's something left for him. You can take it to him after you've eaten."

The hands were indeed waiting in the cookhouse for their meal. Zoey took one look at the motley crew and knew Willoughby had hired the toughest, roughest bunch of men he could find. But she'd never known a man who didn't appreciate a good meal. She hoped the spiked stew tasted as good as it smelled. Steeling her-

455

self against the men's lustful looks, Zoey dished out the stew into their tin plates and set the biscuits on the table. She had even brought coffee, which she poured into their mugs. Then she stood back and waited for them to devour their dinner.

They did. Every last one of them cleaned his plate and asked for more. Zoey had thoughtfully sent a plate out to the guard, which Tubbs brought back empty. As soon as the pie was cut and served, she returned to the house with the empty pot. Tubbs trailed behind her.

"I'm going to bed now, Mr. Tubbs. I hope you enjoyed the meal."

Tubbs merely grunted. "Just remember, I'm gonna be right down here keepin' watch, so don't try any funny stuff."

"You needn't worry, Mr. Tubbs, I'm too tired to think of anything but how soft that bed is going to feel. Good night."

Zoey paced the room anxiously, wondering how long she had to wait for the laudanum to take effect. It had worked fast on her, and she'd used enough in the stew to put out an army.

Seven o'clock passed, then eight. Two hours. Surely that was enough time. Zoey opened the door to her room and poked her head out. She saw nothing, heard nothing. Creeping down the stairs, she peered into the kitchen. Tubbs's arms were folded on the table. His head was resting on them and he appeared to be sound asleep. Zoey made a wide circle around him and exited through the back door.

No one stopped her as she hurried to the barn. If God was with her, the hands would be sleeping soundly in their beds. She didn't light a lamp. She had saddled her horse so many times in the past, she didn't need a light to know what she was doing. Working quickly and silently, she finished the task and led her horse into the yard and through the gate. She smiled to herself when she saw the guard propped up against the fence, fast asleep. Once out the gate, she flung herself atop her horse's back and turned in the direction to Roundup.

Zoey kept a steady pace; the road was well marked in the moonlight, but she didn't want to wear out her mount or risk falling. There was no traffic on the road. With any luck her absence wouldn't be discovered until morning.

It was close to midnight by Zoey's reckoning when she rode down the main street of Roundup and found the marshal's office. The single light shining through the window was a welcome sight as Zoey slid clumsily down from her horse. She could barely put one foot in front of the other as she opened the door and stumbled inside.

The deputy marshal leaped from his chair, reaching for his gun as Zoey staggered into the room.

"I need to see the marshal," Zoey gasped.

Surprised to see a woman, he holstered his gun and steadied her as she wove from side to side. "Sit down, ma'am, you look done in. What are you doing out this time of night?"

"Never mind me, a man's life is at stake. Are you the marshal?"

"No, ma'am, I'm the deputy. The marshal won't be on duty until morning."

"I've got to see him. It's a matter of life and death."

"Relax, ma'am, I'm sure this can wait until morning."

"No, you don't understand. This can't wait. Get the marshal, please."

Deputy Garwood sensed the woman's desperation and was torn. Marshal Kinder was the only regular lawman in this part of the territory, and he was a busy man. Especially with the vigilante activity in the area.

He needed his rest. On the other hand, if a man's life was at stake, the marshal would certainly want to know about it.

"Very well, I'll go get the marshal. It may take a while. Try to relax while I'm gone. You look as if you could use the rest."

"Please hurry," Zoey urged.

Zoey must have dozed off, for she awakened to the sound of voices.

"This better be important, Deputy."

"The lady sounded desperate, Marshal."

"I am desperate, Marshal," Zoey said, coming to her feet with difficulty. "I'm Mrs. Delaney and my husband's life is in danger."

The marshal sighed wearily. "Very well. Since I'm here, you may as well tell me your problem."

"My husband is going to be murdered," Zoey began. "Samson Willoughby sent men to ambush and kill him before he reaches Rolling Prairie."

"You're sure of this?" He sounded skeptical.

"Maybe after I explain, you'll believe me."

It took Zoey nearly half an hour to tell her story. Her tale sounded so improbable, she feared Kinder wouldn't believe her. The marshal didn't interrupt once; he listened carefully as she spoke. When she told him about Willoughby confessing to the murder of her father, Kinder's attention sharpened.

When she finished, he said, "You've made some serious charges against banker Willoughby. Are you sure you're not exaggerating?"

Zoey leaped to her feet. "I'm telling the truth! He admitted to killing my father. Now he's out to kill Pierce. If you won't help me, I'll do what I can myself to stop Willoughby's men."

She took a step and staggered. The marshal caught her and led her back to the chair. "I'm sorry. I'm still not recovered from the effects of the laudanum Willoughby fed me. And I'm . . . I'm expecting a child."

"Leaping bullfrogs!" the deputy exclaimed, staring at Zoey with compassion.

The marshal's gaze never left Zoey's face, as if he was trying to make up his mind. Finally he said, "You must have been desperate to ride all this way in the middle of the night in your condition. Very well, I'll lead a posse out at daybreak. Hopefully we can intercept your husband before he's ambushed. If what you told me about Samson Willoughby is true, he's

460

broken several laws. I'll want to have a talk with him."

"I'm going with you," Zoey said, shrugging off her exhaustion.

"No you're not. I'm going to put you up at the hotel. You've had enough excitement to last a lifetime. Women in your condition shouldn't be gallivanting around the countryside, putting themselves in danger. I'm sure your husband will thank me. Delaney *is* your husband and father of your child, isn't he?"

Zoey's story had been so convoluted, Kinder had a difficult time sorting through it.

"He is, Marshal. And I want him alive to help raise his child."

"I'll do what I can, ma'am. We'll head over Rolling Prairie way and ride toward Butte. If we're lucky, we'll intercept your husband before he's ambushed. You realize we may be too late. If we are, rest assured Willoughby won't get away with it. Come along, now, I'll take you to the hotel."

Zoey went along reluctantly. Every minute wasted increased the danger to Pierce.

Pierce's horse threw a shoe two days short of Rolling Prairie. Pierce cursed his rotten luck. Now he'd have to walk to the nearest community, which was little more than a trading post, and waste precious time having Midnight shod. No matter how much he fumed and fretted over the delay, and worried about Zoey, he could do nothing to make up for the lost time.

After several hours delay, Pierce resumed his grueling pace. When it became apparent that Midnight needed a rest, Pierce stopped and dismounted, stretched out on the ground, and grabbed a few hours sleep. He took to the road again at daybreak.

Thoughts of Zoey filled his heart and mind. He knew her to be brave and resourceful, but she couldn't possibly match Willoughby in strength or cunning. If the cur touched one hair on her beautiful head, Pierce vowed to make him suffer.

The road Pierce followed curved through thickly forested foothills, dense with underbrush. At a particularly dark spot, where only muted sunlight was allowed through the solid canopy of trees, Pierce felt a prickling along the back of his neck. He glanced behind him and saw nothing. The shot that whizzed by him an instant later came without warning. It was so close he could feel the heat as it sped past his head. Ducking instinctively, Pierce hugged Midnight's neck as two more bullets pumped past him.

Suddenly two men appeared in the road ahead of him, materializing from the trees at the side of the trail. Pierce pulled his mount up short, clinging to the saddle as the animal reared against the cruel sawing of the reins. Yanking sharply, Pierce attempted to turn Midnight, but the ploy was thwarted by two riders closing in fast from the rear. Taking to the woods was an option that Pierce was denied. Within seconds he was surrounded by a quartet of fierce-looking thugs.

"What do you want?" Pierce asked, dancing Midnight around in a circle.

"We've been waitin' for ya," a man with a diagonal scar across his cheek said. "Yer late."

Pierce knew this stretch of road had been the scene of many robberies by road agents, which had led to the formation of the vigilantes of Montana.

"I don't have much money on me, but you're welcome to what I have. I'm in a hurry, so let's get on with it."

Carefully he reached into his vest pocket to remove his wallet.

"Keep yer hands on the reins," Scarface warned. "We'll take yer money soon enough, but that ain't all we want."

Pierce didn't like the way Scarface was grinning at him.

"Get down from yer horse."

Pierce dismounted, wondering how many of the thugs he could take out before they got him. Though he would have liked to shoot his way out of this, common sense warned him to use caution. He stood beside his horse, waiting for Scarface's next move, every muscle taut with anticipation.

"Walk toward the woods," Scarface ordered. Scarface and his companions dismounted and walked toward Pierce.

My God, they're going to kill me! Pierce thought wildly. *They're not just run-of-the-mill thugs, they've intercepted me for a purpose.*

"Who sent you?" Pierce wanted to know. "Are you working for Willoughby?"

"Drop yer gun belt," Scarface demanded. "Dead men don't have any business askin' questions."

Pierce made an instant decision. He couldn't sit still while these bastards used him for target practice. No matter the outcome, he'd not go down without a fight.

He was so fast no one saw his hand move

as he pulled his gun and shot from the hip. Scarface made a gurgling sound deep in his throat and keeled over, dead before he hit the ground. Pierce's bullet had found its mark dead center between Scarface's eyes. It was the last thing the thugs had expected. Pierce didn't wait around for the repercussions; he knew his aim had been true. The brief distraction had given Pierce a small window of opportunity. Without a backward glance, he whirled, dashed into the woods, and kept running. Seconds later he heard the thugs crashing through the trees after him, cursing and shouting for him to stop.

Pierce zigzagged around trees and leaped over fallen logs, his mind sorting through all the people who might want him dead. Samson Willoughby topped the list.

The thugs were getting nearer, their stray shots coming alarmingly close. Pierce heard one of the men yell for them to spread out, and he knew a moment of panic. If his body was left to rot in the woods, his brothers would never know what happened to him. And he didn't even want to imagine what his death could mean to Zoey. With those thoughts in mind, he made another instant decision.

He turned and doubled back to the road,

hoping to slip past the thugs to reach his horse. Crouching low, he crept from tree to tree, dropping to his stomach behind a fallen log when he saw one of the thugs directly in his path. The man passed by without a second glance. Pierce paused a moment to catch his breath, then sprinted toward the road. He had only a short distance to go when one of the thugs spied him and called out a warning.

"There he is! He's doubled back toward the road. Don't let him get away!"

Pierce broke out onto the rutted dirt road with the thugs hard on his heels. He ran toward his horse but knew he wasn't going to make it. Daring a glance over his shoulder, he saw one of the thugs taking aim. A shot rang out; Pierce waited for the pain. When none came he took heart and kept running.

Pierce heard them before he saw them. Six riders were pounding down the road toward him. More of Willoughby's men? he wondered dully. He glanced over his shoulder again and was surprised to see that the thugs had stopped in their tracks, staring in confusion at their fallen companion. Suddenly the thugs ran for their horses and Pierce dared to breathe again.

He watched now as the incoming riders

separated the thugs from their horses, cutting off their escape. One of the riders approached Pierce. "Are you Pierce Delaney?"

Pierce saw the man's badge and grinned. "Sure am. How did you know? You don't know how glad I am to see you, Marshal. I heard the government was sending a lawman to the territory."

"I'm Marshal Kinder. We've been looking for you. 'Pears we got here in the nick of time."

"I'm real curious to know what brought you to my rescue, Marshal, but I don't have time to listen to a lengthy explanation. My wife is in trouble in Rolling Prairie, and I need to get to her without delay. These men were sent to kill me by a man named Samson Willoughby. It's a long story, one I don't have time for now."

"I know all about Samson Willoughby, Mr. Delaney. My men and I are going to take these thugs to Rolling Prairie and confront Willoughby with information provided by your wife."

Pierce forgot to breathe. "You saw my wife? Is she . . ." He swallowed noisily. "Is she all right?"

"Your wife is a brave woman, Mr. Delaney. She rode into Roundup in the middle of the night to seek my help. She risked her life by coming to me. Her story was bizarre, but I believed her. We had just about given up hope of finding you when we heard gunshots."

"Where is Zoey now? Did she go home to the Circle F?"

"No, it wasn't safe for her there. I put her up at the hotel in Roundup. I reckon she's still there. She was pretty groggy last night. Willoughby's been dosing her with laudanum to keep her in line. Despite everything she's been through, she found a way to escape Willoughby's hirelings and reach me. You're a lucky man, Mr. Delaney."

"I'm beginning to think you're right, Marshal, though I wouldn't have believed it twenty minutes ago. If you don't need me anymore, I'd like to go to my wife."

"I'd like you and your wife to remain in Roundup until the mess with Willoughby is cleared up in Rolling Prairie. I'll let you know when it's safe to return to the Circle F."

"Gladly, Marshal," Pierce said with a grin. "Zoey and I need some time to ourselves, anyway. We never did have a proper honeymoon."

Mounting smoothly, Pierce gave the marshal a cocky salute and rode off.

Chapter 20

Pierce reached Roundup several hours later. He stopped first at the livery to drop off his horse. The poor animal had been ridden hard and long and had earned a few days of special attention.

"Take good care of him," Pierce instructed the hostler as he patted Midnight's velvety nose. "I'm new in town. Can you direct me to the hotel?"

"Two blocks east, turn left. Can't miss it, it's the only hotel in town."

Pierce flung his saddlebags over his shoulder and started off down the street. He was desperate to see Zoey, to feel her in his arms, to kiss her sweet lips, to caress and love her. They had fought a long, hard battle to be together, and nothing was going to part them again.

A good share of their struggle, Pierce realized, was due to his unwillingness to believe in Zoey. His distrust of women had crippled him emotionally and placed his heart in limbo. Then Zoey had come along and made a mockery of the beliefs and prejudices that had caused him to be bitterly opposed to marriage. If he hadn't met Zoey he would not have found the perfect woman for him.

The hotel clerk was reluctant at first to give out Zoey's room number. The marshal had instructed the clerk to keep an eye on Mrs. Delaney, and he wasn't going to give her into the care of a saddle tramp, which was exactly what Pierce looked like. His clothing was coated with several days worth of trail dirt; he was unshaven and needed a haircut. It took some fancy talking on Pierce's part to convince the clerk that he was indeed Zoey's husband.

"Is my wife in her room?" Pierce asked.

"She hasn't left as far as I know."

Pierce took the stairs to the second floor two at a time. He stopped abruptly before Room 210. His hand was shaking when he raised it to rap sharply on the door.

Zoey found waiting intolerable. Her imagination worked overtime, picturing Pierce lying dead somewhere on a deserted road. She didn't know how she'd survive if

Marshal Kinder had been too late to save him. The waiting was driving her crazy. It wasn't in her nature to do nothing while danger stalked a loved one. If the marshal couldn't find Pierce, maybe she could. Having convinced herself she had to leave, she began gathering up her clothing.

A loud rapping at the door jerked Zoey to attention. Her heart jumped into her throat; a pulse pounded in her temple. The marshal had returned! Fear at what he might tell her kept her frozen to the spot, unable to move or to reply. Her hands spread across her stomach, offering mute comfort to the child inside her, a child who might never know his father.

"Zoey," Pierce called softly through the door. "Let me in, love."

At the sound of Pierce's voice, Zoey's world tumbled back into its orbit. She gave a shriek of joy and stumbled to the door. Her hands were shaking so badly she fumbled with the key in the lock before it turned. Flinging the door open, she flew into Pierce's arms.

Pierce dropped his saddlebags and caught her against him, his arms closing around her fiercely. Whispering his name over and over, she kissed his mouth, his cheeks, his nose, the wedge of flesh showing through the vee of his shirt. Pierce hoisted her off her feet and walked into the room, slamming the door shut with his booted foot.

"Sweetheart, I'm all right." Pierce laughed as she continued to touch him. "Marshal Kinder told me what you did. I always knew you were resourceful, as well as smart and beautiful, I just didn't know how resourceful. I can't wait to hear how you got away from Willoughby. I didn't stick around for an explanation. I wanted to get back to you as quickly as possible."

"I was so afraid for you," Zoey sighed against his neck.

"No more afraid than I was for you. Those four days in jail were pure torture. My imagination worked overtime, visualizing all the horrors Willoughby put you through."

Zoey placed a finger against his lips. "Don't talk, just kiss me. God, I need you. I feared I'd never see you again."

She began pulling at his clothes, working his shirt out of his pants, her fingers fumbling with the buttons.

"Zoey. God, love, I want you, too, but I'm not fit to touch you. I've been on the road for days."

His words had little impact on Zoey. She

had finally gotten his shirt unbuttoned and pulled both his vest and shirt down his arms. She groaned with impatience as she tugged at the waistband of his trousers.

Her need set him afire, sending hot blood spurting through his veins. Soon his own need was as fierce as hers as he began tearing off Zoey's clothing. Half-undressed, they staggered to the bed and tumbled upon it in a tangle of arms and legs.

"Lift your hips," Pierce gasped as he peeled Zoey's denims down her legs. In a fever of impatience, he pulled off her boots so he could get her pants and drawers all the way off.

The moment her legs were free, they came around his waist, binding him to her.

"Zoey, let me get my pants off."

"Later. Please, Pierce."

Pierce tugged at the placket holding his pants together and the buttons went flying, releasing his swollen sex. Zoey felt the hardened tip nudge the moist portals of her passage and moaned her urgency against his mouth. She grasped his hips, bringing him against her as she lifted her hips in flagrant invitation.

"Are you sure you're ready, love?" Pierce whispered. He was more than ready. He was hot, hard, heavy, and primed to burst.

His hand came between them, his fingers delving into her soft folds. Her heat was yielding and sweet beneath his strong fingers. She was wet and eager, and he exhaled raggedly. Flexing his hips, he thrust home, burying himself to the hilt. Zoey screamed, her body rigid as she rose up to meet him.

Pierce froze. "Are you all right?"

"More than all right. Don't stop, love. Don't ever stop."

"As if I could," Pierce groaned. He felt her pulsate around him, and he ground his teeth together to keep from spilling immediately. "You're so tight, love. Your heat is scorching me. I think I'm dying. I could ask for no sweeter heaven."

His hips jerked in and out, sending Zoey higher and higher as she thrashed her head from side to side and writhed beneath him. This was her man, hers to love forever and ever.

"I need to kiss you, love," Pierce said. Tangling his fingers in her hair, he cupped her head in his hands and stroked the seam of her lips with his tongue, then slipped it between her teeth, into the sweet warm recesses of her mouth.

Zoey felt the weight of him against her,

the shape and hardness of him inside her, and felt contractions begin deep within that place where they were joined. Wave after wave of raw feeling traveled over her body, gathering strength, creating a violent force within her.

Pierce felt her climax begin, felt her tightness close around him, and he set his teeth against the excruciatingly pleasurable contractions that pulsed around his sex. Freeing her mouth, he closed his lips upon the hardened tip of her breast, drawing upon her nipple as she shattered. He forced himself to wait until her bliss was at its peak before taking his own pleasure. His groin was heavy and aching as he thrust and retreated, pumping his hips against hers until his seed burst forth in a heady rush of nearly unbearable ecstasy.

"It shouldn't have been like that," Pierce said after he rolled off Zoey and brought his breathing under control. "It should have been slow and easy. I wanted to arouse you slowly, to draw out your pleasure until you begged for release. Damn, you didn't even give me time to get my pants off." He grinned, recalling her eagerness to have him. He hoped she never changed.

"Stop grinning," Zoey said, cuddling

into the curve of his body. "I needed you, Pierce. I wanted it hard and fast. It won't always be like that, but seeing you alive . . . I don't know, it was like I had to have you in that way to convince myself you were alive and well."

"God, I'm exhausted," Pierce said. "I want to love you again, but I don't know if I'd do either of us any good without proper rest."

When Zoey failed to answer, he looked down and saw that she had already fallen asleep. He pulled a cover over them and closed his eyes. Sleep came instantly.

Three hours later, gnawing hunger pangs awakened him. Zoey was still sleeping, so he eased himself from bed and checked the pitcher for water. It was full. He stripped off his remaining clothing and washed the trail dust from his body. Then he cautiously opened the door, found his saddlebags he had dropped there earlier, and dragged them into the room. Digging into the pockets, he found his shaving gear and shaved himself before the cracked mirror.

"I love the way your muscles move beneath your skin," Zoey said in a sultry voice. She'd been watching him from beneath lowered lids for the better part of thirty minutes.

Pierce turned and gave her a slow grin. "And I love the way your skin feels against mine."

She held out her arms and he went to her, stripping away the remnants of her clothing before bringing her against him. "Do you want to tell me about your ordeal with Willoughby?"

Zoey stirred restlessly. "Must I?"

"I need to know, for my own peace of mind. Tell me, love. What did the bastard do to you?"

"He drugged me with laudanum. I don't recall much about the trip from Butte to Rolling Prairie. I woke up in my own bed. I did remember, though, that Willoughby had let slip he had ordered my father killed, and I confronted him about it. He didn't deny it."

Pierce went still. "He killed your father? Why?"

"For many reasons. Me, the land; who knows how the mind of a man like Willoughby works? He couldn't afford to let me escape, so he placed a guard at my door. He told the townspeople I was seriously ill and bribed the doctor to confirm his diagnosis. I'm sure Willoughby intended to kill me. Just like he killed my father."

"Did he say he was going to kill you?"

"He said he didn't know what to do with me."

"I thought your father was killed by Indians."

"That's what Willoughby wanted people to think. He must have paid his men to kill Pa and make it look like Indians did it. Look what he did to Cully. The man is a fiend."

"Marshal Kinder will see that justice is done. Three of Willoughby's men were in his custody. Kinder reached me in the nick of time. You saved my life, love, again. How in the hell did you get away from the Circle F and Willoughby?"

Zoey grinned. "It was quite simple, really. Once I gained my wits, I began making plans." She proceeded to tell him how she used Willoughby's own laudanum to escape his men.

"Laudanum? You drugged Willoughby's men?" Pierce laughed and kissed her soundly. "What a wicked little minx you are. It's no more than I would have expected from you. I reckon I'm going to have to mind my manners around you. You're a dangerous woman. Seriously, love, I was so damned worried about you, I thought I'd lose my mind. Living without you in my life frightened the hell out of me."

"You'll never have to worry about losing me. We're going to grow old together."

"Promise?"

"On my honor." She reached for him, her hands hot upon his body. She placed tender little kisses upon his chest as her hands and mouth roamed over his body.

When her fingers curled around his manhood, he hardened instantly, pushing himself against her palm. "Unless that's an invitation, you'd be wise to stop."

Zoey continued to stroke him, her eyes glowing darkly. "I'll stop if you want me to."

"God, no! I want to love you properly this time."

Suddenly Pierce's stomach rumbled loudly, reminding him that he hadn't eaten in nearly twenty-four hours. He grasped her hand, pulling it away from his body. "Are you sure you don't want to go down to the dining room for something to eat first?"

Zoey considered his suggestion. "Leave it to my practical husband to suggest food at a time like this. Actually, food does sound pretty good. And . . ." she said, smiling mysteriously, "there is something I need to tell you. Something I hope will please you."

"Everything about you pleases me. You can tell me your news over lunch."

Zoey gave him an exasperated look. She couldn't put this off a moment longer. "No, I want to tell you now." Inhaling sharply, she blurted out, "I'm going to have a baby."

"Fine. Now can we — You're what?" His heart slammed against his chest. "Say that again . . . slowly."

"You're going to be a father, Pierce. I'm having your child."

Pierce went still. "How long have you known?"

"A while."

"Did you know when you left me in Dry Gulch? When Willoughby forced you to marry him? When he took you to Butte? When he drugged you? When you escaped and rode through the night to fetch the marshal?"

Zoey nodded yes to all counts.

"Son of a bitch! I'm going to kill Willoughby with my bare hands! What about our child? Is he . . . is she . . . all right?"

Zoey's hands spanned her stomach. "He's still here, Pierce."

"When?"

"In six months. I'm well into my third month."

A shudder went through Pierce as he dropped heavily upon the bed, his empty stomach all but forgotten. "Why didn't you tell me? Dammit, Zoey, what if I had signed those divorce papers? Were you intending to tell Willoughby the baby was his and let him raise my child?"

"I didn't want to mess up your life. I wanted you to want me for my sake, not for the child I carried. As for Willoughby, it was never my intention to remain in that marriage or be a wife to him. After Cully was free I was going to tell Willoughby about the baby and offer him the ranch in exchange for my freedom. If that didn't work, I would have thought of something. I'd rather have died than let him touch me."

Pierce leapt to his feet, grasped her shoulders, and brought her hard against him. "I nearly lost you. I might never have known you were expecting my child."

"You're angry."

"Damn right I'm angry."

She caressed the freshly shaven planes of his face, her eyes misty with tears. "Everything turned out for us, love. I'm fine, the baby is thriving, and you're alive."

"Dammit!" Pierce shouted roughly. He

didn't mean to sound gruff, but he suddenly realized how close he'd come to losing Zoey and their child. He could have signed the divorce papers, or Willoughby could have hurt Zoey.

"I'm sorry, Pierce, I should have told you. I just didn't want to cause you any more anguish than I already have. I disrupted your life once, and I wanted to leave you in peace. My problems were no longer your concern."

Pierce's jaw tightened. He had to think, to come to grips with what could have been a disastrous loss. "I need to be alone. Meet me in the dining room in half an hour."

Pierce had to get out of there quickly, before he broke down like a blubbering fool. Of course he was angry that he hadn't known about Zoey's pregnancy, but it went far deeper than simple anger. He was humbled and deeply moved by Zoey's sacrifice on his behalf. She'd risked life and limb to save him despite her delicate condition. She'd suffered humiliation and degradation. A man could ask for no greater love. He vowed never to take that love for granted.

Stunned and gravely upset, Zoey watched Pierce dress and stumble from the room. Had she ruined everything by not telling him she was carrying his child? Pierce had seemed angry, but Zoey recognized a far deeper emotion. He appeared to be holding something inside, something extremely distressing. She could have sworn she'd seen moisture gathering in the corners of his eyes, and couldn't imagine what she'd said to produce it.

Her mind in a turmoil, Zoey washed and dressed and went downstairs to meet Pierce. She found him seated at a table in the far corner of the dining room. He looked up and grinned at her despite his somber mood. She was wearing those intriguing denim pants, causing a stir in the dining room.

He watched her walk toward him, suddenly glad that he'd had a moment alone to gain control of his emotions. Learning that he was to become a father and then realizing how close he'd come to losing his precious wife and unborn babe had nearly unmanned him. If he hadn't left when he did, he'd have broken down like a bawling baby. Men didn't cry. Unfortunately he was becoming inept at hiding his emotions since meeting Zoey. He'd tried to hide behind anger, but stronger emotions kept pushing the anger aside.

"Sit down, love," Pierce said, pulling out her chair. "I've ordered a substantial lunch for both of us."

"Pierce, I'm sorry if I —"

"No, don't talk. Let's have our meal first. We have plenty of time before the marshal returns to air our thoughts. I meant for this time alone to be the honeymoon we never had."

"But if you're angry with me . . ."

Their meal came then, relieving Pierce of the need to express his feelings. They ate in silence. Pierce was ravenous, doing justice to his meal. Zoey pushed her food around on the plate, too upset to feel real hunger.

"We're sitting here until you finish every morsel on your plate," Pierce admonished. "I aim to make sure you take good care of yourself from now on. Your days of flirting with danger are over."

Zoey remained mute as she concentrated on her food. Everything Pierce ordered was delicious and she should have been hungry, but she couldn't help worrying. If only she knew what he was thinking. His eyes rested on her warmly, but they were dark with some inner emotion she couldn't interpret. When she indicated she could eat no more, Pierce escorted her back to their room.

Once in their room, Zoey rounded on him. "Very well, Pierce, spit it out. Tell me what you're feeling. I know you're angry because I didn't tell you about the baby, but the important thing is that we love each other, and our baby continues to thrive. Are you going to forgive me?"

Pierce sat on the bed and pulled Zoey onto his lap. "Forgive you? You still don't understand, do you, love? Anger isn't what I'm feeling at the present time. It's terror. I keep imagining your panic when you were held within Willoughby's power. You were alone, pregnant and helpless, with no one to turn to. You thought I had abandoned you. Forgive you? No, love, it's myself I have to forgive, and I'm finding that exceedingly difficult. I was too damn stubborn to come after you when you left, even though I didn't want you to go."

"You must be disappointed in me for agreeing to marry Willoughby when I knew I was pregnant with your child."

"I could never be disappointed in you. You did what you thought necessary to save Cully's life. You were pregnant, alone, and still acted with courage and resourcefulness. I'm humbled by your love. I'll never be worthy of it should I live to be one hundred. All I can do is try to be the best damn husband and father in the entire territory."

"If you weren't angry, why did you leave our room so abruptly?" Zoey persisted.

"I'm a man, love, and men are supposed to be strong. For the first time in my life I felt close to" — he cleared his throat — "breaking down. I can't recall the last time I cried, but if I hadn't left the room when I did, I would have been humiliated by my tears."

Zoey regarded Pierce solemnly. Pierce cry? Impossible. Then she smiled radiantly. "You love me that much?"

"That much and more." His hand settled on her stomach. "Learning I'm to be a father overwhelms me. I never intended to marry again after my first disastrous attempt at it, so I never considered fatherhood. Suddenly the notion of having a son or daughter is exciting. If our coming together hadn't been so fast and furious earlier, I might have noticed the differences in your body."

His hands roamed over her lush curves. "You still look damn good in denims, but I hope you'll abandon them for dresses when we return home. Somehow I don't think there's room inside these pants to accommodate a growing child."

"Home," Zoey breathed. A sudden thought occurred to her. "Where exactly is home going to be? I suppose Cully can manage the Circle F without me, but he's getting on in years and it won't be easy."

"He won't have to," Pierce said. "Chad will return one day. He and Ryan can run the ranch without me. I thought we'd make the Circle F our home. It's a fine piece of land."

"You'd do that for me?"

"For us. For our child. Now," he said, working the buttons loose on her shirt, "where were we before hunger drove us to the dining room?"

"Right here," Zoey said, pulling his shirt from the waistband of his trousers.

Between slow, drugging kisses they rid themselves of their cumbersome clothing, arousing each other's bodies until delicious agony licked through their veins. This time their loving was slow and easy and exquisitely satisfying. When the last erotic cry was wrung from Zoey, she closed her eyes and thanked fate for bringing her this stranger to love.

Zoey and Pierce's honeymoon lasted seven glorious, fulfilling days. On the seventh day Marshal Kinder returned from

Rolling Prairie. He called on the honey-mooners at the hotel.

"Come in, Marshal," Pierce invited when he opened the door to Kinder. "We've been waiting for you."

Kinder looked from Pierce to Zoey and grinned. They looked like a couple who had been enjoying every aspect of their honeymoon. "I hope you've been keeping yourselves occupied."

Zoey blushed. Pierce gave a shout of laughter. "You could say that. What news do you bring from Rolling Prairie?"

"One of Willoughby's men feared he was going to be made the scapegoat and enlightened us as to some of Willoughby's illegal activities. Several people have been cheated out of land and money without realizing it. And Willoughby did order the attack upon your father, Mrs. Delaney."

Zoey leaned against Pierce for support. His strong arms steadied her, offering comfort.

"He also confessed to breaking into your house twice to steal documents," Kinder continued.

"Where is Willoughby now?" Pierce wanted to know.

"Unfortunately he's where he can't be brought to justice for his crimes."

"You mean you let the bastard get away?" Pierce all but shouted.

"I mean Willoughby is residing in hell right now. He took the cowardly way out and killed himself when he learned the law was closing in on him. He couldn't face his inevitable ruin. It's perfectly safe now for you to return to Rolling Prairie and the Circle F.

"The newspaper printed a full account of Willoughby's crimes. His men have been rounded up and will get a chance to have their say before a judge. Some had a hand in Willoughby's illegal activities, but a few were unaware of his dirty dealings. They hired on because they needed a job. It will all be sorted out in court."

"I don't know how to thank you, Marshal," Zoey said, relieved to learn that it was finally over.

"No thanks necessary, Mrs. Delaney. I was placed in this territory to protect the citizens and keep vigilante law at a minimum. If you'll excuse me now, I've got reports to fill out."

"We'll be leaving first thing in the morning, Marshal. Zoey and I are grateful for your help. You're welcome to visit us at the Circle F whenever you're in the area."

"I'll remember that," Kinder said, tipping his hat. "Try not to let your wife take any more midnight rides. It can't be good for the baby." Giving Zoey a friendly wink, he left the room.

Pierce turned to Zoey, his brow raised curiously. "He knows? Was I the last to know?"

Zoey shrugged. "I didn't mean to tell him, it just happened."

"Next time it happens I expect to be told first."

"Next time?" Zoey teased, turning in to his arms. "What if there isn't a next time?"

Pierce gave her a cocky grin. "As much as we enjoy making love, there's bound to be a next time."

Zoey nuzzled his neck, inhaling his intoxicating scent. "Think of all the fun we'll have."

"If you don't kill me first," Pierce murmured as he swept her off her feet and carried her to the bed.

Epilogue

Six months later

Pierce stood beside the cradle, regarding his sleeping newborn son with rapt adoration. He was a mite small, a tad red, and as wrinkled as Cully, but there was no denying he was a handsome lad. Pierce reached down and ran the back of his finger along a smooth cheek, wondering how he could have ever believed he didn't want a wife and children. If not for Zoey, he'd still be living a lonely existence, filled with bitterness and distrust. Being forced to marry Zoey had been the best thing that ever happened to him.

"Do you plan on keeping him?" Zoey asked when she awakened and saw Pierce admiring his son.

"You're awake. As for our son, I think I've fallen in love for the second time in my life."

"I feel the same way."

"How do you feel? Doc Colberg said

yours was an easy birth, as far as births go. He said you were made to bear children."

Zoey grimaced. "I wouldn't call it fun, but I suppose I am lucky. Luckier still that he opened a practice in town after old Doc Tucker left so abruptly."

"If he hadn't left, the townspeople would have run him out on a rail. He was never sober long enough to do any doctoring."

His gaze lingered on Zoey's face, on the dark smudges beneath her eyes. "Go back to sleep, love. You need to rest and heal."

"I can sleep later. Cully must be champing at the bit to see the baby. You can let him in if you'd like."

"He's right outside the door, acting every bit like a proud grandpa. I reckon Ryan will show up when he learns the baby has arrived."

Zoey saw a shadow pass over Pierce's face and knew exactly what he was thinking. She squeezed his hand in commiseration. "Don't fret so, love. Chad will come to his senses soon and return home where he belongs."

"It's been months since anyone has heard from him. He could be dead for all we know."

"You would have heard. Wouldn't it be

wonderful if both Chad and Ryan found women to love?"

"It won't happen," Pierce contended. "Both my brothers are confirmed bachelors."

Zoey's eyes twinkled mischievously. "So were you, until you found love."

He gave her a lopsided grin. "Maybe you're right. Neither one has met a determined woman like you. If either of my brothers is lucky enough to find someone to love, I'll wager he'll fall as hard as I have."

"Can I come in?" Cully poked his grizzled head around the door, obviously anxious to see Zoey and the baby.

"Come in, Cully," Pierce invited.

Cully walked into the room, twisting his battered hat in his hand. "You look plumb happy, Miz Zoey. A mite tuckered out, but that's to be expected." He glanced longingly at the cradle.

"Go ahead and take a peek, Cully," Zoey said. "He looks just like his father."

"He's a mighty fine boy, Miz Zoey. Your pa would have been proud as a peacock. What are ya gonna name him?"

"We haven't decided," Zoey said.

"Yes, we have," Pierce corrected. "We're naming him for Zoey's father."

Cully appeared pleased. "He'd be right tickled. Well, reckon I'd best be getting back to the chores."

"Thank you," Zoey told Pierce once they were alone.

Pierce bent and kissed her softly on the lips. "No, love, thank you for loving a stranger."

Author's Note

The towns of Dry Gulch and Rolling Prairie are fictitious but could have very well been frontier towns in Montana during the late 1800s. The Vigilantes of Montana did indeed exist. In the beginning the group was organized to protect citizens from lawless individuals in areas where no law existed. Sometimes the original purpose of the vigilantes fell by the wayside as vicious individuals gained control and used the group to further their own ambitions. In certain places the law became the lawless and the vigilantes became an organization feared by the law-abiding citizens.

In the fullness of time all three Delaney brothers will be given their own stories. *To Love a Stranger* introduced you to the Delaney family, but it was Pierce's story all the way. In my next book, due for release in October 1998, you'll learn what happens to Chad, the brother who fled his home, family, and friends when a tragic event changed his life. In *To Tame a Renegade* you'll meet Sarah, the woman who put his life back on track, taming him with a once-in-a-lifetime love. I hope you enjoy all three books as they follow the lives of three very special brothers and the women who love them.

All My Romantic Best,
Connie Mason